*Drunken danger... and I'm only
an ordinary girl trained to balance books
on her head and swoon. Useless...*

Art didn't move. She watched as the two men jumped over the low wall onto the dockside and fell about laughing. They had spotted Art, of course, and seemed interested in her. They were well-off, and swords were slung lightly at their sides.

"Told you. It's a boy."

" 'Tis so. Come here, boy, and turn out your pockets."

More thieves. Why did they need to? They didn't look poor.

But who was Art to judge; she had never been a thief—apart from that one time on the Lundon Road, and then all she took were a coat and hat—and she had never been a pirate, either.

"Look, the boy's coming over. How dare he?"

"You told him to."

"Did I? Insolent scamp."

Art swung up to them, bowing. Cuckoo Jack's pistol was in Art's left hand, and the pistol's snout was exactly under one of the men's noses—nostril to nostril.

"Box of ducks! The boy's armed!"

FIREBIRD
WHERE FANTASY TAKES FLIGHT™

Across the Nightingale Floor *Episode One: Journey to Inuyama*	Lian Hearn

Across the Nightingale Floor
     Episode Two: The Sword
     of the Warrior
	Lian Hearn

The Beggar Queen	Lloyd Alexander
Beldan's Fire	Midori Snyder
The Blue Girl	Charles de Lint
The Blue Sword	Robin McKinley
The Faery Reel: Tales from the *Twilight Realm*	Ellen Datlow and Terri Windling, eds.
Firebirds Rising: An Anthology of *Original Science Fiction and Fantasy*	Sharyn November, ed.
The Green Man: Tales from the *Mythic Forest*	Ellen Datlow and Terri Windling, eds.
The Kestrel	Lloyd Alexander
New Moon	Midori Snyder
The Outlaws of Sherwood	Robin McKinley
Sadar's Keep	Midori Snyder
Westmark	Lloyd Alexander
Wolf Queen	Tanith Lee
Wolf Star	Tanith Lee
Wolf Tower	Tanith Lee
Wolf Wing	Tanith Lee

Piratica

Being a Daring Tale of a Singular Girl's
Adventure Upon the High Seas

Presented Most Handsomely
by the Notorious

TANITH LEE

FIREBIRD

AN IMPRINT OF PENGUIN GROUP (USA) INC.

To Beverley Birch—who gave Art the time she needed.
With affection and thanks.

And a special thank-you also to:
Beryl Alltimes, who provided the first clue,
Mavis Haut, who provided the second clue,
and John Kaiine—who provided the key to the treasure chest

FIREBIRD
Published by the Penguin Group
Penguin Group (USA) Inc., 345 Hudson Street, New York, New York 10014, U.S.A.
Penguin Group (Canada), 90 Eglinton Avenue East, Suite 700, Toronto, Ontario, Canada M4P 2Y3
(a division of Pearson Penguin Canada Inc.)
Penguin Books Ltd, 80 Strand, London WC2R ORL, England
Penguin Ireland, 25 St Stephen's Green, Dublin 2, Ireland (a division of Penguin Books Ltd)
Penguin Group (Australia), 250 Camberwell Road, Camberwell, Victoria 3124, Australia
(a division of Pearson Australia Group Pty Ltd)
Penguin Books India Pvt Ltd, 11 Community Centre, Panchsheel Park, New Delhi - 110 017, India
Penguin Group (NZ), Cnr Airborne and Rosedale Roads, Albany, Auckland 1310,
New Zealand (a division of Pearson New Zealand Ltd)
Penguin Books (South Africa) (Pty) Ltd, 24 Sturdee Avenue,
Rosebank, Johannesburg 2196, South Africa

Registered Offices: Penguin Books Ltd, 80 Strand, London WC2R ORL, England

First published in Great Britain by Hodder Children's Books, 2003
First published in hardcover in the United States of America by Dutton Children's Books,
a division of Penguin Young Readers Group, 2004
Published by Firebird, an imprint of Penguin Group (USA) Inc., 2006

3 5 7 9 10 8 6 4 2

Copyright © Tanith Lee, 2003

THE LIBRARY OF CONGRESS HAS CATALOGED THE DUTTON EDITION AS FOLLOWS:
Lee, Tanith.
Piratica: a daring tale of a singular girl's adventure / Tanith Lee.
p. cm.
Summary: A bump on the head restores Art's memories of her mother and the exciting life they led, so
the sixteen-year-old leaves Angels Academy for Young Maidens, seeks out the pirates who were her
family before her mother's death, and leads them back to adventure on the high seas.
ISBN 0-525-47324-6
[1. Pirates—Fiction. 2. Sex role—Fiction. 3. Actors—Fiction. 4. Adventure and adventurers—Fiction.
5. Great Britain—History—Fiction.] I. Title.
PZ7.L5149Pi   2004   [Fic]—dc22   2004002409

ISBN 0-14-240644-9

Printed in the United States of America

AUTHOR'S NOTE

As you will see, the world of this book is very like ours and also, it isn't. Names may be familiar—or weird. Some may be authentic old names you might find in a history book—others may be like games played with existing names. All the places (almost) that are mentioned can be found on a world atlas... even though the names aren't quite what you'd expect. But some are in slightly different geographical positions.

So this isn't exactly a historical novel—but it's not exactly a fantasy, either. And it takes place in a time we never had....

The Shakespeare sonnet, though, is still by Shakespeare, even though in Art's world he is called Shakespur.

CONTENTS

ACT ONE: *Molly's Daughter*

ONE
No Angel *3*
Pink for a Girl *10*
Common Talk *16*

TWO
Pistols for Two, Coffee for Who? *26*
Sinking Molly *39*
After the Theater *50*

THREE
Goose and Guest *56*
Breaking the Ice *66*
Port's Mouth Ho! *72*

ACT TWO: *Piratica's Daughter*

ONE
The Port's Mouth Pudding *87*
All at Sea *96*
Changing Faces *106*

TWO

Foe and Fortune *113*
Four Wise Men *128*
Own Accord *132*

THREE

Trade and Traitor *143*
Ships That Pass in the Nightmare *150*
South by Southeast *164*

ACT THREE: *Piratica*

ONE

Setting Fire to Canvas *183*
Blond Bombshell *191*
The Odder Sea *200*

TWO

Treasured Isle *207*
Parrot Fashion *213*
Tidings *227*

THREE

Walking the Planks *244*
In the Same Boat *254*
Trial and Error *262*

Last Scene: Lockscald Tree 273

The action of this novel takes place in a closely parallel world, beginning in the year 17ᕼ2 (Seventeen-Twelvety)— approximate, in our dating, to 1802.

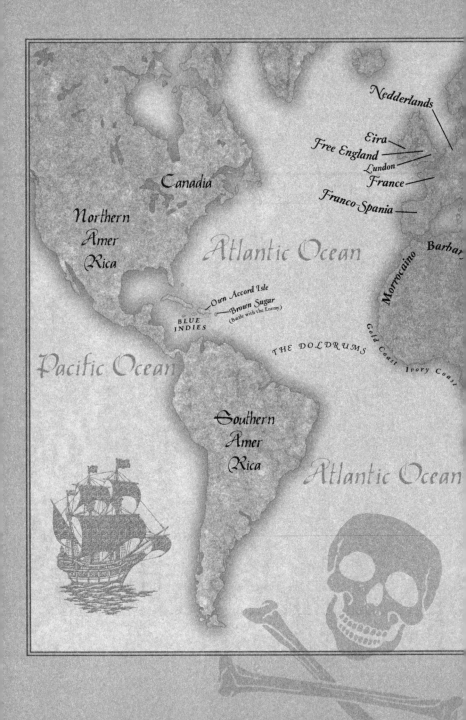

n
w
e
s
Antioch
Egypt
Persis
Cathay
The Inde
THE SPICE ISLANDS
Africay
Indian Ocean
Mad-Agash Scar
Treasured Isle
EASTERN AMBERS
CAPRICORN SEA
Free Cape Town
Cape of Good Hope

"Do not laugh...In tales, pirates always have these.
'Tis a map to find buried treasure."
—Cecilia Dart-Thornton
The Ill-Made Mute
(Book One of *The Bitterbynde Trilogy*)

ACT ONE
Molly's Daughter

⤜ ⤳ONE ⤲ ⤛

No Angel ⟋

One day when she was sixteen, Art remembered her mother. It happened because Art fell down a flight of steps and hit her head on a wooden bannister carved in the shape of an eagle.

She sat there, dizzy, staring back up the stairs at a group of very stupid girls, all giggling and pointing, with large books ridiculously balanced on the over-curled hair that crowned their heads. And Art thought, Who are *they?* And then—

And then she thought of a slim, strong woman, not tall but looking taller because her legs were so long and outlined by the trousers and boots she wore. A woman with strawberry-blond hair tied back in a knot and eyes the impossible green of gooseberries. And this was Molly Faith. This was her mother. Though for six years Art hadn't thought of her, hadn't *remembered* her—this unforgettable and wonderful parent, who had been a pirate captain on the High Seas.

Art—who just ten minutes before had been known, and had known *herself*, as Miss Artemesia Fitz-Willoughby Weatherhouse—shook her head. It cleared, just as her memory had.

She stood up. She said aloud, "The cannon blew apart. Molly's cannon she called the Duchess. That was what knocked it out of me."

Art put her hand to her own carefully arranged hair. It looked, she knew, dark brown, but through it ran, on the right side, a fierce, fox-orange shock, which always had to be powdered over to hide it. As if it should be ashamed of itself.

That orange had happened when the Duchess—or perhaps another cannon, was it—had blown up earlier, when Art was what?—two, three?

Useful, guns, but they had their little ways.

"Are you all right, Artemesia?" cooed one of the stupid young girls—hoping she wasn't, most likely. Injury was always interesting in such a boring place.

Art thought, Am I?

I am.

She ran back up the stairs three at a time, and her long skirt ripped, and she didn't care.

The curly girls fell back before her, and several of their books slid off and went *thump* onto the floor.

They had all been practicing Deportment, Art, too. Deportment was how to walk with a completely straight neck and back—otherwise your head-balanced book fell off. Art's book had—and she had lost her footing.

The odd thing was, although she partly recalled who these people were, and that this big house they were in, with its pastel walls and shiny floors, was the Angels Academy for Young Maidens at Rowhampton (near Lundon), they were all suddenly much less real than the past she had forgotten, and which was now rattling back into her head like a runaway carriage.

"Look out!" someone squeaked then. "Here comes the Evil Eeble."

The Evil Eeble? What was that?

Ah, yes. *Miss* Eeble was one of the Academy's teachers. The kind of teacher who never learned anything herself. Or *taught* anything, except sarcasm or fear.

Here she came, round the corner of the corridor, her dress smooth as a tablecloth, fist faced with pleased annoyance. She liked to catch you out.

"Pray, what is this?"

"Artemesia fell downstairs!"

Evil Eeble glared, first at her informant, then at Art.

Art thought, Do I *know* this woman?

"You've no business, Artemesia, to fall downstairs. You are a maiden of high family. You must be graceful and feminine at all times, an ornament to your female sex. A proper *lady* does not fall down anything."

Art stared at Miss Eeble.

Then, she struck a pose. There in her silly dress, Art threw back her head and rested her left hand on the hilt of the imaginary cutlass that once—six years back—had hung from her left hip. It had only been a small cutlass, she had only been ten. But Art could remember how good—and *proper*—it felt. Unlike a book on your head, the cutlass balanced you just right.

"Madam," said Art haughtily to the abruptly startled Miss Eeble, "what is this nonsense you're spouting like an unblocked drain?"

The Eeble's mouth fell open. She locked it up again tight at once. Only one rigid announcement was let out of it. "Artemesia, I see you must be properly punished for disrespect."

Art smiled. "Poo to you, madam, I say, and poo."

The girls screamed. Books fell like noisy autumn leaves, *bang, thump, crash.* Down the stairs again leaped Art. She whirled across the lower landing, her head full of barking cannon, towering rigging, the creak of timbers, the voice of her mother, Molly. Before her eyes floated the golden coasts of Amer Rica, Persis, and Zanzibari, dolphins springing like silver bullets from the blue mouths of the waves.

"Her father must be fetched!" shouted Miss Eeble. "She has gone mad!"

"Sane," remarked Art. "Gone *sane*."

She bowed to the eagle bannister, which had saved her from all this and given her back her past.

That night was Christmas Eve.

Darkness fell hand in hand with the snow.

All over the countryside, a somber whiteness glowed up from the land at the white somberness of the sky.

England was a Republic. More than twenty years before, the whole country had rebelled against the monarchy and thrown them out. Those had been days of chaos and violence, when the people felt themselves free and powerful—in command of their own lives. Then, as things quietened, if order returned, royalty and royal titles never did. Presently, though a woman might still be called a lady if she were highborn, no one anymore was a lord, a king, or a queen. Art's father, then, George Fitz-Willoughby Weatherhouse, owned a lot of land, but he was called a *Landsir*.

So, Landsir G.F.W. Weatherhouse now came careering over the wintry, snow-falling landscape in his carriage. And when he reached the gates of the Angels Academy, a man rushed to open them.

In the snow, the gate-opening porter looked like a phantom. It was a night for ghosts.

Weatherhouse scowled at that.

His estate, Richman's Park, wasn't more than a couple of miles from the school, and so the letter about his daughter had reached him in the afternoon.

She had gone mad, so they said. Weatherhouse thought, Just like her bloody mother.

The Angels Academy filled a gardened dip among the woods, not far from the villages of Rowhampton and Arrowhampton. Just beyond, too, expanded notorious Wimblays Common, haunted by highwaymen (ten of them to every square mile, according to the *Lundon Tymes*), and particularly the worrying Gentleman Jack Cuckoo. Weatherhouse's carriage, he was glad to say, hadn't had to cross even the outer areas of the Common.

Now the vehicle thundered, behind snorting horses, up the Academy's winter-bare linden tree avenue.

Yellow light spilled from windows. As he stepped from the halted carriage, it caught Weatherhouse's finery—gold embroidered coat, gold buttoned waistcoat, a silver-headed cane, a perfectly powdered wig.

Fluttering daintily mothlike, Evil Miss Eeble and Grasping Miss Grash—the Principal of the school—led him inside and along the polished corridors.

"She is *in there*."

"Then let me at her, madam."

"Oh, sir—do you think—"

"Be quiet and step aside," directed Landsir Weatherhouse, who could out-rude most people.

But the ladies were in a state and a half.

"Sir—we fear she's dangerous—"

"Even armed—"

"Or—

"Be *quiet!* Be *still!* And if you can't be either, be off."

Misses E and G fled. Weatherhouse flung open the doors.

"By God! What's this?"

Art, who was sitting beside the fire, turned almost idly to glance at the furious, over-embroidered, puce-faced man—her father.

Art knew that, only one day earlier, if he had burst in on her in this temper, she would have been upset and guilty.

Now she wasn't. It made her smile.

"Why the devil are you smiling? Look at you! Six years I've kept you in this place—to change you, you skipperty-hop, into a lady. 'Tis for improvement I sent you, not worsening."

"Oh, am I worse, sir?" asked Art.

She stretched her long legs out to the fire. She wore a man's breeches, a boy's boots, a white shirt, and a coat of patched dull velvet. Her hair was uncurled and untied, and through its freshly washed walnut brownness ran that spurt of marigold fire Weatherby had first seen there six years in the past.

"You're like your mother."

"My ma was very fine."

"Not to me."

"Why then, Dad, did you fancy her?"

"How dare you speak to me like this!"

"To who else? You married her."

Weatherhouse roared.

The roar hit the gilded plaster fruit and vines on the ceiling.

Art shrugged. She took a winter apple from her pocket and ate it calmly, while her father stamped about the room, striking table legs with his cane.

"Don't you know your wretched mother—Molly—was the worst kind of woman in this world—"

"She was a pirate."

"If you must say it. If you *must*. A sort of pirate."

Art said, "She was one that boasted she never killed a single person, only took their riches through tricks and cleverness. And that's true."

"You'd forgotten all this rubbish," he snapped. The miraculous obviously made him bad-tempered.

"The cannon blew up. I do remember that now. Then nothing for a bit. Then years of *this*. This school, these fools, this imprisonment. You talk about rubbish, sir," said Art, eyes cool as gray steel. "*This* has been the rubbish."

"Where did you get those brazen and nasty clothes?"

Art laughed.

"Off two stable boys. Their Sunday best. And the jacket and

shirt from the school porter. I paid them—and for the launder-ing. Your money, I'm afraid, but you'd already given it to me."

"I gave it to you for a new dress."

"Well, here it is, my dress."

Weatherhouse leaned by the marble mantelpiece, glowering at his daughter, who now, by heaven, looked so very like his for-mer wife, Molly Faith.

"If you remember so much, don't you remember, girl, the fly and flouncy thing your mother *was*?"

Art turned. She turned like a cat when it sees another cat it doesn't much like.

Weatherhouse, even in mid-glower, gaped.

"My mother, sir, was a Queen of the Seas. She was a Pirate Empress, with a fleet of twenty ships—"

"That play—that *lie*—"

"Her name to this night, sir, rings along the world. Not *Molly*, not *Faith*, nor your name, Daddy, that she took when you wed. Certainly *never* that one."

"She was a common—"

Art stood up. Two clear tears ran from her eyes and down her face. They didn't give her any look of weakness. They were like silver medals her eyes had made from pride. "She was called *Piratica*."

"Grow up. *Piratica*—" sneered Weatherhouse, petty and bru-tal together. "She is *dead*. Dead as the cardboard melodrama she was. Dead and buried—if you like, fish food."

"I know."

"And as for you, Artemesia, they have my orders here. I hope you're comfortable in this room. For this is where you'll stay, my girl, until you come back to your senses. A prison, you said? Then they can lock you in. No food, no nice ladies' drinks of expensive tea or coffee or chocolate or juices. A cup of water. And no more wood for that fire."

"Merry Christmas," said Art.

"I had enough of this," he said, her father, "from Molly. I won't have it from you."

As the doors clanked shut behind him, Art murmured to the fire, "And she had enough of you, sir, which was why she left you and took me with her, when I was only a baby. I've lost six years. That's enough, too, for me."

She stuck the poker in the fire, and then she took it out, black with heat and ash. She wrote large on the clear pale wall beside the mantelpiece, her mother's true name.

Pink for a Girl ⟶

Outside something boomed oddly in the night. It was a deer, belling in the woods, or up on the Common.

Snow fell like white ribbons over the windows.

In the grate the fire sank lower with every minute, and by now the locked room was chilly. Art didn't care. Somehow she was, despite her father's words, the immovable door and windows, going to get out. So she might as well get used to a change in climate.

For now anyway, just as throughout the morning, the afternoon, she was thinking it over, everything she could remember—recapturing all she could. Vivid, the images, as if painted on the inside of her mind.

She saw the different times at sea—calm blue days, raw pea-green ones, others when the skies turned black and thunderbolts blasted the masts, and the galloping wave. The ship then leaned this way, another way, seeming to want to throw herself right over and upside down. Had Art ever been frightened? Maybe only once. One of the earliest memories, this. Molly standing braced, holding Art, two or three years old, in her arms. "What a spectacle!" cried Molly. "Look—how beautiful it is!" And then, "Don't ever be afraid of the sea. She's the best friend our kind have got. Better than any land, however fair. Respect the sea, yes, but never think what the sea does is cruel or unjust. People are that. The sea is only herself. And this ship—she's lucky. She's friends with this sea. They know how to behave with each other." Exactly then, a great green salt wave swamped the decks. Canvas was being hauled in, Molly's crew clutching and swinging like monkeys along the masts. Art and Molly, soaked, and Molly saying, "And even if we went down, don't fear that, either. Those that the sea keeps sleep among mermaids and pearls and sunken kingdoms. You wouldn't mind that, would you, love?"

But Molly's lucky ship—

Not yet. Don't think of that yet.

Instead, Art recalled the "fair" lands and trips ashore. Being taken to white-pillared houses where the governor of this or that place, pleased with the wealth the pirates brought him, invited Molly and her men to a dinner or a dance. Art had often sat on a velvet chair and watched her mother, now in bangles and beads and a frock of scarlet or green, spin about the dance floor with these governors, or other well-dressed men. Fine food was served, real ice creams, and glasses of diamond-dust-sparkling champagne—while on terraces under palm trees hung with stars, Molly's elegantly spoken crew went off with kissing ladies. Everyone loved Molly's pirates. Oh, the sound of the applause and cheers whenever they arrived in port—and the chests on deck overflowing with jewels and coins—rubies, emeralds, gold muhuras, pieces of eight.

Now it was time to think of the sea fights. Well, they had been pretty good, too—Government craft from less friendly ports, or more often rival pirateers, pursued Molly's well-known vessel.

Her ship was called the *Unwelcome Stranger,* and she was like a slick, thin-cut greyhound, despite her toppage of tall masts. The ship's class was that of windjammer, a merchant trader's racer, because on the High Seas, anyone tried to get their cargo in first. But Molly stole the ship, by one of her tricks. And the ship seemed to love Molly for it. She became, the ship, lucky, under her sinister name—obviously, just like Art, the *Unwelcome Stranger* had more fun as a pirate.

The flag, too. Oh, Art remembered the flag! First it had been the usual, much-feared piratic Jolly Roger—white skull and crossed bones on a black ground. But then Molly, one of the few female pirate captains, had changed the flag. She made it, for a joke, deep *pink*. Pink for a girl. And the skull and bones were marked on it in black. After which the crew, and everyone else across the Seven Seas, called that flag the Jolly Molly.

And so, sporting a pink skull and crossbones, the *Unwelcome Stranger* entered foreign ports to applause and thrown flowers. Or out at sea, with enemy vessels bearing down with all their cannon blazing broadside, iron balls and fire parting air and ocean, clouds of smoke like dirty cream, she ducked and dove and flew away unharmed.

As for her own ventures, she in turn bore down on the merchant shipping, sometimes alone, sometimes followed by some or all of Molly's fleet—fifteen to twenty vessels. Art heard in her mind the flutes, whistles, and trumpets screeching and drums banging as *Unwelcome*'s pirate band played their loudest, to scare intended prey. Meanwhile *Unwelcome*'s guns let off terrifying cannonades. But they would fire to disable, never to harm. Molly, once any ship surrendered, treated all those she robbed politely. Nothing rough, either, was allowed from her crews. (Art saw Molly bowing to an anxious young girl, and saying, "And this topaz, you tell me, belonged to your beloved father? Then keep it, madam, with our compliments.")

But if there was a *fight*—Art instead saw Molly with her

dancing grace, her cutlass weaving light as a silver needle. With it she tipped the sword of a man who had dared to challenge her, right out of his hand. Then, the wickedest jest, sheared the buttons of his trousers so they fell round his ankles, and the ship rocked again with laughter.

A lucky ship. Lucky like Molly, who had earned the pirate captain's most needed title: pistol-proof—that is, indestructible, and ever fortunate. A charmed life.

And now Art had unwillingly reached the day that charmed life ended. The Day Her Mother's Ship Went Down.

Sixteen-year-old Art had fallen asleep before the cold hearth. She dreamed it over, then, that final scene, that Day, when she had been ten.

Like this:

Art sits on the deck of the *Unwelcome Stranger,* and admires Molly, with her swaggering skill, climbing down the main mast. Art, too, can climb all the masts. She can help drive in pegs, tie up or unreef the canvas. Art, like all of them, knows this ship backward, under and over. It's home. It's the world.

"Someone chasing us," says Hurkon Beare, who, in the dream, suddenly Art can see very clearly. He is Molly's First Officer. Hurkon Beare is a Canadee, a little short in one leg, grizzled but young (not much older *then* than Art will be at sixteen). But in the dream (the past), Art is only ten and Hurkon looks quite mature. On his shoulder something colorful and untidy is sitting.

Full sail is on, the masts crowded with groaning white. The *Unwelcome* runs full tilt on the wind.

But over the horizon already Art can see the shape of the second ship, the pursuer.

In the dream, also in the past, this second ship is vague, a smoky hole torn in daylight. Are her sails dark, too?

"Ready cannon," says Molly to Hurkon. Molly has arrived by

Art, smiles at Art. No fear in Molly, none in Art. In fact, Art springs up and dashes down to the tween deck, to see the five fat guns swung to their stations, snouts pointing out of the gunports.

Hatches to the deck stand open. Art can still watch her mother striding by, hear her speaking and Hurkon's answers.

Then Salt Walter, the red-haired boy, hustles Art back up the companionway ladder. "Off to your ma." He always treats Art like a child, but he's only two years older. Art, though, doesn't argue. She obeys. In battle, there's never time to waste.

Back on the upper deck, she hears Hurkon say to Molly, "That ship out there's the *Enemy*. See, no flag, but each sail black and with the skull and bones over every one." What *is* that on his shoulder? A feather mop? No, it's alive—it flies up—Art, at ten, knows it's a bird. At sixteen, Art, dreaming, remains puzzled—but anyhow it's gone. And Hurkon says, "The *Enemy*. She never gives up. Wants that treasure map, Molly."

Certainly the *Enemy*, motive explained, is very near. The dark ship rides like a slope of tented house, sails angled, looming forward. She maneuvers neatly.

Guns bellow. There's fire.

Art finds herself sitting astride the single upper-deck cannon, the Duchess. Why is that? Surely she shouldn't be? Maybe she had climbed up for a better view—

They're turning to give the *Enemy* broadside in return of fire.

And then, from everywhere together, there comes, not another bang or thunder, but a clap of hot *silence*. Hot silence—and cold nothing.

Art opens her eyes.

Art opened her eyes, and she was sitting upright on the chair in the locked room at the Angels Academy for Young Maidens.

Not cannon, but a deer again was belling in the outer darkness.

Someone had told ten-year-old Art, later, when she woke up in the crisp starched sheets of a bed so clean and so *tucked in* she could hardly move, told her she had been *rescued* by her father.

Art remembered now the stern Landsir Weatherhouse. At ten, it was the first time she had seen him—as a baby, she hadn't noticed him at all.

Six years younger than tonight, yet he had looked just the deadly same. He had glared at the child and told her he "forgave her" for her "mother's sins."

Art, the child, hadn't understood what those sins had been. Hadn't remembered any sins, or *anything*, until that minute.

Next, sent here to the Angel School, she had known only that her mother was a "bad woman" who had died. That was all.

Until today, Art hadn't remembered *Molly*.

Something was bouncing against the locked windows, out in the snow. Art stared as it caught the fading candlelight. It was both of the colors of her mother's dancing dresses together, scarlet and brilliant green. What was it? Some piece of material, some toy— As the snow streamed down, the object shot all at once the other way, upward, and vanished.

The Duchess had blown up. The ship had been holed by the *Enemy*. Sank.

Art's mother slept now, with her vessel, and how many of her dead crew, among the mermaids and the pearls. Forever.

A strange and alarming noise filled the room. It sounded as if the chimney bricks were coming alive above the marble mantelpiece—

Art sprang round and was in time to see a black thing burst outward in a splash of soot and muck, above the burnt-out fire.

It flew straight at her. *Wings* flailed, showering off soot. Bits of color showed. Green, red.

"Pieces of Eight!" screamed the bird—Molly Faith's parrot from the *Unwelcome Stranger*. "Pieces of Hate—"

"Ma got me away," said Art, watching the parrot flapping

and squawking. "Now I've remembered that, too. The little boat, and they put me in it, just before *Unwelcome* sank. Just me. Only me."

"Pieces of Date," insisted the parrot.

Then it reversed and sprinted back into the chimney.

Art opened her eyes for the third and first true time, and found she was alone and parrotless in the icy, dark room.

Not a sound, except the tocking from a clock on the mantelpiece. She could just make out it was a quarter to midnight, nearly Christmas Day. Had the dream parrot come through the chimney because it thought it was Father Christmas?

Or had Art only needed something to remind her of the chimney?

It led straight up, through the rooms of the house and out to the roof. You could surely climb in and climb up, emerge, and next climb down. The Academy was a four-story mansion of many carvings and stone ornaments, which could provide hand- and footholds. The black, filthy chimney had rungs inside, provided for the chimney sweeps. To a young woman who, when a child, had scurried up and down the masts of a sea-swerving ship, all that was nothing.

Art only wondered, as she eased herself into the chimney space, why she hadn't thought of this earlier and needed the ghost of a parrot to show her.

Left behind in the now vacant room, the poker-written name still waited on the wall: PIRATICA.

Common Talk

Past one o'clock, when she had walked up beyond the woods to where the Common opened into its big round shoulders, Art caught a glimpse of distant lights. It was, of all things, the grand house of her father, two miles off to the east. The other way she saw the lower lamps of the village of Rowhampton. Arrowhampton was hidden by hills.

The snow had stopped as a very sooty Art shinned down the Academy's last ornamental drainpipe. She had landed on the frozen head of a classical statue in the garden. No Eebles or Grashes were about, and all the angelic young maidens, no doubt with headaches from balancing books, were probably in bed.

It was simple to lope across the grounds to the gates where the wall was most climbable. The gate porter's lodge had a light in the window. Inside, Art glimpsed him, drinking hot gin. He never noticed her, and minutes later she was over the wall.

A narrow road ran through the woods. But where it turned off toward the villages of Row and Arrow, Art left it. She took instead a rough track and soon went up with it onto Wimblays Common.

It was a strange night, moonless under the heavy clouds but glowing pale from all the settled snow. The high, bare trees were cased in it like knights in armor with full white wigs. Dense copses of these trees also spread over the Common, and just after she had seen the lights of her father's house, Art halted again. Something huge and powerful was shouldering through the white-dark trunks directly toward her.

Between the wintry oaks and beeches, Art now saw deer, moving like ghosts. Then a tall buck stepped onto the track in front of her. His massive antlers, like the boughs of the trees, were painted in on blackness by collected snow. To Art—for an instant—they looked like the white rigging of a midnight ship. His eyes shone uncanny green.

Art kept still. She watched him. She wasn't afraid. A proper young lady should, of course, scream and swoon. Art smiled. "I give you good night, Sir Deer," she said.

And the buck blew warm white breath down his nose, like

the smoke of two cannon, and, turning, trod away again, back into the mysterious pale shadows.

A good sign, Art thought. A large obstacle had removed itself from her path. Molly would have said a good *omen.*

Art walked on through the night. Once she heard the late clocks of the villages strike two. The sound was also mysterious and very clear across the snow.

Art's aim was to reach the main Lundon Road.

Even at Christmas, a coach went along that road early in the morning, a fast coach that always tried to make the city before midday. Art, if she could, would catch up to the coach when it stopped for a quarter of an hour or so at the village of Hare Bridge. She had enough money in her pocket to pay her fare. And in Lundon? Memory, which had given her suddenly back so much, had fixed on her brain a sort of poster, which read: *The Coffee Tavern.* She knew she might get news here—that was, news of any of Molly's crew who had survived.

She didn't remember the tavern itself at all. But she trusted her instinct now absolutely. It had set her free.

The thick-treed steepnesses of the Common poured over into cauldrons of valleys. The sky had cleared, and a fat moon was setting in the west. Art took her bearings from that—and then again she heard another village clock strike, this time for five in the morning. Dawn would be about half past seven.

Woods closed in once more. But not long after, she searched and found among their columns the Lundon Road, broad and unmistakable, even under snow. To her dismay, however, Art saw instantly the hoof and wheel tracks of a heavy vehicle and six horses. The Lundon coach was early, and Hare Bridge at least another mile away. Art broke into a run.

She heard the confused noise as clearly as she had the church clocks, and long before she could see what caused it.

Treading more carefully and slowly through the trees and bushes, Art arrived on a high bank, where a small deserted cottage gave her cover. The drama went on in the roadway below.

The coach was there, right enough. At first she thought there had been an accident, for it was at a standstill, the horses huddled. Several passengers in furs and cloaks had alighted and milled about. A small yellow dog was barking excitedly. The coachman and his side rider were shouting, too, and somewhere a woman—true proper-lady fashion—let out the occasional shriek.

Only then did Art see why.

Confronting the coach and the crowd was a tall man on a rusty-black horse. He too was in rusty black, his three-cornered hat pulled down above a black half mask, and the lower part of his face muffled too, in a sort of mauve thing that might be a scarf. In his right hand he impatiently waved a pistol that glittered in the coach lamps.

"Stand and deliver, I said," he yowled in a high hoarse voice. "Don't you lot speak English? It means yer keep still and gives us yer stuff. Cat's Wallopers! Make haste. I'll catch me death of cold out here, hanging about for you."

A highwayman.

Used to Molly's pirates, Art thought, He's got no style.

The coachman was shouting again: threats, the Law.

The highwayman replied by pointing his pistol at the sky and firing it. A branch fell and showered everyone with snow, including him, but he only shook himself irritably.

"Cuckoo Jack, that's me," he rasped. "I'm dangerous me, I am. Hand over yer valuables and make it quick."

The woman screamed again. No one took any notice of her. The dog barked and the coachman and his rider were swearing. Annoyed beyond endurance, Gentleman Jack Cuckoo—if so he was—fired his second pistol in the air.

At this the coach horses took fright—either that, or they, too, lost patience. In a tidal flurry of snow, the untended coach slamming and sliding behind them, they rushed off up the road toward Hare Bridge.

At this the coachman—"Me coach—me coach"— turned and ran after, instantly followed by his mate, the eager yellow dog, the screaming lady, and most of the other passengers.

Only one forlorn male figure remained on the snow, standing there looking up at Cuckoo Jack, who was now attempting to reposition—or reload—his guns, dropping bullets all over the ground.

"Go on then, get off too, why don't you? Cat's Wallopers." Jack sounded depressed.

Art could see little of the last passenger. But he bent down and picked up some of Cuckoo Jack's spilled bullets, handing them up to the man on the horse politely.

"Thankee. Bat's Randoms, mighty civil. Now. Give us that ring you've got on."

The last passenger, under his own hat, had hair that was incredibly light in color—whiter than powder could have made it—nearly the shade of the snow. Art had thought he was an old man, but then he spoke, and he sounded young, about eighteen, perhaps. It was an educated voice, too, musical.

"It's not worth much, you know, this ring."

"'S ruby, ain't it?"

"No, afraid not. Glass. I'm only a poverty-stricken artist."

"Glass? Go on." Cuckoo Jack leaned perilously from his shabby horse and peered at the passenger's ring. "Well, what else you got?"

"Only the clothes I stand up in, actually. And they're not worth much, either."

"Go on, gent like you—"

"No, really. I'm skint as flint."

"I'd a done better," observed Gentleman Jack Cuckoo, "if'n

Doll had been with me. Doll Muslin, y'know. She knows how to rob a coach something lovely. But it being Christmas," said Cuckoo Jack miserably, "she said she'd cook us a dinner. She *knows* I'm the one likes to do that, but no, it was 'Out ya goes, Jacko. Go and thieve at that coach for Lun'on.' What a Christmas it'll be now, she'll go on at me—"

"Here, take this coin. My last one."

"No, no. You keep it. I'd best get on."

"Perhaps you should try some other profession, Jack."

"Like what? Like starving, I suppose."

Snow showered up again as the highwayman plowed his horse about. They plunged straight off the road and up the bank, and crashing by, both horse and rider reeling red-eyed and grunting, nearly knocked Art flying as they passed. Something landed smack at Art's feet like a gift from the sky. She thought it was a brick knocked off the cottage. It wasn't.

The second good omen.

Art returned her attention sharply to the remaining figure on the road.

His clothes looked all right to *her*. For one thing, they weren't all black with soot.

She swung straight off the bank and landed on both feet, cat-light, a pace or so behind him.

The young man started round, staring at her, eyes wide.

Art looked him over. He had the handsomest face she had ever seen, better even than those of her mother's gallant pirates. He was so good looking, he didn't quite seem real. And his long hair—yes, it wasn't powdered. He was blond as the ice.

"Hi," said Art. "Stand and deliver."

"Oh," said the young man. He cleared his throat. "So *you're* the highwayman."

"That's me," said Art. With a faultless wrist flick, she brought out the pistol Cuckoo Jack had clumsily dropped at her feet. It was cocked and aimed exactly at the young man's glamorous head. He was about two inches taller than she was, but otherwise only slightly larger in his build.

His eyes seemed a very dark blue, and having looked at her with them, he appeared to think she was a boy, or, like himself, a young man. Her own sooty face was easily as well—or better—masked than Cuckoo Jack's.

"What I'll take," said Art, "are your coat and cloak."

"You must be jesting."

"Remove them."

"In *this* weather?"

"Shall I shoot you," asked Art thoughtfully. "Save us both time."

"Please don't. Besides, you might get a hole in the coat."

"Then get on with it. You can have my coat in exchange. You won't freeze, I haven't. I'll put you in that cottage up there, nice and snug. I'll accept your hat, too."

"Heartless villain," said the blond passenger softly, removing cloak and coat and handing them to her.

He had beautifully shaped hands, though the nails were colorfully dirty—paint perhaps—he had mentioned being an artist. His shirt, she noticed, though worn, had once been good.

Art reached out and touched the ring. "And I'll have that."

"It's not a—"

"Yes, it is. I've seen enough of them to know a real ruby when I look at it."

Art pulled off her sooty coat. She threw it to him, while she put on his outer garments. They were warm, he had made them so, and now he looked very cold. But Hare Bridge village was quite near, once he escaped the cottage.

"It was," said the passenger, "my father's ring."

"Your father's. Does that matter?"

"Yes," said the passenger. He looked down. "Yes."

"Keep the ring then, with my compliments."

Persuading him up the bank to the shelter of the cottage was awkward. He made a dreadful mess of climbing the snowy incline, slipping about so much she considered if he were trying to trick her. She put the pistol to his now hatless head, to all his wonderful hair, and he gave her a beautiful hurt look.

But they reached the cottage finally, and she undid the door and pushed him in.

A wretched place, fireless, grim. Poor fellow.

"You'll remain here till the churches strike for seven of the clock. Get it?"

"You want my word of honor I'll stay put."

"'Tis only this. If you come after me, or the coach, I'll shoot you dead. One bullet will do. I never miss, sir."

"I can imagine. But what excuse will you make to anyone who sees you cheerily murdering me?"

"That you're the accomplice of Gentleman Jack Cuckoo. You were, after all, the only one to stay with him when the rest ran off."

"Just a courtesy. He couldn't make himself hurt anybody, so much was obvious, and he looked so fed up."

"Who do you think would believe you stayed for *that*?"
"You?"

Art bowed. "Your servant." She shut the door on her prisoner and blocked it with the snow-broken limb of a tree, just in case.

Outside, as she washed her face clean in snow, of all things, she heard the man she had robbed begin to sing. It went without saying he had a marvelous voice. Art thought she knew the song . . . couldn't recall from where. She had no space to wonder. Instead, she pelted up the road, trusting someone would have caught the running horses and coach by now and that, after the disturbance, it had not yet set off again for Lundon.

Of course, she would never have shot him.

∞

Bells ringing in Christmas morning woke Felix Phoenix. He opened his dark blue eyes and looked about, rather surprised to find himself in a partly ruined cottage, by the remains of a fire he had tried—unsuccessfully—to light in the grate.

Some creature had leaped down behind him last night, a being like a young leopard with steely eyes. *That* was who had shut him in here.

Anyway, he had promised not to escape until seven, and now, from the sound of it, the day had reached eight o'clock.

"Merry Christmas, Felix," said Felix sadly, running a hand through his ice-blond hair.

He managed to kick open the door after a few tries.

Luckily the sooty coat the leopard creature had given in exchange for his own was fairly warm. A brisk walk to the village should be no great problem. And the sun was out. The sky was blue.

Just outside Hare Bridge, Felix met a crowd packed round the coaching inn—but no coach. Doubtless it was long gone, and the leopard with it, in his coat, cloak, and hat.

People turned to look at Felix as he walked up. Silence resulted—then loud shouts and oaths. Burly farmers surrounded him.

"Hallo," said Felix.

"'Tis him, 'tis Gentleman Jack Cuckoo!"

Up flew the cries like mad rooks.

"No, actually—I think—" attempted Felix reasonably.

"Or his *accomplice*—it's his demon accomplice," hissed a large and aproned woman. "*Worse* than Jack himself."

"This one—"

"—bites off noses—"

"—eats coach wheels—"

"A fiend!"

The leopard lied, thought Felix.

Then he ducked under the waving arms, forced between lurching bodies, and bolted for the road. One long first skid on the ice carried him far off, but as he righted himself, he saw the hunt was already up. Diving off the Lundon Road, Felix Phoenix bounded into the woods, falsely accused, and chased by all the howling host of Hare Bridge.

~TWO~

Pistols for Two, Coffee for Who?

The yellow dog barked all the way to Lundon.

Whose was it? It didn't seem to belong to anyone. Perhaps it had paid its own fare.

Art stayed alert, not trusting any of the other five passengers. Three seemed to think she was still that "delightful young gentleman, Mr. Phoenix," who had been with them before, and two were suspicious she was just what she *was*—an imposter in delightful Mr. Phoenix's stolen outer garments.

Art said little. She pulled "her" hat low and pretended to tiredness but never closed her eyes.

The horses, which had only hurtled as far as the Hare Bridge Inn, had been given oats and were now in a wild mood. The coach made good speed. As the night peeled off the world, it came up in bright wintry colors. Snow silky-brilliant as new marble, sky like turquoise, all the bare trees covered in snow-lace and painted with lines of thin gold by the sun. Bells rang everywhere. It was Christmas. The passengers grumbled, scared, in proper Christmas spirit, they would be late for festive dinners.

But the countryside opened on snowy fields and villages, which steadily seemed to grow together, and at last became grimier and less toylike, clustering in long scaly alligators of streets. By then the skyline of Lundon City lifted in the distance, amazing as an oil painting.

Had Art been here before? She wasn't sure. Port's Mouth, a hundred or so miles to the southwest, that was the English town she must have known best—for Port's Mouth gave on the Free English Channel, and was a place of tall ships—some of which were secretly pirates'.

Art craned at the coach windows. So did the five others in the coach—and the dog. And so they saw: the gilded half orange, with stalk still attached, of the dome of St. Paulus Cathedral, the crowns of Lundon Bridge, the red and white of the Tower of Lundon (where they kept the old crown jewels, and also lions), tall Black Monk's Gate, oily Smoothfield Markets, and marshy Sheerditch.

The coach finished its run under the great clock of St. Charity's Cross on the Thamis Strand. The coachman boasted—the time was only five minutes past noon.

As for the dog, when the passengers got out, it did the same. Wagging its tail, and quite alone, it flew off down the street.

Art stood on the Strand, while a sea of traffic splashed her with slush. She looked between people and buildings, down to the River Thamis. It was the color of bluish lead, and on its banks were huge granite monuments and statues. Ice lay thick on the river, floating in chunks and rafts between the various boats.

"The Coffee Tavern?" The man squinted at Art when she asked him. "That old sty of a place. Beds like pies, pies like beds—fleas in both—West End is where ya go. Ask for Ramble Lane."

Art turned up the Strand and headed west over the cobbles.

St. Martins-in-the-Fields, standing on its meadows of snow, rang gloriously behind her. The Republican Jack of Free England blew on almost every tower or roof, red, white, green, yellow, and blue.

She gave Lundon only half an eye. It was an exciting noisy city. But she had things to do.

⧟

Inside the open door of The Coffee Tavern, the air was brown from coffee fumes and the fudge of tobacco pipes.

Above the door hung the sign of a barrel of coffee beans, and below it, the yellow dog stood barking on the threshold.

Seeing Art, the dog wagged its tail, then darted straight into the tavern. Shadowy figures staggered cursing as the dog shot between them, fetching up in a corner of brownest dark beyond which a window shone. Loud yells greeted its arrival.

"Muck! *Muck!*"

Art froze, listening. She knew that voice.

"Hey, 'tis old Muck, the Cleanest Dog in England!"

"Where hast thou been, ancient doggy?"

"You know Muck. He'll go anywhere."

"Pass the coffee, Walt. The dog'll take a dish."

Art—knew them all.

She moved slowly forward, toward the corner. Coffee drinkers slouched out of her way. To one side there was a wrestling match going on, on the floor. A girl somehow carrying ten coffee jugs sailed by—but everything came and went into and out of the gloom. High as larks on the caffeine, the customers made a din, and raucous songs burst from nowhere and sank back into mugs. Everyone was in their cups.

Art halted by a long table.

Round the table, *they* sat.

Salt Walter, a young man now of eighteen, his fiery hair bright even in darkness. Salt Peter, his brother, a man of twenty, good at cannon. And there, Dirk—*and* Whuskery, and coal-black Ebad Vooms, Second Officer, and Eerie O'Shea, Officer Number Three.

Her eyes were adjusting. She could see them better now. None of them had yet seen *her*.

Art couldn't speak. Her heart hammered in slow huge beats.

They wore the clothes of pirates, exactly as remembered. Shirts of ruined ripped embroidery and lace, coats patched in colors and with golden tassels and braid. High boots of black, broad belts stuck with knives, bullet belts slung slantwise, also stuffed with pistols. Flintlocks leaned by, cutlasses hung about. Three-cornered hats, plumes, jewels, coin earrings, spangles the size of a big pirate's ear.

"Dog's eagerer for coffee than you are, Ebad. He's scoffed the lot." Eerie turned to call for more and noticed the person standing behind him.

Art said, clear and cool over her thumping heart, "The dog came from Rowhampton. He'll be thirsty."

"By the Yak!"

"By the Lord's Armchair!"

Up they rocketed, jumping out of seats—out of their *skins*—but not their gaudy clothes.

They stood in a semicircle round the table, six men staring at Art. One for every year she had been shut in the Angels Academy.

No one spoke.

Across the tavern erupted another song:

> *"Drink your coffee sweet and brown—*
> *Lundon Bridge has fallen down!"*

"By the Topgallants," said Ebad Vooms, soft as dust falling. *"It's Molly Faith."*

"Yeah," said Salt Walter, eyes on stalks. "'Tis a *ghost!*"

Art said nothing.

It was Eerie who said, "That isn't Molly. Can't be Molly."

"No," said Art then, "it's Molly's daughter."

Something dropped like a tattered mop-head out of the cloudy rafters and landed on Art's shoulder. It didn't really startle her. Not after the rest. She turned her head and looked into the pearl-gray eyes of Molly's parrot, Plunqwette.

"Pieces of Eight," said the parrot. "Polly want a Dollar."

"Good girl," said Art to the parrot. Something locked in the back of Art's throat. She blinked once. That was all.

But on the table Muck began to bark, and the parrot, spinning from Art, launched herself beak first at the yellow dog.

Feathers and dog fur flew. Coffee cups rolled and shattered.

"Cockfight!" screamed the coffeed crowd and surged at the table, making bets. "That yeller cock, there, look." "Nah—the green one—" Here came the tavern keeper, too, moaning about broken crockery.

"Oh, it's you lot. Flickety undarned pests—"

"Can't touch us," sang Salt Walter, prancing about on the table among broken china and the fighting dog and parrot.

"We're the Coffee Crew now," said Salt Peter to Art.

Dirk added, *"Pirate Coffee, dear heart."*

Art didn't understand, but neither did they about her. They were on equal footing. She sat down, and soon they poured her a cup of coffee.

"When it happened," said Ebad. "After that."

"You mean when our ship sank," said Art.

"In a manner of speaking, yes."

"It was always Molly's ship," said Walter. He began to cry, and his brother moved the fresh coffee away to save it getting salty.

"Well, we lost Molly, didn't we," said Eerie, blowing his nose. "Lost her for good an' all."

"And after that—well. We've mucked about—not *you*, Muck, you're OK— But we, her most dashing crew, why, by heaven, us. We mucked about, mucked in."

"You survived," said Art.

"That's true. True indeed."

"How?"

They looked at her. Now in the chocolatey gloom beyond the window's glare, everyone could see everyone. Even Muck and

Plunqwette had separated, and, annoyed, the cockfight gamblers had gone away.

"We did this and that," said Dirk. "I'll draw a veil over *that!*"

Whuskery wiped coffee foam from his wonderful blue-black mustache. "*We stuck together.* A band of brothers, we—we few, we happy few—"

"Why didn't you get another ship?" said Art.

"Eh?"

"If you got away when *Unwelcome* went down—"

"No one," said Ebad, "let us *have* another ship."

"Molly would have *taken* one," said Art firmly.

"That's true. Molly could do anything. She cared for us," wailed Eerie, "better than any sister—a mother to us she was."

They toasted Molly in the coffee. Muck did, too. Only Plunqwette sat aloof, preening her disarranged green and red feathers.

Art said, "But what happened to the rest of Molly's fleet?"

No one replied. They were giving Art another very peculiar look now. Finally Ebad said, "Her *fleet?*"

"Yes, Ebad. At least fifteen ships at that time, wasn't it? Did none of them come after to help? Is that it?" But Ebad stared at her, as if suddenly she talked another language. Art thought, That *foul* then. The rest of her pirate fleet—must have abandoned *Unwelcome Stranger,* their flagship, left her to her fate. No wonder these men can't stand to speak of it.

Eerie, proving this theory to her, cried in a falsely hearty voice through the new silence, "But tell us about you, my Art. Your dad got you, didn't he, after we—after we were sunk."

Art frowned.

"By the Wheel," said Salt Peter, "lookit, she's so like her ma—"

"More like Molly," said Eerie, "than *Molly* was."

"Did your da care for you kindly?" snuffed Salt Walter.

Art slammed down her cup.

"*Listen*. I've spent years in prison because of my father."

"Prison—?"

"Some school for refining ladies like sugar. My father is a monster."

"Ah. Well, Molly said he was."

"I *forgot* all this. You. *Her*— Our cannon, the Duchess, blowing up—that blowup made me forget. But now—"

"Well," said Ebad. He nodded. "That explains—truly it does. Fear not, we'll take care of you. By Stars and Sails we will."

"Mr. Vooms, I don't need taking care of," said Art. She stared at them, one by one. "*I* will take care of *you*."

Nobody answered.

She could *hear* their brains clattering together, yelling: *She isn't Molly Faith.*

"We have this job," said Eerie eventually.

"Which is?"

"We help sell coffee."

"*Pirate Coffee*," said Salt Peter. "Drink as much of it as we like, promote it, get room and board and a bit of dosh to go in the pocket. Kind as a silk handkerchief."

Art threw back her head and laughed.

"You *what? You*—sell *coffee?*"

Through his tears, Salt Walter warbled:

> "*Pirate Coffee is the brew,*
> *It's the only drink for you,*
> *Come aboard and join our crew—*
> *Yo heave ho!*"

"Stop it," said Art. "I'll tell you what we're going to do." They waited uneasily. She said, "We are going back to sea."

"Er, Art, er—look—the *sea?*"

"Never heard of it, Mr. Salt? Very well. You've all lost your nerve. Never mind. Molly's crew was the finest. Seven Seas over. Your courage will return—I promise you. We will *take* a ship and make her the second *Unwelcome Stranger*. We'll get rich through cleverness and planning, not by cruelty, just as Molly always did it."

A silence now so total she thought they might never speak again.

Then rather feebly, "We've already got a *sort* of ship," said Eerie.

"The Coffee Ship," said Salt Walter. He went as red as his chair, or the parrot's red feathers. Even in the dark, Art couldn't fail to see it.

"It's an advertisement, you understand," explained Ebad grimly. "We're sailing down the Thamis to cheerful Grinwich, then all downriver, and along the south coast—maybe as far as Port's Mouth. Pirates—advertising Pirate Coffee—you take my drift?"

Felix discovered hours after what had been the trouble. This happened when he saw his own face reflected in silver. *Then* he realized the leopard who had jumped him and stolen his coat, cloak, and hat *hadn't* also given false information to the crowd at Hare Bridge. No, it was Felix himself who had, unintentionally, done so.

Having turned up just after a coach had been stopped by Gentleman Jack Cuckoo and a highway robbery attempted, Felix—by then wearing a patched, old, sooty coat, and having what *looked* like a black half mask over his eyes—had given quite the wrong impression.

The mask was smeared soot. From that fire he had tried to light in the cottage—or even off the coat itself, it seemed to have been up a chimney— And, of course, he hadn't known, he hadn't seen himself that morning. But the crowd took one look—

Felix ran for miles.

He slipped and slithered, skidded in graceful skating slides, hit trees, fell down, got up, ran on.

He lost the crowd. Probably luck—though also, he thought, he had just run off in such crazy directions, now east, now north, fallen in so many snowy ditches, slid at a hundred miles an hour down so many hills that no one in their right mind would ever descend except very carefully—the crowd lost him because they had more sense than he did.

When finally he realized he had escaped, Felix leaned awhile thoughtfully on a tree. He was bruised and battered, but in one piece. He laughed softly at himself, at the world, straightened his hat—remembered he *had* no hat—and walked across a white field, through a stand of trees, and straight into—

"Here he is! You're damnably late, sir. What do ye mean by it?"

"Really nothing," said Felix, looking at the five well-dressed gentlemen, their displeased faces, the table laid with brandy bottles, bandages, and an open box containing two pretty, shining silver inlaid pistols.

"Nothing! Are you light with us, sir? Eh, sir?"

Felix waited cautiously.

"Look at the fellow. Been at a dance and forgot his mask. Don't he know what he's to do? Goat's Gizzards, sir, the cheek of you! Are you taking the Mouse, sir?"

"Seldom," said Felix.

"Dem fellow's taking the Mouse, innit."

One of the men now strode forward and glared very hard at Felix. "I object to this bloke. I wouldn't trust him to put a plaster on a horse, let alone act proper surgeon at this duel."

Oh. A duel. That was why there were pistols on the table. Felix said, "I'm not—"

"Not what? Spit it out, innit!"

"Yes, buck up. I want to shoot this chap here, and get off for my Christmas din-din. We've already been waiting for you an hour, you know."

"I'm not a surgeon."

"Says he's not a surgeon, innit. Hell's Oranges. What *are* ye then?"

The other duelist, who had mentioned his dinner, came stomping over.

"I *organized* a surgeon for today, last night, when you and I, Harry, agreed to kill each other this morning."

"Damn right you did, Perry. I well recall. Just after you said I was a cheat at cards, and I slapped you with my glove and said to expect my bullet in the morning."

United, Harry and Perry, the furious duelists, snarled at Felix.

"Can't do a duel without a *surgeon*. It's against the rules. You'll *have* to be it."

"I know nothing about surgery—"

"You won't need to. One of us'll be shot. The other'll be off to his lunch."

The two seconds had now come up to support the duelists. The fifth man said sternly, "*I* have to be in Republicstown by ten o'clock, to referee Landsir Whack's duel. I'm a busy man, y'know. Got another one at midday."

"See," said Harry to Felix. "Go on, man, stop faffing about. Get your act together, and we'll be off, dammit innit."

Felix was pushed across the snowy meadow. Up in tall white trees, crows sat cawing and laughing. The duelists were choosing their pistols.

The stern referee held up his hand. "One shot to each. Back-to-back, gentlemen. I shall count ten paces, which you will tread as I count. Then turn and fire at will."

"I always like that," remarked Harry, friendly, to Perry, "fire at will—look out, Will, I always say."

Felix stood at the table. The bandages were messy and muddled, and the steel instruments in the box looked medieval and even nastier than the pistols. The duelists were now back-to-back, ready for their countdown, still joking with each other jollily.

"No," said Felix.

"What? What *now?*"

"I won't be party to this. You're friends."

"Friends can still shoot each other," observed one of the seconds, sounding bored.

"I know," said Felix. "There's enough murder in this world to prove it. And I'm *not* a doctor. If you're hurt, I'll be useless. So give it up."

All five men wheeled to face Felix—and couldn't, since he had turned his back and was starting to leave.

"Halt the beggar!"

As one, Harry and Perry fired into the snow by Felix's feet. They were both very good shots. The bullets stung the edges of his boots, and snow fizzed upward in two arcs.

Then both seconds had run up and had hold of Felix. They dragged him back to the table.

"I won't do this," said Felix. "Its bloody ridiculous."

Harry, reloading his pistol, gawped. "Fellow's off again."

Perry patted Harry on the shoulder. "All right, old chap. I'll deal with it. Listen, you," he added, seizing Felix by the shirt front, "either you play surgeon, or I'll have satisfaction from *you*. You're a gentleman, by your voice. You'll do. I'm fighting someone here. You can be it."

"I don't fight," said Felix, pale and still. "I've been told what fighting causes. And I can't shoot, either."

Harry thrust between them. "I've had enough, innit. By the

Caterwauling Stars, sir. Take that"—a slap from Harry's leather glove—

"And *that*, sir, and poo to you, too!" exclaimed Perry, slapping Felix's face with *his* leather glove.

"You are now challenged by both of us," added Harry, bothering to explain. "Damn the surgeon, we'll do without the old grackler. Choose your weapon, sir."

"No."

"Choose it, or I'll shoot you dead anyway."

Felix was stark white now. It made his eyes a blue that was almost black, made his pale hair somehow more vivid. He folded his arms.

"I don't fight. I don't shoot. I'm not a doctor."

But someone thrust a pistol—loaded, presumably—into Felix's hand. He dropped it disgustedly on the snow. No one took any notice. He had been pushed back-to-back with one of them—Harry. The referee repeated his instructions.

"Look out, Will!" cried Harry.

Harry paced the ten paces.

Felix didn't. But when they were counted, he turned. He looked straight into Harry's glittering, bulletlike little eyes.

Harry winked, spun sidelong, and fired from only ten paces, point blank at Felix Phoenix.

As the gun spat fire and noise, Felix fell.

"What the devil—did I *miss?*"

Felix sat up on the snow. "Apparently."

Perry and the two seconds were searching the ground, trying to find the other pistol Felix had somehow managed to hide under the snow.

"I *never miss.*"

"Another one," muttered Felix.

"He fell over," said Perry to Harry. "And he's hid the gun. There, there, don't take on. Never seen a fellow move so quick as he did. Thought he'd swooned. He went down one split second before you fired."

Felix had stood up. Harry was almost tearful, in a tantrum, refusing to be consoled for missing killing Felix.

This time, their Christmas morning spoiled and seasonal spirits damped, they didn't try to prevent Felix leaving. "Good riddance!" someone yelled.

About a mile off, he took the gun—which he had actually managed to pocket when he fell—out of his coat. A duel with one gun—even Harry and Perry couldn't now make that work. Felix would have thrown the weapon away, but then someone innocent might find it. He would keep the pistol till the chance came to be rid of it. Though it weighed like lead on his mind.

Felix, too, was depressed. He stood bemusedly there, examining the pistol. And that was when, in the silver of it, he saw abruptly the dim reflection of his face, with the accidental sooty highwayman's half mask.

Ebad Vooms paused, looking back along Ramble Lane at the tall slim girl dressed like a tall slim young man. Salts Walter and Peter were walking with her, and Dirk, Whuskery, and Muck. The parrot flew back and forth above, upsetting Lundon's pigeons.

Yes, Art was so very like Molly. But Molly's hair had been that pinkly honey shade, her eyes that dark green. Art was taller, too. Ebad remembered well Molly's height, and that she had looked taller, her legs being long—Art was *almost* Molly then. And the difficulty was—

"Is she off her nut?" asked Eerie, melancholy, at Ebad's side.

"*Never.* It's from when the cannon blew up. It did enough damage. And it's affected her memory, as she says."

"Six years back that was, Ebad. Six whole years."

"The girl says she only remembered us at all yesterday morning."

"Give her time then," said Eerie.

"Time and tide wait for no man."

"'Tis a fact, so it is."

Sinking Molly —

They took the horse bus to Grain Dock. Ten horses pulled the vehicle, which was packed with Christmas Day travelers, their baskets exploding with uncooked or ready-roast geese, bottles, tangerines, presents tied by gilt ribbons. A huge Christmas tree took up most of the front four benches. The air was heavy with the scent of pine, smoke, horse dung, of Christmas dinners at varying cookery stages, and Christmas puddings boiling in pie shops along the road.

"Not a single mince pie have I had," mourned Eerie.

"None of us will have a Christmas."

"Such is the life of the advertiser."

At Grain Dock, the snow piled upon either side of the steps, and ice stuck thickly out by the embankment. Ships stood off on the river, their masts stripped bare as winter trees. They were mostly rusted merchantmen that plied the Thamis up and down, solid and heavy-bottomed, unsuitable for pirating.

Art looked searchingly about for the ship the men had spoken of. Would it be any use? (They always referred to it—as *it*, not "she"—that didn't promise well, did it?) But they had told her the vessel was supposed to travel, not only on the river, but along the south coast—to Port's Mouth even, Ebad had said. So it must at least, this It-ship, be seaworthy.

But Art wasn't certain, wasn't happy. There was something very wrong with her mother's crew. In six years they had lost their stamina. But it was more than that. They had been *pirates*. Among the most famous ill-famed in the world. Apart from anything else, how could these men be roaming the Lundon streets, taking work as adverteers? Some ports (like Port's Mouth itself) were often lax with their kind, letting them come and go, relishing the wealth English rogues brought England. But Lundon wasn't the same. In the capital, Law was held up like the Republican Jack. The fate of any pirate here, as with any highwayman, was, when once caught, to face trial at Oldengate Prison, and next a hanging on Execution Dock.

Yet here they were, quite undisguised, larger than life—and walking free.

Had they been pardoned? Had they all gone *mad?*

Gone mad—when she had finally *gone sane?*

She hadn't pressed them. She was watching them. A dark distrust had settled on Art. She hadn't really expected to find any of them so soon. But to find so many of them, and so swiftly—and then, *this.*

Well. She must wait, watch, see.

Then the ship came, towed upstream to the dock.

Oh, dear. The ship.

"There's a nice little boat, now."

"That—is *yours?*" Art inquired.

"It's the Coffee Ship," said Salt Walter.

It was.

Painted a rich coffee brown, with bright red and yellow trim, it was a sort of pirate ship done small. Very. Only about thirty feet stem to stern, it had three thin masts of no great height, and hung with some dainty cream-colored sails that looked as if the first real wind would split them. On the side of the ship was painted its name, the *Pirate Coffee.* Below her matchstick of a bowsprit leaned out a figurehead of a lady with a coffeepot. Worse than all else—Art's eyes journeyed, disbelieving, *believing,* upward—the *Pirate Coffee* flew the Jolly Roger. Only not quite. On a black ground was painted, instead of a skull, a fine white bone-china cup, above two crossed coffee spoons.

"If you step aboard that—*thing*—" rasped Art, "the curse of every ocean rover born will fall on all our heads."

"Chin up, Arty," said Ebad. But he sounded strained.

Then Art saw it was already too late. The curse must have fallen. For some of Molly's crew *were* on board. Over the rail of the Coffee Ship leaned two other known faces from her past. The bad-tempered black stubble of Black Knack, with black eye patch over one eye. The round moon face of the Honest Liar, topped by red handkerchief and brass earrings.

"Ahoy, mateys!"

"Avast, ye sea slugs! Hove over. Thou shalt pipe us aboard."

Muck barked. "Shut up," said Art unfairly. But Muck went bounding off down the just-placed gangplank, with Molly's parrot flying over very low, swooping in now and then to bother the dog.

"Look who we found," called Eerie, presenting Art.

Black Knack stared, then took the eye patch off his perfectly healthy eye to stare harder.

"We don't need any more on this trip. Not enough money being paid for *us* as it is."

"Black Knack—'tis Molly Faith's daughter."

"That's never her daughter. It's a lad. Go on, be off, you boy."

Art stepped on the gangplank. She strode straight across to Black Knack. And as she went, sensing the shift of timbers (even on this silly little deck), a loosening and relief washed over her muscles. Then she was facing Black Knack, eyes to eyes.

"You should be ashamed, Black Knack. And you, Honest. Look at this streak in my hair. Who am I?"

"All right, I know you."

Honest blushed. He hung his head. "I did know," he said. Then he grinned. Pulling out the whistle, he started piping her and the others aboard.

Art still confronted Black Knack. "I don't only mean for not knowing me, sir. I also mean for *this*."

"The ship. True," said Black Knack. He looked away. "In our day we were the best. We're mighty fallen."

Ebad was there. "Stow it for now. We'll talk about that later."

"Tell me one thing," said Art, "who's going to captain this craft?"

"The sponsor wasn't much bothered. One of us . . ." Black Knack paused. "Some man," he said.

Art walked off along the deck, but Ebad and Eerie had joined her. They showed her hatchways, ladders. The Captain's Cabin. It was the size of a large chair, and in any case was full of sacks of coffee. The belowdecks were also full of similar sacks and barrels.

"Here come the sailors," announced Salt Peter from the tiny quarterdeck.

Art's head turned very fast.

"Sailors?"

A group of deckhands was now trooping on, tarry, beery men who might have come from any of the merchant ships around.

"We," said Art, "are the crew."

"Not here. Not now." Ebad's voice was grave with worry.

"We need no sailors!"

"The Coffee Sponsor—his company—" Eerie said quickly. "It's their show. They decide who does what."

A boy was swinging up into the rigging of the teeny mizzen-mast. It must be stronger than it looked.

Art sprang. She sprang to the central main mast—the only one, in fact, she trusted to take her weight.

Up she went, hand over hand, quicksilver in the sunlight, hair like a banner. Reaching the top cross-spar, she sat there, smiling up now at the blue winter sky. Here—*here*—despite everything—was her dream, partly realized.

"She's Molly's all right," breathed Ebad. "She's never forgotten how."

"I wish to God Molly were *here*."

"Molly's dead," said Ebad. "You and I, all of us, we saw her. *We* were lucky to get off alive. So was the kid—Art."

"Gently we go," said Eerie.

"Or would it be better," broke in Salt Walter, "to up and out with it, straight?"

They stood with eyebrows clenched, while alien sailors swarmed the slender masts, and Art sat high above, smiling at the sun.

Pirate Coffee sailed down the Thamis to Grinwich and the Isle of Hogs.

As the afternoon grew smokier and the west began to pinken, people still waved to them from the banks, and soon shook their lanterns. Street lamps were being lighted along the quays. Glints of yellow sparkled in the ice-bitty water.

"This ship and we, we're just like Cleopatra's barge in the Shakespur play," said Whuskery. "Dost remember, Dirk?"

"*Do* I, dear," said Dirk. "Be hard to forget after that night at—"

"Hush," said Whuskery. "There's Art."

Dirk looked nervously along the rail. Art, too, stood there, looking out at the passing shore. The monuments and massive buildings of Lundon had long since changed into trees, reedy islets, and docks of ships keeled over at their cleaning.

Art had stolen up like a shadow. Molly had been like that. Silent. Sudden—wonderful.

"She ought to be *told*."

"Up to you, dear, if you want to risk it," said Dirk, trimming his nails by the light of the Coffee Ship's lanterns.

They reached Hog's Isle in the gloaming. Passing Budgerigar Wharf, with its tall black towers and warehouses, the little Coffee Ship sailed under and through a pale reflection of Hawksmoore's pillared Egyptian church, St. Edwige.

"Dock here tonight. Show starts tomorrow."

"First," said Ebad, "the theater. We'll go there."

Art looked aside at Ebad in the coming of the dusk. His darkness behind the lanterns hid him well.

"A theater now."

Inside Art, somewhere, some strange thing stirred. It was like a lion roaring in the far distance from the Tower of Lundon. She shrugged.

The Coffee Ship bumped home in shallow water, not needing much depth. Rafts of ice sailed by. They went ashore, the pirate crew, a walking advertisement always now for Pirate Coffee.

Pigs grunted and rummaged over the river on Hog's Isle, heard but invisible by night. The main streets of Grinwich were lit by street lamps all the way to the theater.

"*Why* are we here?" Art said.

"Just look, Art. Look at that great gray wall all aflap with bills of old acts and plays and performances."

Art looked unwillingly, and only to please them. Although she had recalled the crew so well, now they seemed, every minute, more unknown. Strangers—*welcome* strangers—?

She had brooded some while on how she had gone up the mast that afternoon, sat on the cross spar. Fooling herself she was on a proper ship at sea.

Walter was enthusing over a long tattered poster.

"'The Great Zimbaldo,'" he read, "'Magician and Reader of Minds'—I recall *him!* A genuine fake—and here. 'Madam Clora Snutch and her Talking Hens'—"

"I've heard some things about *her,*" sniffed Dirk, "*and* those hens."

Ebad had a key to the Stage Door. The front entrance to the theater had been boarded up. Art had gathered they were supposed to bed down here tonight. It wasn't inviting.

"Breaks my heart," said Eerie, "seeing the lovely old place gone to ruin."

They went in, and Peter lit a lantern. They eased up a flight of narrow twisted stairs. Cobwebs hung like solidified smoke.

"Takes me back," said Eerie softly.

Back where? Oh, Art thought, he must have seen some play here once.

The theater was a warren. Corridors ran everywhere, none lighted. The lantern glare lurched and crashed about, reminding Art of things (silently) blowing up—until more lamps were lit.

All the crew were now suddenly very lively. They were laughing and striking poses, drawing their cutlasses and making pretend charges at one another, telling jokes, reciting things that sounded like bad poetry—worse even than the coffee song. The dog, quiet for once, stayed at their heels. Art didn't know where the parrot had got to.

Why did Molly's men like this theater so much?

Ebad said, "Art and I, we'll go along now and see the stage. Glance at that room where—see the room."

"Ebad," Art said, "*I've* got no interest in this theater."

"Art, just come with me."

"All right. If it's that serious."

Alone, the two of them walked off into the maze of darkness with Ebad's lantern. The theater was icy, but a colder apprehension was gathering in Art's bones. *Could* she trust Ebad? She thought, I've still got Jack Cuckoo's pistol.

She hated to think this. But if any of them was now her enemy—he would regret it. You didn't have to kill a man to stop him.

The stage opened beyond them like a wide cave. It was scattered over with forgotten things—props no one had wanted or remembered to take—a faded tree made of painted wood, a moth-eaten curtain, a broken stool, a plate. Where the footlights ran below, their glass bowls were smashed, and they hadn't any candles in them.

Why would Art know about footlights? Had *she* ever been to a play as a child? No, she was certain not. There had never been time—she had been at sea with Molly.

"Notice up there." Ebad dramatically raised the light and pointed.

Ropes hung down, weird wooden apparatuses for lifting or carrying, most of them now skewed at awkward angles. Somewhere high among the shadows, wings flashed like colored papers. The parrot? A pigeon.

Art turned to Ebad.

"What's this about?"

"You don't know, Arty, do you?"

Art waited, looking into Ebad's familiar, unknown, ebony eyes. (Something moved behind the stage—pigeons? She couldn't decide—)

Ebad said, "Come and see the dressing rooms."

"For what?"

"You've not seen them."

"Then, Ebad, I won't. I've seen sufficient."

"Nay, my girl. Thou hastn't. This way. Follow me."

Art was cold now as the ice. She felt again the dizzy feeling that came when her head hit the eagle bannister in the Angels Academy, and all her past flooded in like a high tide.

She found she *must* follow Ebad, on two numb booted feet, follow the splurging lantern.

Down another stair. Along another corridor. To another door.

On this door, the remains of another poster, mostly intact.

Ebad posed once more, holding the lantern high.

"Read it, Art."

Art read the playbill. It was about an old performance, years before. Though she read it and read it again, somehow it didn't make sense.

She read the poster three or four times, and still she didn't know what it said, or what the picture meant, the black-and-white woodcut at the poster's head . . . three things stuck up from a long cheese-wedge shape—What was it? And was the printing in some language Molly hadn't taught her—Persian, or Nedderlandish— Art had a good smattering of French, Spanish, even Africayan—so it couldn't be those—

It wasn't that.

Ebad, looking at her, saw she hadn't understood. He shut his mouth. He didn't know what else he could say. Aside from the blaring truth—

It was Black Knack, who had come after them on cat-soft feet, who spoke up now in a harsh, ringing voice, reading every word of the playbill out to them—from memory?

" 'For the Delight of our Patrons, that Wonder of the Lundon Stage: Mrs. Molly Faith and her Peerless Troop, the Pirate Crew of the Notorious *Unwelcome Stranger*. Tonight, and for Six Succeeding Nights, behold the Daring Ventures of the *Unwelcome*'s Crew, as they Rob from Zanzibari to the Coasts of the Amer Ricas. This Entertainment ending most Splendidly, and with *No Expense Spared,* in a Terrible Sea Battle with *Unwelcome*'s Ancient Foe, the Golden Goliath, as played by Mr. Trevis Wilde, aboard his Evil Cutter the *Enemy*'—"

"That's enough, Black Knack," murmured Ebad.

But Black Knack didn't stop; he ringingly read on. " 'Never will you have witnessed such Startling Spectacles, as Cannons Blaze and Vessels Sink below the Salty Brine—Should our Presentation be any more Realistic, you would Believe Yourself at Sea'—"

"Black Knack."

" 'Do not miss this Glittering Opportunity to Experience the Exciting Victories and Tragic Overthrow of the Famous Pirate Queen, feared and loved by all: PIRATICA. Stalls one shilling only for this Limited Run. Special Concessions for sailing men: Proof of a Nautical Profession may be Required.' "

Art shook her head. It cleared.

She said coolly, "You're saying someone made a play about Molly and the ship and all of you."

"No, Art," said Black Knack.

Art stared back at the poster. The peculiar drawing was of a ship. She could see now. Three masts. A tall windjammer with greyhound sides—

"It was us," said Ebad.

"You mean like this advertising lark. I have it now. You and she—you came here and acted out, as a play, your life at sea."

"Art," said Ebad, "there never was a *life at sea*. Only on the stage. Only up there on those boards you saw—they were our deck, those and others—half the theaters, from Lundon to the Scottish Borders. And the ship was false, built of light wood, balanced in runners, strengthened very cleverly, so when the wooden waves rocked, so did she. It was a magnificent show. We were the toast of the town. And so was Molly, our shining star."

"My mother was Piratica. She was a pirate captain."

"Your mother," said Black Knack flatly, "*played* a pirate captain. *Piratica*—that was her *character*. Molly made her famous, and we made her crew famous."

"You're pirates—"

"We're actors, Art. *Actors. Molly* was an *actress*. So were you. Child prodigy. Very popular."

"I remember," said Art, hearing her voice miles off, "the deck plunging under us—"

"Machinery, I said. Like the wooden waves."

"Wooden—no! We were drenched—"

"Girl, sometimes they threw buckets of water at us to make it more realistic for the crowd."

"Masts—I climbed them, so did you—"

"How many more times? I *said*. The ship was special and well built."

"The cannon," said Art's miles-off voice, "gunpowder—"

"Gunpowder the same as for fireworks. And thunder made by banging metal sheets."

"The fights. We can *fight*."

"Stage-managed. Stage-trained."

The Governors' palaces, said Art, but now she was no longer speaking aloud.

Black Knack anyway answered her.

"All scenes. A play. We brought the house down. And when the ship sank each night—machinery again—and you were put off as a little child and escaped all alone on that little boat into the wings—not a dry eye in the theater."

Pirates, thought Art, not speaking, Oceans—

"Never been to sea in my life," said Black Knack. "Even that river makes me wobble in my insides."

Ebad put his hand on Art's shoulder. It was a measure of her horror, greater than rage, she didn't thrust him off.

"But our Molly, she did die, Art. That last night. Something went wrong. That cannon, a stage cannon, the Duchess. Too much powder in it. It blew up. You were thrown clear, but the whole of that heavy-built set came down on us. The ship sank, right enough—dropped right through the floor of the stage into the cellars below."

"Alas, poor Molly," said Eerie from the unseen dark of the stair behind Black Knack.

Vaguely Art became conscious all of them were now standing about there.

Eerie said, "A Molly of infinite jest, most excellent fancy. Like a queen and a sister and a mother to us all. That at least, Artemesia, you remembered true."

After the Theater

Usually enough, Christmas left Grinwich at midnight, rung out by the bells of St. Edwige.

Art stood on the docks.

All about, the winter forests of ships' masts, and above, the high yellow moon sailing to the west.

It was like before. Art found she had only the dimmest memory of pushing past all of them, still cold as ice, and finding her way—too easily, as if she knew it—out again by the Stage Door.

She had dreamed it all.

Molly wasn't a pirate. Art wasn't. There was no ship, no lost, astounding life to go back to. Nothing.

Art kicked at the pebbles.

Somewhere real sailors were roaring a sea chantey from some real deck hung with lamps.

"But I remember—"

No, she thought. You don't. The sword fights and sea fights, the dinners in great houses, the jewels, the wind in the rigging, the dolphins leaping—the tricks, the *skill*— They were all make-believe.

Yet it had seemed, *still seemed*, so real. More real—than anything else.

So what am I to do now? Go back to darling Daddy, ghastly Landsir George Fitz-Willoughby Weatherhouse—or rather the Angels Academy? Never.

Art glanced over her shoulder, up the bank at the luminous white of St. Edwige. Downriver the sailors had left off their singing. Instead, a new and more threatening sound was scrawling along the street beyond the church.

The noise got louder and louder. Pebbles crunched. A bleary shout—they were definitely coming this way.

Drunken danger—and I'm only an actor. An ordinary girl trained to balance books on her head and swoon. Useless.

Art didn't move. She watched as the two men jumped over the low wall onto the dockside and fell about laughing. They had spotted Art, of course, and seemed interested in her. They were well-off, and swords were slung lightly at their sides.

"Told you. It's a boy."

"'Tis so. Come here, boy, and turn out your pockets."

More thieves. Why did they need to? They didn't look poor.

But who was Art to judge; she had never been a thief—apart from that one time on the Lundon Road, and then all she took were a coat and hat—and she had never been a pirate, either.

"Look, the boy's coming over. How dare he?"

"You told him to."

"Did I? Insolent scamp."

Art swung up to them, bowing.

"Ho, quaint laddy."

"Ho! Ho!" they warbled.

But Cuckoo Jack's pistol was in Art's left hand, and the pistol's snout was exactly under one of the men's noses—nostril to nostril.

"Box of ducks! The boy's armed."

"Dastardly custard!"

Art reached delicately forward and drew the rich man's sword, light as a breath, from its scabbard.

She stood back and twirled the blade, this in her right hand, all ways as it looked at once, and she smiled as she did so.

"As you say, pockets turned out, gents. Lay your money kindly on the stones."

Yawping and hiccupping, the two unfortunates who had happened on Molly's daughter did as requested. Then they begged to go home.

"But I love your company, sirs," said Art, having pocketed the unpocketed valuables.

"Oh, likewise, likewise—but please—supper waiting, you know—hate to upset Nanny."

"Come, how ungallant. Won't one of you give me a little dance? Take your sword out, you there that still has one. We know you can thieve off people on the docks, if they let you. Let's see who can fight here."

Even by moonlight, and the gleam of St. Edwige, the Egyptian church, Art could see how green and sickly the two highborn gentlemen had turned. But the one who still had a sword plucked it out.

He moved in fact quite fast, but Art much faster. His weapon went spinning down toward the Thamis, and next instant all the buttons had been cut and flew off his trousers: Molly's masterstroke, even if only on a stage.

His trews round his ankles, the gentleman stumbled off along the dock. The other threw himself on his knees, bleating.

"Poo to you, sir. Get up."

"Don't kill me."

"I never kill. Never need to. I'm too fly for that. Give me your scabbard. I'll keep your friend's sword. It prefers me."

He never argued.

With the sword attached to her own belt, Art left him there. The other had vanished, back over the wall. Art fleeted along the shore. Laughing herself now, she ran up the gleaming ice-slippy pebbles. She had no thought for anything, and nothing else came at her or got in her way—as if the night now knew.

"I've gone sane," Art reminded the Grinwich Docks, the safe round-hulled merchant ships, with their antlered masts, clunking faintly at anchor as the Thamis tide came in. Above, the saucy golden moon Grinwich-grinned back.

The pirates who were actors were no longer in the theater. They were down by their Coffee It-Ship, putting other ships, these small and made of folded, printed, waxed paper, carefully onto the river. In each of these little vessels burned a wick in a tiny crock of oil. As they sailed away, this miniature fleet, the flames fluttered like butterfly flowers on the dark. The dog trotted up and down, barking at all things equally.

"A custom of the Inde," said Whuskery, not looking Art in the face, "these papers with lights. Wrong season for it— couldn't get to do it the right time this year . . . brings good luck."

"How do you know all that if you've never been to the Inde?" demanded Art.

"Oh, 'twas in one of the Piratica plays," said Dirk, "ever so swish. Audience cheered for hours. But look, this wax has *ruined* my nails—"

"Have none of you ever been to sea?" asked Art.

Glancing at her, they saw she was now relaxed. She was smiling at them, nodding at the charming little lit-up ships floating away. She was patting Muck.

Relief spread visibly over the crew. They started to look at her properly again. She would settle down, their Art. She was Molly's girl. They would care for her, poor lass.

"Well, not *one* of you?" she asked again.

"I," said Ebad.

"You, then, went to sea."

"What else. I was brought to England from Africay, when I was nine, as a slave. I had a choice, work my passage or lie in the stinking hold and rot. I worked. I've climbed up masts, I've bailed out water in a storm, I've swabbed a deck."

"A slave—" said Art.

"Yes, in England, too. Then the Revolution happened here. The people of England rose up and threw off their chains—and threw off mine. The Republic set me free. So then I was an actor. Now I advertise Pirate Coffee."

Art stretched out her hand, businesslike. Ebad shook it.

"What's this?" she said.

"For you," he said. He held before her one more sheet of waxed paper.

"You want me to make a paper ship, Ebad?"

"Not out of this. We've been using the coffee posters. But this I give you now is different. A souvenir, maybe, of the past."

Eerie leaned in and said, "This is the Great Treasure Map. The one the Golden Goliath was after, on his dire ship, the *Enemy*. In the—er—play."

"But," said Art, "there's no real treasure, is there?"

"It's just a prop. Part of the act. Sentimental value, that's all." They put the map, folded, into her hand.

As she opened it up, Art noticed the others had moved away, back to watch their lighted ships. Only Ebad and Eerie stayed near her, watching *her*. Eerie seemed transparent as clear water. Ebad, though—Ebad seemed, had seemed almost from the first, a man of secrets. No doubt he had good reasons . . . he had been a slave. In the past, though—in the past had he been, even then, so—unreadable?

Art looked at the map, the prop. Drawn large, an island in a navy-blue sea. Dolphins leaping. A ship at one corner, like the ship on the playbill in the theater, the ship she hadn't recognized because *it* wasn't real.

Letters were written along the edges of the island—some invented code? They spelled nothing except nonsense: OOP, TTU, F . . . A . . . B . . . M's—H's . . .

How cold it was. Frost starred the waxy paper. But, too, the map's lower edges ended wrongly, oddly blackened.

"The bottom of the map—and of the island—is scorched off," she said. But Ebad and Eerie had moved on after the others, watching the burning boats.

A bird circled over. Pigeon? Gull? Parrot.

"Pieces of Slate!" cried Molly's pet. "Polly want a Doubloon. Polly want a Golden Louis."

Art held out her arm. "Here, Plunqwette."

Plunqwette swept down and fastened her claws into the cuff of Art's stolen coat. The air crackled with frost about them, as if with fire. "In the blowup," Art said to the parrot. "That was when the map was scorched, eh, girl? You and me," Art said. "Me and you." The parrot craned, pecked at the hilt of the stolen sword none of the others had apparently noticed, and winked her lizardlike eye.

❦ THREE ❦

Goose and Guest ⟶

Felix got the first coach to run the day after Christmas. He had by then walked to Hammer's Smithy over snowy fields and commons. Seeing his appearance—hatless, sooty, patched—innkeepers turned him away before he could show any money. Inn daughters, wives, and servant girls, however, seeing his eyes, hair, face, and figure, sometimes ran after and gave him mulled wine, bread and cheese, half a pineapple, a muffler, a cap. Felix had always been lucky through his looks, but prone to disaster otherwise. Or so it seemed to him as he trudged on.

At Hammer's Smithy he slept overnight in a barn, sharing the space with several fleas.

The coach, once boarded, was a slow-coach. It stopped everywhere, every village and hamlet, even at a couple of well-known trees—Early Court, Barnes Court, Yorkister . . .

He began to wonder why he still bothered to reach Lundon. The job he had been offered had been meant to begin yesterday—Christmas Day Evening, when he had been hired to draw portraits at a large party in a fine house near Lundon's Eastminster. He doubted they would want him now.

The day was crystal with hard frost, and the coach not much warmer. Also, one of his fellow travelers, a nosy man in holiday clothes, became over-interested in Felix's personal belongings.

"Ruby ring, is it?"

"Glass."

"Looks like a ruby."

"No."

"Thought to myself, there's a cranky thing now, a young man of no obvious great wealth, judging by his garb, and he's sporting a ruby ring."

"Glass, as I say."

Nosy kept on. He was like a piece of clockwork that could only repeat certain phrases. But he crowded Felix, and the barn fleas, which loved to meet new people, soon colonized the nosy man, and he drew away, scratching and glaring.

"Tramps shouldn't be permitted on the coach," someone else remarked.

Felix was now shunned. And therefore left in peace.

It had puzzled him slightly, he thought, weary and half asleep as the slow-coach trundled to Knight's Bridge, stopped, started, how the leopard who robbed him had also seemed to think the fake ruby was real. Surely, such a practiced thief should know better?

When Felix woke, they were bouncing into the yard by St. Charity's Cross. Looking from the window, Felix saw at once a pack of persons gathered there, perhaps waiting for the coach. He noticed several others clad in the black and brass buttons of the Lundon Constabulary. Were *they* also waiting for the coach?

Too late, Felix saw a new possible problem. He wasn't wrong.

A big whiskered face, topped by a black constabulary hat, was shoved in the coach. It had eyes only for Felix.

"Welcome to Lundon, Cuckoo Jack."

The mob in the coach turned to Felix in fury.

"Sat here all this way with us—"

"No doubt expecting his villainous accomplice to ride up—then rob us all!"

"And he's given us *fleas!*"

Felix was hauled out onto the icy cobbles. The watching crowd raised a loud cheer.

"They've caught Cuckoo Jack!"

"It will be useless to tell you," said Felix to the whiskery one, "I am *not* Gentleman Jack Cuckoo. Or his accomplice."

"You can tell us anything you like. Attempted robbery, threatened violence—even disrupting two gentlemen's duel, so we hear—oh, yes. A fast rider galloped in yesterday from Hare Bridge by Rowhampton and reported your doings, and that you were at large, seemingly making for the capital. Perfect description, I may say. Surprised no one's caught you afore, seeing how individual you look. Got your black half mask and other disguises in your pockets, no doubt."

"No."

"Ah, cunningly dumped them along the way."

Other jolly constables had gathered close. They were slapping one another on the back, even slapping Felix on the back, they were so happy to have caught him.

Cuckoo Jack hadn't seemed very able at his highwaymanning. However had he earned such a powerful reputation? There were ten constables, all armed to the teeth with sticks and flintlocks.

"You'll come along with us now, to the handy law station by the Temple," the constables helpfully told him. "Then it's off to Oldengate. Jail won't take much of your time. Quick trial. You'll be hanged inside the week," they congratulated him. "Anything you say will be used," they added, "in evidence against you."

To the salutes of the crowd—strangely veering between outrage and admiration—he was being marched now down a side street.

The cobbles were glassy-slick with ice. Icicles stabbed down from roofs and drainpipes. Ahead lay the river. They had been saying on the coach, the Thamis had frozen overnight, solid, from the Strand to far beyond Lundon Bridge. Felix now saw this was accurate. The water seemed to have turned to hard, white cake icing.

But the guards were now propelling him into another street. Or, they tried to.

For something came from this street and out at them, something also icing sugar white, squawking, hissing, and beating two huge white broomlike things, behind an orange dagger on a long white tube.

Everyone ducked to avoid it—and so collided instantly with the man who came belting along behind it, cursing and howling at the top of his lungs: "Stop that goose!"

"Goose?"

"Thought it was a angel—" cried members of the Constabulary.

But they were sliding and slipping, knocked sideways on the ice, all going over now together, with Felix lugged over in their midst.

But somehow the running man chose Felix to grab—he attempted to hold himself and Felix upright, and they did a kind of rapid slithering polka together, stamping and hopping on the lethal cobbles and the bodies of fallen, unpleased policemen.

While they did this, the man insisted on telling Felix his troubles. "Told me it'd be *plucked* and *ready-roasted*—but there it was, still alive—flew straight off—I've been chasing that egg-blatted goose since Christmas Eve—"

The man abruptly got his balance. He let Felix go and dashed off down the road toward the river—where the goose had gone. Felix, using the force of their last slide, hurtled after him.

The Constabulary floundered. A few managed to get up, and with trodden-on marks on their smart black uniforms, reeled after.

"Stop that goose!"

"Stop that man! He's Gentleman Jack Cuckoo!"

All down the street, bending to avoid being hit in the face by the still low-flying, bad-tempered goose, people clutched each other and slid into walls—windows opened and heads poked out, and dislodged windowsill snow crashed on all the running figures.

"Stop Cuckoo Jack!"

"A cuckoo? That big white thing? That's not a cuckoo—it's a *goose*—"

"Gentleman Jack Goose? Never heard of the fellow."

At the end of the street, the embankment opened, lined by polished, snow-capped statues of lions and tall statesmen of the Revolution. The goose flapped off over the railing and up into the clear blue sky above the river.

Felix, also intent on flight, tore down the first available river steps, so fast he never slid once.

Behind him the goose chaser had halted, shaking his fists, the Constabulary still toppled, the curious crowd surged and got in the way.

Below the steps, the snow was crisper on the rough pebbles and shale of the bank. Felix leaped and raced over this track, the frozen river on his right.

Soon, however, the ice had begun to bundle in up the shore, in big chunks, humps, and strange fluted shapes like shells.

Felix stopped then. Panting, he looked back. But no one was there yet.

Out on the solid river, though, was another small crowd. They were slowly dancing on the ice—no, they were skating.

Two young ladies, in fur-trimmed velvets, waved to Felix. Soon, in ever-widening arcs, they sailed toward him, leaving their companions behind.

"Isn't it wonderful—the Thamis has frozen! Too brill of it."

"Wonderful, indeed," said Felix.

"We're skating down to Grinwich—or Sheepwich—I forget w(h)ich—come with us, pray, why don't you? Look, we've got our brother's skates—he wouldn't come, in a bad mood since yesterday—and hot chestnuts and chocolate—and sandwiches, those new things with bread."

Smiling prettily, tempting him. He didn't need tempting. They spelled escape, and under cover.

"You're too kind," said Felix. "But has the river really frozen so far down?"

He hadn't ever skated in his life, hadn't ever had the chance. But Grinwich sounded a satisfying distance from the Lundon Law. No one would be looking out for a skating party.

The girls' companions had already set off, but Felix was in more of a hurry to join them than either young lady.

Assisted by them, he put on the skates as instructed, got up—and promptly sat down again. Linking his arms on either side, they helped him get up again and said they would show him what to do.

Everyone wheeled round in dreamy circles, cutting silver coils in the ice. (Felix glanced often up at the embankment.) The water was invisible below its icing, and the police so far invisible on the bank, though vague shouts were sometimes wafted over.

Soon anyway, Felix and the girls took off.

"Have a hot chestnut, dear Mr. Phoenix."

Practiced skaters, the girls fed him chestnuts and chocs as they glided along the great curve of the sleeping Thamis.

"We're off to see some silly thing our uncle's organized. He's in coffee, you know."

"Really?" said Felix.

"There's a goose!" the girls exclaimed sweetly. "Look, bless it, it's going south for the winter!"

Lundon moved by now very swiftly, rolled away from view on either side, like a wound-up ball of ribbon—that was still somehow always there in front as well. With exercise and snacks, the chill became exhilarating as they soared along. Felix was aware, too, that the fleas had deserted him on the coach—or fainted from the cold.

The two girls had told him they were called Fan and Ann Coffee. They never caught up to the rest of their party. But neither did any representative of the Law catch up to *them*.

Parklands, high gates, churches, monuments stood tall on the banks above. Bridges spanned the river, rushing toward them, arching over, flowing off behind. *There—gone—there—gone.* All in a spurt of spangled ice. They traveled faster than any slow-coach.

"That's the sponsor, Art."

He was a short fat man, and his coat was of the finest coffee-brown brocade; and over it he had furs, and on his head a hat with a crimson plume. There was a gold brooch on one lapel of his coat, and on his hands rings without number. Worth robbing, actually, the sponsor. He wasn't friendly.

He strutted about the deck of the *Pirate Coffee*.

"You were supposed to sleep at the old theater, Vooms, not a tavern. That was why I gave you the door key to the place."

"It was a cold night, sir."

"Cold?" The Coffee Sponsor flicked his furs. "Couldn't you have lit a fire somewhere?"

"The whole building might have gone up."

"Good riddance." The small eyes moved and saw Art. "Who is that boy? Not one of the sailors I hired."

"No, sir." Eerie had stepped forward, bending in a fawning bow. "My nephew."

"You," said the sponsor to Art, "who are you?"

"Art Blastside," said Art. She swept the small fat monster a bow beyond all bows—arrogant as if she had slapped him instead.

"*Blastside?* Some stage name."

"Truly, sir. A cannon blew up once on the boards of a stage and blastsided me. 'Twas my christening."

The sponsor clumped off, inspecting the Coffee Ship, making sure they hadn't spoiled the coffee by sleeping or leaning against the barrels and sacks on deck and below. (Of course, they would be doing both during the "voyage," there was nowhere else to sleep or lean, except the cabin, which they had offered to Art.) They all reeked by now, rather deliciously, of the coffee, even the yellow dog, Muck, who already seemed to like the belowdecks best.

"River's freezing up, Lundon way," said the sponsor to Ebad. "Tell me, have *you* ever *seen* snow before?"

Ebad's face for a moment turned as arrogant as Art's bow. Then—stupid. "Hey!" said Ebad. "I wonder what da white stuff be."

The pirate-actors scowled, concealing laughter.

Ice too lay in thin top-skins all over the river here. The sponsor had kept speaking of it.

Now, "Best be off," he commanded. "I don't want this barge ice-locked."

"And our payment?" said Ebad.

"Oh, don't worry about that. You'll get it at Port's Mouth."

"That wasn't as we agreed."

Art watched. She didn't make a move. She was waiting, having her own plans, now.

The sponsor wasn't happy at all. Ebad had quietly kept on requesting payment. "Confound it then. Here's a pair of guineas. That'll do you for now. And keep that filthy dog out of my coffee."

"Muck's clean!" cried Walter.

"No such thing as a clean dog. And what's that bird?"

"A parrot."

"Does it talk?"

"Does it talk, Plunqwette?" Art asked of the parrot.

Plunqwette spoke with exquisite precision.

"Pirate's parrot. Parrot's pirates."

The sponsor leered—his first smile. His teeth were so appalling he seemed to have made them like that on purpose. "Good, good. Make it do that for the crowds. Oh, and see about appointing a captain. Can't have a pirate band without."

"Ah, lookit de *snow*, la!" chortled Ebad, fist closed on the two guineas and jumping about.

Eerie smothered his giggling in a handkerchief.

The sunset was red that evening, for Felix Phoenix, Fan, and Ann, with a flame of crazy green beneath. A parrot sunset, had they known.

Along the margins of a river now frozen rigid as enamel as far as Camber Well and Deep Ford, occasional braziers burned like the eyes of tigers or torches like red rags on poles. Then, though, the ice grew thinner and chancy. Rifts appeared. The skaters detoured to the bank.

"We shan't risk Grinwich tonight after all. Shall we hire a carriage?" asked Fan.

Ann said, "Uncle was saying if the frost really set in, he'd have to send them off at once—and look, it *is* freezing up ahead, but not quick enough for our skates. So, we've missed them, innit."

"What," asked Felix, "have you missed?"

"Oh, only his silly advertisement ship. It's not important. Aunt's house is up at Black Death Heath. Let's go there. She'll love Felix. Supper first, then, as you *vowed* to us, Felix, you would, draw our portraits!"

Torches burned, too, at intervals over night-black Black Death Heath, leading the way from the village to the enormous house of the skaters' aunt. As they drove there in the carriage, Felix had sights pointed out to him, including Grinwich Observatory, where Time was made, rising from the trees on its high hill.

Lamps lit the Coffee Aunt's drive.

Felix had been in many grand houses in his various roles—of singer, of artist, even long ago, of guest. (Come to that, long, *long* ago, he had *lived* in the grand house of his father. But Felix wouldn't think about that often.)

Used to such things, nevertheless, he fitted into the most splendid of such places with great speed. Despite his unsuitable coat, cap, muffler, Aunt Coffee soon welcomed Felix, as predicted. And then he was sitting in a vast drawing room with salad-green walls and classical statues from Greece, before a strong fire, and with refreshments on a blue china service, and everyone was having a wonderful time—

Until the door opened.

"Mr. Harry Coffee," announced the aunt's butler.

"Harry, whatever are you at *here?*" grumbled the aunt. "You were meant to be busy at a duel in Rowhampton, weren't you?"

"That was yesterday," said Ann.

"And things didn't quite—" began to add Fan.

"Just so," shouted the arrival in the doorway. "But, Aunt, some blatterer turned up and wrecked it. Hadn't the heart for it, after. Smirched Christmas Day for me. For poor old Perry as well."

Felix Phoenix knew by now that the gods of Unjust Fate were entirely capable of exactly this sort of unfair trick.

And as Harry's little greasy bullet eyes landed on Felix, and Harry's fat mouth burst open to swear very horribly, Felix was already up and bowing.

"Why dem ye, sir, ye's already *here*—what are you, innit— Are you *haunting* me?"

"Is this gentleman the one you were to duel with?" asked the aunt, perking up. "Why, then, he is our guest, so could we not still arrange something violent?"

"No way," said Harry. "By the Yak. This man is, I gather, Cuckoo Jack—worst highwayman in England. Has a price of fifty crowns on his head, which, now I know who he is"—here Harry's anger melted to grisly joy—"*I* shall claim. Pilchard," he added to the butler, "go at once and send for the Black Death Constables."

"Oh!" cried Fan, "how exciting. But, Auntie, before Felix goes off to Oldengate to be hanged, please may we just show him Uncle's model of the Coffee Ship in the dining room? He's awfully keen to see it—a last treat, and all that—"

Before Aunt, Harry, or Pilchard could collect themselves in their now rather confused state, the girls had bustled Felix from the room by another door.

"There's the model—"

"Don't be *daft*, Ann. Quick, down this corridor. Now out the window—see the Observatory tower all bright-lamped up there? Just over that hill's the way to the river—"

Felix got out of the window and dropped neatly seven feet to the snow.

The shining Observatory seemed miles off, and Oldengate Prison much, much nearer. But, as with grand houses, Felix was getting used to running away.

Breaking the Ice

Art had read the list of ten or so ports they were to call at. Such places as Till-We-Bury, Margaret's Gate, Battering-Ram's Gate, Dover, Dungeon's Nest, St.-Leonard-and-the-Dragon, Brig Town . . . Hugging the coastline all the way to Port's Mouth, and halting at each port in between, it would probably take them a good month. Or longer, depending on the winter weather.

But the Coffee Ship was so flimsy. She would *have* to hug the coast.

And now anyway, despite the fussing of the sponsor, last night they had run into thick ice at Rottenhythe. Down went the toy anchor. And the hired sailors—the *true crew*—off *they* went ashore, and into the nearest town. They hadn't yet returned.

"We're becalmed. Like the Doldrums, off down from Northern Amer Rica." This from Eerie.

It wasn't remotely like that, Art thought; they were partly trapped in ice, more like the Antarctic. Even so, "How do you know about the Doldrums," she asked, "since you've never been to sea?"

"We *acted* we were there."

Now, at midday, the ice was letting go. But lacking the "proper" sailors, they hadn't moved yet.

Was the ice familiar? Yes . . . icebergs floating like green-white sails . . . And the Doldrums, she knew those. When the *Unwelcome Stranger* had had to be towed by the three jolly boats and their oars, because there was no wind for her to move by.

"What are you looking at there, Arty?" inquired Salt Peter.

Art blinked, and saw, instead of imagined ocean, the riverbank.

"Something's running along," she said.

"One thing running, then some other *riding* things—the second lot are on horse—a hunt? A *man*hunt?"

"Oh look," said Salt Walter, joining them, "he's jumped off that little bridge there out onto the ice. Wow! What a landing. Now he's skating—no, he's just sliding along the river."

They watched, and up aloft somewhere the parrot cackled, having a better view than anyone else.

East of where the Coffee Ship had been wedged in by the ice, broad areas of open water now showed after a morning's sun. Back toward the shore, the ice so far stayed firm. Last night the frost had knitted it in so tight, the little ship had groaned. Now the river was half and half.

"He'll go in, he will. In that icy water."

"There, he nearly did," added Eerie, also at the rail.

On the wooded bankside, among some sheds and warehouses, the men on horses were riding up and down, obviously deciding *they* didn't want to risk the semi-frozen treachery of the river.

"They're constables."

"He's a criminal running from justice, then," said Walter.

And I recognize him, thought Art.

In fact, she recognized his *coat*—it had been hers. The man she had robbed on Wimblays Common?

As he ran, he was looking up at the ship, sadly. The *Pirate Coffee* was exactly like the model he had glimpsed yesterday, when Fan and Ann hurried him past to the window. All that night he had been a fugitive. Cold with winter, or warmed by the exercise of *escaping*.

In the ship's blue shadow, Art noted Felix's white-blond hair.

At the same moment, Felix reached the edge of the ice. He stopped, staring at the ship, and the water between him and it.

Back on the bank, a flintlock discharged powdery smoke, a bright purple-yellow flash and sharp crack. Attractive, deadly.

Art pointed down at Felix.

"Get him aboard," said Art.

"But he's a felon," suggested Eerie.

"I doubt it," said Art.

Ebad anyway was already slinging the end of a rope over the side, down to the ice.

Felix looked up at the crew now, and so saw Art.

"Hell's Kettles! He can't climb!"

Also seeing the rope, however, more police fired their guns

along the shore. They were bad shots, or their police-issue pistols not much use.

"You down there! Grab the rope and hold on—" bellowed Eerie.

Felix nodded. He grasped the rope. As they hauled, Felix jumped clear over the gap of water, his feet striking the vessel's side, and up the flank of the Coffee Ship they dragged him.

His pale, weary, handsome face swung back and forth, getting nearer and nearer, till they pulled him in over the rail.

Felix sat on the deck. Molly's crew regarded their catch.

The men back on the shore were yelling. *Crack, crack* went their guns. A couple of bullets thumped into the hull. And Plunqwette, who had been sitting up on the mizzentop, thrashed off behind the sails with an aggrieved shriek.

Art leaned across the rail. She had Cuckoo Jack's pistol, which the highwayman had managed to reload before dropping it. She shut one eye. Of course, she had never fired a real gun—it had all been an act, and the bullets fakes. Nevertheless, she aimed, and eased home the familiar trigger. The shock hit the socket of her arm—hadn't she ever felt that before? On the bank, a man's brass-buttoned hat flipped off his head, sparkling in the sunlight.

Art fired again, the second shot took off another hat.

"Bullets?" she asked idly, watching the shore.

"We don't *have* bullets."

But Felix was suddenly beside her. He handed her the three bullets of Cuckoo Jack's that he hadn't returned and also the silver-inlaid pistol from Harry and Perry's duel.

Art weighed this in her hand a moment; it was a lighter weapon. She raised it higher, fired, took off two hats together.

There was some bother among the policemen. Some of the horses had bolted. Either that, or some of the constables had.

Art reloaded methodically, as Molly had taught her, hands steady.

The crew, gathered behind her, watched in dire silence.

Only Felix's silence was quite different. It was calm and very bleak.

Eerie said, "You can leave off, Art. Look, they've all run away."

"She *forgot*," said Black Knack, sullenly, "we are *actors*. Now she's made us wanted men, and all on this rocky boat."

"Only I fired at them," said Art. "Only I am a wanted *man*."

"And I threw the rope down. There's a freed slave for you," said Ebad. "Manhunts dismay me, sweet friends. Yep."

He strode off along the deck.

Eerie followed him.

"You attempted to wound no one," said Felix to Art. "It wasn't poor shooting, even I could see that. Why?"

"I told you once. I don't inflict great hurt. I don't kill. I'm too clever."

"True. I remember you told me that."

He looked at Art. Yes, she *was* a woman. And she still wore his coat and cloak, though not his hat. Her hair was a rich dark brown, with an extraordinary streak running through it on the right side, russet as a fox's pelt. Was she more like a cunning fox than a dangerous leopard? Both, he thought.

He hadn't meant to keep any bullets, had forgotten till now he had. It had been when his hand closed, on a reflex, as the highwayman had gone on about the ring with red glass in it.

"What do I owe you for my life?" he asked the leopard-fox.

Art glanced at him. Eyes like steel.

"Nothing. You were my excuse for some necessary pistol practice. We'll put you off at the next stop."

"The constables will report you."

"But," said Art, "we can pretend it was *you* firing at them. Not us."

Felix laughed his musical laugh. It caught Art's ear half a second, but only that. It was time, she felt, to take the chance that had come so early.

She strode for'ard.

"Listen," she said to the pirate-actors who were standing about there, in their lace and plumes, coins and cutlasses. "The ice is all broken up ahead. Let's get off before the Law comes back."

"Those sailors are still ashore—" gasped Walter.

"Never mind," said Art. "*We'll* crew her."

Ebad was standing under the forecastle. He watched Art, unreadably.

Eerie said, "Artemesia, we can't crew a ship."

"We have done it a million times," said Art.

"On a stage."

"What's the difference? Boards—a deck—machinery causing us to rock—or river currents."

Black Knack pulled a face. He banged off across the deck and threw up loudly over the side, making his point that way.

"You see? That's us, Art," said Eerie.

Ahead, the already broken ice gave a yap, splitting, offering them more open water.

Art gazed across at Ebad.

"Raise anchor, Mr. Vooms."

Ebad shrugged. Slowly he drew himself up. "Aye, aye, Captain Blastside. To it, men. Anchor aweigh."

Salts Walter and Peter exchanged glances. It was the Honest Liar who gamboled serenely over and began to work the small anchor's chain about the capstan all by himself.

Felix stayed by the rail, looking away from them all, observing the receding shore. Art could just picture him, this elegant, graceful young man, walking with a book on his blond head for the sake of deportment.

Salt Peter, then Dirk, went to Black Knack's rail and threw up. They were doing it on purpose, Art thought, as Whuskery and Eerie joined them.

The parrot flew over the ship in circles, keeping close. Art moved aft to take the wheel and steer them among the lingering slabs of ice. She knew exactly how to do it, even if she never had. Below, among the coffee beans, she could hear the dog, Muck, howling like a wolf.

And there was a change in the air. That was why the river was choppy. They had a following wind. The little sails croaked and squeaked as they filled. They were sailing downriver toward the sea, at last, and suddenly now, Art could smell, even over all the oily sweetness of the coffee—sea-salt *brine*—

Port's Mouth Ho! ⟵

"But the whole idea of the coffee advertisement is to make a show. We must stop everywhere and perform the act."

"There'll be constables at Till-We-Bury Docks. There's heavy river traffic and a fort," said Art.

"They'll be looking for *him*," said Black Knack, jerking a black-nailed thumb at Felix. "Not us."

"As I pointed out before. But I've thought since. And you, Black Knack, were the one in the right. They *will* be looking out—for all of us. They will know we helped a felon escape."

"*You* helped—you and Ebad Vooms—"

Felix himself stood unspeaking, eyes lowered. He hadn't offered to leave the *Pirate Coffee*, and no one had asked him to. Eerie said, "At the next Channel port, maybe, we can stop. News may not have got down so far."

"We're not stopping at any next port," said Art. "We're making on directly round the coast. We have enough stores for such a brief voyage, despite your sponsor's stinginess. I've checked, even with Whuskery's constant efforts to prevent me."

"But Art—Art—the *advert*—the *sponsor*—!"

"Why are you courting him? You want to marry into coffee?"

"He pays."

Art stood, her long booted legs braced apart on the deck, which, though they were currently at anchor, still lurched. Even so, she noted, though the water was so frisky here, most of the crew had got over their seasickness. "I've a nicer notion. Listen, we sail straight to Port's Mouth. That's where we'll put on this show."

"'Tis not what Mr. Coffee wants."

"It's what *I* want."

They stood staring at her. Only a blot of green on the forecastle rail—Plunqwette—and Ebad, sitting back on a coffee barrel, slowly smoking his pipe, were watching her with another sort of look—considering, thoughtful.

Muttering. But it was Black Knack who thumped up to Art, thrusting his bristly, eye-patched face into hers.

"You'll wreck us, girl. You'll get us all hung. You're only a bit of a kid—a baby—who are you to tell us—*I want this, I want that*—flouncing back into our lives—you're never gone without anything—never lacked a button—rich Daddy saw to that. We've had to struggle. No one would give us work—thought us bad luck after what happened with Molly and that exploding gun. I'll give you, your mother, when she was alive, took care of us. She'd order us about, and we took that. Fine. But *you*—"

He paused because Art had reached forward, pulled off his eye patch, and slapped him across both unshaven cheeks.

Black Knack went the color of boiled beetroot in a red wine sauce. He raised his fist—Eerie and Peter roared together and started forward—but Art had ducked Black Knack's blow with the perfect weaving motion of the trained fighter. Swinging back, she punched him instead with a sharp thwack on the point of his shaveless jaw.

Black Knack's eyes rolled up. He keeled straight over and landed with a crash that further bounced the deck.

Almost everyone else had crowded round. Not, though, Felix, who had walked off to the stern and was looking out there at something fascinating and nonexistent in the river. Nor Ebad, still parked on his barrel, thoughtful. The parrot preened.

"In Pirate Law on the High Seas," said Art, "whoever doesn't agree to my terms can fight me. That's fair." She added, friendly, "You're all gentlemen. I know you won't try to fight me except one at a time, in proper order. Otherwise, I'm ready for any combat you wish. Though *that* with Blacky hurt my fist. I'd prefer blade—or pistols next time."

"Artemesia," said Eerie.

"Call me that name again, and I'll run you through anyway, Mr. O'Shea. I hate to remind you, but my sword is a real one. I'm Art Blastside. Or, if you prefer, *Captain* Blastside."

"Art—oh, by the Sacred Golden Pig of Eira—" Eerie raised his eyes to the sky.

Peter and Walter looked merely nervous, in a red-haired way. They had seen Molly fight, grown up seeing that on stage. Art fought like Molly. But then, Molly had trained Art, all those six years ago. It had been *stage* fighting—only Art had somehow turned the illusion—into a *fact*. The Honest Liar simply grinned, nodding and nodding at Art.

"Well," said Art presently. "Anyone?"

Whuskery spoke up in a bluster. "Art, this isn't right—"

But "Don't get her wild!" hissed Dirk. "See her eyes—hot-cool—she'd run us *all* through as soon as look at us."

Down on the deck, Black Knack grunted and coiled himself into a sitting position, rubbing his jaw.

Art walked over.

"Settled, Blacky? Or do you want another bout?"

"You've a cruel fist, Art," said Black Knack, "nearly broke my jaw."

"You have a cruel jaw, Mr. Knack, nearly broke my hand."

Black Knack nodded. He got up. "You win. For now."

Above, the canvas squeaked on the little yards.

"Trim sails for the Channel," said Art. "Who's going up? I'll choose then. Honest, Walter, Peter."

Still grinning, the Honest Liar leaped for the main mast at once. Walter, lighter of frame, eased himself unhappily onto the mizzen, clung there like a desperate dormouse to a stalk of corn, then—began to climb very expertly. Peter took the foremast, only hesitating to check brother Walter's safe progress.

Art shouted, "Take down that flag with the cup and spoons, Honest!"

"Aye, aye, Cap'n."

"What colors'll we fly then, Art?" said Eerie, seeming dazed.

"For now, nothing. But let's get some coffee brewed and I'll demonstrate."

"All planned out, Arty?" Eerie gazed at her, and said, "You mentioned we'd give a show in Port's Mouth—what *type* of a show, Art?"

"Prizewinning," said Art.

"The advertisement?"

But Art had turned her back.

Soon, from the for'ard galley, the rich smell of the coffee rose. Whuskery appeared with his tray of pots and tin cups.

"Not at all," said Art. "Put all that back. Tip it in the stew pot."

Whuskery glowered thunderously.

Dirk whisked Whuskery's tray of pots and cups away, gibbering, "Oh, she's a wild thing—*wild*, I tell you—don't provoke her."

By late afternoon, the Coffee Ship had lost all its colors but brown and white. Indeed, other than its sails, it was brown from stem to stern. They had used the thick staining coffee, brought in relays from the galley, to paint over the canary yellow and scarlet trim, and run up a white flag made from half an old shirt, decorated with a brown stripe—that looked innocent and might have meant anything.

The ship's name had also been defaced, by Art and Honest, hanging off the side. The *Pirate Coffee* looked now like a small, distinctly odd, pleasure craft, which had run perhaps, into some heavy weather, causing less harm than a total loss of smartness. All that was visible as identification on its side was an apparent trade name: *irate Co.* Also vandalized, the figurehead. She had lost her coffeepot. "Wanton damage," moaned Eerie.

Nevertheless, despite disguise, they slunk through Till-Bury Docks by moonlight, creeping among the flares of the quays and lanterns of other ships, lying law-abidingly and fugitiveless at anchor. The grim old fort, however, peered out to sea, looking for the French. Still themselves a monarchy, they were always reckoned on the verge of invading Free England. The fort had no eyes for a little brown three-master.

Beyond the docks and the port, the estuary yawned on the Free English Channel, where banks of fog ghosted in the distance. Rime coated the masts, but there was neither snow nor ice.

They kept close to shore till sunrise, when the sea was undone before them. How wide it was, and charcoal gray, under the opening eye of the sun.

"Is that far shore France? No, it's only fog again—"

"So much water! Look—it's everywhere! Oh—I'm going to be— Urrrk!"

"Where's the dog? Where's Muck?"

"Swum off last night, the bloater. Spotted him at it. He went straight ashore at the docks. He's got more sense, that dog, than to go to sea."

Had she always been so lonely?

Yes, Art thought she probably had—since Molly died.

After that she had scarcely seen her father, and certainly never *wanted* to see him. The Angels Academy was full of girls and young women who all seemed exactly like one another, and none of them like Art.

But these men had been Art's family. The only one she ever had. And now—they weren't.

Perhaps she should, she thought, simply have tried to join them in their *Act*. But it was no use. She couldn't remember any of that, not the stages, not the machinery that worked the green waves and the stage-set ships and the metal sheets that made the sound of storms— Only the lash of wind and water, the colossal skies and oceans, and the golden coasts and the coasts like ivory and emerald.

This—that gray choppy Channel—even with Whuskery puking in it just beyond Art's cabin—that was the reality.

But she was alone there.

The parrot, seated on the coffee barrel beside her, gave a whistle.

"Yes, Plunqwette."

"Pieces of Skate," said the parrot.

"You *don't* talk, do you," said Art. "I thought Molly taught you lots of words and phrases—didn't she?—so that she could hold a conversation with you . . . or seem to."

"Molly—" cried the parrot, ruffling up, "Polly want a Molly!"

"You've only got me, old bird. I'm sorry."

"Gold Muhuras! Pieces of Plate!"

The door was politely knocked on. *Felix.* Oh, he would do that, of course, knock. The others just burst in—luckily she could hear most of their unsea-legged trampling long before they arrived and fell against and through the door.

"Yes, Mr. Phoenix, come in."

He walked into the cabin and shut the door and gazed at her.

"Well," she said.

"When am I to get off your boat?"

"Ship, Mr. Phoenix. It's only an It, but it's still a ship. As for when, when we stop somewhere, I'd suppose."

"I'd thought I might be off at Till'-Bury."

"Evidently not. You seem impatient to leave. Should we be hurt?"

"My presence has caused you problems."

"Possibly. You're actually a minor problem, Mr. Phoenix."

"Well, Miss Bla—"

"Captain."

Felix raised his dark brows. Strange that, thought Art, his lashes were very dark, too, even with that blond hair.

"Captain then," said Felix, "I don't really belong with a band of cutthroats, robbers, and—pirates. Sorry."

Art stared. Then she smiled.

"Haven't they convinced you, sir, they are *actors?*"

"I don't know *what* you all are. But this isn't the place for me."

"Don't fret. If we get good weather and following winds, we could be at Port's Mouth in a week. Then you can scamper off."

"I don't mean to be ungracious," he said. "You and the—er—*your men*—maybe saved my life."

"Oh, I'm sure we didn't, Mr. Phoenix."

"Pirate parrot," said Plunqwette.

"So. Port's Mouth," he said glumly.

"Unless you want to swim off at the next port, sir, like Muck, the Cleanest Dog in England."

"I can't swim," said Felix. "Half your *men* can't, you do know that?"

"Most of the English Navy, sir, and almost every pirate or sea trader from here to the Blue Indies, *can't swim,*" said Art. "It hasn't stopped any of us."

"Thank you," said Felix, turning back to the door.

"For what? Are you grateful for *nothing?*"

"Sometimes. Sometimes I prefer it to *something.*"

Outside the cabin, Art heard some of "her men" begin to question him anxiously. They liked Felix, naturally—he was like one of their own, dramatic, gorgeous. The explanation he had given of mistaken identity as the criminal Jack Cuckoo, they had believed at once, even before Art confirmed it. He had sung them a song yesterday, on request, in his beautiful voice, and Eerie had exclaimed, "Why, you could make a fortune on the boards!" They knew more about him, too, than Art did. Because he talked—to *them.*

But really, Felix didn't matter. He only bothered her because he was here, and somehow in the way—and yet, by *appearing* on the ice, had started her plan ahead of itself.

Time to go out now, too, and prowl the deck, making sure what they were all at. Who could she trust?

The parrot hopped onto Art's wrist, waddled up her arm and onto her shoulder.

"Treasured Isle," said the parrot, and dug about among her feathers after one of Felix's last fleas.

During the next days, *irate Co.* sailed round the frilly edges of England's coast, keeping out of deep inlets and bays, avoiding the fishing villages, coastal towns, and shipshape ports that crowded her cliffy shores. The weather assisted them, staying calm, but the landscape was bleached by winter. Sometimes mist veiled the shores. Art didn't recognize them. They were alien to her and unknown—it was everywhere else she knew.

If anyone on land noticed the ship, and probably they did, they took it for nothing special. Which definitely wasn't what the sponsor had intended. But the crew worked together now, if rather untidily, assuming roles and duties Art had handed out—which were the same as those they had had in the play.

Whuskery was the worst cast. He had acted, perhaps, a wonderful cook—but what the tiny galley now produced was fairly horrible.

Ebad served as First Officer, where he had been Second, Eerie as Second, where he had been Third. They had no word of Hurkon Beare, who had played the stage part of original First Officer. "Gone back to Canadia," suggested Salt Peter. "He was a Canadee."

"Broke his heart," said Walter, "when—when Molly died."

The seas got rough just past the dimly sighted inland hamlet of St.-Leonard-and-the-Dragon, and the coffee stain partly washed off the ship. They redaubed it, once the usual members of the crew had stopped being sick.

Ink-and-paper-colored gulls, and a few pigeons, followed the ship, screeching, high on the coffee scent, and with a mad need to taste the beans. Sometimes they landed aboard, squabbled, pounced at the barrels and sacks—sometimes the screeching parrot fought them off, dashing and diving. Gull doings and assorted feathers gave the *irate Co.* a new black, white, and green trim.

"Art and that parrot. Two of a kind. Fighters. Bullies. *Cracked.*"

"Nay, Black Knack. She's Molly's girl. Be patient. She'll come to her senses, so she will."

To Art, they sounded—and looked—sometimes now even more like genuine pirates. Their speeches, too, were often more ornate, as in the play—or as on a pirate ship, where bravado and threats and flights of fancy were normal, surely.

Watching them, Art would see them strutting the deck in their gaudy coats, hands on the hilts of cutlasses, flaunting. These weapons, along with the pistols and bullets in their belts, were fakes. They didn't look it.

Passing by Brig Town on Sunday morning, oh, woe! There

were red-and-yellow banners out along the shore, reading clearly: WE WELCOME PIRATE COFFEE.

The non-advertising pirates swore and complained. There was almost another fight. Art performed Molly's trick a second time, and Whuskery's trousers landed on the planks. Peter had to sew the buttons on again.

Only Honest threw himself into his new life, beaming.

Only Ebad was contained and unreadable still, while acting his role of First Officer without a hitch.

And only Felix kept utterly aloof, and wouldn't be part of any of it. Except to sing to them, Art's crew, when they requested, and to draw pictures of them, posing or stalking about. But Felix had told them of his artistic abilities. He was one of their kind—and also, a voluntary outsider.

"Just you and me, girl," said Art to Plunqwette.

Sometimes she wondered if they would all try to run off at Port's Mouth. Even Muck had abandoned ship.

After Brig Town, the land expanded as if breathing in, puffing itself out, and the sea deepened in color and in actual depths. The ship took on a swimming movement that set some of them off again at the rails. (Was their sickness true? After all, if the machinery of the stage had created just this rocking and bounding—why hadn't they been sick then? Maybe only because they had known, *then*, they *weren't* at sea. Black Knack was the worst. It was so regular, she wondered if he were forcing himself to it. But also she half admired his infuriating knack of turning the event of throwing up into an aggressive protest.)

It was sunfall, and Port's Mouth had appeared, about a mile off the starboard bow, some of its taller buildings flashing golden-white, and windows mirroring the sun, like doll-size pirate sequins.

"See, it exists," Art mocked.

Everyone, for once united, gazed toward the port, with its round bay and long harbor arm, crowned by a fortressed lighthouse. The water there was stacked high with ships, keen and glittering, even at a distance, with paint and cleanliness, sails down or firmly reefed, all rocking soft as cradles on a winter sea that looked nearly like summer, and was the color of Felix Phoenix's eyes. Gulls wheeled everywhere now, white flakes stirred in blue sky.

I know this town, thought Art. I have been here. They'll tell me I haven't. But even if I only pictured it in my mind—it's *familiar.*

Another thought in her brain said, quietly, kindly, Well, Molly must have showed you paintings and drawings of all these places. That's how you recognize this one.

Then, thought Art to her thought, I'll recognize them all.

Between them and the port and harbor lay the small offshore island known by the name of Spice Isle. Warehouses perched there, and on the evening breeze came the smell of ginger, cinnamon, and toffee—which perhaps explained why *irate Co.*'s escort of coffee-gulls was already deserting in droves, to join other birds—gulls, pigeons, ravens—sailing over the island and the port.

"We'll put in at the Isle," said Art.

A few ships lay already anchored there, more battered in appearance and smaller in size than those in the harbor.

"But," said Walter, "after that—what?"

"I, and a couple of you," said Art, "will go ashore. We'll use some little boat we'll pick up. I can see several from here, pulled up on the shale."

"That's stealing."

"No. We'll be bringing it back."

Walter dithered. "But—"

"And you, Salt Walter, will row us over."

"I've never rowed—truly, Art—"

"You have. On stage."

"There, Walt," said Ebad suddenly. "Art, I'll take thee across."

Art's eyes rested on Ebad. She nodded. "Tack for shore now, mates. The Spice Isle, under the wing of dark."

They obeyed her. They had heard and obeyed such orders a thousand times or more, if never at sea.

Art went along the deck to where Felix stood, on his own, looking over the waves at Port's Mouth.

"And you, sir, will sing us in. In that fine voice—something charming."

"All right, if I must."

"I want us heard and seen a little, friendly, lawful traffic, nothing to hide. And would a wanted felon sing?"

The sun slipped down like a golden coin in a pocket of red velvet. The dark swelled up and stars lit their lamps, and one by one all the lamps along the shore, and among the gathered shipping, answered them.

And Felix sang.

It was a Shakespur sonnet. The tune they didn't know. But every actor on the ship pricked up his ears, and Art stood above the little bowspirit, listening, too.

> "Shall I compare thee to a summer's day?
> Thou art more lovely and more temperate:
> Rough winds do shake the darling buds of May,
> And summer's lease hath all too short a date:
> Sometime too hot the eye of heaven shines,
> And often is his gold complexion dimm'd;
> And every fair from fair sometime declines,
> By chance or nature's changing course untrimm'd;

But thy eternal summer shall not fade,
Nor lose possession of that fair thou owest;
Nor shall Death brag thou wander'st in his shade,
When in eternal lines to time thou grow'st:
So long as men can breathe, or eyes can see,
So long lives this, and this gives life to thee."

Eerie, at the wheel, wiped his nose. "Ah, 'tis Molly. Could be Molly's song—could've been written for her—"

Otherwise they listened silently. Only the slap of waves, the creak of timber and bunching linen sound of sails, taking the current and the wind for shore, only that between them and the song.

Whuskery had popped up like a rabbit from the galley hatch. Honest and Peter, attending the sails, hung like monkeys, next to Plunqwette scanning ahead. Dirk and Black Knack had left off rolling a coffee barrel. Ebad, adding pipe smoke to the dusk, still thoughtful, said, as Felix ended, "Encore, Mr. Phoenix. Once again."

And Felix sang the sonnet over.

Art thought, Yes, for Molly. Course unchanged, sails trimmed. Not wandering and lost in the shade of death. Still alive in memory.

PIRATICA, she thought. My ma.

ACT TWO
Piratica's Daughter

∽ᦅ ONE ᦅ∽

The Port's Mouth Pudding ‾‾

Mistress Hornetti, black of hair and needle-eyed, came into the main room of her inn, her sausage-shaped dog under one arm, and the rolling pin under the other.

Customers looked up and greeted her with careful—and noisy—respect. Otherwise she was not above clouting them with the pin or setting her dog, Ratskin, (worse than he looked) on them. *They*, the customers, were a dodgy lot, too. Here in this low-beamed, sulfur-lighted tavern sat a collection of men, in a ragged finery of patches and earrings, quilled with beards, unshaved stubble, and barely concealed weaponry.

"Missus," said one of the serving girls, "someone's a-tapping on the back door."

Mistress Hornetti swept by and down the passage. In a couple of side rooms as she passed, more quilled men, playing cards in menacing noiselessness, also raised their tankards to the owner of the inn.

At the back door, which led to a side yard, Mistress H paused, listening. *Tap-tap* went the door, and in a particular pattern.

Mistress H undid the bolts and flung the door open.

There before her was a tall slim man, his face muffled in a mauve scarf, his three-cornered hat pulled low as low over invisible eyes.

"Doll!" exclaimed Mistress Hornetti.

"Dot!" exclaimed the muffled man. He had a woman's voice.

Into the inn he (she) came then, lugging a saddlebag. "I've hidden the horse in the dark of your shed, like always. By the Bat's Earpiece, Dot, what a mess my Jack made of things over Christmas. Half the constables of Lundon Town are after him. Though luckily, so far, after the wrong man."

"Come in the parlor. I'll take a look at your loot, dear, and we'll drink some gin."

"Sherry, Dot," said the highwaywoman. "You know I can't stand the gin."

Soon seated either side of the table, by a cheery fire, drinks in place and the door locked, the highwaywoman removed her hat and muffler. She was blond Doll Muslin, Jack Cuckoo's close friend and accomplice—actually, if truth be told, she *was* Jack Cuckoo, or pretended to be. The coaches that went in terror of Gentleman Jack were usually being successfully robbed by Doll.

On the table Doll laid the goods, pocket watches of silver, rings of gold and pearl, a diamond buckle, some necklaces of brilliants, and a snuffbox of ivory set with amber and jet. Mistress H did a roaring trade passing on such items, both from the several highwaypersons and also the smuggler and pirate crews who visited her inn.

"I'd appreciate a bed here tonight, Dot. I've ridden from Rowers, all this way. The snow's still bad, and all those Jack-seeking constables are everywhere, thick as fleas."

"You stay, Dolly. We'll have a party, you and I. Drink up. All the way from the Franco-Spanish port of Sherry, that sherry is."

The boat they had "picked up" (stolen . . . borrowed . . .) was a leaky little thing. It let lots of water in, and Art became aware maybe someone had just thrown it out on the beach of the Spice Isle to rot.

However, they got across and bumped in on the gravelly shore alongside the outer reaches of Port's Mouth Town.

"Where are we going?" asked Walt, who after all had come with them, rowing strongly and well under Ebad's guidance.

"There's an inn," said Art. "I remember."

"Port's Mouth Pudding," supplied Ebad.

"But that's not a real place—" cried Walt. "It was only in the play—"

"'Tis real, Mr. Salt," said Ebad. "That play of ours named and used a number of real things. The Pud's famous for the bad company that keeps there. Cheer up, though. The Golden Goliath never drops in there anymore."

Art stopped Ebad as Walter and the silent Felix got out of the boat. "Golden Goliath was real, you say?"

"Yes, Arty. A pirate of the worst sort. The *very* worst."

Art said coldly, "The poster at the theater said he was played by a Mr. Trevis Wilde."

"Trevis *played* Goliath in the drama. But Goliath is a real man, for sure. If such a monster can be called a man. He was feared from here to Barbary—I say *was*. Half the French Navy took after him and caught him near the Indias. They sunk him with his ship. Down he went. No one's heard of him since."

"But that black cutter with the skull and crossed bones on every sail—"

"That was her. He had a fleet, too. Six, seven ships. Never kept many by him at any one time."

"But his vessel was called the *Enemy*."

"Yes. If a ship can be anything, she's like her master. That ship—was an evil thing. The audiences used to shriek when she hove into view—or seemed to—on the stage. And they loved it when Molly and us fought that ship, and in some of the adventures, bettered her. Goliath himself, I said, was feared and

hated. Vicious he was, a killer always. No one and no ship survived his attacks unless they were strong enough to fight him
off. Those he took he finished. He let no one surrender. The
merchants and traders who lost their cargoes—lost their men—
their crews, their friends, to G. Goliath: number them like the
stars of night."

They walked quietly up the cobbled lanes, between lighted
taverns and low-lit or darkened shops.

The Pudding was exactly where Art remembered it to be.
Molly must have drawn her a map.

Opening the door, Art strode in first. Ebad followed, then
Walt and Felix.

"Why's she come in here?" whispered Walt. Of all people, to
Felix.

Felix shrugged. "Why do you think, Walter?"

Walter looked no wiser.

But right then, a strange rumbling cheer broke out around
the crowded, brandy-scented room. Men were getting to their
feet, raising glasses and mugs at the door. Only a few sat back
and jealously growled.

Was this for Art? She didn't think so. She looked round, as
Ebad and Walter were doing, to see who else had come in.

Felix grimaced.

Then Art heard the greeting. "It's Cuckoo Jack! Heard he
was headed this way. Hey, Jack! He saw off the Lun'on police!
Yay, Jacko—come and show us the loot!"

One huge drinker was swinging over. Instead of an earring, a
small knife was slotted neatly through his ear. He beamed at
Felix, reached across everyone else, and wrung the young man's
hand.

"I'm not Gentleman Jack Cuckoo."

"Course y'are. I've seen you about. Tall and light of figure
and white-blond of hair. Besides, that horse of yours is in

Mistress Hornet's shed. Seen it. Can't miss that horse—wears a half mask, like you, Jack, when you're at your robbery work."

"Oh, God," said Felix in obvious utter disgust.

Art clapped a hand on his shoulder. "Jack's modest, Mr. Knife. But we thank you for your warm welcome."

Avoiding a hundred offers of eternal friendship, they got to a corner bench and sat down at the table.

The potgirl approached even so bringing a tray laden with free drinks. "On the house, sirs." She winked at Felix. "Never knew you were so pretty, Gentleman Jack."

"Thank you," said Felix wearily.

Ear-the-Knife bowled back and packed himself onto the protesting end of their bench.

"Any pocket watches today, Jack? Or a necklet? Something for my old lady."

"No."

"Nice ring—how about that red ring?"

Felix shut his eyes. Walter, concerned, put an arm about him.

Art saw Ebad was laughing, for the first time since she had remet him, that she had seen. Ear-the-Knife was also intrigued by this. When Ebad stopped, Art said, "Jack's in bad bother with the Lundon Constabulary."

"So we hear!" chortled Ear-the-Knife.

"He's worn out, as you can see. Rode all the way from Row-hampton."

"So we hear, too. Famous that ride'll be."

Art leaned forward. "What ships are going out—seaworthy ships of good rig. We need to find Jack safe passage out."

Ear-the-Knife sighed. "I knows 'em all. Though me pirate days are done, I can still judge a ship. It's like marriage, you know," he added confidingly. "Faithful to one. But yer can still have a look."

Felix said, in a low, gentle voice, "Get this clear, gentlemen. She isn't asking about ships for *my* sake."

Ebad said nothing.

Walter opened eyes and mouth wide.

Ear-the-Knife stared at Art. *"She?"*

Art turned suddenly coy. She simpered. She knew precisely how to do it—though she would never have thought anything taught at the Angels Academy might be any use.

"Ssh," she twittered to Ear-the-Knife. "Don't let on."

"Oh, ah." He grinned. "I get you. Sure thing. 'Tis safe as porridge with me."

Then he sat back and spoke about all the ships in the harbor. Their origins, shipshapery, owners, destinations, dates of going out.

Ebad and Art listened. Walter, too, began to listen, surprising himself, apparently, by his own knowledge of seaworthiness and voyages.

Felix put his head on the wall and went elegantly and silently to sleep.

He woke up because their potgirl was back, leaning over the table, shaking him by the lapels.

"Gent Jack! Rouse yourself—there's trouble!"

"Of course there is," said Felix.

He saw that Ebad, Walter, and Ear-the-Knife were having a comradely drink over at the tavern counter. Only Art was still sitting at the other end of the bench.

To Felix, she looked—nearly frightening. Her eyes burned with a far-off light. Even her hair was electric. Frightening—and something else.

Like what he had heard of her mother, Felix thought, on stage—you couldn't take your eyes off her.

Had she even heard what the potgirl said?

But the potgirl was prancing about, pulling at Art now.

"What is it?" said Art mildly.

But what it was suddenly bashed its fists—several of them—on the Pud's back door.

"Open in the name of Free England!"

Felix stood up, flexing his hands ready for the shackles. He knew they'd never chance his escaping this time. Art, too, stood up, eyes cool again and hand on sword hilt.

Then into the room swept a woman like a tornado, with piled up clouds of raven hair, a rolling pin clutched firmly in one hand, a steaming gin tankard in the other. Broomed along yapping and slavering in her skirts came a dog shaped like a long black sausage.

"It's the constables, lads!" she cried. "They're after our own Gentleman Jack—do your stuff or you'll never drink here again."

The place erupted. Literally, it seemed.

All the rogues on the benches were in action. Some dived and some leaped. Cutlasses sparkled and fists flailed. Flying bottles and cups filled the air. A most incredible brawl had begun.

The potgirl grabbed Felix in motherly arms. "Don't panic, darling. All this lot pay bribes to the local Law. They're safe enough."

"So glad," said Felix.

"I mean, the Law must go a bit careful with them—which'll help slow the constables up no end. It's only you as they want anyhow. I'll sneak you out the special side way. That's what the missus'd want. Funny—I always thought you were a *woman*—"

Art avoided a descending beer mug and shoved off a fighter who had got carried away and was trying to brain her with a chair. Ebad and Salt Walter emerged beside her from the fray.

"Oh, Art—" baaed Walter.

"They're only *acting*," said Art, bashing a smilingly violent someone else hastily on the nose.

Art and Co. squirmed out through the chaos, following the girl who was helping Felix escape.

Through three or four side rooms that opened from one another everyone ran. (A pair of card players, ignoring the racket from the main area, were busy having a private, *un*acted fight in one of these.)

Soon the helpful potgirl reached a chamber packed with barrels, pressed a stone in the dank windowless wall, and revealed a sort of chute that vanished steeply downward into wet and dark.

"Fine," said Felix.

"Out and quick!" supplied the potgirl. "It's the smugglers' exit." She kissed Felix so forcefully it knocked him into the chute.

Art herself sprinted to the chute. The others jumped and landed after them—or on top of them. Down they all slid, through scraping darkness and the rich smell of brandywine. The end of the trip was an open drain, into which they fell, one by one.

Walter was the only one to be vocally upset. "It's my best coat!"

"Not anymore," said Ebad.

Beyond the timbered corner of the Pudding, loud sounds had broken into the street. Peering around this corner, they saw three constables exploding out on the cobbles, one with a slavering mad black sausage attached to his leg.

"How about if I give myself up?" Felix asked.

"They'll hang you," said Art. "I know you prefer nothing to something, but that is too much nothing."

"By the Wind's Heart," said Ebad, "let's go."

Art and Ebad dragged Felix between them into the shadows of the unlit alleys of Port's Mouth Town, Walter stumbling at their heels, whiffling about how you got alcoholic sewage out of broadcloth.

"You gained what you went for," said Felix to Art.

"Did I."

"You know you did. Your list of likely ships. That wasn't for me, was it."

"No. You're your own difficulty, Mr. Phoenix."

"I never said I was anything else."

"Delightful," said Art. "I never saw you angry before."

"I was never driven to be angry! No," Felix said, quietening, his eyes going back to the night water, over which Ebad and groaning Walter were rowing them. "Once I was. Just once. One anger that lasts me forever."

Art seemed relaxed. (Like a lioness, he thought, after a successful hunt.) She murmured, "Yours sounds like a sad story."

"One you'll never know, madam."

"I'm happy not to know it, sir. I have sufficient of my own."

Startled, for a second, Art stared at Felix, realizing she had, as had he, let out the hint of a secret pain. She hadn't meant to.

But it wouldn't matter. As Felix didn't. Felix could still easily be put ashore later. Her own plans were set, hazardous but concrete. They were, she had to admit also, quite *theatrical*.

Anchored in Port's Mouth harbor that night, the captain of the Free Republican Ship *Elephant* marched about his lean, tall-masted and orderly vessel, glancing at faultless arrangements of bales, barrels and ropes, rolled canvas, jolly boats, cleanest decks, and galley and hold stuffed with goods. She was in excellent form, the ship, a trader of the fast class of windjammer, bound tomorrow for the open seas, on her way to Own Accord and the Blue Indies.

Puffed with reasonable pride, the captain withdrew to his own neat cabin and poured himself a glass of budgerigar wine. Not knowing he was, next morning, now due to meet Art Blastside.

All at Sea

Morning opened the doors of the sky.

On the thirty-footish deck of *(P)irate Co(ffee)*, Molly's crew sat eating slabs of cheese on bread. Whuskery had also undone the greengage jam jar for a celebration. They were going ashore, weren't they, today? To put on, at last, the sponsor's show and earn some dosh. As for any worries over the Law, most of them seemed to have forgotten it. They had bought the idea, perhaps, that with Felix soon to be off-loaded, no blame could still attach to them. And they all knew, from years of experience—not all of it on stage—how to lie well.

Standing on the forecastle, Ebad Vooms watched, through his spyglass—a prop that was in fact quite real—the beautiful neat white shape of the tall ship FRS *Elephant*, gliding out from harbor, letting down, as she went, her ranks of snowy sails.

"A fine sight," said Eerie. "Look how she moves. Like a swan."

Art came from her cabin, with bright green, unswanlike Plunqwette on her shoulder.

"Here's trouble," muttered Black Knack. "She wants something again. Look, it's written all over her."

Salt Peter stood behind him. Very flatly Peter said, "Art was telling us about that ship out there—the *Elephant*. She said last night, *Elephant* is bound for the Blue Indies."

Felix alone hadn't joined them. He had told a concerned Walter and Dirk that he was seasick, and lying up in the hold among the coffee beans. Possibly this was his tact—his way of showing them he would be sure and keep out of sight until he could get off. He hadn't been taken sick before.

Art moved to the midpoint of the deck.

She looked out to sea, where the *Elephant* was now breasting the long blue waves. Then round at all of them. Her eyes were steady. She smiled slightly.

"If this were our play on stage," she said, "what would happen now?"

No one spoke. Then the Honest Liar cried, "We'd go after—take that ship out there."

"A tempting prize," Art agreed. "She's loaded with goods for the Blue Indies, and stacked with enough stores for just such a long voyage. She's big, but highly maneuverable. And she's armed."

Eerie said dolefully, "Yes, she's got cannon, the *Elephant*—seven of them. I've counted her gunports."

"How piratical of you, Mr. O'Shea," said Art. "But one more reason, in the long run, to take her."

The Coffee Ship gave a sudden lurch, as if it too was now becoming nervous or excited. Black Knack immediately threw up over the side.

"Molly," said Art reasonably, "wouldn't have got in a fight, though, would she, not unnecessarily. She'd have taken the *Elephant* by means of a trick."

Eerie remembered an episode of the drama. "Maybe by pretending distress—having to be rescued."

"That's right," said Art. "Let the *Elephant* rescue us. And once aboard—" Art paused, thoughtfully. "Raise anchor. We are going after that ship."

The men made just the noise she had expected. Bellows of protest and sarcasm, mocking laughter.

She stood there. When the expected noise ebbed a little, Art added, "But I see you've forgotten why. We promised we'd get Mr. Phoenix safely on board an outgoing vessel. You don't want the Law to take him, do you? Or us, for that matter, if we still have him with us?"

Everyone looked at her, at one another.

"For our honor," Eerie said, "we have to get him away. But he's seasick, Art, lying in the hold on the coffee. He's missed the boat."

"Never mind," said Art.

Honest had already set about the anchor chain. Walter joined him.

The small sails hadn't even been taken in.

Art took the wheel. Salt Peter went below to tell Felix the good news he was to be put on a really good ship, bound for the safe Blue Indies.

However, Peter met Felix on the ladder. Felix didn't look sick, only grim and rather wet.

"There's water coming in down there."

"*Below?* Art!" yelled Peter, bounding back off the ladder. "We're taking water—"

There had been noise before; now there was a loud blank. Out of it Black Knack snarled, "*She's* holed the ship. Mad bloody girl—"

"We'll drown—"

"Hell's Porcupines—"

Art frowned down at them from the wheel station.

"I haven't holed the ship. It'll be just an inch or so of bilge coming up."

"Look," said Felix. He pointed at his boots and trousers, wet to the knee.

Black Knack yelled at the crew of fear-stricken actors, "She's crazed and heartless, this girl. She'll do anything to get her own way, this cracked plan of hers—"

"None of us can *swim*, Arty," said Eerie, more in horrified sorrow than terrified anger.

"I *can* swim," said Ebad.

"Lucky for *you* then—"

They could, all of them, feel it in the ship now. Though it accepted the offshore wind and advanced along the waves, it wallowed and bumped.

Far behind now the Spice Isle, farther still morning-shining Port's Month.

And the perfect white *Elephant* sailed before them, about half a mile away. It looked like a thousand.

Art spoke clearly. "Walt, Honest, Peter, Whuskery, Dirk, Ebad—get the coffee barrels up. Throw them overboard and the coffee, too; lighten her. We've no jolly boats thanks to the lovely sponsor. So we'll use the barrels, the empty ones. We can hold on to them, float. Signal that ship."

"How?" demanded Black Knack, a world of venom in his voice.

"Set fire to your drawers, Mr. Knack. Anything. *Shout!* You've all got the lungs of actors—use them. It's only half a mile."

In any case, it seemed the *Elephant* had already taken note of their plight—Ebad, pausing to use the spyglass, saw men clustering at the big ship's rail, pointing.

Felix stood amidships, waving his (Art's) sooty, too-small coat over his head. Honest yowled, Dirk hooted, Whuskery and Eerie boomed. The rest bayed in harmony.

It was no good wondering if insane Art had done this to them, or wondering whether or not Felix wanted to escape to the Blue Indies, or if *any* of them wanted to end up in the sea.

Shout! Art had ordered, and they shouted.

Coffee barrels were emptied, barrels and sacks were heaved, splashing over the sides into waves that rose nearer and nearer. Coffee beans carpeted the sea. The little ship bucked and rolled. Black Knack, cursing Art with every spare breath, forgot to throw up.

Dirk clutched Whuskery in a final embrace.

The *Pirate Coffee* dipped nose down in the water, sinking her dainty woman figurehead, without even the coffeepot they had knocked off before Till'-Bury to comfort her.

Down the deck everyone slid, rebounded, hit the ice-cold sea. Where most of them screamed, gulped water, bubbled.

Art saw Plunqwette whizz upward like a scarlet-green cannonball, just before the stinging salt sea shut over her own head.

Ebad propelled Art to the surface.

"Don't struggle. You're safe."

"Don't be a fool, Ebad Vooms. I can swim better than *you*— Molly taught me—see to Eerie. Get him clear or he'll go down with the ship's undertow."

Treading water, Art glanced round, checking her men.

Whuskery and Dirk had grabbed coffee barrels and were afloat, if sprawling and unhappy. Peter, oddly, could also swim and had hold of Walter, who was howling and so filling his mouth with sea. The Honest Liar, who Art would have sworn couldn't swim, had somehow learned the moment he landed in the water, and, best fellow, was enjoying himself. He waved to Art gleefully and struck out, doggy-paddle, for FRS *Elephant*. Ebad had reached Eerie just as the new Second Officer was going down for the third time. Black Knack had also found a barrel and spun in circles, spouting swear words. Above them all, a small feathered goddess, Plunqwette soared, offering encouraging squawks.

Everyone was now clear of the last sinking moments of the *Pirate Coffee*.

Almost everyone. Felix Phoenix was missing.

Art sucked in the cold air and dived again under the colder sea.

Of *course, he* couldn't swim. Where was he?

A dull *glug-glug,* a gush of darkness and bubbles roared down past her. It was a piece of the Coffee Ship—the figurehead, snapped off from the bow. The coffee lady smiled inanely at Art and sank away, and, instead, Felix appeared, drifting through the icy blue dimness, his hair unfurling like a silver banner.

Art grabbed him. She pushed and kicked and thrust them both up to the water's top.

The moment air slapped his face, Felix stopped being a beautiful, lifeless statue and threw up water into water.

As the spasm subsided, Art turned onto her back, and began to tow Felix backward with her, toward the other ship.

She could already see it had put about, was closer, coming—to rescue them.

"Did you?" Felix murmured in a musical croak.

"Don't talk."

"Did you put a hole through the keel of the Coffee Boat?"

"*Ship*. No. Shut up. Lie still. You're safe, I've got you."

He said nothing else.

The *Pirate Coffee* had vanished into the arms of the sea.

Everyone swam, floated, flailed, until they met a long, narrow jolly boat.

They were helped over the side by bad-tempered and contemptuous sailors, and presently were hauled up the flank of the tall-masted windjammer *Elephant*.

Burly and neatly bearded, the man positioned on the quarter-deck wore the smart, deep red uniform coat of a captain of a trader vessel, three-cornered hat trimmed with showy gold braid. A medal, for some gallant or shopkeeping deed, burned on a ribbon among the lace at his throat.

He wasn't, Art thought, quite like her father. And yet—that same disdainful look of displeasure. That same bad smell under his nose.

The captain strode bowleggedly down the short ladder and swung on across the wide bleached planks of his clean, clean deck.

All his visible crew—about twenty of them—shuffled back respectfully. Aloft among the snow-white, exquisite canvas, faces peered over.

"Who's in charge here?" the captain of FRS *Elephant* demanded.

Art stepped forward. "I."

"*You?* You're a boy. Voice not properly broken. What d'you mean by it?" The captain eyed Art as if he had just found her floating—not in the water—but in his cup of tea. "I tell you what, if it *is* you, laddy, you've lost my ship a lot of time here, with your silly adventuring. You can have a boat off when we go past the Isle of White Lion, and not before. And I'll see to it, sirs, you're all fined for time wasting. What possessed you? What kind of a tug were you on?"

"A ship—and our bloody ship *sank,* sunshine!" bawled Whuskery.

"'Pon my soul," said the captain, "I'll have none of your banana-caper insolence. Scum you are, the pack o' ye."

Art took three more steps. She came almost up against the captain, water dripping from her garments and hair, but not from the pistol she had produced, apparently magically, out of nowhere. She pressed the nose of the gun to the captain's lips. He closed them, and went cross-eyed, looking down the barrel.

All around, the *Elephant*'s crew gave off an audible collective hiss.

"Pray, sir," said Art, "hold your noise. I want only to thank you from the depths of my heart."

The captain angled his head back and spoke.

"Put down that pistol, or I'll have you clapped in irons. The English Revolution is over these twenty years."

"To thank you, that is," ignoringly added Art, "not for your paltry rescue, but for giving over to our care your so supersweet ship, with all its goods."

The captain lunged. Art kicked him hard in the leg, and he went to one knee. Behind her at once she heard a scuffle, two or three cries, a series of thuds. She didn't look.

"Pay 'em no heed!" the captain shouted. "Their powder's wet—they can't fire. No way, by thunder."

Art put the pistol to the side of the captain's head.

"We keep out powder dry, sir, in sharkskin pouches," Art lied. "Shall I prove it by blowing off your ear?"

A shot cracked instantly. The captain yelped and clutched his ear—it was still attached. It wasn't Art who had fired; it was Ebad. He had aimed, playfully it seemed, over the ship's rail. His gun smoked handsomely. Naturally, it was an actor's prop and hadn't had any bullet in it—but no one on the *Elephant* could know that. Certainly he had proved the idea of dry powder.

Art glanced swiftly behind her. She saw the pair of men who had come running to the captain's assistance. They had been felled by Honest, Walter, and Peter. Honest sat smiling on *his* man, a second uniform with a nasty face.

"You may take your personal valuables," said Art to the captain, "and you may cram into one of your ship's boats. Row for Port's Mouth. We allow it."

At her back, as she had also seen in that one glance, every actor had drawn pistol and cutlass. Dirk, flourishing cutlass and knife, had sprung up to where a couple more officers stood with mouths wide open. Black Knack and Whuskery had meanwhile turned as one and banged together the heads of two creeping-forward sailors. The rest of the *Elephant*'s crew seemed stunned. "Draw and yer dead," Black Knack also advised them.

"By the Pike's Twinkle," said the captain, still kneeling on one knee before Art, as if in the act of romantically proposing marriage. "You're a confounded *woman*."

Indeed," said Art. "Art Blastside at your service. And these gentlemen here are my merry men. Let me explain, since you seem, sir, a little slow. We're *pirates*. We *steal* things. Ships . . . *lives* . . . Now get up and go away. Before I change my mind about your so blowable-offable ear."

Art heard a menacing rushing rustle above. She slipped the knife (thieved last night at the Pudding) out of her sleeve, and threw it in a fierce blink of light and speed. The mast-descending sailor gave a wail and hung there, pinned by the seat of his pants to a spar. His own spent dagger dropped harmless on the deck.

Salt Walter fired another smoldery blank up in the air. Every actor struck a menacing pose, in a scything-up of blades.

"Let's tear out the livers and kidneys of them!" cried Walter, red haired as blood, brandishing two cutlasses at once.

"Let's sling them on the keel for the fishes!"

"Fill 'em full of lead, by the Lord's Armchair."

Very suddenly the spirit of the *Elephant* collapsed.

There was a scuttle toward the boats, while everywhere the pirates bounded, leering and declaiming, their weapons and patchy piratical finery flaming in winter sunlight.

Even Felix, who had been lying in a swoon on the deck, managed something. He woke up and threw up all over the Fourth Officer's shimmering buckled shoes.

The captain rose, cautious, eyes on Art.

"I'll see you hanged, Missy."

"I'll see you never," said Art, with the briefest bow.

Even the cook was hurrying up from the galley, carrying apparently his favorite ladle and eager to escape. A shame, maybe. Perhaps (undoubtedly), he had been better at the job than Whuskery was going to be.

The single boat went down into the cold blue sea. Sailors swarmed over the side to pack it. It seemed, very soon, ready to sink under its passengers.

Only the captain hesitated at the rail, still trying, under the snouts of the pirates' pistols, to have the last word.

"Devil take you!" was all he could manage.

And Plunqwette, flying in abruptly from a sea tour she seemed to have been taking, had the last word herself.

She enormously pooed on his hat from her godlike height.

"What have we done? Oh, songs of my innocent cradle—what?"

"We were defending *Art*. Couldn't let them attack her."

"Why not," despaired Eerie, "look what she's brought us to."

Bemused, the pirate-actors balanced on the strong driving deck of the *Elephant*. Their swashbuckling had given way; they were like burst pumpkins.

"It was the stagecraft caught us up," said Whuskery. "*Habit*. A million times we've acted it."

"And acted it here, got hysterical, and *now* look."

Ebad kept silent. Felix, propped against the side of the midship deckhouse, also had nothing to say.

Art addressed them all in a quiet, carrying tone.

"Gentlemen and friends, tell me honestly, would you rather *advertise coffee?* If really you would, then leap into another boat and row for White Lion Isle. But otherwise, only think of this. You're *actors*. That seasickness of yours—that was stage fright. But you are now on the biggest stage in the world—the ocean. And every land of the world sits waiting—to be your audience."

They stirred, staring, hearing, despite themselves, Molly on the forecastle of a make-believe ship. Hearing the dream—or nightmare—coming true. Even Black Knack, for half a second, had stars in his eyes—even the one under the eye patch.

Then Dirk said, sulky, "If the sea's the stage, dear, and the land's the audience—where's the dressing room?"

Felix opened his eyes. Art was standing now in front of him. "We'll put *you* off at the Isle of White, Mr. Phoenix."

Felix watched them strutting about, watched them dressed up now in the dry clothes they had pilfered from the ship's many chests. Peter brought Felix clothes, blankets, and later Whuskery gave him a pewter cup of some of the worst soup Felix had ever tasted. Otherwise, Felix was seemingly forgotten.

And when he noted, over to port, the Isle's pale cliffs, known as the Pins, and the background land that formed the shape of a lying down lion, lost in their own self-amazement, nobody approached to shove Felix off in a boat. Nor did he offer to go.

Felix's thoughts: Actors? No, they *were* pirates by now. Had become so the moment Art returned to them. And though she had saved his life—twice—Felix understood that she had become his deadly enemy. For that very reason he wanted to get away from her. And—for just the *same* reason—had decided to *stay*.

Changing Faces

Now there was no time to lose. While they were in English waters, the Republican Navy, duly alerted by the *Elephant*'s furious captain, would be looking out for them. Not to mention anyone else they had offended.

But flight—they were used to that. Had acted it so often. Even Eerie consoled himself with the comment, "On a stage, I used to believe every word and act, while I played my part. Now it's real and I don't believe it at all."

The coast of England, the Isle of White, were painted out behind them by winter haze and distance. By hours. Evening.

Night fell, and in the light of oil lanterns, they ate the revolting supper Whuskery had prepared.

They were quiet (even about the food), cautious, catfooting around one another. Art, too, said little. But she kept mostly out on deck.

She set the night watches, putting Ebad on a watch at the time she would go into her cabin to sleep. Mysterious Ebad, it seemed, was helping her. He looked as if he intended her to succeed. If she asked him why, she imagined she wouldn't get an answer.

Though not huge in size, the *Elephant* had everything. Stores, cannon, *dry* powder, pistols, comforts. The food, despite Whuskery, had potential. Great jars of fruit marmalades, conserves, pickled greens, slabs of dried meat, soups, apple barrels, barrels of sweet water, live chickens busy egg-laying in coops under the quarterdeck—Plunqwette would visit these frequently, scornfully parading past. As for the Captain's Cabin, it had been a model of orderly tight charm. But Art soon disarranged the crisply made bunk, scattered clothes, and books from the captain's private library, on the floor, opened the glass port so spray wetted the maps pinned to the wall. The maps, however, were wonderful. They showed the world. There it all was, the countries of Art's returned memory—Africay, Persis, Zanzibari, Gold and Ivory Coasts, the Amer Ricas, the true Spice Islands, the Blue Indies. They were all colored in, honey and brown, with ripe blue sea around them, and drawn animals—dolphins and sea dragons, octopuses, whales that pulled or puffed water at the corners, and imps and cherubs who blew curly white winds. On the landmasses were drawn landmarks—towers and tigers, bears and beacons. Fleets of green icebergs sailed across the Antarctic Edge. Mountains craned to the Afric moon.

Strangely, perhaps, it was when she looked at the maps that Art felt her first deep doubt. Excited, seeing the hugeness of the world, *remembering it*—yet knowing that her mind had somehow twisted her recollection—that she hadn't *ever* seen it—all at once she glimpsed how vast it was, this thing she had taken on. For it was more than a ship, or Molly's crew, more than her own life. What Art had taken on, and she knew it, *was* the world.

But she pushed the doubt out of her thoughts. Out of her heart. In a battle—and what else was *any* of it—there wasn't ever time for arguments.

Art woke up because Plunqwette was standing on Art's ribs, digging in her sharp claws.

"*Ow*, old bird. Move thy talons or I'll bite you!"

The parrot slightly altered her stance.

"Treasured Isle," Plunqwette announced. "Map and all."

"Yes, there are maps in here, Plunqwette. Don't do a do-dah on any. I like them."

"Land ho!" cried Plunqwette. The parrot's voice had altered. It sounded—more human—more—like *Molly's*? "Beach by cobhouse. Ten miles up. Fifteen paces left."

Art sat up slowly, and Plunqwette bounded into the air with a screech.

"*What?*"

"Pieces of Mate!" racketed Plunqwette.

"*Plunqwette*. Are you talking about a treasure map?"

But as she said it, the doubt rose like bilge. Even if Plunqwette somehow was—they had only been lines from the play.

"Go to sleep, Birdy. It's dawn in an hour."

Plunqwette, showing off her mimic skills, sat on the captain's desk and clucked for an hour like a chicken.

In the daffodil dawn, Art walked the length of her ship. There would need to be changes.

Deep in the hold she had seen blocks of tin and bars of refined English steel, crates of books, and of Scottish whisky, soapwood, woolens, and china plates. She didn't spend so long on these—trade goods had no appeal for her. Her (false) memory supplied only casks of jewels, gleaming weapons, and the bright money of a hundred lands.

Art's ship wasn't, now, a trader.

They would sell off this dull cargo at the nearest port that liked it, take weight off the hold, save only what was needed to support the ballast.

Meanwhile, the elephant figurehead must be removed, though *kept*, for all figureheads had power—there were tales of them coming alive or answering questions. Treated with courtesy, the elephant could be stored.

The name of the ship must change, too. But here, there were proper materials to work that sorcery—lime, paint, varnish.

A flag? Peter could sew, and down in the hold Art had also discovered some lengths of deep pink cloth. . . .

Whuskery must *cease* being cook. He would poison them all. Or merely drive them mad.

The crew were still ambling about, stunned. Sometimes they struck piratic poses—or cowered, glaring at the wide sea, not a dot of land on it now, but for the faintest penciling to the port side, which must be France, and soon would be Franco-Spania. No other ships.

Ebad could read the ship's instruments—compass, sextant, charts. That, from his days aboard the slave ship, where it seemed they had trained him for their own amusement. He had shamed them by learning faster than they.

Art had little patience, either, with any of that—charts, instruments. She wanted only to forge on. She knew this was a weakness, and let Ebad lesson her in the skills.

They hit turbulent weather one morning about two hours after sunrise. The sea shook, the sky clotted to rifts of dark and light, that let forth freezing blasts of wind.

Above, the elegant mastheads leaned and were gilded with rime.

Art climbed up, carelessly sure as any acrobat among the ducking tent-forest of the canvas, the prickly rime sticking to her fingers.

She wasn't afraid of the ship, but hadn't got to know her. So she was learning to.

From the mizzentop Plunqwette (speechless) let fly a white decoration on the deck, just missing the tiny far-down figure of Black Knack.

Coming off the mizzen, Art met Black Knack at normal size.

"Cap'n." Black Knack bowed humbly.

Art looked at his humbleness. His bristly humble face and eye patch. Distrusted all three.

"Yes."

"Wanted to say, I'm with you now, Arty—Cap'n. Never was, as you know. But now, I *am*. The way you took this ship. It impressed me. And—I don't want to advertise *coffee!* I never did. None of them did. I want my freedom, and this could be the way to it. So I'll act now, like I did before, that I'm a pirate, and I'll fight, and rob the seas over. We'll make a whole pile of gold."

"Maybe, Mr. Knack."

Black Knack nodded.

Art went into the Captain's Cabin—her own—and once more confronted the maps of the gigantic world.

The sea was calmer now. But the sea—was the sea. Ever changeable. Could they man this vessel with only nine people—Felix, naturally, being a passenger, and useless. Art had heard of such small crews. (But where? The play? Or was it true?) So far here it happened, it worked—even when the sea grew rough. They weren't even being sick anymore.

The ship kept her proper course southward, following the line of the lands eastward—the French-Spanish coast, later the coasts of Africay—before turning out full west toward the islands of the Blue Indies. The *Elephant* had been meant to voyage that way. Who now would suppose she still would?

Near midday, three French ships, flying the Lily of the Bourbon King, sailed over the horizon, seen vividly in Ebad's glass. They paid *Elephant* no attention.

But like the weather, at sea, you never knew—unfriendly ships were as common as storms, and besides, there were phantom things. . . .

Felix was keeping to the belowdecks, the crew area in the lower forecastle.

She was glad not to see Felix. She didn't like him. He made her feel—what was it—in the *wrong*. Like all those others in her life, the ones she had had to *resist*.

Someone yelled. Art, standing on the forecastle deck, looked back.

Ebad at the wheel, Walter aloft, Peter in the galley at his new duties of cook—Whuskery and Dirk, Black Knack, Honest, and Eerie peering down over the port side—were they being sick after all? No—then what?

"What is it?"

"See, Art—a great black fish—aaah!"

"It's a *woman. Drowned.* I tell you," snapped Whuskery.

"She's not drowned, either. She's—waving?"

"Better haul the lady out then," said Art.

Something was there certainly, something dark, trailing long black ribbons and veils, floating there, just under the top-skin of the waters. It had been caught by some of its—*drapery?*—against the ship's side.

"Tis a mermaid," declared Eerie.

They seemed inclined simply to talk about the object. Art directed them to throw over a rope with a grappler and hook the thing out. She could see it wasn't human—and not alive.

Up it came, wiggling its slimy ribbons.

They were weeds, seaweed out of the depths. It was thick in silt, but as they hauled it over the rail, a pale hand poked out, and Whuskery screamed.

"It's a statue," said Eerie. He knocked his knuckles on its side and produced a wooden noise.

Walter, from the crow's nest, called down. "I can see what it is! 'Tis the figurehead."

Honest ran up with a bucket of water and sluiced off some of the mud.

"By the Cat's Elbows, it's the old one, off the Coffee Ship."

It was. The figurehead of the little *Pirate Coffee* had followed them. Lying there now, darkened and made sinister by the deeps below, there was nothing *nice* about it. Nothing—welcoming.

"Don't clean her up," said Art. "We'll blacken her worse."

The pale hand, which had held out the coffeepot, stretched forward now from her muffled shadow, in a distinctly menacing gesture. *Give me!* the hand seemed to say.

Third good omen.

Art said, "Forget our old figurehead. We have our *new* figurehead. Gentlemen, pray greet the *Unwelcome Stranger*."

᥆᥅ TWO ᥅᥆

Foe and Fortune ⟶

Running over the blue horizon came a ship that looked black as a piece of yesterday's night.

This was a warm sea. And there was a warm strong wind that blew this ship, a cutter, where she wanted to go, and her sails were turned sidelong or taken partly in, adjusted for the wind's pressure.

On the quarterdeck, surveying the busy sailors, was a small, slender figure. Hair curled and black, eyes very green. Boy or woman?

The figure spoke. She was a woman, of about eighteen years.

"Well, Mr. Beast. It seems the game is on."

"Aye, Cap'n," growled Mr. Beast, First Mate.

(He *looked* like a beast, too, shaggy and craggy and dressed in unmistakable pirate finery, much stained by action. True pirates, these.)

The young woman tossed something up in the air, and it fluttered to the top of the mizzen, where it sat, looking surprised. Not a parrot: a pigeon.

"That's the expected pigeon then? You *trust* him?" asked Mr. Beast, not meaning the pigeon, and picking his beastly teeth with a small dagger.

"No. Nor would my dad. But he's ours."

She showed Mr. Beast, though she knew, this girl, quite well, he couldn't read the piece of paper the carrier pigeon had carried out to them, finding its clever flight path here all the way from Port's Mouth, England.

"I never," said Mr. Beast, pretending to have read the paper they both knew he couldn't, "trust a traitor."

"Nor I, Beastie. But this I do believe. I've been waiting for it," declared the young woman. She was beautifully dressed, with a green silk coat, gold and jewels stitched on, and green feathers in her three-cornered hat. In her belt were a brace of silver-chased pistols, a cutlass, and a couple of handy knives—of which she had a few others stored about her person. Every finger was ringed. "My father," said this being, "taught me a lot. I trust *him*. That is, I trust his memory."

"The Golden Goliath!" exclaimed the Beast, clapping one murderous paw respectfully to his heart. "He was a Lord of the Seven Seas."

This girl, then, was the daughter of Golden Goliath, the notorious, and *real*, pirate.

"The main fact of it is, Beastie, these actor fools have got the *map*. Or part of it, apparently. The edge is burned off, or so our informant says in his letter."

"*Treasure.*"

"Enough we can live like kings."

"GG was always after that map."

"I *know*, Mr. Beast. But *we've* never quite known where it went, have we? Even thought it got burned right away in their unlucky stage cannon blowup. Then we believed it got hidden in some theater—but which? And we couldn't find it, despite the dad's best efforts. By the Starry Wheel, it's only just surfaced again. And *she's* got it, damned Molly's daughter." The black-haired girl threw back her head and let out a fearsome shriek. Below on the deck, her pirate crew nodded and applauded, as they applauded almost everything she did. Her father, the Golden Goliath, had trained them cruelly and well. And she, this glamorous girl, was *worse* even than GG—"*Piratica*," said GG's daughter, with awful scorn. "We'll teach them a lesson, won't we, Mr. Beast."

Down on the main deck, someone took a potshot at the pigeon, but missed it.

Offended, the bird flew off looking for another safer perch— it was used to such treatment, here, but it would be a long journey back to England.

"One thing," said the Beast, "do Molly's boys know the map's worth anything? Aside from our traitor knowing it, of course."

"He's not sure. Nor am I. They do or they don't. But we *do*. So, set a new course, Mr. Beast. The Blue Indies is where they're bound. Own Accord Isle. *Wicked*."

The *Unwelcome Stranger* sailed down the chart of the world. (A routine had been established. Masts to be greased, decks cleaned, all parts and areas checked for repairs. Unwillingly, the crew got the hang of it. Acts they had performed lightly—as *acting*—became ordinary life.)

In this way the ship had gone by the sunny coasts of Franco-Spania, to follow the white beaches of Morrocaino, and there sold off the bulk of her cargo for a fair price, Art and Ebad haggling with merchants under orange trees and old painted walls.

Such ports as they now visited were used to their apparent kind. No one doubted for a moment they were what they appeared, a very flashy, dashing collection of pirates.

Palm trees pillared up, crowned by dark green plumes, markets swarmed with life and color, ancient castles teetered on rocksides. Cutthroats in garish clothes strode about, and spat at, or bowed to them in the way of brothers.

(And Art had seen all this before—*knew* it—somehow. . . .)

At the edges of the Morrocaino coast, they sat in dusty taverns, and all the *Unwelcome*'s crew drank and sang and bragged, as if they had robbed over every inch of the oceans, from here to Australia.

But so far they had done nothing.

At the last Morrocain tavern, Art had other business. She stood with Felix, looking over a brown donkey track that led away up a brown hill with brown donkeys trotting along it, loaded with barrels and baskets.

"I've offered to give you a share of the cargo money, Mr. Phoenix, to start you off. I offered that, also, at the last port. And the one before that. You could have been away at France, if you'd wanted. They hate the English for throwing out the English kings. You'd have been entirely safe in France from English Law. So why won't you go?"

"Laziness?"

"I'd think you wanted to join us. But you don't."

"Sincerely, I do not."

Art looked at him. He had accepted new clothes from the ship's store and looked—as always—handsome enough to make your eyes smart. But he hadn't done anything on the ship save make drawings, sing, and tactfully listen to the men's troubles. Those were his three talents. He couldn't fight, didn't want to, and wouldn't take on any of the ship's duties. Even Whuskery had now mastered climbing the masts, and Peter had proved himself well able to cook. They all took their watches, trimmed sails, saw to the general upkeep and cleanness. All but Felix, the passenger—nonpaying.

"Then," said Art, "*sincerely* I tell you, you must leave us. We sail on tonight's tide. And the first ship we encounter after that—we *take*."

"Yes," said Felix.

"Which doesn't please you."

"No."

"Then why stay? Do you think you can stop us?"

"No," repeated Felix.

"What then?"

Felix turned to Art. His eyes were intense and beautiful.

They had great depths that reminded Art irresistibly of the sea itself. But where she liked to gaze deep into the sea, Felix's eyes angered her if she looked into them too long.

"I think you might say," said Felix quietly, "I want to understand why you're doing this. And how—if you *are* able to— you're *able* to."

"A riddle."

"I mean, how can you even consider it. Let alone *do* it."

"It's easy, Mr. Phoenix." Art drew her pistol and held it under his chin. "Like this. That's all."

"But you've said you won't kill."

"I shan't. Nor will my crew. You saw what happened on the ship, when it was still the *Elephant,* and we captured her. If you're canny, you can commit acts of piracy by bluff. Like Molly."

"No," said Felix. "That worked in the drama. In real life it *might* work, now and then—but in the end—"

Art flicked the pistol over and slipped it back into her belt.

"Well, you won't be there to lament over our end. You must take your leave of us here. No more debate. It's a fine town. All arches and donkeys."

Before Felix could reply, Eerie spoke soulfully from the tavern door. "Don't send him off, our Felix. He's our lucky talisman, Art, so he is."

Felix smiled and lowered his sea-deep eyes.

Art said, "We don't need him. And we *may* need one or two others who can crew with us. What say you? Do we want a useless load?"

She saw the loads on the donkeys as she said it. All useful, no doubt.

"But we can't leave him here, Art!" cried Walter from inside the tavern—they had all been listening. There was now a chorus. Out they all trooped, all but Dirk and Peter, who had gone to buy cheese and oranges in the town, and Black Knack, Ebad, and Plunqwette, who had stayed to mind the ship.

The air twanged and droned with calls for Felix to stay aboard.

"And don't go saying you're Cap'n," added Whuskery, "coz, by the Whale's Knitting, on a *pirate* ship, we *all* get a say."

Half amused (or furious?), Art decided not to provoke them.

They weren't bonded yet, not completely. They didn't believe what they did, thought it still a play—which had helped push them along, but was a problem on the practical side.

She thought, once Felix Phoenix witnessed what they could really do in the pirate line, he would probably jump over the side.

Dusk came, eastern swift. Under the blazing upside-down footlights of stars, they flaunted off, anchors aweigh.

Unwelcome Stranger, a tall pale ship, with the faceless figure-head of a black-veiled woman, gesturing in a menacing, grabby fashion. The sails glowed, and phosphorous sewed along the water.

A lamp at the masthead lit the rose-pink flag. Its black skull and crossbones looked peculiar that way, funny—almost crazy—like a dream.

Darkness gathered round. How alone, the ship, in the midst of the sea. As Art felt *herself* alone, among these men. The moon lifted at their back, casting their black shadow forward.

Felix gazed down at this, while Art's crew performed their sailory chores. From the galley came the smell of decent cooking.

All their guns were real now, and probably stuffed with bullets.

Felix felt a sadness heavy as time and stood turning the ring of ruby glass on his finger.

"What would you say to me, Father?" he asked the evening softly.

Only a faint lightning answered, winking at the sky's edge.

And the next morning, there on the wide, well-lit stage of the sea, with not a strip of land in sight, *another* ship.

A trader, with a round-looking hull and plenty of canvas up, she trundled cheerfully along, flying red, blue, and purple flags of France and Spain. Her name was visible. Written in Franco-Spanish, it meant *Royal*.

Art leaned out like a cat watching a bird, Ebad's spyglass to her eye.

"She's ours."

And her reluctant crew—they *cheered*.

Art had no time to be astounded.

With a flourish, Black Knack started the band.

The pirates' cannon thundered, three of the seven, a broadside, that landed, deliberately short, in the flounces of the sea. Nevertheless, the trader vessel juddered. She skipped. Then she opened fire in turn.

Art yelled her orders. *Unwelcome Stranger* slewed to starboard, and the trader's shot missed her. The trader had only two cannon.

"By the Prancers! Our Art's good. How in the name of angels did she learn *that?*"

"On a stage," said Dirk acidly.

The windjammer swerved, settled.

The band had started their hellish dance tune—Honest on the two drums, Whuskery on squalling trumpet, Walt with whistle, just as they had in every play.

In fact, these and other instruments had been aboard their new ship, a cargo meant for somewhere or other that liked music. (Fourth omen?)

Unwelcome racked back into her proper orbit. Then ran straight at the unlucky Franco-Spanish ship.

Above, Molly's pink flag with its deadly black signal and a green-and-red parrot darting round the rigging.

Another cannon shot left the trader—badly aimed, it went foaming off far to port.

Art, up on the forecastle, the bowsprit wire above her, laughed at the panic on the trader's deck.

She had the sense, like that of a god descending on machinery in the theater, of flying down at them. She called loudly: "Here we are! Good morning, sirs."

She did this twice—once in French, once Spanish. Molly had taught her both.

Next minute *Unwelcome* lightly struck the *Royal*, and the fatter ship staggered. *Unwelcome* slung over her grapplers and held firm, a hound bred for running and seizure. It had been judged to a hair's breadth.

The trader deck now gushed with alarm.

Art seized a rope and swung straight across the gap of open sea. She landed in their midst, a pistol now in either hand, one of which she fired instantly directly up, and hit their main mast, which showered a quick wooden rain. But she was always a crack shot, it seemed.

Just as she had always known.

"Yield!" Art shouted, once more in both languages—in English, too, for good measure. "Surrender, or we'll slay the pack of you."

The *Royal* seemed quite crowded. As several of Art's crew also swung over on the ropes and dropped with great elegance beside her, cutlasses drawn, guns out, their victims burbled, screeched, and wept.

Then the *Royal*'s captain arrived, a small plump gentleman in flawless uniform, starred with medals and gems.

He fell on his knees before Art and spoke in French. "Mighty prince, do not destroy us."

"That's not our goal. We want only your valuables."

"Everything—" cried the captain. He drew or threw off rings and earrings—another rain, this one of gold. "There are purses bulging cash in the belowdecks—"

"Then fetch them. And no tricks. My men are vicious as unfed wolves."

The captain got up rapidly and ordered his people to bring the goods. "We have Indian silks—pearls from Cathay and Antioch."

Art put a friendly arm about his neck.

"*I* will trust you, sir. One false move, however, and I will kill you, sir."

"Oh—by the Sacred Blue of Heaven—"

"Believe me. A clean death at my hands is better than what any of my men would do to you."

The captain glanced at Art's men. Gibbered.

Unwelcome's company stood rampant, training their blades and pistols in a deadly array of force on the *Royal*'s crew. Their faces were proud and terrible—*successful*—pitiless. Perhaps no true pirate had ever looked so capable of doing his worst.

Art smiled at the captain.

The remaining crew and passengers of the *Royal* held their breath, while up from the hold came the caskets and the bales.

"Are you a woman?" the captain whispered, pale as washed washing.

"Yes. Have you never heard my name?"

"*Forgive me*—never! May I inquire?"

"I am known, sir, as Art Blastside, the Daughter of Piratica—and she was the most fearsome female pirate to cross the Seven Seas."

The captain fainted. Art caught him tidily and handed him to his Second Officer, who bowed very low.

"Your lives are in no danger, providing you offer us no difficulty."

The *Royal* rang with mooing chants of obedience.

Then a man rushed forward. He cast himself at Art's feet.

"Glorious sir—madam—let me come along with you. Let me serve under your banner. I will die for you, meself."

Art looked at him thoughtfully. He was tanned and brawny, a Spaniard perhaps, doubtless well trained in the crewing of a ship.

"Why?"

To her surprise the volunteer switched to English with a strong Lundon accent. "I was pirated off another ship—useless, they were—escaped but ended up here. Me name's Glad Cuthbert. And I can play the ol' hurdy-gurdy—got me own an' all. Do for your band."

The captain had revived in his Second's arms.

"Take the fellow," he begged. "He is an English *pirate*. And his playing—by my King!—it stinks."

As they leaped back on the ropes from the ransacked *Royal*, Glad Cuthbert leaped with them, porting his instrument, a hefty wooden box with keys and a handle.

The pearls and silks, the gold and ornaments of the *Royal* also went with them.

Even Plunqwette flew down to see.

Such ease. Was it possible?

Just like in the theater.

"You were very fortunate."

"No, Mr. Phoenix. We were very *able*."

Now the seas were the violet of a peacock's feather, and with just those same flashes of bronze and green. Oh, yes, the dolphins leaped, silvery. Great shoals of fish, colored pewter with blue—and pink as the flag—escorted *Unwelcome Stranger* for miles. Winter was far away. It was always summer, here.

Like gilded honeycomb in sunlight, the coasts of Ivory and Gold rose on the port side. Lawless harbors were everywhere, welcoming the *Unwelcome*.

Men black as Ebad Vooms, and clad in vermilion robes, rowed out to bargain with the ship as she lay at anchor offshore. Palm-leaf baskets full of pineapples, white bananas, mangolines, and coconuts came aboard.

Aquamarine lagoons, fringed by palms in feather headdresses of dark emerald, later drew them ashore. Honest splashed in the waters, Ebad sternly attempted to teach Eerie to swim. Eerie resolutely sank. "Man, I'm not a *fish!*"

Art, like her men in shirt and under-leggings, swam like an electric eel.

Felix, having been rowed ashore, too, sat under the palms with Glad Cuthbert, learning, not to swim, but to play a hurdy-gurdy.

"Named meself Glad, after me old missus. Gladys," Cuthbert explained, along with explaining about the musical instrument. "One day I'll see her again, the old bag. Real pain, she is. I miss her every waking hour. Dreams about her, though, and in the dream we're always having a good ol' row. Cheers me up no end. Who've *you* left behind?"

"No one much," said Felix.

"Nice pretty feller like you, must be someone."

"Lots of someones," said Felix. "No one in particular."

"No family then?"

"No."

"How'd you hatch then? Out of a bird's egg?"

Felix laughed his melodious laugh. He glanced at the pirates, swimming—or semi-drowning—in the romantic blue lagoon. Art sprang suddenly from the water, her walnut hair shot with its narrow orange-marigold powder burn streak, glittering off water drops. But she dived straight down again. And presently just-about-swimming Walter yelped as an invisible Art pulled on his ankles.

"Like the look of our captain, do you?" asked Glad Cuthbert.

"Not much."

"You coulda nipped off with that Frenchy ship I left. They'd've took you. Only need to say you're not a pirate and beg help. You know that? Yes. So why stay?"

"Everyone asks that. I have reasons, apparently."

"You don't understand why a man—or a woman—takes to the pirate life," said Cuthbert. "That's a fact. But we've *our* reasons, too. *Apparently*."

No one had told Glad Cuthbert he was the only genuine pirate aboard. Felix didn't enlighten him, either.

Above and to the back of them, where the palms gave way to lush forest, full of roaming large animals they glimpsed but avoided, birds colored like rainbows clattered in affront as Plunqwette, wet(te), landed among them.

"That there parrot can swim, too. Never saw that in me life. Thought they talked, those birds. Bit on the quiet side, that one, isn't it? For a parrot . . ." mused Cuthbert. "All those other birds up there, real racket. I miss the pigeons of ol' Lundon."

Walter, who had just scrambled from the water, nodded. "Pete and I kept pigeons once. We flew them to carry messages. Earned some money that way. You'd never believe how far they can travel—"

Peter, emerging also, tapped Walt on the shoulder. "Forget all that. Let's hear a song. Cuthbert on his hurdy and Felix to sing."

Under the lagoon, staring through turquoise jade at fish igniting like tiny flames from the shadows, Art slightly heard Felix singing on the bank.

When she rose out of the lagoon, she was frowning.

She knew what she wanted and was getting it at last. The new *Unwelcome* she had managed. And these men, they too were beginning to break free and find their true calling. They had acted pirates better than any pirate ever could. And luck had changed for all of them. The future was open as the seas. No end to possibility.

But Felix Phoenix. His chisled, thoughtful, dejected face. Why did he stay? What did *he* want?

"Ebad," Art said to her First Officer, who was now hauling her Second Officer O'Shea out of the water like a wet sack of spluttering potatoes, "that young man over there must be sent packing."

"Oh, by the Butters of Eira, I'm that full of water I'm a sponge," moaned Eerie.

Black Knack (who also refused to learn to swim) spoke round the edge of a banana. "Aye, don't trust that Felix, Arty. We'll bounce him off at Blue Indies. No excuse for him to hang about once we get *there*. If he won't, he can go over the side."

Out in the lagoon, Dirk, Whuskery, and Honest swam on their backs in relaxed formation—till Whuskery suddenly sank. Honest hoisted him back up.

Felix's song ended.

"Never swam," said Glad Cuthbert. "Never bloody will, neither."

Plunqwette shook out her feathers on the trunk above, and soaked him.

The next ship they ran down and boarded was a well-rigged clipper, coming up from Southern Amer Rica.

Walter spotted her from the crow's nest in the early dusk, setting her course shoreward for a cove.

Turning to the evening wind, *Unwelcome* stole after, smooth and almost soundless on the darkening sea. She was, *Unwelcome*, exactly the ship Art had thought her. Powerful yet maneuverable. Taking in her sails, they crept along the lip of the cove, under the cover now of settled night, all lanterns put out.

Well practiced from a hundred such deeds aboard their fake theater ship, the pirate crew were skillful and noiseless.

They lowered a jolly boat with scarcely a ripple. Armed to the teeth, Walter and Peter rowed, and Ebad, Eerie, Art, Whuskery, and Black Knack (armed also to the teeth) crowded the boat, ready.

The clipper was herself a ship of the Amer Ricas, and flying their striped Flag of Liberty. She lay at anchor, garlanded with lights. But the deck had only a scatter of watch about on it—the rest, from the sounds, were at dinner in the saloon and in the crew's quarters below.

Up the side of the clipper swarmed Art Blastside and her men. The five sailors on watch were overcome in a trio of minutes—their grunts and squeaks not heard above the loudness of eating and drinking just under the deck.

Tied up with cords brought from *Unwelcome,* the watch soon lay looking miserably up at the stars.

Art, Ebad, Eerie, and Black Knack went down into the officers' quarters. They slipped along the narrow passage between, and reached the saloon.

The door burst open on a candlelit scene of startled captain and three officers blundering to their feet, in a crash of dishes, as a tall, slim, young man (?), with long brown hair, landed in the midst of their table, pistols pointed over the roast and the smoked cheeses.

"A good dinner, gentlemen. Forgive our interruption. We won't keep you a moment."

"Pirates—!"

"Flaming ferrety renegade reivers!"

"Congratulations on your eyesight," confirmed Art. "Yield, and we'll do you no injury."

The captain pulled out a gun. Art shot the weapon precisely from his hand. It sped over the room and landed splat in a cake on the sideboard.

Ebad and Black Knack had disarmed two of the others. Eerie was patting the third, the youngest officer, who was sobbing in his dish—"I *told* Uncle I never wanted to go to sea!"

"There, there, now, lad. We'll only skin ye alive if ye *resist*," promised Eerie.

The clipper carried scented wood, rice, and chalk, and three crates of gold and shell statues from ancient tropical temples.

Her crew brought them up from the hold and laid them before Art, as she held their captain in a loving arm, and Eerie boomed about removing lights and livers.

Last of all, Art extracted the key to the Captain's Cabin from the dismayed captain. She locked him, his officers, and several of the crew in the small room, crammed tight together. The rest of the crew she ordered back below.

"Finish your supper, sirs. If any attempt to annoy us after we leave, you'll find yourselves quaintly full of holes."

Hardly anyone dared, it seemed. Over the silk of the night their boat scudded away. Only once a head poked above the clipper's rail. Art combed its hair for it with a bullet, and after that no one else tried even to look.

They had reached *Unwelcome Stranger* before they heard, carried across the warm stillness, the smash of timbers as the captain and his packed-in men broke down the cabin door—maybe only by pressure from inside.

And they were aboard, and already making way, before pistols powdered out red shot along the clipper's bows. They had not one cannon, it seemed. Without any loss then, lucky as cats in custard, Art and her crew floated off along the balmy night.

Four Wise Men ⟋

Right at the center of Lundon's High Admiralty Walk stood the Navy Building. A silver oar was fastened over its doorway, which was flanked by large, sandstone statues of sphinxes, brought from Egypt ten or so years earlier.

Landsir George Fitz-Willoughby Weatherhouse paid these creatures no obvious attention. But the look on their female faces had, however, reminded him nastily of his long-ago wife of one year, Molly Faith. Cool, canny, serene only with getting her own way.

Up the marble stairs his landsirship stamped, rapping his silver-headed cane on the steps and bannisters—*stamp, stamp, clunk*— So anyone hearing him would think he had three legs.

Two high double doors were opened for him, and in he marched.

"What's all this nonsense?"

"Ah, George," said the man in the big white wig and big wooden chair, all across the polished wooden floor. "Good-day."

"What's good in it? Why am I dragged up here?"

"Oh, did they not say? How thoughtless. It seems to concern your daughter."

G Fitz WW checked. "Daughter? He said piracy, that's what he said, that pompous asp you sent to me."

"Pray be calm. Both piracy *and* your daughter, it seems. The newspapers are full of it. Don't you read, George?"

White Wig, who went by the name of Landsir Snargale, indicated a man in the clothes of a wealthy merchant captain. "This is Captain Bolt, who until recently ran the trading vessel FRS *Elephant*. And this other gentleman—"

"Name's Coffee and *trade's* coffee," barked the other gentleman, who was short, fat, and wore a brocade coat the color of coffee with cream in it. "I sponsor half the coffee market in Free England. I organize advertisements of a spectacular nature. I'm famous for it." (George Fitz looked at him as if he were instead famous for insanity.) However: "And your *daughter*, sir—"

"One thing at a time," said Landsir Snargale mildly. He had been a commander of a fleet in earlier years. Now his importance lent his words great weight.

Ruffled, everyone else stood puffing, even the bowlegged Captain Bolt.

Landsir Fitz remarked sullenly, "In any case, I disowned the hibberty-flappit, if it's Artemesia you mean."

"Art Blastside is the name she gave *me*," rumbled Mr. Coffee, still on the boil.

"And myself, 'pon the Giraffe's Earlobe," added the captain.

"While in point of fact, I admit I took the gnat-batty wench for a *boy*," confessed Coffee.

"She fooled *me* never for one moment, sir."

Fitz WW rapped his cane again sourly. "Like her mother. Acting. Molly—no holding her. No holding her daughter. I did my best. I had them lock Artemesia in the school. Up the soot-socked chimney she goes—off into the snow and ice. I thought the vixen had perished. *I* shed no tears."

"No, George. I believe you did not. Sirs, please—" as another outburst threatened from all sides. "We will all tell our stories, one by one. That gentleman in the corner, Mr. Prawn, the clerk, will write everything down."

One by one then—although sometimes also shouting and at the same time after all—three aggrieved men ranted out their tales.

Fitz WW had the tale of the thankless Molly, an actress, who had run off back to the gutter and left him, only to die on stage ten or fifty years later, when some theatrical gunpowder blew up. After which he had, from pure generosity, rescued their child from the low-down life of the theater, and had her trained to be a lady. Which hadn't taken. At Christmas last, she had stormed off. He hadn't seen or heard of her since. Had he looked for her? Why should he?

Next, the Coffee Sponsor entertained them by his tale of the brazen boy on the advertising ship, *Pirate Coffee*, who had soon after *stolen* the ship, *sunk* it, and run off with Mr. Coffee's hired crew, a band of idiot actors, leaving him with a loss amounting to many hundreds of English pounds.

After him, Captain Bolt charged bowleggedly about, telling in great detail how he had kindly saved eight or nine highly stupid people—as he *thought*—from drowning, just off Port's Mouth. Only to find they were piratic thieves, who forced him at gunpoint off his own ship. The actors formerly described, he had now no doubt, though they had seemed both dangerously violent and experienced, at the time, in what they did. The girl was the worst. She said she was their leader. Mad, Captain Bolt had decided, mad as a hatter.

"To all this I must add the information I've since received," said Landsir Snargale. "It concerns a number of trading ships fired on, or otherwise boarded by tricks, and most of their valuable goods removed. This, between the Africas and the Caribbean waters of the Blue Indies. It's thought the criminal's ship, which they call the *Unwelcome Strangler*—is now heading west for the Isle of Own Accord. Where indeed Captain Bolt meant to take said ship, when she was his, and known as the *Elephant*. I've said, all Lundon papers carry this and the other stories. That the pirate captain is female, and English, has proved a source of great interest. And I fear, sympathy. The journalists hold the young woman up as a fantastic heroine—a swashbuckling star. Even the *Lundon Tymes*, I regret to say, praises her 'Gallantry and Cunning.' The poor and the low people love their highwaymen and pirates. Daring and lovable rogues—that's what they think them and call them. But I know, sirs, having seen evidence of it, the loathsomeness of the pirate kind. I—*we*—know, don't we, to call such villains by the name *vermin*."

No one else spoke for a while. They stood about, blowing down their noses like horses, glaring at one another, the floor, the walls, and a selection of shipshape decorations.

Landsir Fitz muttered at last, "*Unwelcome Strangler*—that's not it. Mouse take it, its the same as the name of the damned ship in Molly's play—*Stranger*—*Unwelcome Stranger*—"

"Mr. Prawn," said Snargale, "I trust you have that corrected? There is also one other popular felon with Artemesia's crew," he continued. "It seems a most unstable and worrying highwayman, known in the area of Wimblays Common as Gentleman Jack Cuckoo, also attached himself to the pirates—either at Grinwich or Sheerditch or even Port's Mouth—accounts vary."

"I saw none like that," declared the sponsor. "There were only two other odd ones—a yellow dog and a green parrot."

"Gentleman Jack could now be any of the pirates," said Captain Bolt, "by the Shark's Handshake. They only had one extra—blond fellow who swooned. Seemed out of place."

"Nay, sir, a swooner? 'Twould *never* be Cuckoo Jack," said Snargale. "Let's be wise on this matter."

"Nay," agreed the Captain hastily. "No way. Neither up nor down."

"Well," said Fitz, "we've had all that now. Again, why am I here?"

"George, if all this is true, as it seems it is, your daughter is now a pirate. Not *acting* piracy, as you say her mother did, but *living* piracy—like many others on every sea of the world. She has preyed on French and Spanish ships, also on our allies of Amer Rica. That is bad enough. But she's insulted English ships, too. Captain Bolt's to begin with, and three more since in the mid-Atlantic—she is now a wanted criminal. Our own patrols, and every lawful governor between here and the ends of the earth, has been, or will be, alerted to her villainy. Mr. Coffee here and Captain Bolt are already joined in setting up a ship to follow and find her. When caught—either by English naval vessels, Mr. Coffee's seagoing ship, or anyone else who has a grudge against her, and has signed treaties with England—your daughter, and her *men,* will be brought home. And by home, George, I regret to say I mean to Oldengate Prison and the hangman's rope."

George Fitz-Willoughby Weatherhouse lowered his scaley eyes. His puce face mottled with a duller tone.

But all he said was "Then be damned to the fool. Let her swing."

Own Accord

Sun, a golden guinea, kissed the face of the Isle of Own Accord.

It lifted from sea the color of cornflowers.

But the island was itself so green—it was green like a new color. And the land there built itself up like a castle, the lower terraces leading to massive inland towers: mountains were there, covered with a dark exotic fur of forest, out of which poured rivers like shiny frayed white wool.

"Milk River," recited Ebad.

"Black and White River," announced Eerie.

"*Sugar* River," said Black Knack, and smacked his bristly lips.

"And the sea here," said Peter, "they say, is so blue from all the spilled pirate cargoes of sapphires—"

Liberated from slavery at the same time as the English and Amer Rican rebellions against the monarchy, Own Accord took its name from its declaration of independence. "Herewith," said the charter, "our island, Ours. By Our Own Accord."

Port Republic appeared—Porto Rex as it had been known. White buildings massed along the harbor. The beach gleamed like daytime stars.

Scarlet birds flew out to look at the ship, then flew away. Plunqwette, unconcerned, preened on the foremast.

"Own Accord flourishes on ordinary trade. But it's known the island also welcomes well-mannered pirates with coins to spend and goods to sell. Especially those from Free England and the Amer Ricas."

Whuskery squinted over his mustache at Art.

"That's what was said in the play. But is it true?"

"Behold," said Art.

The port was lined with waving figures. Cheers and flags greeted the approaching tall ship. Small children rushed toward the shoreline. Flowers dazzled out across the lapping water of the bay. While on the ships already at anchor there, sailors craned to see who came in, grinning, and they, too, raised a cheer.

"By the Topgallants—'tis just like our drama—"

"The clapping and *bravos!*"

"Do they know who we are?"

Black women in dresses of canary gold and peony red showed their matchless teeth like white crescent moons. More flowers were flung.

"Fine-looking people. Do you hail from here, Ebad?" asked Peter.

Ebad shook his head slowly. "Not here, nor the coasts of Ivory and Gold. Nor Zanzibari. My land," said Ebad in a low and thrilling voice, "is Egypt, above the Nile. I am descended from kings."

"Coo," said Dirk. "Get you, darling."

Eerie cried, "No, he is so, so he is. As I am, from the fiery kings of Eira."

"Shut up," said Art, "the pair of you. We're Republicans now."

The coil of harbor closed around them, and *Unwelcome* anchored just outside the shipping and the flowers.

The spontaneous reception was anyhow ebbing away, people going back to their own business.

"Who goes ashore, Cap'n?" asked the Honest Liar, yearning out toward the lovely land that now seemed, good-naturedly, to be turning its back again.

"Cuthbert and Peter will take the first harbor watch. The rest of us—"

"No, Cap'n Art, let me go ashore," groused Salt Peter. "If Walt goes, so do I."

"There you are wrong, Mr. Salt. You're staying aboard." Peter sulked. He too turned his back, not good-naturedly. "No fuss," said Art. "You'll have your turn. Now, everyone to his quarters. Use the crew bath. Dress in the best. We can sell and buy excellently at such a trader's port. Besides gain useful hints on the tastiest shipping in the region. This place should be a *Who Is Who* of robbable vessels. But they won't take us up if we're messy."

Felix stood as always behind the others, leaning at the rail, out of Art's way.

Art walked over to him.

"Mr. Phoenix, we are putting you off here. What do you say?"

"You've made up your mind. What can I say?"

"This is, I agree, Something rather than Nothing—Something being that thing you say you hate. Never mind. Just as Cuthbert and Pete'll get their turn ashore, I'm certain, you can sing and draw and charm yourself aboard another vessel.

Try the Amer Ricas, Mr. P. They say a young man can do well there. Meanwhile, the dress code applies also to you. Spruce yourself."

Art turned into her cabin. She was jaunty. She had heard the cheers, seen the flowers, just as she recalled. And she knew exactly how to behave on the island, and where to go.

As she pulled the bath out from under the sofa (Captain Bolt had not been one to travel without his comforts), she remembered, too, the old name of Own Accord Isle. It was Zaymaxa—*Place of Many Waters*.

Plunqwette almost joined Art in the bath, sitting on the side, dipping in her beak, then spitting out the perfumed water.

"Oh, look how high the mountains are!" exclaimed the parrot, in Molly's voice. "And the crystal rivers rushing down."

Art jumped. She flipped water at Plunqwette, who flew up to perch on the bookcase. Speech left her again as she bit interestedly at Captain Bolt's books.

Dressed in their best, bathed and scented, combed and gorgeous, the pirates parrot-preened along the deck in the moist, hot noon sunlight.

Then there was Felix Phoenix.

"By the Cranes of Connor! Will you look at this."

Felix too had put on fresh clothes from the ship's stores. He wore a coat of ice-white satin one level lighter than his hair, trimmed by silver braid and pearl. At his side hung a dress sword (for show only) in a scabbard of silvery hue that matched his tight and flattering trousers. His boots were the palest fawn leather, embroidered with curlicues of silver and gold. He had several rings on his fingers, and that white hair of his, long, thick, and springy from washing, laved over his shoulders, to match the white lawn shirt with its sewn knots of pale green ribbon. He raised his black brows, and Dirk pretended to faint.

The crew were all gaping in theatrical appreciation, when their captain's cabin door opened.

"By the Swans of Sausage—!"

"It's Molly," said Ebad simply. "By the Lord God. Our Molly Faith."

Felix, amused and touched by admiration, also turned to see. And then there was Art Blastside.

They didn't know how long she had hesitated before the row of dresses found in the passenger storage, remembering Molly in her ball gowns of red or green. All of five minutes Art faltered. Then she turned on her heel and went elsewhere. She had *worn* skirts for six years. That would do.

Plunqwette had sat watching Art, head on one side, as Art dressed up. Next Plunqwette helped, by spinning round and round Art's head, pulling at her newly washed hair, squawking, until Art swore at her.

Then Plunqwette swore back—better.

But now, Plunqwette waddled along the deck behind Art like a proud maid who, single winged, had done everything to make Art look wonderful.

Art *did* look wonderful.

Felix stared at her.

She wore a man's clothes still, but now they were those of a rich and artistic landowner. Her coat and breeches were paired amber silk, her shirt a fantasy of cascading white lace that mimicked the rivers pouring off the mountains high above. If Felix and the men had put on four or five rings, Art had put on ten or so. And all of them real—agate, topaz, diamond.

From her left ear swung a huge amber raindrop. Her hair, drying, was curling in the heat. Its fox streak looked deliberate—a plume.

Magnificent, Felix thought. A leopard, a lion. But what is she? Actor—thief—madwoman—murderer?

Glad Cuthbert punched Felix's arm, light as nothing.

"You're love struck, you are."

"I beg your—"

"Seen it before. Seen it in meself. Go on. Give in, Felix, me son. 'Tis yer fate, already."

Felix, white as his coat, stalked away up the deck. He stalked past Art, not bothering to give her a glance. But she, turning to gaze at *him* in open appreciation, put her fingers to her mouth, and blew the whistle common on the streets of low Lundon. A sign of maximum approval.

Her crew roared and applauded.

"Well, we'll have no problem shifting such a beauty," remarked their captain.

Spoiling Art's own effect, Plunqwette alighted on her head.

Up the ladderlike walks of Port Republic, past the clamoring market, to the pleasure gardens of Belmont Park—with its racetrack for tiny carriages drawn by cockerels. Next to the park lay Doubloon Street. Off *that*, in a yard crowded by palms and blooming frangipani and marzipan flowers, lay the Punch of Sniff, a tavern, favored by more wealthy sailors—and others.

Art blew in at the door in full sail, her officers and the rest of her pack behind her.

The tavern crowd glanced up, nodded, looked back down—at its tall tots of rum and liqueurs, its chocolate-laced coffee, and games of cards, dice, dominoes, and unlawful scheming. Art and Co. obviously passed the test.

They chose a long table under a window.

Outside, flowers. Air sweet with marzipan scent.

Drinks arrived.

Plunqwette let out a shriek.

So did Walter.

"Muck—*Muck*—the Cleanest Dog in England—"

"Cleanest dog in Own Accord—"

"Hail fellow, well met, old doggo!"

For once, two outsiders together at an inexplicable event, Art and Felix wriggled freaked-out eyebrows at each other.

How could Muck be here? "Stowed away on some other ship," decided Eerie. "Never thought he'd take to it, being without us too long."

As a barking yellow thing landed on their table amidst outcry and delight, Art was reminded of first finding them all in Lundon.

Like that other time, too, a young woman's voice spoke then, from the tavern shadow beyond the sun.

"Another round of brews, my mates? I'll pay. I'm feeling gracious this afternoon."

Everyone, including Muck, looked round and up.

Three figures stood there, who moved forward into the light without any delay. A richly dressed, but shaggy, beastly man with his hat on, another, also richly dressed, thinner and less beastly, with hat off. A beautiful young woman, better got-up than either, with a mass of long black curls, ice-green eyes, and full-skirted matching dress.

Muck yapped and, turning right round, leaped off the table and under Walter's chair. Plunqwette, who had been investigating the drinks, flew onto Art's shoulder and sank in her claws.

"Pieces of Hate," said Plunqwette, clear as three bells.

The woman in green smiled beautifully. She said, "Let me introduce myself. My name is Little Goldie Girl. And herewith, my First Officer, Mr. Beast, and Second Officer, Mr. Pest."

"How dee do," sang the men in chorus.

Art rose. Standing, she was an inch or two taller than the girl in green, and slightly stronger in frame. The green eyes *greened* up at Art, all surface. A still sea with sharks in it.

Ebad had also risen.

"I know her."

Little Goldie Girl nodded. "I know *you*, Ebad Vooms."

Art said, not taking her eyes off Goldie, "Who is she?"

"Daughter to that murdering butcher called the Golden Goliath."

Art opened her memory. She saw the deck of her mother's ship, and the black ship with its skull and crossbones on every sail—bearing down. The *Enemy*, run by Golden Goliath—who had *killed* Molly.

Only, that had been in a play. Though they had used the character of Goliath, none of them had ever met him. How could they have?

There was a razor's glint in the green eyes now. Goldie looked at Ebad, who had called her father a butcher.

"Thanks for your compliment, sir. 'Tis true he let no one live he could send to feed the fish. My da liked aquatic animals."

"He's dead, ain't he?" blurted Walter.

"Dead, yes," said Little Goldie Girl. "Off the shores of a rotten land, ended by villains calling themselves the Royalist French Navy. Forsooth, not cool."

"What do you want?" said Art.

"I'll sit down," said Little Goldie. And slid into the seat facing Art's.

Felix had put his head down on the table, shaking visibly.

"Hush," said Dirk.

Felix raised his head—he was laughing insanely. He, too, got up and strode off across the tavern and out of the door.

Goldie said, "I'll come to the point. You've got something I want."

"What the hell could that be?"

"A map."

One by one, all the stood-up pirates thumped down in their chairs. Behind Little Goldie, only Messrs. Beast and Pest remained standing.

"What map?" said Art.

"Don't thou know? Well, groovy, thou art a klutz."

Art leaned over the table and put a tiny knife point foremost at Little Goldie's exquisite cheek. "I said, *What map?*"

"The one hid in some theater in Lundon or at Grinwich. Vooms hid it years back, then brought it out and handed it to you. *That* map."

"It's a *stage* prop, Golden Litty. For a play."

"You think, Madame Know-Nothing? 'Tain't. 'Tis a true treasure map. It shows the most obscure and sought-after islet in the whole history of pirates and quests. The Treasured Isle."

Art's face changed. It went quite blank. In her head she heard Plunqwette, who that time had intoned: *Treasured Isle.* And later. *Map and all*—and perhaps directions—*cobhouse—ten miles up—*

"It's lost," said Art. "So sorry."

"As lost as a found thing. It's not lost, you popped yacket. It's somewhere about you, now."

"Nay."

"Yay and yeah."

Art withdrew the knife. As she did that, she slapped Little Goldie lightly and stingingly across the other cheek.

Springing up, Little Goldie did something surprising, though maybe not to Art, who had guessed. With a ripping motion, the green skirt was peeled right off. Under it Goldie wore fine black trousers and boots, and a fine cutlass, which drawn, she swirled high up.

Art dodged backward, was on her feet, her own blade in her hand.

The table went over with a bang. Chairs erupted. Muck erupted, and with Dirk, Walt, and Black Knack, ran for cover. Ebad also galloped away, as the women's two swords sliced together and nearly took off his nose.

"Hold—stay—wait a minute—" yelled Eerie.

Sword skithering on sword, neither woman took any notice.

They snaked across the sunlit floor of the Punch of Sniff, and other patrons bounded away before them, plastering themselves to the part-safety of the stairs and walls.

Strang! Clang! The blades met, crossed, slid. And sparks exploded.

Little Goldie fought playfully, like a cat. But Art fought like a *big* cat, harsher and more definite.

This, Felix saw, standing now appalled in the yard door of the tavern.

It seemed to him either of these women was about to kill the other—then, one blade lifted high—too high—took flight— As it arched over, more patrons ducked and dived.

Little Goldie's cutlass landed, edge down, embedded in a far-off table. Ebad was there next instant, and had hold of the hilt.

"Well," said Art Blastside. "Whatever shall we do now?"

What they did *now* was get out.

Because the owner of the Punch of Sniff came down the stair of the tavern like a rockslide.

He was a black man about seven feet tall, bulky and broad, muscular and impressive. Aside from his linen trousers and leather apron, he wore nothing, and across his shoulders and arms spread the most intricate tattoos, filled in by gold leaf. Eyes, tattoos sparkled. So did his teeth—white, but for one central tooth that was also all gold, and set with a tiny, delicate diamond. His name was Teeboa Sinjohn Sniff.

He spoke in a voice like a vast, velvet drum.

"Wretches! This is my pad, O fiends! Look what damage ye've done—tables upended, chairs bruk! Customers upset. Now. Pay up the damages, and in proper biteable gold. Or never again shall you enter this special house of rum and rightness, for trade, plot, drinks, or cards. Or, if not . . ." Here Teeboa Sinjohn Sniff *swelled*. He grew—enormous as a thunder cloud. "If not, I'll bring down the hammer of my fist, and after cut you into bits, then sew those bits into a sack, and throw that sack into the deepest deep depths of the darkest of Blue Indies waters. There shall ye lie. But the souls of ye shall walk, restless, crying, forever, up and around, trudging the basement of the Caribbean, till the last and final trumpet. Whereat, I tell ye, shall ye be judged what ye are— makers of trouble—and the torments of the well behaved shall be visited on you and last you out for eternity. An'ting."

Art and her pirates, Goldie and her pirates, paid up and left as fast as they could.

Teeboa Sinjohn Sniff watched balefully from the door as they made off. At least he had not punched any of them. (His tavern was called for his one most famous punch—which had knocked thirteen pirates together straight through a wall.)

✑ THREE ✑

Trade and Traitor ✦

Art halted under the plantain trees of Belmont Park. She couldn't fail to note that rather than separate, Goldie and her two Mates had stuck fast to Art's crew.

Now there was much worse. From among the plantains and hydrangea trees came swaggering fifteen further men, all looking enough like Beast and Pest that they, too, must belong with Goldie.

"Isn't this nice?" said Goldie. "Perhaps Mr. Slavey Vooms would consent to handing back my weapon now."

"Return the lady's blade," said Art.

Ebad did as she said without a word.

Goldie resettled the cutlass in its brass- and gold-studded sheath. Then, with a coy look at Felix, wrapped round her again her flowing skirt and buttoned it in place.

"I believe Molly's Daughter asked what we should do next," said Goldie. "Let's see. I think that we should accept that I have seventeen men here, and she has—three? Four? Who can say. So what we should do, perchance, is *she should give me the map*."

Art shrugged.

"I can't, madam. It's not on me."

"We can search you."

"In fact no," said Art definitely.

"No," added Ebad.

Eerie and the others echoed him in fiercest pirate mode. On Art's shoulder Plunqwette screeched and sharpened her beak.

Mr. Beast began, "Captain—just say the word—" And stopped, because Art had thrown one of her collection of small knives into his hat, sending it flying away down the sanded path.

The Beast liked his hat. He swore and tutted, and went to pick it up, dusting sand off it tenderly as a mother with a fallen child.

"This map," said Art crisply, "is in my cabin aboard the *Unwelcome*. Since you're so keen to have it, I'll sell it you."

Little Goldie let out a new laughter, less pretty than the other. "*Sell* it—"

"Yes. Personally I reckon it's worthless, and so does every authority I've consulted." The lie sounded quite believable. "But if you're so obsessed, poor Miss Gittle Loldy, you can have it for three pieces of silver. That's all I'll charge you. I don't much like to cheat such a silly gosle."

"*Gosle?*" Goldie clapped her hand to her hip, where the cutlass still was, under the skirt. Mr. Pest grabbed her arm. She thrust him off.

"No, no, darling Cap'n"—his little uneasy eyes oilily rolled over Art's crew—"if we can get it peaceful like—what's the odds?"

Art couldn't resist glancing behind her.

Quickly she studied the crew of *Unwelcome Stranger,* and for a moment nearly laughed herself.

It was what she had already seen—they looked more terrible, more bloodthirsty and rabidly ready for vile and vicious action than any of Goldie's bunch. Indeed, Goldie's men were all looking nervous, snarling and tugging at their guns and cutlasses—while behind Art her crew already had the pistols out, and pointing.

Farther down the park, happy shouts and cockerel crows resounded from some race.

Here, it was a standoff. Any second, bullets and blades must come alive.

To Art's utter astonishment, suddenly Felix Phoenix walked right past her, up to the crew of the *Enemy*, up to Little Goldie Girl, and stood there looking down at her, with the strangest, most intense and hypnotizing look.

"Gorgeous Captain," said Felix. And Goldie looked back at him—*up* at him, for she was about five inches shorter. "Don't provoke them. Don't risk your beautiful person."

"Risk—who are you to—"

"I'd never forgive myself if a woman of such evident delicacy and worth fell before the heartless and barbaric weapons of such as that evil uncouth tyrant queen, Art Blastside there. Listen, I've no fear of them now. They took me prisoner and are keeping me to get a ransom for me. It will be paid, and they must have me in one piece for that. Otherwise—God knows—I'd be afraid to come between you. Take her offer of silver for the map. *Take* it. Spare yourself and your faithful men any more truck with such as these vipers and ravening dogs"—offended, Muck yapped on his cue—"or I'll be forced to risk my life after all, to save you."

Goldie—*fluttered*. "Why, handsome sir, I'm well able to take care of myself. Nevertheless, your gallantry is admirable. What can I say?"

"Say yes."

Art's face in turn was a picture. She looked frightful—dangerous.

Goldie seemed to consider. Perhaps she was recalling Art's swordplay earlier.

She said, "We'll accept the terms then. I'd not like to distress this adorable gentleman further."

"Done," said Art. Her mask of apparent fury—perhaps it was real?—didn't change. She snapped, "Get back among my crew, Mr. Phoenix."

Felix bent and kissed Goldie's small white hand. Long-lashed eyes downcast, he returned to Art's side of the path.

"Well, then," said Goldie, "we must go to your ship."

"Or we to yours."

"Ours is elsewhere, well concealed. Forget any plan to visit it."

"My place, then," said Art.

"I shall come aboard with twelve men."

"Then you come not aboard."

Again, the now samey rattle of deadly cutlery and the beaks of pistols—and parrot—rising.

Art spoke in a bleak, hard tone.

"We must have a compromise. We'll go to the harbor. There we'll leave you a hostage. We'll take one of your men in exchange. He, I, and Mr. Vooms will row out to my ship, get the map, come back. You and I then exchange the goods and the men. Fair trade."

Goldie looked at Mr. Beast.

"What would my dad have done, Beastie?"

"Blown big openings in the lot of 'em."

Art said, "Mr. Beast, if you don't shut your row, I'll put one of those big openings you refer to straight between your eyes."

Something worse than anger now in Art's face, made the Beast step backward. He trod heavily on the toe of the pirate behind him, who howled and cursed and managed to shoot the *path*, presumably by accident. Uproar.

In a hideous shriek, Little Goldie Girl shrilled her men to order.

"Stow it, you pigs!"

It was stowed.

"Agreed then," said Goldie to Art, with great disdain. "I'll choose that hostage now, too. I'll take that unsavory fellow with eye patch and bristles."

Growling, Black Knack went forward, as Art's crew slapped him on the back. He gave Goldie a mocking salute, and lined up beside her.

Art ran her steely eyes in turn over the ranks of her foes, and called, "You, with the tattoo on your nose."

Tattoo paced over. He was a stocky man, who looked fit and fleet, and handled his armory well. He would almost certainly be useful, therefore missed—Little Goldie would want him back.

More cockerel crowing came from the distance.

Not to be outdone, Plunqwette crowed louder.

Muck fell in behind his pirates with a watchful expression round his whiskers, as everyone left the park and, in a cold unfriendly mass, descended to the harbor.

Glad Cuthbert was unfazed by the return of only Art, Ebad, and the man off the *Enemy*. Salt Peter, however, seemed put out, chewing his nails and staring at Tattoo with perhaps unneeded menace.

Art and Ebad stepped into her cabin.

"Don't give her the map, Arty," murmured Ebad, the instant the door was shut.

"Don't mean to, Ebad. There are enough other maps in here."

"Art," said Ebad. "It's not so simple. I'll swear they *know*, or very nearly, what kind of a map our one is. What it looks like."

"A prop from a play."

Ebad dropped his voice even further. He had, of course, the actor's trick of being able to speak almost silently but also audibly. "It's real."

Art nodded. "I was just beginning to think so, too."

"'Tis a long story."

"You must tell me sometime, Mr. Vooms. Not now."

"Not now. Art, if you take a map off the wall here, it must

seem *like* the map I gave you. It must show a remote island. And the paper has to be *burned* off along the lower edge."

"They know that too, do they?"

"I think," said Ebad, "we have a rotten apple in our barrel. Some rat among this actors' troupe of ours, who turned thief and two-faced before the rest of us." Ebad's features were set in thought—his brilliant black eyes as ever unreadable. "He knew our map was real and tipped them off."

"How—if he's been with us?"

"He'll have noted I'd unearthed the map at Grinwich. Maybe he was on the lookout for me to do just that, there, or somewhere else—once you'd reappeared in our lives. No one else but Eerie knew the hiding place. Some have thought the map destroyed—otherwise it could have been a hundred and one places. I took care, Art. In case it was ever worth . . . trying it out. So, during this time since Grinwich, our traitor, whoever he be, passed word to mad Goliath's madder daughter. He's sent her some message—through another ship—we passed plenty on the river—even by carrier pigeon. Port's Mouth then, probably. They keep flocks of 'em there, even on the Spice Isle, for just that purpose of messaging ships. And, Port's Mouth being what it is, pirate ships are included in the customers."

"Only you and I and Phoenix went to the Port. And Walt. The rest stayed on the Spice Isle—then again, at the Pudding someone could have slipped away; I didn't have my eye on both of them all the time we were there—"

Art scanned the walls of the cabin more closely. "*Look.* That one. Unnamed remote islands off upper Canadia—a lovely chilly trip for them. It even has dolphins and a drawing of a ship, just like our map."

"Let me see. That may do. Except our map shows only one island. They may know that, too."

"I'll put a cross on one of these isles. The one here at the bottom. Light your pipe, Mr. Vooms. We'll burn off the lower edge."

Outside, Glad Cuthbert and Tattoo had fallen to discussing old times a few years back, behaving badly along the piracy shipping lanes.

The scent of tobacco stole out under Art's cabin door, and had them reaching for their own pipes.

Peter only gnawed his thumbnail.

"Here."

"Why, *thank* you, Miss Art. And how neatly rolled inside this sealskin wrapper. Which is rather damp—never mind." Little Goldie Girl sniffed. "A smell of smoke, *still—*"

"Ebad lit up."

"Naughty Slavey Vooms. You might have burned another piece off it." She opened the map fully, and, concealing it with care from all the *Unwelcome*'s people, Felix included, glued her eyes on the paper. Presently Goldie said, "Seems I have caught someone out in a lie." Art said nothing. She looked impatient only, not interested. Goldie glanced at her. "Don't bother yourself. Someone gave me a wrong direction on this map. He said he was hoping for a share, too. Dear, dear. But I should have known he lied. I never found anything in the area *he* said."

"If you're satisfied," said Art, "the agreement was three silver pieces."

"Oh, pay her, Mr. Beast. What a stickler for her pathetic bit of loot. One thing," she added to Art as the coins were produced and put in Eerie's palm. "Won't you let *me* ransom off poor Mr. Phoenix, there?"

Art saw Felix glance up—his face alight with *hope*.

"Be damned to you," said Art.

Tinkles of glass beads—Little Goldie's laughter—spangled round the harbor. Now Felix looked away as if bored.

Art and her men, with the restored Black Knack, piled into their jolly boat and took off again across the bay. Felix gazed back shoreward—wistfully? "As I thought," said Art. "The woman's a dunce."

Tattoo and the rest left on shore, jibing, watched Art's company go. The crew of the *Enemy* said similar things regarding Art Blastside.

Two hours later, when Goldie and her men were celebrating at the other favorite of Port Republic's inns, the waterfront tavern Dizzy Lobster, a bird walked in across the floor.

"What's that?" the drunken crew asked one another, as it pottered to their table.

"It's a chicken."

"Here, chick-chick!"

"No, 'tis a cock from the races."

The smart black cockerel scratched on the floor with coral claws. It was tame and seemed glad enough to meet them. A paper was tied to its leg.

"What's it say, Captain?"

Too wildly furious to tease them now by showing them words they couldn't read, Little Goldie Girl told them with a hiss like poisoned steam:

"From our *friend*. It says, *Overheard Eb. and A. Wrong map, Goldie.*"

Ships That Pass in the Nightmare

Felix watched the sunset rush away behind them and sudden night come down on the coffee-dark sea.

There had been fireflies in the air near the port. Out here, instead, the vast liquid Caribbean stars opened their eyes.

Beautiful. He had often heard this spoken of, long ago, such voyages, such nights.

Felix leaned his head on his hand. His eyes were wet, but was it pain or rage—or frustration?

Unwelcome Stranger sped forward, urged by a warm salty wind, her canvas turned to catch every breath, and grunting on the yards.

The pink flag with the crossed bones and skull waved joyfully.

Felix jumped. Art, as he now realized, stood just behind him. She had come from nowhere. She could aways approach so silently, stealing up—well, she was a practiced thief, so what else? How had she learned it all? The others had told him a little about her, all *they* knew, all she had told them. What puzzled him most was how she had—not gained the skills in the first place, as a child—but got them back so swiftly at the age of sixteen, six years after all that had ended for her.

"Mr. Phoenix, my *deepest* regrets." Felix stared. "I mean, sir, for not permitting you to go off and be the pampered pet of that green-brained skipperty-hop, Goldie. It didn't fit my plans—not under the circumstances—to leave you on Own Accord. Goldie may realize, you see, she's been tricked. I don't think you'd find her so sweet then."

"Undoubtedly not. But you are never sweet, so I know exactly where I am with you."

Art smiled slightly.

"Have patience. You'll be off this ship soon enough. Plenty of ports along the Amer Ricas."

That afternoon, before leaving the bay, she had talked things over with Ebad and Eerie in her cabin. Both of them had always known the map of the Treasured Isle was no fake. Plunqwette, it seemed, knew it, too. The parrot perched on the bookcase, looking at each of their faces as they spoke.

(Once only did Plunqwette offer advice.)

"How did you find this map, Ebad?"

"At sea."

"Ah—on the slave ship." Ebad didn't reply. "I think you must have stolen it, then."

"We had a plan," Eerie broke in, "to save up our money— only we never made any—charter a ship, try to find the blessed Treasured Isle. They say, they do, there's one single chest there, buried, and loaded with the biggest fortune on earth. The Cunning Crows of Eira know what *that* can be, to fit in *one* chest."

"Let me suggest," said Art to Ebad, "this was the reason why you alone made so little fuss about coming back to sea."

"'Tis part of it, Arty. But I meant you to know first that you'd never been a pirate—save on a stage."

"But now we are."

"Yay. But not quite the general pirate fashion—evil murdering cowards that normally they are. Like Goliath's filth. Besides, I wanted to think. I'd say the map was a true one—but no one has ever found this island, and maybe *'tis* a pack of lies. On the other hand, now you've tricked Goldie out of it—"

"We'd better see if we can use it," finished Art.

This had been when the parrot spoke up. (As she had that other time to Art.) "Land ho! Beach by cobhouse. Ten miles up. Fifteen paces left."

Ebad started. "She's not said that for six years."

"What *has* she said?" Art demanded. "Are those actual directions to find the treasure chest? There are none written on the map, nothing but these letters—O's—T's. And Plunqwette says *Ten miles up?* You shake your heads. And *Beach by cobhouse—* what's *that?* A shed storing nuts? Again, head shakes, you look all puzzled. But should I trust you? *You* said the map was a prop."

"By the Wind's Beard, Art—" "By the Cheeses of Eira—"

"Very well. Then where's the *island?* I mean where is it reckoned to be? Do you know *that?*"

"All I know," said Ebad, "is it lies out from the Indian Ocean, on the Capricorn Line, past Mad-Agash, the pirate isle off Africay."

"That's a journey, Art," said Eerie sorrowfully. "South through the wide Atlantic, the dire Doldrums. Easterly round the Cape of Good Hope that makes men hopeless with its storms and hurricanes."

"But we'll do it," said Art.

Eerie said, "I'd never have thought you so eager for money, Art Blastside, Molly's Daughter."

"Things can be done with money, Eerie. It's useful. But it's more than that."

Ebad said softly, "She wants to do what everyone else may have tried and *not* done. Art likes to win."

"We'll all win. So plot our course, Mr. Vooms. Before you do, one last question. If the Treasured Isle is at all close to Mad-Agash Scar—the pirate's isle, as you say—then don't *they* try for it? Has none of them ever found the island—the treasure?"

"The island—" Eerie paused. "There's this tale Ebad heard— the Treasured Isle's *magical*. It sinks from view—comes up only when it wants to be found. All that sea there, south and east— strange—bewitched."

But "Polly want a Gold Muhura," said the parrot in practical tones. "Pieces of Fate."

Standing now beside Felix Phoenix, both of them not looking at each other, watching only the night sea, Art, her mind still mostly on treasure, felt a curious deep twist inside herself.

Yes, she thought, I know. This young man means something more to me than I believed. Well, well, Art. Well, well.

Art glanced at her (unwilling?) companion, sidelong. She was still half smiling at the idea that Felix Phoenix had come to mean anything at all.

Ships That Pass in the Nightmare - 153

Seeing him with Goldie—that had woken Art up. She hadn't questioned him, couldn't decide if he really *liked* the look of Goldie, and was prepared to ignore Goldie's other, less appealing qualities. Or if he had only meant to stop a fight in which he, and the actor-pirates, of whom Felix did seem genuinely fond, might get hurt.

So now she said, "Tell me truthfully, Mr. Phoenix. That act of yours in the park. Would you have gone off with Goldie Girl if I'd let you?"

"Yes, madam." Perfect profile turned to starry darkness, Felix said, "I've been looking for her—without knowing I was—almost all my life."

Art *scowled*. Wiped the expression off her face. "You have very bad taste, sir."

She, too, turned and strode away, lightly punching the hilt of her sword, and called up a too-hearty hallo at Honest in the crow's nest.

A half hour later, Honest, still aloft, began to yell.

"Ship—ship—a cutter off starboard stern!"

Art was quizzical. She said to Salt Walter and Whuskery, who were standing by, "Plenty of ships in these waters. Own Accord's just behind us, Brown Sugar ahead."

"Bad 'un," yodeled Honest from the masthead.

Dirk ran to stern. He had Ebad's spyglass to his eye. Up from the galley Peter and Cuthbert came clattering, Peter with a stirring spoon in his hand.

"She's after us!" shouted Dirk.

"Let me see." Art snatched the glass. She squinted down the distance—black glimmer of waves, phosphorous—*saw*. A lean flying shape, full-rigged—looking as if leaning forward—dark, darker than the young night.

In her head Art hears the voice of Hurkon Beare, clear in six-years-ago recollection. "The *Enemy*—she never gives up. Wants our treasure map, Molly."

"*It's them,*" Art says.

And Molly says in memory, "Ready the cannon."

"Cannon," repeats Art. Her face is strict and cool as ice water. "Cuthbert, Peter. Get to work."

She reckoned two or three of them could handle the seven well-kept cannon of the *Unwelcome*. Plus Glad Cuthbert had held the job of gunner on his own pirate vessel. Yet now all her crew hesitated—looked crazily round—

"Art—"

"Jump to it. Do you want those scurvy tail-tufts to get the better of us?"

"We can outrun—"

"Nay, Mr. Salt Peter. We can't. Goldie's ship's a *cutter*. She *cuts* her way through the water. But trim sails. Walt, Dirk, Whusk. Let's get up what speed we can."

Now they all ran to obey. Dirk and Walter flailed up mizzen and foremast. Whuskery darted everywhere, adjusting spars, ropes, and tackle.

But the sails already possessed most of any speed the brisk wind could lend them.

Art plucked a completely relaxed Plunqwette off the ship's rail, carried her to the Captain's Cabin, and shut her—squawking—in.

"Black Knack, break out more handguns—include the musketoons—powder and shot."

Black Knack—the only one, apart from Art and Ebad, to have changed from finery to more workaday clothes—stuck there gaping at the approaching problem. Art shouted again. He woke up and made off at an unsteady slouch.

The *Unwelcome*'s cannon, as mostly in the play, were stationed just below the top deck. Rasping sounds came now as the hatches there were loosed, and then clanking as the guns rolled forward on their wheels—

Art checked down over the rail. Her ship rode slightly lower in the water than at the last flight, weighted by goods she hadn't, thanks to Goldie, been able to sell on Own Accord.

Art could hear Plunqwette shrieking angrily in the cabin, even through its stout timber walls. Poor old bird. *She* at least always seemed ready to take on a battle.

Salt Walter's shaky cry penetrated through cannon rattle and parrot din: "Art—what's *that?* Another ship eastward—*all lit up!*"

Art raised her eyebrow.

"Courage, Mr. Salt. 'Tis the moon rising."

And the moon rose. It was nearly full, yellow as a ripe plantain. It hit *Unwelcome Stranger,* her masts and prow, her shrouded sinister figurehead. At her back, too, it drew in the crinkled waves, and farther off—but not, now, so far—the cutting shape of the cutter *Enemy*—which suddenly just then turned half-side on, so all her angled sails showed foursquare to Art and her crew.

This way, the other ship seemed really like a knife. Her bowspirit very long and finned with canvas. But also—

"By the Blast of Hell. Would you look at that."

In Art's memory, Hurkon's voice, again. "Each sail black and with the skull and bones over every one."

Had Art remembered *Enemy* like this?

For the *Enemy*'s Jolly Roger was not a flag.

It was instead painted, huge and staring white, and in joined jigsaw sections, over all the ink-black canvas. The first third of the skull on the main royal, the second third under it on the main topgallant, the last portion, with its jolly grin, over the main upper topsail. The two bones meanwhile, big as those of monsters, crossed on the main course sail below. Then stretched away to decorate most of the mizzen sheets and foresheets on either side, finishing up at the stern, on the spanker, and at the bow on the jib.

She needed no other banner.

The black cutter, caught in the stage lighting of that actor's moon, balanced—and so *became*—an ultimate of pirate imagery, all one giant, skeletal, *oncoming grin*.

It was—fearful. Horrible.

How many had it cowed, before even the guns on *Enemy* sent out their fire?

Art said, "Well. There we have it. What did I say? *Bad taste*."

Ebad laughed. Eerie and Dirk echoed him less strongly.

With a jangle, Black Knack slung down musketoons, powder flasks, and leather strips of bullets, extra swords, and daggers. "Case they board us."

Art gave him one look of disapproval. But there was no time for that.

Through the spyglass she scrutinized little figures springing, dwarfed by *Enemy*'s enormous horror of skull and crossbones. If she made out Goldie Girl, Art wasn't sure. But she saw the flicker of lights, barrels of powder left on the forecastle, and the mouths of cannon poking eagerly out, as now the cannon of *Unwelcome* did.

"Veer to starboard. Mr. Vooms, take the helm. Mr. O'Shea, the deck is yours till I relieve you of it. Walter, Peter, Whuskery, down to top deck. I may call for other help with the cannon. Otherwise, all of you, arm, get cover, mark your targets— ship and ship's furniture, not human things—and *brace* your- selves for one of two *bumps*. Mr. Knack, this also means you."

"Right, Captain. You want the impossible. 'Twill do my humblest best."

Art jumped down the companionway ladder into the oil and tinder gloom below.

Unwelcome was turning, pivoting like an athlete on one foot.

The cutter had noted their maneuver. She was the readier. Across the jet-black glittering field of water, her guns shouted, One! Two! Three!

Peter squealed.

Art gritted her teeth. With no one here to see their performance, were they going back to being fightless scared actors?

"Peter. Steady. Their miserable scum-boat's too far off to strike us yet."

But they heard the whistle of great shot coming over. Flame or fiery steam fiendishly lit the underdeck through its ports. The *Enemy*'s first three cannonballs smashed into the water, rocking *Unwelcome* roughly. Suddenly Plunqwette's raucous complaints, till now heard over everything, fell still.

Art had turned her ship so four of their own seven guns were now facing the *Enemy*. She hadn't counted how many cannon the cutter had—but many more than seven, she had seen. They also had at least one cannon secured on the top deck, judging from her view through the glass.

And Goldie's impatient, thought Art. Can't wait to get her claws in us.

Art looked out of the gunport, around chains and the metal of the gun.

Near enough now, she thought.

She took the touch light from its container, dipped it in fire. At least Glad Cuthbert, the gunner, had properly prepared things, loading and priming the shot. He looked steady, too.

"Now."

Unwelcome's return cannonade was also One! Two! Three! Then—as Art sped to spark it—Four!

Despite the narrowing gap, two of the smoking, screaming balls fell far short of *Enemy*. One, though, landed right beside her, and a waterspout blazed up into the moonlight. The fourth shot—Art's—arced over the cutter's deck, tearing through her lower main course sail.

Flame blushed up.

"Reload ball and charge!" We need more men here, Art thought. She too dragged shot across and loaded it in. Then bellowed up the hatchway for Whuskery and Black Knack. They, and Peter, had been the ace gunners in the play, and performed to good effect when they had taken the Franco-Spanish ship *Royal*. One figure hurtled down into the underdeck—he looked quite keen. Only Black Knack delayed. Art leaped up the companionway and past him. "Get to the guns, Mister."

As he obeyed, she had the urge to slap him. Why was he hanging about—

And where, by the way, was Felix? She hadn't thought. Should have done— Hiding, probably, under a bunk, like Muck, who had raced below at Honest's first yell from the mast. *I hope so.*

Art ran up onto the quarterdeck. Even back here, she could see now, not needing the spyglass, water had been bucketed against *Enemy*'s burning lower sail. It was already out. But smoke curled everywhere—as in Art's memory, like dirty creamed mashed potato.

Enemy fired again.

Art watched the shot explode—six guns speaking at once.

How slowly the balls moved—how *fast*—

"Hard to port, Mr. Vooms! Quick as you like."

Unwelcome nearly seemed to somersault. Walter, standing at mid-deck, fell over. Peter sat down.

Yes, several of the *Enemy*'s cannon were on her upper decks, stuck out through the wood below the rail.

Art raised the brass-bound musketoon she had chosen to her shoulder.

Aim for ship and ship's furniture. *Molly never killed.*

That was a *play*—

No.

With a peculiar clearness, like that of the spyglass she no longer used, Art saw men scurry off the forecastle, leaving it empty but for barrels.

She swiveled with the musketoon. It was more accurate, she knew, than any pistol. And—familiar as her own arm. She fired.

The bullet whizzed, unseen, over the sea between the two ships. (Distance apart now maybe less than forty yards.)

The bullet struck, as Art had meant it to, a smoke-wreathed barrel of gunpowder left on the forecastle. Which blew up like a firework of pink and primrose. The gun called Duchess had blown up. Gunpowder. Molly—the deck—the *stage*—giving way—

Not now. Forget all that—

The cutter jerked, gave a staggering forward curtsy.

Art dived off the quarterdeck and roared through an open hatch down at the gunners, "Fire! Keep *firing.* Are you asleep? Aim for the hull of her and the masts."

Red-hot now, the guns of *Unwelcome* boomed and kicked.

On *Enemy* a whirlwind of men and water round the exploded barrel and its resulting fire. But at the same instant *Enemy*'s cannon cranked forward, shuddering, loosing another broadside. They had more crew—but less *guts*?

The dividing space was getting always so much less—

Art, in that second, as she jumped back to the quarter, found Felix Phoenix there, like a ghost—or an idiot—an *audience*—at the rail—*watching*—

"Down!" She pushed him. He dropped and so did she, as a black smoldering roar passed over their heads and cleft the mizzenmast of the *Unwelcome Stranger* from root to main royal.

Art, seeing half the rigging, half the wooden mast cracking out, *spilling* toward them, packed Felix against the ship's side and quickly cast herself over him.

"Keep *still*. It may come down."

"I thought it had. Thought it *fell* on me. Oh, was it you?"

But, groaning and splintering, the mast held together. It had been split shallowly, but like a peeled stem.

Small shot from pistols was now sputtering across from the *Enemy*. At *Unwelcome*'s rail, Dirk and Eerie sniped back—and another powder barrel coughed into flame.

Art removed herself from Felix. "Get up and get below to the forecastle hold, Mr. Phoenix. You are useless and in the way."

"My apologies."

Above, the split mast whined piteously, like a wounded harp.

Keeping her head down, Art looked across the area of narrowed sea—was it only a yard or so now? But the *Enemy*'s pistol fire seemed over. Ah. One of the previous round of shots from *Unwelcome*'s guns had messily burst in two of the other ship's gunports. Both cannon there had bucked and toppled partly out, hanging now in a gape of jagged wood, muzzles in water.

"Neat," said Art.

"For a nightmare."

"No doubt you fear injury to your best girl, your Goldie. Don't fret. They've not taken more than a scorch or two."

All the guns of *Enemy* had fallen quiet. Most of her crew were taken up with putting out fires, or bailing at the bashed gunports.

It seemed Goldie's pirates after all were unused to much resistance. Or perhaps only to accurate shooting.

But a single cannon—the last, as it turned out—belled from the underdeck below Art's feet. The ball launched, flighted, and solidly thwacked into the *Enemy*'s foremast.

"Cuthbert," Art decided. "You can't beat proper training under fire."

A ragged cheer rose from *Unwelcome Stranger*'s decks, a wail of dismay from the now-crippled *Enemy*, as down shattered a good half of her foremost yardarm, complete with two black sails carrying the white ends of crossbones. Swarms of men dashed everywhere. Smoke hid the view.

"We've done for her, Art." Peter jumped up and down. He was in tears.

"Not quite, but it may serve. Please return below and give my congratulations to Mr. Cuthbert."

Black Knack, too, was up on deck. "Why not finish her off, Arty? She's no chance as she is."

"A Fox on you, sir," said Art. "I don't kill. Let the fool go. Now, Mr. O'Shea, anyone hurt?"

"No more'n splinters and bruises, Cap'n."

"Then we'll make on for Brown Sugar Island. *Unwelcome* needs her own repairs. I doubt they'll come after. Even with our mizzen spoiled, we can outrun them now."

The *Enemy*, control mostly lost, was already banking choppily away behind, tossed by the unchecked night wind in her uneven rigging. Small fires were still busy, and her broken side was now gulping water. If anyone had stayed at the wheel, you would never know.

Felix at Art's shoulder, said, "And if their ship goes down, what then, O Captain *Neverkill*?"

"*Enemy*'s not so badly holed. Besides, they've got their boats," said Art icily. "Their best bet for that damage will be at Own Accord. They can be there, even rowing, by sunrise."

Honest walked down the deck, head lowered. Felix had noticed Honest in the fighting, not taking enough care—seeming, too, to fire wide. He hadn't looked afraid, only unhappy. Felix had a feeling the Honest Liar disliked firearms as much as Felix himself.

Now he said, "Do you think you're free of Goldie? Remember, Art, whose daughter she is."

"And I, Mr. Phoenix? I am a pistol-proof captain, and the daughter of Piratica."

No one came to harass them on Brown Sugar. There wasn't a hint of the *Enemy*.

The crew lazed in the humid green sunshine, and the lawless bands of men, who didn't help with the sugarcane, but knew ships, carpentered and caulked and over-keeled *Unwelcome* back to her best.

Yellow bananas, ginger tea, budgie wine, pink snapper cooked in the pot, the scent of brown sugar.

"Let's stay, Art. It's heaven."

"Walter," she said, "we have something else to do. Mr. Vooms will tell you."

Mr. Vooms told them all.

"This treasure then—it's really real?" said Black Knack.

"Maybe."

"Then we'll—be rich—" cried Whuskery.

"Oh—" said Dirk, "our own company of actors, dearie—our own *theater*—"

Most of the others were silent in wonder.

Felix said to Art, "You understand now, I shan't get off this ship."

"I'm not asking you to, am I? But I believed you'd prefer to return to Own Accord. Goldie will have gone there for repairs."

"Goldie will follow *you*."

"I see." Art looked long at Felix. She poured him a glass of wine, then leaned forward and tucked a flower into his collar. "But otherwise, you are a mystery, Mr. Phoenix."

"No. I'm straightforward. Unlike yourself."

"There's nothing to me. I just like to be alive. Don't you?"

"Must I answer that?"

She shook her head. She had seen he had taken off the ring of ruby glass. Why was that? She didn't ask, nor anything else.

Eleven days they were there, on Brown Sugar. When they took to the sea again, there was still no evidence of any enemy—

or of the *Enemy*. But there was yet a traitor with them. And they would need to find out who he was.

She had limped, as predicted, back to Own Accord—decks thick with the fog of smoke, one mast wrecked, hull holed, moans and arguments everywhere—the cutter, *Enemy*. Mr. Pest went about, armed with bandages, splints, and other implements, setting a broken arm here—shrieks—a dislocated shoulder there—more shrieks. Firefly flittings of sparks were still going up—smothered or doused again and again.

On the quarterdeck, Little Goldie, too, was sizzling, to herself and to Mr. Beast.

"They'll *pay*. By the Wheel's Wiles, pay with *blood*. And he *too*, that *Phoenix*, with his delicious tricky charms—for yes, he's a trickster like the *rest*. Oh, I'll make him *suffer*." She nodded. "Then I'll marry him."

"Worst punishment of all for him then," chortled Mr. Beast unwisely. His chortle ended as Little Goldie tossed her lovely head, turned, and booted him in the stomach.

South by Southeast

"Couldn't we go another way?"

"Ships don't sail overland, Walt."

"There's no other sea route to the East," added Ebad. "It's this way, and catch the Trader Winds."

"But these Doldrums—is it as bad as 'twas said in our play?"

"Yeah."

"Then—"

"And—" (Eerie) "the dreaded Cape's worse—hurricanes, ghost ships—the cursed Flying Dutchman, who brings bad luck to all that see him."

They sailed sou'southeast. The sea changed slowly, as if trying to deceive. It didn't. From sparkled blue it merged to greasy bluish-gray. The sky copied it, and seemed to hang down each day lower, as if on ropes. Soon it looked as if you might bang your head on that low, dense sky. It was hot.

"We must honor the old gods of the sea here," said Eerie.

"Yes, that's the tradition," agreed Glad Cuthbert, not looking glad at all. "I've seen some bad things done to others, crossing the Line. Worse," he added, low, to Ebad, "on regular ships—me ol' pirate vessel warnt too bad."

They were almost at the Equated Line, halfway mark on the earth between the South and North Poles.

The pirates became actors. They dressed up in invented bizarre costumes, colored their beards, if they now had them, or their mustaches, and certainly their hair—green. They declaimed long speeches from Shakespur to Neptune, the sea god, and broke out the rum, and Cuthbert cheered up. Art, dressed for the occasion in a green wool beard and an eye patch, offered rum to the sea.

But with the Line crossed, nothing improved.

At night the stars had turned unusual colors—brownish, reddish-mauve. . . . The quarter moon looked hollow and was marked all over with shadows.

To begin with, winds were everywhere, sprinting in from the east, west, north, south—constantly *Unwelcome* trimmed and tacked. There was no land to see, not even the occasional haze-vague coasts of Southern Amer Rica, nor any of the tiny islets there. The winds skittered away. Art and her crew watched them go, running nimbly over the waves. Now a heat came in like a shut room above an oven.

Then all motion stopped—or nearly. Windless, the windjammer, built for winds, stood stock-still, on a soup-thick ocean. Which, with no warning, every few minutes *churned* like an upset stomach.

Muck howled, on and on. Plunqwette dauntlessly flapped round and round the sails, perhaps attempting to make a breeze and move them.

Art looked disapprovingly at her men. Plenty of them were back at the rail, honking and puking. It served such a sea right, maybe, for persons to be sick in it. But two days had passed this way.

Art, Ebad, Glad Cuthbert, and strangely now Dirk and Black Knack—strangest of all, Felix—had no qualms. The rest, even Honest, slumped at the rail.

"What now?" said Black Knack. "We're stuck. That's what this hell-kettle does. Sticks you down. And she—I mean our best beloved Goldie Girl—she can catch us up here."

"Assuming she knows our direction."

"She did last time."

"Lighten up, Blacky," said Art. "We've got the boats and the oars."

Retching and grumbling then, her able and sickly crew together, lugged the three clinker-built jolly boats off the deckhouses and placed them down on the repulsive ocean.

"Rope on, Eerie, keep the wheel. Blacky, keep for'ard watch. Walt—no, you can't, can you? Whuskery, you're better? No? Yes, you are. Get up to the crow's nest and take lookout. All hands else with me. How are you at rowing, Mr. Phoenix?"

"I've never tried."

"Well now you shall. What a treat."

"Nay, Art—yaarght," puke-protested Walter.

"You'll be better, sir, with something to do."

Glad Cuthbert cackled. "She's harsh. Reminds me of my ol' girl at home."

Ebad said, "You could never argue with Molly, either."

Plunqwette dashed off the crow's nest, which she sometimes used as a parrot's nest, as Whuskery landed beside her. Craning over, he then projected vomit in a spectacular arc into the water below.

"Well *done*, Mr. Whusk. You missed my parrot, and not a spot on the deck!"

"Art, you *are* heartless."

"Mr. Dirk, you forget. I'm *Captain*."

"Chance to forget would be a fine thing. He may fall off!"

"Never. Look, he's fine."

They climbed or toppled down into the boats. Ebad checked the ropes now attaching them to *Unwelcome*'s hull.

The Honest Liar raised his green face to Art. "Feels better down here."

"Less roll."

Art had put Ebad and Cuthbert, judged the strongest, alone in one boat. Felix and herself, the lightest and perhaps—or not—least strong, she divided between the other two boats, each of them with two other rowers.

They positioned the oars.

At first it was chaos. Even Art found herself flailing and knew a raving irritation. Normally now she had learned herself able to do anything she needed. But her first oar efforts, she scathingly thought, were worthy of a Young Maiden of the Angels Academy.

Then the oars ceased splashing and striking. An intent, muscle-ripping rhythm was established.

Ebad glanced across at Art only once. Of course, she had known how many ships got themselves through the dreaded Doldrums, where, as often happened, winds ended. He wasn't amazed at all.

Up on the forecastle, Black Knack glared. Aloft, Whuskery had stopped being sick. Eerie held the wheel and tried to sing a hiccuping lament.

Three days then they towed the *Unwelcome Stranger* through

the thick hot waters, under the low and windless sky. Drowned in sweat, every fiber in arms and back screaming for rest. Moving like snails. Too stiff, exhausted, and pained for anyone to throw up.

Sometimes they took a little break. Or Art changed Eerie, Whuskery, and Black Knack over with three others. (She herself never switched with another. She joined in every rowing stint.) At night her men lay whining along the deck, the quarters below being even hotter.

Muck had given over howling. He padded up and down and licked his friends' hands consolingly.

"He's a good dog."

"Best dog in England."

"England—oh, England—will we ever see those cool pale coasts again?"

Plunqwette, though, would fly down to assist Art in the boat, perching on her head till Art shouted swear words at her, or on the oar, waving her wings, bursting off just before it met the water, landing on it again as it came up.

"Plunqwette—I'll—*kill* you—I'll put you in—a *pie*—"

Plunqwette, by then one-legged on Art's boot, cleaned her beak with a talon.

"Pieces of Late."

That evening, during the rest time, Felix sat beneath the awning stretched under the forecastle, drawing. His fingers were slick from sweat and the white shirt stuck to him, as the Doldrums had stuck the sea to the ship.

Art came by. She looked down at him, and next at what he did.

"Not too sore from the oar to wield a pencil? What a pity you should waste your energy."

For he was drawing Little Goldie Girl. Goldie's heart-shaped heartless face, wide eyes, clustering black curls. An exact likeness. He was obviously making sure of that.

Felix said nothing, nor did he leave off.

They had covered some miles, Ebad assured them. But nothing seemed changed. Sky and water were the same, only deepening toward sunfall. At night the heat would become merely more airless.

Black Knack said to Salt Peter, "I never knew a captain row with the men."

Salt Peter looked awkward.

Plunqwette hit the deck with a white splash.

From higher up, Dirk called in a crazy voice, "I can see a wind coming!"

"Yer can't see the wind," said Glad Cuthbert.

But they turned where Dirk was yelling them to, northward, and Cuthbert was wrong. You *could* see it.

The waves were abruptly running and alive, like gray-blue dogs, parting in troughs, and racing toward them, while huge clouds, like vast pale blue heads of cauliflower, were bumbling up over the horizon. The ocean became a saucepan, boiling.

"Raise the boats! Sails—get to the yards—"

The pirate-actors flung themselves, yelping at oar-strained arms, up into the rigging.

Muck barked them on.

A rich coolness struck the ship, and everything—humans, dog and parrot, sea, atmosphere, sky—breathed *in*— The sheets swung and turned bow-shape, full of thrusting air.

Unwelcome, too, took off like a mad thing, bowling down the edges of the waves.

"Won't last," said Black Knack.

The wind got Felix's drawing, too, as he turned, staggering on the insanely woken-up ship. The image of Little Goldie fluttered off on its own, like an innocent white bird.

"*Such* a shame," said Art. But there was no time to gloat.

The wind kept up till the third watch of night—then at the clink of the ship's bell, mystically flattened, sank into the sea, was gone.

"Told you so."

"Shut your bristly gob, Blacky," replied Whuskery through his mustache. "Thou art a pain in the Royal."

"But oh—*listen*—" moaned Eerie. " 'Tis the *drums*."

There in the renewed and total silence, all of them stood listening in awe to the weird and superstition-making noise that, reported in a hundred dispatches, had given the area its name.

A thin sharp tapping, now on one side, now another. *Tpp–tpp–tppp*—like the rapping of the drums of tiny mechanical soldiers. *Doll Drums—* A whole hour they heard it. Even the moon came up to hear. It showed nothing but ship and sea.

When the uncanny sound at last died away, the wind stole back, strong yet more manageable. All that night then they blew away to the south and east, toward the sheltering ripe lower coasts of Africay, where lawless lucky towns gleefully greeted pirates, and all their wealth and goods.

Unwelcome stayed a brief while around those rough-built, growing towns. Stayed for fried fish suppers and palm tree nights, with the stills for brewing yellow brandy out under the stars. Slender black locals crowned everyone, especially Felix and Ebad and Eerie, with flowers, and offered them wives. (Eerie was evidently quite keen. He had to be dragged back to the ship.) Even Art was offered a wife. Art smiled and said, alas, she already had one in England.

Lions paraded the streets of log-built Free Cape Town, under its purple cliff of mountain, lions with beads in their manes, and painted claws. Zebras ran in striped herds down to the bay, where whole fleets were parked: whalers, traders, undoubted pirates under other flags. At Art's order they had struck the pink Jolly Molly before entering the first port. They went in under the colors of the Republican Jack. They had non-piratical business here.

Once some of the cargo was shifted, some of the money spent, some boxes of uncut diamonds stored (uncut, they weren't at all what Art expected), they stocked up on fruit and general stores. They persuaded Walter not to buy a zebra—"Just think of that stripy thing, kicking and neighing all night." And so set out again.

"Beyond this point," recited Eerie, arms dramatically outflung as they put off on the morning tide, "lies the Cape—the place of Meeting Oceans. Above, the close-knit lands separate Atlantic and Pacific, like stern parents keeping apart two lovers. But here, none stays them, and the great seas run together. And what are we and our small barque, crushed against their fierce embrace?"

"It's from the play, that speech," commented Dirk.

"I know," said Art. "I remember." But aside from the dull diamonds, she thought she remembered—*all the rest, too.* She had even remembered Free Cape Town. *Surely* she had been there before?

The storm came at midnight.

First there had been mist, and out of the mist partly showed the rocks of a shoreline no longer friendly or flowerlike. The image they saw, indeed, flowing in and out of the mist, was like, they believed, a skull and crossbones.

"A bad spot. A spot for terrors—"

"Belt up thy chops, Eerie. Not *now.*"

The sea was calm and the wind still soft, then. Art set the watches and sent the rest of her men off to sleep. She herself went to her cabin. Felix was up on the quarterdeck. She called a good night to him—he never answered. Deep, she thought, in dreams of Goldie.

In the Captain's Cabin, Plunqwette was drinking chocolate and clicking her beak at Captain Bolt's maps, which, like all his books, were turning rusty green from former Doldrums damp. (Waxed and stored, the treasure map wasn't affected.)

"I can smell more blowy weather, Plunqwette. So can Muck—he's off below again."

"Oh, the ship!" shrieked Plunqwette in another (unknown) voice. "Help! Help! Save our Soap!"

"Shush."

The crystalline ports of the cabin were steamed over, and anyway veiled with dark and mist outside.

Art lay down to catch an hour's sleep.

She dreamed she had, in fact, caught all the night in a vast net. Molly stood with her, Molly young and slim and wonderful, with her gooseberry-green eyes like no other green eyes on earth. Together, mother and daughter, they hauled in the net. In the dream, Art was happy. And over the deck, Ebad stood, smiling too, looking also young and full of pride in something or other.

Then Molly and the ship were gone. Art was falling over a tall precipice into a web of whirling darkness and lashing salt sea spume, with a hard thump at the bottom.

She came to on the cabin floor, pushed right off the bunk by a sudden keeling tilt of the ship.

The door had come open, too. Eerie stood yelling at her. A thin lace of gleaming water spurled along the floor, with Plunqwette hopping and cursing in it—"Poo upon it, and thrice poo, say I, by the Yabbits of the Kraken—"

"Mr. O'Shea, calmly now. All hands—shorten sail."

Art threw herself out on deck as Eerie tottered away.

It was the first storm she had seen since the tempests of memory. But this too—*this too*—she recognized. And with the startled clutch at her insides, came also the rush of pure exhilaration.

The sea was in the sky. It stood on its side, the sea, and the ship heeled right over before it, yet somehow just keeping its upper deck above the wet fury that thrashed and moiled below.

Most of the crew had been sleeping for coolness on deck. Now all of them were deckside, bellowing and calling—but Art could hardly hear any words, not even Honest's whistle, in the tumult of wind and liquid.

Lightning cracked the blackness. For a second the sea was lime-colored, the sky white as scoured china.

Then black crashed back on everything, and everything else seemed to crash down across the *Unwelcome Stranger.*

Above her, Art saw the sails were being crowded in. The masts dipped over, and for a moment she wondered if the repair to the mizzen would hold—

Even though she couldn't properly hear the voices of the crew, the voice of the ship herself was very loud. She was crunching, growling, and *meowing* like a huge fighting cat. A stretch of canvas, left untended on the mizzen and escaping from tackle and stays, slapped and tore with a noise like a breaking tree.

"Lash on!" Art wove her way along the deck. But they were already at work, things were secured, hatched over, or being tied. On the cabin tops, the shackled jolly boats wobbled and clacked.

Art vaulted across a lake of sliding water to the wheel station. Ebad had the wheel. His face, like that of a statue made of basalt, he held them as steady as was possible. And she saw in his face in that moment, he might indeed be royal, the descendant of true kings of Egypt.

Unwelcome now threw herself the other way. As she went, the also-heeling-over sea descended on her. Water closed all things—eyes, nose, breath, night, and world.

This century underwater ended in perhaps three heartbeats.

Art found herself grappled to the mizzen—which had held together perfectly well. Behind her, Ebad shouted her name. She shouted back. Above, the torn canvas croaked.

Art sprang up to the yards. Hand over hand, through the colliding jig of the ship, she climbed as far as the rent topgallant. Locking her legs around the spar, she began the task of pulling home the flyaway canvas.

Everyone else was now down off the yards. They were lashing *themselves* to the galley and deckhouse and the masts. She counted them, even Felix. Safe as they could be, every man. Muck shut below. Plunqwette? Oh, there, claw-gripped to the deckhouse roof.

Up the ship bounded like a white horse across a midnight mountain. The sail tamed, there was no sense now in struggling to get down. Art had roped herself by now to the wood of the mast. She flung back her head and saw stars beyond the banners of the storm, reeling and spinning like silver daggers. She *laughed*. She laughed, and heard her mother saying, all those years before, when Art had been a child—perhaps even a baby in Molly's arms—"What a spectacle! Look—how beautiful it is!" "Yes, Ma," Art sang in the teeth of the gale, challenging it, fearless of it, loving it—"*Yes*. And this ship, she's lucky. She's friends with this sea, eh, Ma? They know how to behave with each other. This isn't a war, only like two cats playing at a fight—"

Up through the glass-splintering of another wave *swam* a green-and-red feathery fish. Plunqwette, sopping and snorting, landing by Art, digging claws now into the spar.

"Hold on, girl!" cried Art.

"Hold on, girl!" Plunqwette cried back, in the voice of Molly Faith.

The sky turned over. They dipped toward the shattered depths of the sea, and stars snowed down on them. The wind itself was like a canvas sail that tore.

Art's crew howled in horror. Art sat grinning far above.

It had never been—had it? How could it have—like this on a *stage*.

"What's that sound?" chittered Walter to his brother.

"How do *I* know? What noise— 'Tis *all* noise—"

Three paces along, by the deckhouse, Glad Cuthbert shouted to them, reassuringly, "It's only a wave got into the bilge—will pass."

But Walter shuddered as the rumbling of the wave ran back and forth below in the guts of the ship, sounding like several of the heavy horse-buses of Lundon racing there.

Felix, lashed to the deckhouse with Cuthbert and Eerie, had put back his head to watch, through the streams of sea and wind, Art the Leopard, high up in the falling sky. He murmured, "She's insane."

"Aye," said Cuthbert. He spat out a mouthful of sea. "Tell yer what. A good woman nearly always is. But a good cap'n— *always*."

"Why?" Felix's voice, even in this fix, was cold.

"How else, sir, would the damn fool dare put to sea in the first place and drag a load o' others with him?"

Eerie was praying. He told them to hush up. God might not hear him if *they* kept yattering on.

The wind was now screaming. It came head-on at them and they were thrown sideways, backward, prow rising far above stern—so even Art and Plunqwette, high on the mizzen, were washed a moment under a wave. Then the ship set straighter, yet circling round and round, as if about to be sucked directly down some supernatural drain.

"Need more'n one at that helm," said Cuthbert.

Felix saw Cuthbert had cut himself free of the lashing. From his place under the main mast Black Knack rasped a warning. Dirk and Whuskery roared. Salts W and P screeched from the galley. But Cuthbert was gone.

"Is he over the side, Mr. Phoenix? I daren't look."

"No, Mr. O'Shea, he's with Ebad now, holding the wheel. And Honest's there, too."

"Bless them, all three. But that wheel—it'll snap off its standing, so it will." Eerie wept. "We're all for the sea's black cellar."

Felix turned and took Eerie's hand. "I've heard of such storms, Eerie. A ship as good as this one can weather them."

Eerie coughed. He asked, through a momentary lull, "How do *you* know? You don't know the sea."

"I knew some once who did."

"Could you trust the beggars?"

"Yes. They were my father and my uncle."

The wind came up again and silenced them.

Another hour the storm, at a single pounding pitch, had its fun with them, or—if Art was right—the ship had fun with the storm.

The end came as unannounced as the start.

Two waves loomed before them like two black brick walls—split and folded away. And there hung a moon, low, and pumpkin-orange, over a lively but no longer stampeding sea.

Out of the mouth of the tempest they hurtled, and *glided* down into a different night, another universe.

"Here's me hurdy-gurdy, right as rain in its ol' waterproof."

"*Unwelcome* stinks of sea mud, fish, and weed."

"There's fish landed in the crew's quarters. Muck's eaten one—bloody dog—"

"Chickens are all wet, lost four eggs—"

"Look at these broken plates—thought they were made of proper pewter—"

"My hands—just *look* at my hands—ruined!"

"Aye, Dirk, you'll never play the harpsichord again."

Beyond the storm, the sea kept busy that night. By the glow of the rising pumpkin moon, things stirred up from the water by the wild spoon of the wind covered the surface. Rafts of flotsam that gleamed green, pearly chains of sea wrack. Flying fish broke the ocean top and soared, gold on darkness, black across the moon. Later, serpentlike eels also filled the cauldron of water, coiling and glittering, luminous blue and white. The air was sharp with ozone. Starfish floated by in groups, like coral islands.

Above, little running clouds pranced past the stars. Sea and sky, both in motion, both dark yet full of moving lights, were reflections of each other. And the moon and the ship sailed on.

Next day they cleaned and cleared *Unwelcome Stranger*. There was pumping out of water, scrubbing decks, regreasing the masts. Carpentry was attended to and tar plugs put in.

The wind was harmless, helpful. Clever Cuthbert snipped and sewed canvas, climbed and repaired the torn mizzen topgallant.

Dusk came, and big stars, and supper, and the wind grew more harmless, and less helpful.

A lull began.

It wasn't like the deadly stillness of the Doldrums, only a becalming. The ship rocked quietly.

"Take the opportunity," Art told them. "Get some rest."

But then the moon rose too early, rose on *every* side.

Everyone went to the rails.

A brilliant shining rimmed the horizon in all directions. They were caught at its center in a total darkness, like a black stone at the center of a burning silver ring.

"Mr. Vooms," said Art, "what's this?"

"Something left over from the storm, Captain."

Eerie said, "Nay, 'tis not natural, by the Porpoise's Eyebrows."

"Rubbish, Mr. O'Shea."

"Listen, Cap'n Art," said Eerie. "These waters now. Have you never heard of the Flying Dutchman?"

Art frowned. Everyone else stared at Eerie, who was uncannily lit by the fiery ring on the sea.

Curiously, maybe, it was Felix who spoke. "Mr. O'Shea, that is a legend. Not a truth."

Eerie shook his head. "He was a Dutch trader—or a whaler captain, some say," intoned Eerie. "He called on fiends to help him, and so used the hurricanes of the Cape to speed his ship to better profits. Then one day the fiends claimed him. They slew his men and left him alone and immortal, doomed forever to haunt these seas."

"And those that witness his phantom ship," said Black Knack in a truly horrifying voice, "one of their number must *die*."

Art spoke. "My. I just remembered. You are *actors*, gentlemen." She clapped. "Bravo."

Black Knack slunk aside.

The others gloomed but hovered. No one was inclined to go below to sleep. Art didn't insist.

Something in the air made her skin prickle. "Ebad, by your reckoning, are we into eastern seas?"

"Here's the border of them. I'll admit to you, as Eerie said, strange things can happen here."

"Keep that from the rest. Keep it from Eerie. Mr. Phoenix"—Art crossed to him—"thanks for your words of good sense."

"No thanks are due me. I don't believe in ghosts. The dead don't return—nor is anyone immortal."

They stood under the quarter. "You never find otherwise, Mr. Phoenix? Sometimes they do come back—sometimes they *are* immortal."

He nodded. "But only in dreams."

A fearful, low, warbling cry wavered over the night. Who or what had uttered *that?*

But Felix and Art and her crew turned together eastward, even Muck, silver-lit and hackles raised, even Plunqwette, her feathers pointing out from her wings, disturbed as any dog—

Felix dropped his hand on Art's shoulder. His touch was as electric as the night.

"There."

From the witch light of the weird ring, a shape had bloomed up like a shimmering blot. It was a great ship. Long and wide and squared with full canvas. Swiftly forward it sheered, all along one curve of the glowing circle, driven by a wind that didn't blow, illuminated by a light that showed nothing of it, beyond its faintly glimmering silhouette.

"It's the Dutchman!"

"Ill luck to all who see—"

"One of us is marked for death—"

Art shook herself. She opened her mouth to thunder at or reassure them. In that instant, the ring of light itself *died*. Only solid black filled in sky and water. And besides *Unwelcome*, no other ship of any sort was there in it.

ACT THREE
Piratica

~ ONE ~

Setting Fire to Canvas ⟶

Having turned the corner of Africay, *Unwelcome Stranger* sailed up into eastern seas. Far ahead lay the Indian Ocean. Nearer, the pirate land of Mad-Agash Scar.

It was on a morning of lilting blue weather that Mad-Agash came in view.

A small country more than an island, set adrift in water. Mountains rose far off to the east, and among them one tiny volcano puffed its pipe, clearly to be seen.

The breeze was firm and refreshingly cool, angling to the land, so they tacked and turned to catch it.

Mad-Agash had been, for two centuries, a pirate stronghold. Countless pirate landsirs kept their domains there, and practiced trade and truce with any who called by on friendly terms. Here there would be news and clues of all kinds.

Noon came and passed over the ship. Under Ebad's piloting, they sailed in toward the western shore.

Up that coast then they moved, a mile or so out beyond the shallower depths, which, here, showed a murky green. The little volcano far inland kept pace with them, smoking away. But nearer, the plains looked grassy and lush, with herds of creatures galloping—deer or other bouncers.

An hour or so later, they noted a couple of strongholds up on higher ground. These were log-built, and massed in trees, waving high bright flags. But in the spyglass, six-pound cannon were also visible, pointing from the wooden walls.

Not till late afternoon, however, did anyone attempt contact or investigation.

Then a group of narrow boats came around at them, skimming all at once up the sides of the crocodile-green waves.

"Brace yourselves, gentlemen," said Art. She loaded the musketoon, and then stood waiting. The crew copied her.

The approaching boats were ten in number, all rowed skillfully, and each flying a white-and-scarlet flag.

"Do you know what flag that is, Mr. Vooms?"

"It will belong to some resident here and be an invention, for show."

The men in the boats were a mix of black, white, and brown. One in the nearest boat stood up and hailed *Unwelcome* through a horn.

"Lay up and declare thyselves, mateys."

Art called clearly back. "*Unwelcome Stranger* under Captain Art Blastside."

"English, be thee?"

"Aye."

"Ye've struck no English holding here. You must follow us in. We'll guide you round the bar. Then you'll come ashore along of us, and state your business to the Governor."

Every man in the boats was armed. There were about forty of them.

"Very well. We'll do as you say."

The boats sniffed about *Unwelcome*, then escorted her in as promised—or threatened.

A vast deep bay lay around a headland where trees hung in curtains. Birds shrieked and wheeled overhead, and Plunqwette lifted her emerald face, interested—*parrots*.

In the bay also stood five quiet ships, spars empty, at anchor.

Though green, the bay water was clear as glass. White sand lay far beneath, and fish spangled through below, in endlessly shifting colored ribbons. *Unwelcome*'s anchor was lowered.

"Who is this 'Governor'?" Eerie wondered.

"Whoever, we must make friends with him," said Art. "We may need also to lie. For example, the rest of our fleet, if it comes to that."

"The rest—"

"We will playact, Mr. O'Shea, that our own friends are just behind us."

Not attending to this debate, Cuthbert had noticed one of the other ships—or rather, her figurehead. It was of a buxom lady with dark hair. "Cor, what a stunner!" Cuthbert read the ship's name out—despite the previous warning, the name was written in English: *Saucy Mrs. Minnie*.

The narrow boats clustered in again.

"Is this all your number?" called up the Mad-Agashy who had spoken before. "Ten—eleven—persons?"

"On *this* vessel, yes," said Art.

Surprising Art, the Mad-Agashy only seemed curious for scientific reasons. "By the Dragon of the Deep, how'd this few of you work your ship?"

Art smiled. "It can be done. But, of course, we can call upon other men when we need them."

Art selected her landing party, including Ebad. She left the well-armed and cautiously alert Whuskery and Black Knack, with Muck, aboard the ship. She was also surprised to find Felix had joined her.

"I don't advise your coming ashore, sir. This mightn't be a picnic."

"Then you must ignore your own advice."

"More trying to understand the pirate kind? It could be dangerous."

"That'll make a pleasant change."

"Stay to the back then, with Honest and Walt."

No one demanded they give up their weapons. The men in the boats were polite as they rowed *Unwelcome*'s crew to shore.

Through the dripping drape of trees, a hill appeared. On the hill stood a very grand mansion, reminiscent of scenes from Art's memory—or the drama. It was the color of gingerbread and trimmed with white paint. The windows beamed with sun. A flag flew over the roof, white and red. A Governor's house for sure.

Once the boats grounded, their guides led them up from the beach and along grassy slopes. The grass was tawny, and waist-high in places. Abruptly, out of a stand of trees, a group of white furry beings came madly leaping and jumping along, clowned over the path immediately in front of them, and vanished into other trees beyond, making hooting noises.

Everyone was amazed. Walter screamed: "Men—men with dogs' heads!"

"No," said the guides' spokesman, whose companions were laughing. "Lemuras. Animals native to the land."

"But they walked upright—had white trousers on—and long black dog noses," insisted Walter.

He kept on and on about this as they climbed up through yellow-tasseled trees, and emerged on a terrace, walled, and with statues. Through the open wrought-iron gates lay a garden, and a bubbling fountain. The Governor's important house stood at the end of a sanded drive, mountains and volcanoes making an artistic backdrop.

They all stopped under the carefully gardened ornamental trees, watching, waiting.

Art very slowly opened her eyes wider. Down the driveway, a man was unhurriedly strolling to meet them. The Governor? Richly dressed—silk coat, lace shirt. No wig, and hair curly and grizzled. A way of walking, lagging a little—familiar. At her side Ebad sucked in his breath.

Peter said, "But it's—is it?"

Plunqwette squawked and took off like a feathered cannonball—straight at the Governor, who was—

(Art spoke) "Hurkon Beare."

After the splendid dinner (spoiled only by the sunset wailing of lemuras outside), Hurkon took his guests on a tour of his house.

"We use torches for walks after dark, rather than lamps—keeps off the mosquitoes, indoors and out."

His accent was the same, the mellow notes of the Canadee mountains, but trained to actor's pitch. To Art, it was the voice that came back to her, with her mother's, the first, that day when everything came back.

They saw huge rooms with floors made of marble mosaic, and huge staircases with gilt bannisters. There was an indoor fountain, and in some walls, shells had been set. But everything was rather empty, save for several statues, boxes, and brass-bound chests.

"See here, my friends." And Hurkon undid a chest with a whip of the thin sword worn at his side. The lid fell back and torchlight dazzled on heaps of the most impressive jewels—chunks of wine-red ruby, leaf-green or yellow topaz, ropes of pearls, and coins—French gold louis, muhuras from the Inde, Spanish doubloons, even the parrot's favorite pieces of eight.

"Fakes," said Hurkon. "An old actor's jest. Any real wealth of mine is in the bank at Port Liberty, in the Amer Ricas."

Plunqwette, dozing on a bronze statue, seemed to have lost her fascination with Hurkon. She yawned and snapped her beak.

A few of Hurkon's men had stayed to dine, and now came on

the tour, too, his four captains off the ships in the bay, and three officers. This was Hurkon's fleet, though now, he said, they seldom went in for piracy. He was more a respectable trader along Afric and Arabic coasts, merely one who kept useful piratic connections, and so traveled safely.

"I'd hang in England," said Hurkon. "Probably in Canadia, too."

He had said little about those first days after he left the actor's band in Lundon. Said less about his own days of real piracy. But now, "I fell into that life," he said, "half by chance. Ebad—d'you know what I mean? The old tale—a ship attacks the one you're aboard. 'Tis a pirate. They offer you death or the pirate's hat. You take the hat."

" 'Twas what happened along of me an'all," agreed Cuthbert. "Who's goin' ter say, well, kill me quick, for I'll never serve with a pirate crew?"

Felix stood pale and grave across that room where the unreal jewels drizzled from the chest. He said in a dull, expressionless voice, "Some might, Mr. Cuthbert. Some have."

"Well good luck to 'em. But not me."

"Nor I," said Hurkon. "Come on, Ebad, old mate. Tell me you understand why I did it?" Hurkon's face was all laughter. Laughter that cloaked unease.

Art turned to look at Ebad. He seemed able always to hide so much—all he couldn't hide was that he *was* hiding something.

And Ebad, low and dull as Felix, said, "I'm no better than thou, now, Hurkon."

"Much better, for I gather you've stuck to the code of our play. To Molly's code. Taken not one life."

Art said, "You're saying you've killed then, Hurkon?"

"In self-defense."

"There are usually other ways to defend yourself, Hurkon."

Hurkon glanced away from Art. "You're like your mother,

and you judge too harsh. You're young, Art, and you've the luck of seventeen devils." He sighed. He said, "Which is why I know you've kept that map, Ebadiah, or more likely, given it to Arty, here."

They were evenly matched, eight to eight. There in the flick-flick of the torchlight, Art and her seven crew, Hurkon with his seven men.

But no hand was put to blade or pistol.

Art said, "What do *you* think of the treasure map, then, Hurkon, old friend?"

"It's worth a fortune."

"Have *you* never tried for that fortune?"

"Yes. Never found it, though. I said, my luck's only an ordinary thing. But you, Captain Art, well, I believe you are"—Hurkon paused, and his eyes gleamed; he spoke up like a bell—"the true Piratica."

"But Piratica, Mr. Beare," said Art, "was only the character Molly acted in a play."

"Once she was. But you have made Piratica—*come alive*. Come on. I see Piratica *there*, where you're stood. Piratica, with the luck of seventeen devils. I don't deceive you. You're all my old mates. Someone should get their mitts on that treasure trove. I know you mean to try. And I'll help you all I can."

With a flare of his silk coat, he limpingly turned and led them off up another, narrower stair.

(Must it always be like this—old friends refound, but not to be trusted any longer?) Art ran her eyes over her company.

Plunqwette flew after them in slow wheelings. Ebad's face was a shield of darkness, and Felix's face a shield of white enamel.

The rest were drunk and quite jolly.

She sensed strongly Hurkon had not credited the idea Art also controlled a fleet.

They came into a—*picture gallery*. There were thirty or forty pictures hung there. In the torchlight, their images—of palaces, countryside, people—seemed to move.

"My one indulgence," said Hurkon. "Worth a bit."

They passed down the double line of paintings.

Each canvas, catching the torchlight fire Hurkon held near to it, shone like a lamp, then went out.

Ebad murmured, "This is where *his* fortune lies. And some of those gems he showed us—a heap of glass, with some genuine stones mixed in—or I'm a lark."

Felix said, very softly, "Among these paintings are three at least by classical Italian masters. Worth in price half this island."

At the end of Hurkon's gallery were two last pictures. They were of landscapes, and—peculiar after all the other cunning scenes—not well painted.

"Now here it is," said Hurkon. "I was brought these long ago, because my men knew my weakness for artistic objects—and, at that time, my other weakness—which was to search for the Treasured Isle. And in front of you now, on canvas, *is* that Isle."

They stared. The torchlight stared with them.

"Which painting is it, of the two?" asked Peter, finally.

"Both."

"But—"

The two pictures were not like each other, though each showed a long, long stretch of coastal land, lapped by a rough sea, while behind rose a cliff, bleak and forbidding, with what seemed, in each case, to be gulls flying about its top.

Otherwise, the foreground land couldn't have been less similar.

In the first painting it was smothered in shrubs and flowers, with trees laden with orange, green, and golden fruits. In the second painting, the land stretch was black and littered by weird debris. And though there were a few trees standing on it, they were blasted and withered—seemingly dead.

Hurkon appeared to take delight in their bafflement. Although Art kept quiet, he let her crew ask one another questions, while behind them the men of Hurkon's ships also smiled patronizingly. They knew, too, it seemed, the joke. Whatever it was.

At last Hurkon picked up his recital.

"There's a legend you'll have heard—the island *sinks—hides*. Certainly the sea, which is called, there, the Eastern Ambers, is treacherous and bewitched—dangerous. But this man, who painted the Treasured Isle, he found it—*twice*. Though he never unearthed any treasure—maybe never even had a true map, though there is more than one, as several know. One time he saw it; it was a sun-laved shore, all fruit and blooms. The other time like a thing pulled up from Hell, scorched and foul, stinking and fearful. So the Treasured Isle has two faces, mates. And where the treasure lies on it, none know, if they have a map or not. Both paintings have the same name."

Art moved forward. Something had caught her eye.

She looked at the writing on each canvas, scribbled there on it in paint, and below, the signature of the one who had painted it. As Hurkon had said, name and title were the same in both.

Then the light was swept off like a broom. Hurkon was away again, some of *Unwelcome*'s merry crew galloping along after. Eerie was with them.

Art glanced at Ebad.

"You saw the words on the canvas."

"Aye, while the light was on it."

"Title and artist: *Beach*," said Art, *"by Cobhouse."*

Blond Bombshell

Hand in hand, the pirates sang songs together. They downed everything—rum, wine, the brandies of Africay, the home-brewed lemon ciders, coffee in which a knife could have stood upright.

"You must stay in my house," said Hurkon, the perfect host. "The beds are good—nicer than a ship's bunks."

Art's crew cried happily that yes, they would stay.

Art said, sitting relaxed over her coffee (the only drink she had joined them in), "No, sirs. Back to the ship with you. Discipline," she added to Hurkon. "They forget who's captain. I, and my two officers, will stay in your fine house tonight, with thanks."

"And your passenger, Mr. Phoenix?"

Art shot Felix a long look. But she found she was always, now, looking at him. "Yes, he'll like a comfortable bed."

Grumbling, Art's troupe set off for the shore, escorted by two of Hurkon's men. Hurkon seemed glad to have kept the four he had. The talk went on some while—most of it sentimental chat of the actors' past.

Finally Art sent her men to their beds. Up the broadest set of stairs they all went, by corridors with wide windows, showing palms and other trees, and embroidered stars. It was two in the morning.

"Mr. Vooms," said Art, "one half hour. Then everyone is on his feet, and we're away out of here."

"My own thought, Cap'n."

The house was soon in utter silent blackness but for the starlight trickling in.

Eerie was the only one taken aback by Ebad's suggestion that Hurkon wasn't to be trusted, so everyone should now leave both house and Mad-Agash Scar.

"But I'm worn out, so I am. And there'll be hot chocolate in the morning—and a bath!"

However, Felix had caught the drift of suspicion without trouble.

The four of them (Plunqwette hooked to Art's shoulder) crept down the narrowest stair. No one was about. If Hurkon Beare had meant to keep them prisoner, he had set no watch on them. Perhaps he had gambled on their stupidity.

Perhaps, too, thought Art, Hurkon might have been all right, if *we* hadn't had a *map*.

The great mosaic front hall, when they reached it, lay open and full of faint echoes. The front door was barred but not locked, and was undone with ease. But outside they froze into the shadows of the verandah, seeing two men patrolling through the garden.

"What *are* they at? They carry on in a funny way—"

"Look, one's gone right up a *tree*—"

Art chuckled. "And they wear white furry trousers. They're lemuras, those things from the grasslands—they've got in over the wall."

There was a sentry they *did* find, by the gate. He sat in a chair, a flintlock over his knees, head back in slumber. A drained bottle lay by him on the ground.

"Down to the shore!"

They descended the moonless slopes, keeping among the grass and trees, going fast. The *Unwelcome Stranger* appeared below, sat out on the water of the bay, just beyond Hurkon's fleet. Hurkon's rowboats lay at the shoreline, where his men had left them—and a kind of camp was now visible farther along the beach, where lamps burned bright. They would have to avoid that place.

It had occurred to Art, too, how powerful Hurkon must be in this area, if he left only so slight and unreliable a guard on his house—presumably, no one *dared* attempt a break-in, or raid.

As they went through the last mass of trees, someone came bounding toward them—pistols flew out—and another lemura passed them with a hair-raising gargle. Plunqwette opened one eye.

"Nearly shot the blasted thing," Eerie complained. "What kind of a beast is that, now? Shouldn't be allowed."

As they reached the last tree, a tall shape they had thought *was* a tree turned and screamed into Eerie's face. Eerie, well panicked, shrieked back into its doglike one. Another lemura. Fortunately, thought Art, the creatures themselves made so much row, the outcry of Eerie would never be heard.

They gained the shore at a crouching lope.

"Here's a boat. Take the oars, Mr. O'Shea."

"I? But, why not Ebad—he's *sober*—" Eerie added accusingly.

"If any are looking out from Hurk's ships, and they see Ebad returning, they may get nervous. And anyway, some exercise will rinse some of the coffee and booze out of you. The rest of us lie flat down. (Also you, parrot.) As we pass the ships, Eerie, if any challenge you, you curse me and say I sent you back alone."

"Aye, Cap'n. 'Tis easy to curse any that makes you row when ye're fit only for your rest."

However, despite his state, Eerie kept them carefully wide of Hurkon Beare's fleet. And though lamp-lit at prow and stern, no watch seemed active on those five decks. No challenge came. They reached *Unwelcome*, found the ropes, and hauled themselves up her side.

It took a further fifteen minutes to rouse the peacefully snoring crew, especially Black Knack, who was found asleep in the crew bath. Five more to inform them they were now in retreat.

"How to set sails, Cap'n? They can't fail to hear us reefing—"

"We'll row her out, like the Doldrums. This time muffle up the oars with rags. Come on."

They obeyed her. Even through the fog of gone-bad goodwill and sleep, some curious sense of menace spread now all across that night. So *Unwelcome Stranger,* towed by her oar-muffled jolly boats, slid nearly noiseless from Hurkon's bay, and back away on to the wide waters.

"Eastern Ambers, Mr. Vooms. Was that a clue worth having?"

"Maybe. It's about the right area, and I've heard of them, too. Though not many charts carry that name. South again, east again, as we thought. The Capricorn Seas. Odd currents— magnetic— The South Pole below us, India high above us as the moon."

"Do you think he'll pursue?"

Ebad stared off toward Mad-Agash. "He may. I sense he won't. He's got lazy, Art, lazy, trustless. He's not who he was, Hurkon Beare."

"Look, Mr. Phoenix, that group of stars that sparkle like cut gems. The South Down Cross."

"Some sailors call it the Southern Buckle."

"Yes. So they do. Did you ever see anything more beautiful?" Art didn't expect an answer. Yet she got one.

"Yes."

Then she glanced at Felix. She thought, He means Goldie, or I'm the Flying Dutchman.

"Well," said Art, "I note you know all your star maps any-way, Mr. P. And that way lies the Pole. We may spot icebergs in these warmer waters."

They stood on the forecastle. Before them the arrow-point bowsprit of the ship, the shrouded figurehead below. Canvas and stars and sea everywhere else.

He had been a practical help, escaping Hurkon. He had worked in harmony with her men. Useful. As well as decorative.

Felix said, "It's time I told you why I came with you."

"I thought you had no choice. And then gave up."

"No. There's always a choice, Captain Blastside."

"You may call me Art, sir, in our relaxing moments."

"Oh, do I dare?"

Art smiled. "Maybe you don't. We'll see. It's there if you wish. Always a choice, as you said."

Felix stayed silent a long while after that, and so did she. They leaned together at the rail, shoulders not quite touching.

Behind them, most of the crew were at a hearty dinner. The oceans were calm tonight, but who knew what even the next hour would bring? Storms, enemies catching up, the sight of some remote lost isle—which might be the very one they sought.

"My father," said Felix.

Another pause.

"My father was a man whose name was Adam Makepeace— for like you, Art, I've changed my name since. I only knew him till I was about eight years of age. He died then. I'll come to that."

Art waited. In her side her heart beat heavy. She had kept her own mother only two years longer.

"My father was a rich man, Art, a landsir. But he was also a kind man, a noble man. He took care of his own people, not just his family—my mother, his other children, me—but any who worked for him. His estate was covered in well-built cottages and houses where his people lived rent-free. And in the town he looked out for any in distress. Anyone could come to him and go away better off in all ways. He gave money and much of his time. The whole of that countryside depended on Adam Makepeace. I tell you, Art, they tried to rename the area for him—*Adamsham.* He wouldn't have it. He laughed. He laughed a lot in those days."

Again came silence. She watched Felix as he remembered. Through the back of his dark blue eyes ran shadows and currents, as they did in the heart of the sea.

At last she said, "What stopped the laughter?"

"Oh, Captain, Captain, don't you *guess? Pirates* stopped it. Your own charming kind."

"Ah."

"Ah. He was a trader, my father, Adam, that's where he'd got his wealth, and got enough he could always give it away in armfuls and still make more. His pride was a ship, a windjammer—like yours—and one of the best ever built, so he'd say. She was called the *Voyager,* and she voyaged over the Seven Seas and brought back riches. The captain of that ship was my father's brother, my uncle Solomon—Sol. I say brothers, but they were more friends, the best friends in the world. One day Sol was to take out a special cargo, a new venture for Adam. The ship was to cross almost the whole earth and reach the Indias. That is a perilous trip, as you'll know, but she was sound and well stocked, and in the hands of a man who knew his business better than his own skin. There was great investment in the voyage. Even some of the Admiralty fellows had a share in that. But there were passengers, too. Among them, my mother's sister and her husband, their children, and three close friends—they thought nothing of any risk. Sol was captain. They would be safe. That night before Sol went down to Port's Mouth, my father and he quarrelled. It was over some trivial thing—something to do with the family. I suppose, now and then, in the course of their lives, they had quarrelled before, too. But I was only a child; I'd never seen it happen, didn't understand. They made it up, but stiffly. They didn't part in the usual generous way. My father made some sour joke I overheard, about at least avoiding a duel. . . . Later on Adam said he wrote to Sol, sent the letter ahead of him to Free Cape Town, to find Sol when he got there."

Another great gap of speechlessness came then.

Art said softly, "And—"

"And one midday between Guinea and the Hope Cape, three

lean ships bore down on the *Voyager*. They flew the flag of murderers, the Jolly Roger, as you call it, the flag of death. Cannon blazed, back and forth. But *Voyager* was no match for three such fiends. They brought her low, two masts down. Then boarded her. Pirates, Art. Not like your warrior notions of honor, Molly Faith and her play-actor's code—oh, no. They killed everyone aboard my father's ship, men, women—*children*—yes, children, too. They fired her, and they sank her, and went away with all her goods. Only one man escaped. He lost an eye and a leg, but he got off by playing dead on a plank in the sea. Another vessel picked him up by afternoon, or he, too, would have died. It was this man told the story. It was to this man my father, when he finally met him, gave the last of his wealth. It wasn't much by then. For the sinking of his ship ruined my father. He lost all he'd ever made. And much more than that. My mother died of shock and grief for her sister. One by one his other sons sickened and died, too. By then we lived in a slum, and my father's hair had turned white as salt—and no one knew us anymore."

"Didn't any help?"

"None. There were one or two he had hoped—but we saw nothing of them. Adam was pulled down by his financial loss, and by what in turn that loss caused. The town, too, was wrecked by it. They cursed him, Art, for entrusting so much on one ship. As if he were to blame for it all, not that scum of the seas who sank her. He lived four more years. Then he was gone. It was the county workhouse for me after that."

"How did you survive?"

"I could sing when I was a kid—better than I do now. And later I could draw likenesses. People took me up. They said I spoke so nicely, what a nice-looking little boy—only look at his nice hair, so blond. It's not blond, Art, my hair. I used to be black-haired, like my dad. I went white, too, very young. When I was eight, in that workhouse."

"Felix," she said.

"Yes," he said. "Felix. That means 'Happy'—did you know?"

". . . You took off the ruby ring your father gave you."

"It's not a ruby. It's glass. It *used* to be a ruby. That was how Adam paid the man who got back crippled from *Voyager*—with the real ruby out of the ring. Then Adam had red glass put in. It was all he left me when he died. I can remember them throwing it to me. You have it, they said, it's not worth anything."

Behind them, the pirates were singing a loud song. The bell rang for some o'clock or other.

She thought, I was two years old when you were four and the *Voyager* went down. I was six when you were eight and your father died. You were twelve when I was ten and Molly—was killed.

"Thank you for your confidence," said Art. "Of course, I won't speak of it elsewhere."

"Ebad Vooms knows. I've already told him. And Glad Cuthbert."

Art was stung. Then resigned. Men—who could understand them?

Then he delivered the cannon blast.

"Which brings me," said Felix, "to *why* I'm here. The one confession I've not yet made to any other. I am here to see what you do, you and your bold pirateers. I make drawings of it all, all your acts of robbery, and I write a journal, too, recording these crimes. When I'm done, I shall take the material to England, where, along with my own evidence, it will prove entirely useful in bringing each and every one of you to justice. I don't like pirates. Perhaps now you see why not."

Art stared at him, her gray eyes wide and brilliant as the stars above. Her beating heart had stopped.

"But then, sir, I have no choice but to—"

"Kill me? But *you* don't kill, nor your pack. A riddle for you, Captain."

"I shall find some other way," she said, "to prevent your plan."

"The only way is my death."

Art's lips tightened to a thin line. "Don't fuss yourself. There'll be others. For now, sir, I'll leave you your privacy in which to plot and make your notes. Otherwise, from now on, you will find yourself, I regret, less free on this ship than you have been."

"I've not been *free* for ten years. Good night, *Captain Piratica*."

When the calm yet disturbed night had passed, the sun rose in front of the ship. The sky was blue, but not the sea. The ocean had altered and was the color of clear tea in a white china cup.

The Odder Sea

In the midst of that strange amber sea, the *Unwelcome Stranger* ran lightly, with a flighty, circling wind. They let the wind guide them. They trimmed only to steady the ship. The air smelled of flowers and growing plants—but there wasn't a strip of land in sight. Once, a rock passed them, stuck up from the sea like a fence post in a flooded field. "They say bells chime under these waters." "They say the kraken, the biggest monster in the ocean, dwells here." "Oh, shut up." Plunqwette sat on the crow's nest, scanning the view, sometimes crying out unhelpful alarms: "Polly want a Dollar!" Or, "Pieces of Crate!" Muck, too, was lively, running up and down the deck with a foot of tongue hanging out, wagging his tail. "Something energetic in this sea," said Eerie. "I feel it as well—like strong coffee. Or strong tea, which is more its color."

Meanwhile, day to day, and in the blue-amber evenings, the main debate went on.

"Is Felix our enemy then? Will he truly betray us to the courts?" Walter.

"He says he's hid all the drawings and notes where we'll never find them. And we *can't* find them." Peter.

Black Knack said, "Let's string him up, Cap'n Art. Eh? That's what he's got in mind for us, in England."

"No," said Art. "Let him do as he wants. He can be confined to belowdecks, or tied up if necessary, when we reach the Isle."

"*If* we reach it. *If* it exists."

"*Beach* by Cobhouse," said Art. "Ten miles up. Fifteen paces left."

"Did Hurkon Beare never figure that out? He had the two pictures."

"He may not have had an accurate map. He *didn't* have Molly's parrot."

Art spread the map before them again. There in the indigo map sea, the brown island lay, map and Isle burned off in an uneven shape at the bottom. (What clues had been lost in that burned area?)

Down the map's side ran the mysterious letters, which surely were some kind of clue:

OOP, TTU, FAB, MMN, RRS, AFC, HHI, YYZ, FAD.

"These double letters must mean something important," said Whuskery. "OO—TT—HH—"

Cuthbert, leaning at the main mast, commented, "They mean a dose o' indigestion."

"Why didn't Ebad let us in on this before? Come on, you tell us, Eerie—he told *you!* and *her*—" Black Knack.

Art stood up. The sword she had drawn like a whisk of sleek flame touched delicately the tip of Black Knack's nose.

"*Her*, Mr. Knack?"

Black Knack said, "True, you're no girl. You're a demon. But—a hell of a captain, I'll give ye that, OK. Beg pardon, Cap'n. It's my nerves."

"See your nerves," said Art, "cause no other problems—or accidents. If harm comes to Mr. Phoenix, I shall know exactly where to look—your *nerves*. Don't break our code, Mr. Knack. I tell you for your own good."

"Ebad, is it possible *Felix* is our traitor—by his own lights he wouldn't be. He was *never* on our side."

"Aye, 'tis poss., Art. But betray us to *Goldie*?"

"He *liked* Goldie. Maybe he knew her before—thinks he can reform her from her piratic ways."

"Felix doesn't strike me as a total fool."

"Someone tipped her off, as we know. Someone also, Ebad Vooms, or so I think, holed the Coffee Ship at Port's Mouth. That *wasn't* in my plan, though it helped us. It could have *drowned* us—for all Mr. Phoenix knew. And he was below in the underdeck. So was it him?"

"Neither could *he* swim, Art."

"Perhaps he was pretending."

Now in the crew's quarters under the forecastle, Felix sat on his bunk.

He was still drawing, from memory, the portrait gallery of everyone he had recently met. Two of these drawings were particularly excellent. One a girl with cat's eyes and black curls, one a girl with steel eyes and dark hair parted by a single shining streak. Goldie. Art. Misters Beast and Pest were also there, and Tattoo, and one or two others of the crew of the *Enemy*. Hurkon Beare and his captains had been recently added. All Art's company were present.

Felix, finishing the latest sketch (of Art—there were quite a lot of Art, in fact), got up and walked along the dark tweendeck, to the apple barrel left handy for everyone. He drew out the apples. The constant taking on of more exotic fruit had made reliance on this barrel slight, and there were a lot there. Under them, sacking. He removed that, too. Felix threw the latest artwork of Art inside. Back went the sack, the apples, the lid.

Then he stood, looking at the shut barrel.

He didn't really care if they were found. He had stowed drawings everywhere on the vessel, and none of them *had* been found. It was all a game. Because, if they were, he could always draw everything again, and perhaps even better. Unless Art broke her code and ran him through.

He had had to tell her. Although he had been mad to do so. And she, of course, had alerted the men.

Black Knack was the only one who had threatened Felix. At which Ebad and Cuthbert had dragged Black Knack off.

Black Knack seemed also the only one who might be prepared to kill a fellow human. Felix had heard, Art had promised Black Knack that if he did so, they would maroon him on some islet of the Ambers.

Up above, Felix could hear the Honest Liar playing Cuthbert's hurdy-gurdy. Honest had just picked the instrument up and, not needing to be taught, had *played*. He had been like that with swimming.

Honest was a good and innocent man, and young, not much older, Felix thought, than he himself. Walt was not much more, nor Peter. Dirk and Whuskery yearned mostly for stage life, saw treasure as a way to be successful and famous actors. Eerie longed for Eira. Ebad, who had been a slave, deserved every fine thing he could ever get. And Cuthbert wanted to go home to his "ol' missus for a proper row—the kind with thrown pans—and a cuddle."

And Art. Well. She wanted her mother.

Her mother had been her father, too, judging from the little Felix had heard of Art's actual Da.

So Art remade herself in Molly's image, to bring Molly back.

Or was it only that?

No. Too simple—Art—

Was Art.

Art—

Was Piratica, as the wealthy, trustless Canadee pirate Hurkon had said.

Soon after this, Walter came to let Felix up on the top deck for air.

Walter squinted unhappily at Felix. Wouldn't talk.

Ebad said, "Take your walk around, Mr. Phoenix. No one grudges you. You have had a lot to burden you."

But no one looked at Felix, spoke, or wanted a song. No one, naturally, wanted his picture drawn. But he was used to being alone.

Art Blastside paced her cabin. She was busy shoving Felix out of her heart—where he had got lodged, somehow.

Before his "confession" she had been making plans to win him. But now she must be done with him. Molly would have been.

Days and nights, nights and days. The amber ocean glowed as if with subsurface fires. Sometimes very odd currents tossed the ship. Once they hit a miniature tempest, whirling and cracked at by forked lightnings, rained on—the rain was salt—until spun loose of the storm. Beyond it, everything was still. The tempest lay behind them, rearing and clashing on the waves like something alive, furious—and very small.

The day after, they saw an island.

"Is that the *Isle*?"

It wasn't. Only a few yards all around, it lay there like a flattened cake. A single palm tree grew on it, black and metallic with coatings of salt.

Both Felix and Black Knack gave this place a wary glance. On such horrid rocks, pirates marooned those they disliked or thought disloyal. But no one was put off.

Afterward, a whole stream of such little isles went by, dotted about as if spilled from a careless island-making hand. Some had nothing on them, were all blinding white sand. Some were stony. On one, a broken deserted boat lay, a wretched reminder of someone else's awful mishap.

By nightfall they were sick of these dreadful tiny isles.

"They'm like a rash of boils on the sea."

"By the Whisker Pole, will we never look at real land again?"

They sat down to a dinner on deck. The pirate band played, and Honest on the hurdy-gurdy. (Felix didn't sing, though they had let him up again for food and airing.)

"Thank you, God, for the gift of greed."

They tucked into salt fish and new-baked bread, a pot full of malted cabbage and meat soup.

Stars undid their doors.

Muck strode up and down, growling for no reason.

Plunqwette sat silent as a toy.

And Art—glittered by starlight.

"Cap'n Art—"

"Yes, Mr. Walt Salt?"

"There's parrots all over our masts."

Art, who had been worrying again at the theater map in the cabin, turned to Walter in surprise.

"You don't mean Plunqwette?"

"Not unless she's split into fifty or so others."

Out on deck they all stood, save Felix, confined below.

Along every spar and bar of the masts, along the rails, atop deckhouse and galley and Captain's Cabin—Parrots. They were like colored flowers. Azure and black, yellow and cerise, honey, cherry and white, gray and purple, crimson and jade.

All of them, though, as Plunqwette often was, voiceless. But perched there, they had that look—as if, Art thought, staring in astonishment, they were a great parrot chorus, trained for a work by Mr. Haydn, the composer, and about to break into—

"*Land ahoy! Land—land—land—!*"

At Whuskery's howl from the crow's nest, every parrot on the masts exploded into a kind of *pleased* squawking. Grown men clapped their hands over their ears—and rushed for cover as the deck was adorned with parrot droppings.

But Plunqwette came waddling from the chicken coops.

"Cluck-cluck," went Plunqwette. She looked up at Art. "Now shall the world," said Plunqwette in the voice of Molly, "be thine, sweetheart."

Then she fired herself away, up among the rigging, the parrots, unscathed through the sheet of poo.

And also through it, *they* saw the landmass ahead of them. First a hill, crowned by a coil of trees. Beyond that, a stretch of whitest sand. Across the sand more trees, flowers, blossoms—all parrot shades of cherry and gold and green— Far off lifted a rocky towering cliff.

Around the shore, the sea flowed a healthy deep blue.

It was the island from Cobhouse's second painting. It was— *must be*—the Treasured Isle.

~❀ TWO ❀~

Treasured Isle ─

Young fruit beaded the nearest trees. Farther along it was ripe—
rosy or peachy in color. Flowers made a carpet or climbed the
trees in ropes. All this lay just beyond the sand, which itself
sparked as if diamonds were in it. After the sand, flowers, and
fruit trees, a small forest lay in green velvet ruffles. Out of which
the bald cliff raised itself. But to start with, hardly any of this
was visible.

For off the cliff, out of the forest and the shoreside orchard,
more parrots flew—in thousands, it seemed—so many they were
like vast swarms of bees.

Meanwhile the parrots that had already settled on the ship
left her and settled on the beach. Instead of going away,
they went round and round *Unwelcome*'s boats, round the heads
of the crew, flying often so low they knocked off hats. Occasion-
ally hundreds of the *other* parrots dived across to join in. Feathers, droppings—the air was rainbowed with a type of parrot
snow.

Spades brought for digging, ropes for climbing, fell, clattered
and tangled.

"What is it? What's the matter with 'em?"

"Flap 'em off, Whuskery—look, one's messed my coat now—"

"By the Lord's Loud-Hailer—"

"Pah!"

"Yuck!"

"Damnation in a sock!"

Muck yapped, trampling everyone, bouncing off spades and

legs, springing at parrot after parrot—missing them all. Plun-qwette—was gone—*lost* among her fluttering peer group.

Art shouted above the noise. "Fire in the air, Mr. Vooms, Mr. Dirk. Your best shots. *Don't* hit the parrots. Everybody else, keep still."

She added her own pistols to the bang of guns.

The parrot swarm screamed and swirled away, around again into the heart of the island. Plunqwette, presumably, went with them.

Rather in a mess, the crew stood dabbing at their clothes.

Art gazed in at the Isle through Ebad's spyglass.

Something black lurked among the forest's green. She wasn't sure at first what it was. On the other hand, the top of the cliff had a faint blush of vegetation along its rim.

Looking back the other way, the hill still stood out, heavy with its trees. Separate from that, the beach ran back into the blue sea. The hill seemed like an extra to the island. (At anchor, on the sea's blue border, *Unwelcome* rested against a tea-brown ocean. Only two men had been left aboard. Salt Peter, who had drawn the shortest straw, and—tied by a long, tough cord to his bunk—Felix Phoenix, their unfriend.)

Black Knack said, "Well, Captain. Where do we start to dig for the treasure?"

"Not here," said Art. "I'll tell you my idea, gentlemen. This part of the Isle, down here, it gets regularly swallowed by the ocean. Oh, maybe not every day, but every so often. You see that blackened place inland among the trees? That's still getting over being smothered in subsea brine—it's been *pickled*. The rest has already recovered."

"She's got it," breathed Eerie. "That's why they say it *sinks*. It never does, just this beach and these trees, and the inland forest area—high tides come in, and they *drown*. Everything underwater dies. Then the sea goes again, and everything's left black, pickled, like she says—"

"Until gradually it heals over and the leaves and fruit and flowers come back," finished Whuskery. "Till the next high tide and drowning."

"The map is burned off along the bottom," Art said. "Maybe that isn't an accident. I think the burn is deliberate. It shows how the sea covers the Isle—and shows the only piece of the island always left above water—which is the *cliff*." She pointed. "There's vegetation up there. That's where those parrots go, when the rest is under the sea. On the other hand, sailing past, you might not see anything much up there, that is, nothing to make you think it was worth going to investigate."

"How'd we know when the sea's going to come in again?" asked Whuskery uneasily.

"We don't. The tides are strange here. I do know this. No one who grasps that fact would bury treasure anywhere down here—nor on that hill, either."

"Then where—"

"Top of the cliff, gentlemen. Where else?"

"But Cap'n—it's sheer rock—who could scale it, even with rope?"

"Let's see if we can find out."

"Peter!"

Salt Peter, fretful on the deck, heard Felix calling down in the tween deck.

Peter went below and looked into the gloomy, bunk-shelved room.

"What?"

"Untie me, if you'd be so kind."

"Not I."

"Peter, I'm not dangerous. I can't fight and I can't swim. I'll give my word of honor to do nothing at all. But I'm stifling in here."

"No," said Peter. "Really sorry. No I'm not, you swine. Anyway, she'd skin me."

"Who? Art? But Art doesn't kill. That's her boast."

Peter said nothing. He went back up the ladder and slammed the hatch.

Felix sighed, and resumed his slow destruction of the cord that bound him, with the small file he had found on deck the previous day.

The way through the island forest, a distance of about half a mile, turned out, to begin with, very exciting.

"Look! Look! *Jewels!*"

Everyone peered past orchids at the fern-fronded ground. "It's flowers."

"No, you twit. Lookit—a sapphire big as my eye!"

It was.

Art, conscious by now she couldn't tell real from fake, said cautiously, "Is it glass?"

"Never. Genuine as daylight."

They kept the sapphire, at first. By pirate law, all loot was common property to be divided almost equally—two shares to the captain, one share each to all crew members.

But then they found six gleaming beryls, then seven red garnets. After that, in one of the still unhealed, sea-scorched corridors, they noticed silver coins in handfuls, and bits of gold, greenish from water, caught in bare tree roots with the fish bones and shells of ancient sea things.

"There's a fortune lying about."

"What colossal *other* wealth did they leave here," whispered Eerie, "that they could abandon trinkets the like of these?"

"Whatever else they left, these are offerings to Fate," said Ebad. "Let them go, mates. It'd be unlucky. Even the sea's not taken them."

Sullenly, they threw the treasures down again, back among the mud and shells. Very superstitious, actors and pirates both.

As they came out of the trees empty-handed, the sun struck them like a blow.

The cliff reared up, sinewy, yet surface-smooth.

"Unclimbable."

"There must be a way," said Art.

"Ten miles up, that's what that parrot said. It *looks* it. Even with a rope—not a handhold, barely a crack."

Art took out the map. Crouching, she spread it on the ground. Everyone else crouched, too, and stared at it.

Then they all sat. The sun beat on them and on the map with the burned edge. . . . And on the impossible cliff. And on the unreadable code of letters—all the O's and T's, H's and R's and Y's . . .

"Great thundering earwigs—those birds are coming back—"

Appalled, they all glared skyward.

Like a wing-clapping, multi-tinted, jabbering cloud, parrots fell toward them from the sun.

As they came, they filled the air not only with fluff and other stuff, but with *language*.

Each parrot was now shrieking out words—incomprehensible, insane words—in English, but also—Art heard French and Spanish, Latin even from the ancient world—and other tongues she had never heard in her life, let alone been taught by Molly.

Her crew were also registering the variety.

"Greek?"

"Africay—I know that dialect—"

"Mandarin Chinese. Can't speak it, heard it spoken."

"Hindi from the Inde."

The parrots had landed.

Now they stayed put, didn't fly round and round. There seemed to be much more than two hundred of them. They all stood there on their short, tough feathered legs, wings held in, tight, or stretched stiffly sideways, heads nodding with the vigor of their shouts. Pearl-button eyes blinked. Beaks clicked, black parrot tongues darted.

Out came slices and sections of the most bewilder-making, mad phrases—

"Bird of bone!" "Through eight and eight more!" "Hit me right!" "Sixteen paces—" "Twenty-one paces—" "Upright or fallen!" "Raise the lid!" "Through the nineteen!" "See how pale I am!" (This last from a parrot colored a violent purple, black, and turquoise.)

And how could you make head or tail of it? The babble of crazy screeching voices—some sounding very human, some sounding only very parrotish.

Then through the tumult broke the trumpet squawk of Plunqwette herself, no longer sounding a bit like Molly. "Ten miles up! Ten miles up!"

In despair, the treasure-seeking pirates, who had only ever found treasure chests on a stage, looked at one another. If this was any sort of clue or code, how could they ever break it? Whoever had trained these birds had taught only pieces of the whole to each and every one.

Hundreds of pieces, like a scattered, half-seen jigsaw or a smashed plate no one could ever hope to mend.

When Felix came up on deck, Salt Peter, the only one of the crew left on guard, was staring jealously at the Isle. He had attention for nothing else.

Felix walked up behind him and quietly, reluctantly, put the pistol—one of many still in the stores—to Peter's neck.

Peter leaped in the air.

"I'm sorry. But help me lower a boat."

"Captain said—"

"I'm going ashore."

They looked at each other mournfully.

"Why do you want to go ashore? More notes for your evidence against us? To get us nicely hanged?"

"Perhaps. And I intend to see this treasure they're after—if it exists."

"*You* want a share? No way, you scurvy rat."

Felix lifted the pistol. "I want to learn if this dream-nightmare we're all in is actually real. Now. Boat." He thought, I've learned the proper method to threaten, heaven help me. Look, it works.

Peter had quailed. "If you go over, then I'm coming, too."

"Then you can row us, Mr. Salt. I've had enough rowing to last a lifetime."

"What makes you think you'll *have* a lifetime, when Art sees you?"

Rowing away. The *Unwelcome Stranger* left standing on a glimmering tail of reflection behind them, just there, where blue water met amber. Not another isle, not another sail in sight. Sea empty. Just the island ahead, and more parrots zinging over the wooded hill, their sunlit wings flashing like rubies and emeralds, sapphires and topazes, diamonds and gold—the hottest treasure in the world: beauty.

Parrot Fashion

You must fathom this code, Art Blastside. If you're Piratica now, Art thought fiercely, *do* it. Molly would have. Would she? *Could* she? (I think back to those six years at the Angels Academy. I've forgotten everything about them. It's *that* part of my memory that's missing now. And Molly is clear as if I saw her yesterday. So what is real?)

Art thought of Felix, tied in the boiling underdeck.

Don't think of Felix. Felix *isn't* real.

She sat and looked at him in her mind, then pushed the sight away, and stared again at the aching bore of the map and the code she couldn't solve.

Most of the others had retreated back to the shade of the forest's edge. They were eating the fruit, which were kinds of mangoline or peach—but apparently salty. Muck lay exhausted (like all of them) by parrots, panting under a tall liana-webbed palm.

The birds still walked around, between the cliff and the trees, mostly quiet now, but sometimes babbling in bursts. Others flew about far off, not approaching, uninterested.

The Honest Liar was coming over, his round face serious. He held out to Art a peach, with the leaves still on.

"Thanks, Honest. I'm not sure anyone should eat these."

"They're all right to eat."

"How do you know?"

"I know."

"You always seem—" She hesitated. "You seem to know things the rest of us don't."

Honest lowered his eyes, now going red as his head handkerchief. "I've never been taught. Leaves me more room."

Art considered this. She bit into the fruit. It was salt, but eatable—more like a huge juicy olive than a peach. She said, "Honest, maybe *you* should have a proper look at this map."

He came and kneeled down by her, and stared at the map.

"These letters written along the side, there," said Art. "We've got those. And all these parrots. But—" She thought of Felix. Refused to think of him. Returned to the moment and saw Honest staring on, his face round and blank as a cloudy moon.

Art lay back on the ground between unscalable cliff and shady forest. She shut her eyes.

"'Tis numbers of letters, Captain Art."

". . . What?"

"On the map. These O's and T's and the rest—they're letters of the alphabet. And the alphabet has twenty-six letters. A is number 1, B is 2, C is 3—Z is number 26. I forget all the letters between—"

"Honest!" Art sat upright.

"So the numbers the parrots are saying are the numbers of these letters. Seemingly the numbers of paces, that is. If you match the numbers the parrots say in the same order as the letter-numbers on the map— 'Tis then you'll get the paces right, and the other clues that go with them in the right order, too."

"My God. Honest—I think—you've solved it—"

Art pulled a stub of pencil from her pocket. It would barely write through the wax. She sharpened it with a knife, licked it. She wrote by the side of each of the letters on the map its number in the alphabet:

O-15, O-15, P-16. T-20, T-20, U-21. F-6,
A-1, B-2. M-13, M-13, N-14. R-18, R-18,
S-19. A-1, F-6, C-3. H-8, H-8, I-9. Y-25,
Y-25, Z-26. F-6, A-1, D-4.

She read them out.

Like a whirlwind, most of the hundreds of parrots opened their wings and rushed up into the sky and away. Only twelve parrots were left, standing there around her. Their beaked faces—did she only imagine the look of strained patience on them?

"They were waiting—for that signal. The others—they were the ones who had been taught all this in different languages— the French and Spanish versions, the Chinese and Arabic— except, where the alphabet *itself* is different—as it would be in

Chinese or Arabic—*their* clues must be different, too—" Art gazed at the twelve remaining parrots. Plunqwette, she now noticed, was among them.

Parrots could live a hundred years or more. Was that when the hundreds—thousands?—of versions of the code had first been taught to them?

But how to make them speak one at a time, and how to line them up.

"Wait," Art said. "*Plunqwette's* the first. She must be. *Beach by Cobhouse*, she says that. I think that means, without the beach and the forest above water, there's no method of approaching the correct part of the cliff and finding the way up. Even if you were in a boat—you couldn't find it—that way would be under-water. But then, what does she say—ten miles up—10—that would be J. But J isn't one of the letters on the map. Let's try something with them." She stared at Plunqwette and said clearly, "Fifteen."

"Land ho!" cried Plunqwette. "Beach by Cobhouse. Ten miles up. Fifteen paces left."

Art frowned in thought. She said again, more clearly still, "*Fifteen.*"

A gray-and-black parrot stalked forward, wriggling its tangerine-lined wings. It said, "Fifteen paces more. Lift up your feet. Sixteen paces left."

"*Yes,*" said Art in a long, dry hiss. She checked the map. OO and P-15, 15 and 16 taken care of. Next the double T and U. To the parrots, Art announced, "Twenty."

A scarlet parrot with a beak like iron bounded in the air, yelling, "Enter rock. Twenty paces in and twenty more."

One by one, Art interviewed the parrots, cueing them like nervous actors not yet sure of their lines. To each letter-number, if spoken in the same order as on the map, a different parrot replied. Where more than one had the same letter, and so number, they spoke in a definite order that stayed the same—as with Plunqwette and the gray-and-black parrot, who both had 15. Some had only one number and a set of other clues. Some had two or three numbers all to themselves.

"What's our Art doing?" said Walter by the trees. "Ah, how sweet. She and Honest are chatting to the birds."

When Art came running at them like a brown-maned electric storm, Honest trotting behind her, twelve parrots whizzing round her head, her crew were slightly alarmed.

"Pon the Drum, Cap'n, steady as she blows—"

"Take it easy, Cap'n, know what I mean—"

"Stow it. Listen." Art cued her chorus.

Each parrot spoke.

Altogether this was what all twelve of them had to say:

"1) Beach by Cobhouse. Ten miles up. Fifteen paces left. 2) Fifteen paces more. Lift up your feet. Sixteen paces left. 3) Enter the rock. Twenty paces in and twenty more. 4) See how pale I am. Hit me right, which is to say left, twenty-one blows. 5) Pass through me. Six paces forward. One pace left. Two steps to the lamp. 6) Climb till climb is done. Thirteen paces right and thirteen more. Raise the lid. 7) Free of the dark. Fourteen paces forward to the bird of bone. 8) Eighteen paces right and eighteen more. Through the nineteen, whether upright or fallen. 9) One pace forward. Six paces right. Three paces forward. 10) Through eight and eight more, whether upright or fallen. Nine steps down. 11) Twenty-five paces left. Twenty-five paces forward. Count twenty-six on the ground. 12) Read by the sun. Six paces north. One pace west. Four feet will take you to me."

"That ties in exactly with the way the letters are written on the map," Art told her gaping men. "Honest figured it out. Congratulations, Mr. Honest." A confused cheer rose from the confused crew. "Now all we need do is find where the pacing *starts*. And understand these tricky clues."

Ebad had risen. They all had. Everyone was on his feet, panting like Muck, or as if they had run for miles.

Ebad said, "Something will be marked or written on the cliffside, Art—something from that first clue of Plunqwette's. Not the *Beach*, we've got that now. It's the *Ten miles up*, that's the start sign."

"Nothing here goes ten miles up," grumbled Black Knack. But he had dragged off the eye patch. Both eyes shone like dirty but polished knives.

Dirk said, as Art had, "Ten is a number—letter J—"

"J's not on the map. I think it means something else."

Eerie said, "We will go, my boys, with our peerless Captain, our pure silver Piratica, and we will *look* like hawks over every inch of that blasted rock, till we find the place to start."

Muck, heaving an intolerant sigh, got up and followed his leaping comrades to the cliff.

The sun was going over. The cliff threw down a little hem of shadow.

The twelve parrots accompanied the treasure seekers, ready to speak their helpful (or unhelpful) clues again.

"Who trained these birds? They're better than Clora Snutch's chickens."

"About a thousand persons, at a guess. And in about a thousand languages. Nor will every set of clues be like ours."

"True, for the alphabet of the Inde isn't like our own. Nor the Greek."

They searched, peering and scratching along the flank of rock.

It was Walter who found it.

"Thought he stepped on a snake from the yowl he gave."

In the stone, something had been cut, just above their heads. This: *Here be Yacoby Tennmile's Up. What that he maketh for his Capn and ship-meets, this Year of God's Grace 16↓2.*

"It's a *name*—Tennmile—"

"Sixteen-twelvety. A hundred years ago—maybe to the day."

"What is an *Up*?"

Eerie turned on Black Knack with the scorn of a poet confronting a factualist. "A stair, unthoughtful man. *Up*. It goeth *up*, d'ye see, by the Monkey's Precious Whiskers?"

"Where is it then?"

Art said crisply, "Inside, Blacky. *Inside* the cliff. Let's start the paces and find the way *in*."

Now the parrots, in response to each correct number, cued *them*.

Fifteen paces left they went, from the carved message on the cliff. Then fifteen more.

"Lift up your feet!"

A shallow ledge was there. They got onto it and teetered along, counting the next sixteen paces left.

"Enter the rock . . ."

"*Enter the rock—where?* There's not entry *here*—"

Art, first in the moving line, showed them a wound creeper, and through it, a slender parting in the cliff.

"Not *there*. It's much too small. Only a cat could get in there—and probably not out again."

"I can get in, sirs. Let's see what I find." Art tore down the creeper and slid into the rock like sword into sheath.

It was dark enough inside, close-sandwiched between the outer barrier and the inner wall. But scraping bruisingly through and along, Art found how the space suddenly widened. She could move after that with complete ease. She called back.

One by one the crew forced themselves, swearing and yelling as the rock tore their flesh, garments, hair, and Dirk's nails, into the inner space. Only Whuskery and Eerie were a moment stuck. The others pushed or pulled them through. Cuthbert, who looked too brawny to fit, in fact seemed somehow to fold himself down—like a shut umbrella—and went through nearly as well as Art.

The parrots swiveled in like cautious, accurate fish around a reef.

"Twenty paces is where it widens. Now twenty more."

They counted them.

"Twenty-one!" Art cued the parrots.

Blue-and-purple called back, "See how pale I am!"

"Yes, look, the stone of the cliff shows paler here—almost luminous."

"Hit me right, which is to say left, twenty-one blows."

"Riddles, Art. Worse than the weekly acrostic in the *Tymes*."

Art said, cool as ice cream, "*No*. It means to *get* it right, you hit the left side. Twenty-one times. We'll use the hilts of weapons. You will strike two blows each. And I, as captain, five. Begin Mr. Vooms, Mr. O'Shea."

They struck the pallid piece of cliff. They saw now it was pitted—dented by the blows of other treasure seekers? It gave off a hollow boom at each thump.

At Art's fifth blow, the twenty-first, Yacoby Tennmile's clever trick door in the cliffside, yawned grindingly open.

There they stood—paralyzed by success.

"It's pitch-*black* in there."

"*You're* all right, Dirk. But don't *you* go in, Ebad," quipped Black Knack. "We'll lose you."

Even in the confined area, Dirk turned and slapped Black Knack across the face.

Art barked over their voices.

"Shut thy row. Are you off your heads? This place may conceal some tricks—we are dealing with the map and plan of *pirates*. Beware. No more fights. No more of your idiocies, Black Knack. First, block this door open—some of the spades will do. And when we enter this cavern, you'll keep your wits about you." There was quiet. In it, Art spoke to the waiting parrots: "Six!"

The parrot voice came at once. "Pass through me. Six paces forward. One pace left. Two steps to the lamp."

Moving now with worried care, there was still a collision

and some stumbling in the total dark. Ebad struck flint and tinder. Through the wavering on and off of light, Whuskery tripped on the two low steps. Muck yipped as Dirk stood on his paw.

Then they had the lamp. A sealed flask of oil was by it, the oil still good. Filling the lamp, they struck a firmer light and ignited the wick.

They were in a broad black chimney. Down from its roof stabbed fangs of rock or solidified water. Veins like dull gold glinted in walls. A stone stair rose in front of them. Up—and up—and *up*.

"Ten miles high, so it is indeed," said Eerie.

But they climbed it. And at the top, forty full minutes later, puffing and groaning, took thirteen paces right and thirteen more, till Ebad, their tallest, reached up and pushed off the hatch of shrieking, corroded metal. Beyond showed daylight. They had gained the cliff top. Out flew the parrots and paraded along the edge of the hatch, as one by one the flightless humans swung and hauled one another also up and out.

All along the cliff top, which seemed to cover at least another mile, ran tall thick grasses. Low trees, not visible from beneath the cliff, spread here and there and crowded toward the center. Vines and orchids draped them.

The rest of the parrots had vacated this area for the time being. Only the twelve parrots armed with the clues of the English alphabet flitted back and forth.

A stream bubbled out of the cliff. They drank from it gratefully, and the water was sweet, but with a faint bitter aftertaste.

"Fourteen paces forward to the bird of bone."

"What's that? A bone bird—it'll be too small to see."

It wasn't too small.

As they traipsed through the tough high grass the correct amount of steps, Dirk let out a cry that sent all twelve parrots shooting upward. Rather than desert, however, they descended on a single, oddly spreading palm.

Below the palm—

"That's never a bird."

"Yes. D'ye see the beak of it?"

"'Tis a monster, the fabled Roc of the Arabic Nights."

"I've heard of such a creature," murmured Ebad. "Prehistorical. Ten feet high."

"It's like a parrot—a huge great parrot—"

The bird had fossilized, there beneath the tree. It was sallow, the skeleton ridged and strong with creepers. Another little date palm was springing between its claws. One wing had fallen away. The other spread like a strung harp. Its beak was like two hooked ivory hammers, one curved over the other.

The fourteen paces ended exactly in front of it. Dirk and Walter stepped aside. But Glad Cuthbert seemed delighted. "Just think what the ol' missus'd say if I brought home a live one of these in a cage—never hear the end of it."

"Eighteen paces right, and eighteen more. Through the nineteen, whether upright or fallen."

"*Stones,*" said Art.

"They? I thought them trees."

"'Tis the creepers. They're upright stones—or fallen stones. We'll count them."

There were nineteen stones, seven were leaning low and had become fossilized in looks as the giant parrot. Plus two were down, barely to be noted in the grass and red fever flowers. Through they went.

"One pace forward. Six paces right. Three paces forward."

"More stones."

"Count. There should be eight, and then eight more—"

"No. That's sixteen. These are only fifteen."

Eerie pointed down at the ground. "There." It was a single

stone, all broken in the roots of a three-foot flame tree, long fallen, smothered. "Sixteen—eight and eight."

"But now it's nine steps—there *aren't* any."

"Yes, right by your feet, covered in creepers. Hack them free."

The nine steps were freed. They went down them.

The eleventh parrot directed: "Twenty-five paces left. Twenty-five paces forward. Count twenty-six on the ground."

"What's *that* mean? *On* the ground? Aren't all the paces counted that way?"

"Twenty-five and twenty-five first," said Art.

She took the paces. The others fell back, watching her, quite drained by anticipation and stairs.

Art, though, soon found if she could go twenty-five paces left, taking the next twenty-five forward was not so likely.

The ground had given way there. Crumbles of stone and soil, parched uprooted plants, blocked off both the way and any exact assessment.

She stared forward, over the subsidence.

Count twenty-five forward, then twenty-six on the ground. Twenty-six what? Paces? Inches? Yards—

The eleventh parrot flapped right past her, across the jumble of stones, and landed in the grass. Another stream was there, overhung by reeds.

Art jumped the gap the parrot had flown. Her feet back on the ground, she looked about her. Had she covered the proper twenty-five paces?

Yes! For there, half hidden in grass, a heap of short gray poles lay stretched. They were antique oars, maybe a hundred years of age. She walked around them and counted them, and there were twenty-six, *on the ground*.

Then the others came rushing, flying over the fallen place, landing on grass, on the oars, in the stream. Whooping. Muck yapping.

"One more—only one more clue—"

"It's a group of three more clues, Mr. Whuskery, from parrot number twelve."

This, though—the last—was the bit they had all somehow instantly memorized.

They chanted, along with the twelfth parrot, "Read by the sun. Six paces north. One pace west. Four feet will take you to me."

It was simple to judge the northwest reading from the sun, now about an hour down from the noon height of the sky.

They did it, and a cool breeze blew along the cliff top, rustling the grass heads like silk tassels on a curtain.

Four feet will take you to me.

Elation lapsed. The last clue was after all the strangest. They were so tired now. They wanted the treasure.

"Four feet?"

"Do we go on all fours?"

"*That's* never four *feet,* you imbecile. It's two hands and two knees."

"What has four feet?"

"Lions, goats, horses—"

"*Dogs.*"

"Muck—here, old chum. Muck, here, laddy—"

"How can it be Muck?"

"He's got four feet. Look—*see.*"

Muck ran up and down the grass, snuffling and whuffling. Something there abruptly intrigued Muck, it seemed. Then he began to dig.

"*Go on, my boy!*"

"Best Muck—*Cleanest* Dog on Earth!"

"A *genius* among canines—"

"Thou shalt dine off a *gold* plate, Muck—"

Muck dug up his treasure. He was thrilled and vain about it. It was a nine-inch-long giant parrot bone.

Chuffed as a world conqueror, Muck bounded over the grasses—chased by comrades who now swore they would wring his neck.

"It's here," said Art. "Somewhere very close. *Here*. Keep still, or we'll lose our bearings."

They slumped at once down on the ground.

The breeze was cold against them now, cold though the day stayed hot. The bronzy eye of the sun leered on at them. The parrots walked about the grass, preening, snapping self-satisfied beaks.

Art stood up slowly.

"And here," said Art, "is precisely where we dig. Spades forward, if you please."

"But that's still only where the last ol' paces stopped, Captain."

"Think, Mr. Cuthbert."

"I'm thinking, Cap'n. Not much happens. Story of me life."

"Anyone? No? Four feet," said Art. She hefted her own spade and struck it into the earth. The turf was hard and impacted, but had no feel of rocks. "Not four feet to run on, gentlemen. It means *dig four feet down*. A shallow burial. Pitch in."

They only rang on something ungiving, the spades, when they struck the top of a great square box.

Sunlight rayed sidelong over the chest. It was of grayed blackwood, uncarved, but with faded brass fitments and a large brass plaque, like a page of metal, nailed in on the lid.

They read what was written there, chiseled into that brazen page:

"We are the Pirate Kind. We live by blood and murder.

"We end our days on a rope, or under the pitiless acres of the Sea. After which, we are told, we must suffer forever in the Kingdom of Hell, for our Sins.

"Our kind then, though often we grow rich, seldom leave Heirs to inherit our Wealth or keep Our Secrets.

"For this Reason, One Hundred of our Great Number have made a Pact, and, under Pirate Truce, brought and laid down, each man, an Example of his Vastest Gains. Here these Treasures lie, together, in one place. It is our last—for some, their only—Good Deed. May it, in the Balance of Heaven, be weighed against Our Sins.

"To the End that the Treasure may be found, we have left about the World some very few Maps and Clues. But they are not easy come by. Besides, there will, no doubt, be copies made, and these not to be trusted, all filled by Mistakes. Yet, You have chanced upon a True Map and Clue, or else, now, You would not stand Here.

"Therefore, because of Your Wit—and Luck—you, who unearth This Box, we make, unreservedly, Our Heir.

"Take up the Spoils. Drink deep of the Golden Cup. Prosper."

The men of *Unwelcome* stood, dumbfounded, before the box. Before the unthinkable, unknown treasure—the blessing of those hundred who had left in it their "Vastest Gains."

No one could move.

Then Ebad strode forward. He set his strong hands on the box. He wrenched—damp kinked hinges squealed.

"For Molly Faith," Ebad said, too low for any but the dead to hear, "Queen of Women. My only love."

And flung back the lid.

In a horror deeper than a pit, those people there—actors, pirates, human beings—gawped down into the insides of the treasure chest, as if turned to stone.

Till Walter wailed what each of them was otherwise silently—surely—wailing. "'Tis full of old paper! *Paper!* Nothing else."

Tidings —

Zebra-striped grass shadows lay over the folded or rolled papers in the chest.

The sun had got a little lower. Was it an *hour* they had stood here—shattered and unmoving?

Then they began to turn away.

"Oh, it's always like this—life—everything you try—"

"Fortune poos on us."

"Well, I wish I'd never bothered to come."

"I rage at heaven! I bellow at Fate! Really. I mean it."

"Wait." Art's voice, now, had little effect.

Black Knack was beating his fist on a rock. Cuthbert held a conversation with his not-present wife.

Even Ebad had stridden off.

Art ignored her theatrically complaining men. She walked over to the box, knelt down, and pulled out a handful of the papers.

Crumpled and dulled, a little mildewy at their edges—not much, for they too had been waxed—she turned them up, free of shadow, to catch the sun.

The crew left her there.

"She's gone nutty again."

"Mad as a Shakespurian heroine. Knew 'twould happen."

"Well, it's enough to make anyone mad, this."

Even so, when Art shouted in the stage-trained war-voice she kept, normally, for ordering her ship, they stopped, turned, and looked at her.

"Gentlemen, you give up too soon. True, there is no obvious treasure piled in this chest. No gold coins, chains of brilliants, chunks of amethyst and emerald."

"Too right, dearie."

"What's here, however, are some hundred odd maps. That's what the old papers are, gentlemen. Maps. *Treasure* maps.

Showing incredible, and never before revealed treasure hoards, buried in almost every country on earth, to the world's four corners—and beyond."

They came running.

They cast themselves down, plucking out maps, jumping up again, prancing on the grass, Muck pouncing round them, with the giant bone still clamped in his jaws.

Plunqwette flew up to Art's shoulder.

"Hi, Plunqwette. Thou are a clever old bird, thou are."

"Pretty Polly," said Plunqwette.

The other eleven parrots had vanished. Perhaps frightened off by the yodels and mad laughter of the crew.

"It says here—a million freshwater pearls and seven sets of gold plate once belonging to Spanish royalty—"

"It says *here*, the entire fortune of three rajas of the Inde."

"And here, in Africay—cut diamonds to the value of two million English guineas!"

"Some of the maps are in foreign languages."

"We'll get them translated!"

Now the wind blew cold along the cliff top. It had a cold, bad voice, but no one heard it or heeded.

Art, standing with Plunqwette, saw the late arrivals first.

They came pushing through the grasses, seeking the place not by means of clues, not needing that now, guided there with no trouble by the noise.

"Mr. Peter Salt. And Mr. Felix Phoenix. Shouldn't you both be on the ship? Indeed, Mr. Phoenix, shouldn't you be tied up belowdecks?"

They stood looking at her, looking at the over-the-moon pirates. Peter grinned—nervously.

Felix said, face like ice, "It was simple to find the way. The cliffside seemed to have been mauled by an angry wildebeest—a creeper handily torn off to reveal the entrance—and the cliff door standing open inside, held so by four spades. Even a lamp left kindly burning at the head of the long stair, to assist our climb."

"You didn't even put the lid thing back over the way out," said Peter.

Art said, "Well, you're here. Peter, you're a fool. Mr. Phoenix, I see *you* are a villain after all." She called to Ebad, who came over to her at once. She observed he didn't seem as exhilarated as the others. "As we note, Mr. Vooms, our ship now stands unattended on the uncertain sea. Get the men together. We must go down."

The chest was heavy. It took four of them to heft it—Ebad, Black Knack, Whuskery, and Cuthbert.

Felix's hands had been tied—Black Knack's suggestion, which Art agreed to.

With Art at their head, they began to move back across the cliff top. It wasn't such hard going, only at the subsided area was there some scrambling. Weariness was settling on them, however. Victory had, for now, taken the last of their energy.

Besides, it was growing bitterly cold, the wind aggressive, blowing in long bursts. Above, the clear sky had turned milky gray. Parrots, though, were coming back to the cliff in droves, either that or flying in windblown spirals overhead. Their strung-out shrieks pierced the wind-woolly air.

They had reached the group of nineteen stones, when suddenly the light entirely changed.

The sky above—went *green*.

"Storm coming up," decided Cuthbert.

Muck let out a wavering howl (still taking care not to drop his bone).

"How much farther? This trip was quicker coming across than it is going back," grumbled Walter.

"What is that?"

It was Peter, the truant off the ship, who pointed away over the sick-lit landscape.

"A tree."

"Nay, 'tisn't."

"Unless," added Whuskery anxiously, "trees walk."

Something certainly was there. It seemed to have come from a stand of low palms ahead of them. It was neither tall nor large, very dark, and shapeless—robed, maybe, or wrapped in a sort of *sheet*—behind it in the wind blew a black gauze—perhaps a veil. One pale something was outstretched before it.

"Is it an animal? One of those lemura beasts?"

"Does it live up here? Did it climb the cliff—"

"All stop," said Art. She halted.

Everyone else did the same.

They watched the veiled black-draped shape, which with one white hand and arm outflung, as if to claw, glided on through the stormy grass toward them.

It was Walter who gave a little cry. But the rest of them, even Art, by now could see exactly what the approaching *thing* was.

It took Eerie to say it.

"God save us. It's the figurehead off the ship."

Art answered briskly, "I doubt it, Mr. O'Shea."

"She followed us afore—"

"She swam after us when the Coffee Ship went down. We draped her in black and veiled her face—look, with her sinister hand held out to *grip*—"

In that moment, a huge rumble came from somewhere—either sky—or *sea*—or both. And as if that got it properly moving, the figurehead of the *Unwelcome Stranger* broke into a springy run, straight at them—while at its back, from the trees, other figures—other forms—dark—bright—burst into motion.

"Pistols," Art rapped. "Fire wide and at the ground in front of them!"

"Too late, Cap'n—they've got us—"

"Covered."

Art and Co. became stock-still. Before them, the nearing glitter of unfriendly drawn guns and cutlasses. And foremost of all, their own figurehead.

Which, in one able sweep as it leaped to join them, threw off its veilings and laughed with perfect pearly teeth.

"Surprise!" cried Little Goldie Girl.

"Yeah, merry meetings," elaborated twenty-three crewmen of the *Enemy*.

"We crept in so cleverly, but no one was even keeping watch on your ship, Captain Blastside. We've been following you since Mad-Agash. Dearest Hurkon, an old friend, let us know. But then, we already had more than some notion of which way you wended. By the Wheel, it's been so easy."

"Easy once you'd repaired your ship," said Art.

"Repaired? Oh, that. 'Tis nought, innit. It takes more than your poor unbaked cannon to harm a vessel such as *Enemy*. Hurkon, as you know," added Goldie, "guessed the rough direction of this Isle. The secret of it has always been, providing you believe in it to begin with, less its location than how to crack the map's naughty code. But I think also Hurkon's afraid of this place. Well, he's too old. However, he did say *That girl of Molly's—she has the luck of seventeen devils. It shines off her*. He said you would do it—if you came to the Isle, then it would be above water, and you would solve its riddles." She looked at Art, smiling lovingly. "My remarkable da, he was so keen to have your map—long ago. He knew it was one of the true ones. I'm sure he's singing in his sea grave now. But I wonder if even *he*, the wonderful Golden Goliath, would have had the genius to let *you* do *all* the work for him, as I have. Hurkon expects half shares, of course. Well. Maybe I'll go all forgetful about that."

Art watched Goldie. Goldie was just out of reach. She prowled up and down, tossing her lovely hair, which even the wind had only combed into more flowing curls.

"Perhaps I should reward you, Art, by telling you who your Mister Traitor was—I mean, aside from Hurkon Beare, who anyway has always been on my side. I must say, Mr. Traitor has been quite clever, too. First he sent me a messenger pigeon. Then swam ashore at Own Accord and sent me a messenger *chicken.* Only one stupid move. That was when he tried to sink you all at Port's Mouth. But luckily you survived. I can tell him, it isn't as simple as he seems to have thought, fishing a map back off someone who is drowned. Much better to let you bring the map to me yourself—or, as it turns out, let you keep the map, solve it, and dig up the treasure for me. But then, he's just a traitor. A lesser form of life, eh?"

Art's crew were turning to one another, writhing with added horror and rage. Only Eerie, Ebad, and Art—and, of course, the man himself—had known about a traitor in their midst.

In the squall of wind, under the pea-green sky, now every face of her own men was like that of a ghost beneath the sea.

"Well, Little Goldie," said Art, "tell us, pray, who betrayed us."

"He shall tell you himself. Step forward, sir," said Goldie. "You're with *us* now."

No one moved.

"I see," said Goldie. "A coward. Well, that, too, a traitor always is. Come out, Mr. Knack. *Enemy*'s pistols will cover your escape."

Black Knack broke from the circle round the chest. He bolted straight over to the ranks of the *Enemy* and stood there, grinning, both his unpatched eyes alight with triumph—and fear.

Art's men made an uproar. It didn't matter. At least they were all one again. Had she suspected Black Knack? Perhaps. She had half suspected all of them—except for Ebad and Eerie . . . and she should have tried to find the traitor, yes, even though, by then, she had thought he could do little to harm them—

Art held up her hand to silence both her men and her thoughts. Silence came.

"Very well," she said. "He holed the Coffee Ship. He sent you pigeons—and *chickens*—with messages. Also you say he swam ashore at Own Accord. So Black Knack could swim after all."

Goldie patted Black Knack's shoulder. "Do go on," she said encouragingly.

Black Knack spoke up. "Of course I can swim. I'm not deranged, going out on a ship—you wouldn't have caught me doing that without knowing how to keep afloat. I made out I couldn't at Port's Mouth, when I sank that boat. I acted well—I'm an *actor*, aren't I? The other time, off Own Accord? I'd heard you, Arty, and your so-called officers. All that chat about your brilliant double-cross. Safe in your Captain's Cabin—you forget how easy it is just to find something to do quite near—and hear every word. So before we set sail, while the crowd of you were playing sailors in the bay, I slipped off back to the waterfront. Nice warm water, that time. Didn't take long. I'm a strong swimmer. And, after, plenty of dry clothes to change into. None of you knew."

"A round of applause for cunning Mr. Knack," said Goldie.

Unwelcome's crew made not a sound. The crew of *Enemy* jeeringly crowed. Black Knack looked most uncertain.

Goldie said, "So there you have it, Art. Those you trusted

have sold you to me. And I've sat comfortably and let you find the treasure for me. How dismaying for you, madam." The pale green eyes glowed, then shifted elsewhere. Goldie looked at Felix Phoenix. She made a sympathetic face at his tied hands. Then smiled divinely at him. *Fear nothing,* the smile said to Felix, *soon you'll be mine.*

The wind stamped. Plunqwette, with a loud clap of wings, flew in among the other men by the chest—Muck was already sheltering there.

"Stormy weather," said Goldie. "Best settle up, and get going."

There was a pistol in her hand. It was of chestnut-colored wood, fitted with brass—an artistic object. It pointed at Art.

Art stood expressionless, her eyes meeting Goldie's. Art judged Goldie's eyes—and saw the pistol was not really for *her.* And in that instant, Goldie swiveled and raised the gun to Black Knack's heart.

"Even when they're useful, I don't like betrayers, Mr. Knacky."

Black Knack shrank away. "Your own father took me on, Little Goldie—all those years back—said if I could get him the map he'd reward me well. I've *done* what you both wanted. He— you—promised me my share."

"*Here's* your share."

Black Knack turned, from Goldie and from her gun. He ran away, the following wind buffeting and thrusting, adding to his speed as if he, too, were a ship—

He pelted back across the cliff—heading plainly toward the hatch that led downward through the rock.

Then Goldie fired.

Fire flash. The silliest sound—like a huge twig snapping. Black Knack seemed to jump—that was all—to jump forward— forward—

The jump took him right past the hatch that led down to Tennmile's stair—it *threw* him instead to the lip of the cliff. And over.

Black Knack was gone.

Goldie wiped the nozzle of her gun as if it had sneezed, smiling also tenderly at it.

"She killed him," said Whuskery. He began to cry.

Dirk said, "Hush, darling."

Peter said, "I saw Black Knack act *Hamlet* once. He was the best."

Cuthbert said, "Shot in the bloody back."

"He was a poor thing, but still a man," said Eerie.

"Is he dead?" whispered Walter.

"Farewell," said Honest.

"Art," said Ebad, "Don't—"

As she sprang, Art saw Mr. Beast rearing, cutlass and pistol in the way, and landed a fist of ringed knuckles at the base of his nose. He dropped.

Art's sword lifted Goldie's gun into the air. It flew up like Black Knack and arced into the grass.

"Draw," said Art, "you slatter shad."

Her face was white, her gray eyes inky. Goldie stared at this and backed a step, almost as Black Knack had done. "Why— Miss *Blastside*—"

"*Draw*, lady. Sword out and meet me. It's time you learned how to fight."

Goldie shot a look at her crew. Only the Beast had attempted to intervene, and he had failed. Now Art was too close—they couldn't risk a shot, for Goldie might be included in it. Instead, *Enemy*'s men just stood there, their own eyes gleaming like those of hyenas.

"Give me room then," said Goldie. She flipped back her coat's edge. Instead of the cutlass, one of those little knives came zipping out, straight for Art's throat. Art dodged, batting the knife away as she did so, with the blade of her sword. Deflected, it too dropped in the grass.

"Oh, dear, by the Wheel's Whim, I see I shall have to kill you by the long way," said Goldie regretfully.

And the cutlass was out, catching the ill light along its curve.

Both crews pressed back (Art's dragging the treasure chest), leaving an area for the fight. Soon this area would widen, as the fighters ranged over it.

No man spoke now. They left the concentration of battle to the women.

Goldie seemed more fly, better prepared for Art's skill.

Felix, standing among *Unwelcome*'s crew, his hands locked behind his back, watched with a feeling of lead in his guts. Goldie was a swordswoman, too, so much was evident. And besides, she had killed—killed with as little hesitant remorse as when shooting Black Knack. But would Art now break her vow—her mother's vow—was Art now ready to kill?

For Art there wasn't a thought in her brain. There had been horror and disgust and freezing anger—but she had sent them packing. It was only an actor's trick. Throw away yourself, and let the part—the *other*—in. But the other, of course, is also *you*.

Art didn't fight this time merely to disarm. No. She had another goal in mind.

Goldie's light cutlass played quite gracefully over and back, under and through—each time Art evaded its attack. Her own method had now very little elegance. She hacked forward with her blade, grass-cutting at Goldie, and Goldie sped each time out of range.

Five minutes had passed. Nothing to show for it, on either side.

But already the combatants were expanding their ground,

and the two groups of men, though keeping far apart from each other, made room.

Goldie fought with little occasional squeaks of spite—or frustration, as she missed her target. Now the squeak came out with a lilt to it. Art, closing in with scything motions of her sword, had finally come within Goldie's reach. The edge of the cutlass caught Art across her left shoulder. Scarlet budded out through the coat.

Art seemed unaware of the wound. Whether it was slight or bad was hard to tell.

But Goldie, pleased with herself, pressed forward, and now one of Art's swinging thrusts caught the dark-haired woman across the right arm—a grating gasp went up from the men on both sides—but plainly it was only the coat fabric that was torn. With a curse, Goldie ripped the whole sleeve off. She threw it in Art's face, but Art shook the green silk away and came in again. This time the flat of the hacking blade slammed against Goldie's waist.

Goldie staggered—juggled about—kept upright. But before she could recover, Art's sword turned over and whacked Goldie across her legs, just below both knees.

With a screech, Goldie went down. She was kneeling there on the grass, and instantly Art cut down at her.

It was a most vicious swipe. Walter and Peter and several others, seeing it, thought Art had cut off Goldie's head— certainly something fell away— It was a great cascade of long black curls.

Goldie scrambled up. She found another knife from somewhere in her clothes and threw it at Art's eyes. Art wasn't quite quick enough this time. The knife cut her thinly along the right cheekbone.

But Goldie, they now all saw, was bleeding at the temple where the hair had been sliced away.

Goldie threw herself back several feet. She stood there shriek-ing foul names at Art. Art, though, came straight on at her again, and Goldie ended the rudeness in order to defend herself.

Art isn't fighting to kill, Felix thought. He felt dizzy and sick—with revulsion? Fear?

The two blades slicked and slapped and grated with a ter-rible sound over each other.

Oddly, the wind had fallen, ended. Above, around, the dark greenish atmosphere hung like—truly like—a backdrop in some play.

Snick—Goldie's blade cut Art again across the left arm—*slurrh*—Art's blade cut Goldie, too, this across the right shoulder—only a little blow, but enough to color the shirtsleeve there bright red.

Both women were dotted and striped with red. Blood ran from seemingly small wounds along their upper bodies and both arms and over their faces—Art's from the right cheekbone, Goldie's from the left temple—

But anyone might see—Goldie was giving ground. Goldie, before the hack and crack of Art's apparently unstoppable sword, was tiring.

And *swash* went that sword. Another fountain of black hair flew off, and *swash* again, and more hair, and *clackety-clack*—jeweled buttons off the already ruined green silk coat.

Goldie gave a shriek. *She* was the cat, *she* was the one who toyed with her prey—

Suddenly Goldie screamed, "So you *loved* him—Black Knack—all this—for *him!*"

Art answered. Her voice was low—not one of them didn't hear what she said. "He was part of my crew."

Goldie gave another scream—this one again wordless. She turned and swung her cutlass round in an arc—Art was jump-ing back—but the end of the surging steel caught her now across the waist—

Art didn't make a sound. But for a second she, too, fell back, her hand going to her side. Blood streamed there. She didn't even look at it, and took away her hand.

Then she ran straight at Goldie.

If Art had moved swiftly before, now her movements were almost too fast to see—definitely too fast to be sure of until after they were done.

Her sword—was like a windmill gone crazy. So it seemed. It appeared, from the speed with which she used it, to be not one but four blades crackling round in a ring.

Out of this whirlpool whirled cut swathes of black hair, pieces of gold-embroidered green silk.

Inside it, Goldie squeaked—it was now a rather frightened sound.

Her cutlass flailed. Suddenly—it was gone.

Disarmed, as before by Art Blastside, Goldie crouched on the ground.

Art stood there, breathing as fast as she had moved, but her eyes and face as still as those of a statue.

"Pick it up."

Goldie made a small sound.

"Pick it up, Little Goldie Girl, pick up your dashing blade. We're not done."

Then Little Goldie turned her face—pale and bloody and watery-eyed, framed by a mess of uneven chunks of tangled black hair. She turned to the crew of the *Enemy*.

"You lazy pigs—come here and help me finish this bitch."

Art didn't even glance at Goldie's pirates. But *Unwelcome*'s crew erupted—Ebad growled at them, "Wait, you. *Look*. Are any of *them* moving?"

None of *Enemy*'s men had stirred.

They stared at their captain, crouched among the wreckage of her clothes and hair, bested—and not one of them did a thing.

"I shall fry you in batter," Goldie squealed at them, "keelhaul the pack of you—rub salt in your filthy wounds—" She reached for her cutlass and stood up and dived at Art all in one motion.

And Art sidestepped, as if in a dance. And caught Goldie with her fist between Goldie's right wrist and elbow.

Arm numbed, Goldie again let go of her blade.

"Pick it up."

"How can I—you *bitch*?" Goldie had begun to cry. She sniveled and her nose ran.

Art flicked with her sword and cut off a single curl from Goldie's hair. Goldie screamed once more.

"So sorry," said Art. "Pick up your blade. Let's get on."

Goldie rubbed at her numbed right hand. From her right sleeve she pulled out one more knife. She pitched it left-handed at Art— Art slapped the knife away with the hilt of her sword.

Goldie stood there, half bent over, unlovely and snotty, sniveling.

Art crossed to her, picked up Goldie's cutlass, and pressed it kindly into Goldie's hand.

Goldie dropped the cutlass.

"Oh, dear," said Art.

Once more she picked up the blade—as she straightened, Goldie tried to clock her one with her left fist—Art struck the fist away, lightly. Art handed the cutlass to Goldie.

Goldie clutched it after all. She made another pounce at Art.

This time Art struck Goldie's cutlass up and backward with such force it took off along the cliff—and also overturned Goldie. Who, losing her balance completely, toppled backward, too, landing on the grassy rock at Art's feet.

"No more," said Goldie.

"I beg your pardon?"

"*No more!*" shrieked Goldie. "I surrender—no *more*—no *more*—no *more!*"

"Ah." Art looked down at Goldie. "Surrender. I think your father, the Goliath, never allowed surrender."

Stricken, Goldie stared up at Art's white, bloody, black-eyed statue face.

Art leaned over her.

In a sort of silent terror, both ships' crews watched the silver sword go *snick and snack* across Little Goldie Girl's face.

Art straightened.

Then the watchers heard Goldie sob, "What have you done?"

"Left you something to remember me by. Think yourself lucky, miss. You bear the mark of Piratica."

Goldie reached up and felt at her right cheek, just beside the upper lip.

Yet *another* scream. "She's scarred me—cut the crossed bones on my face—my beautiful face—*kill her,* you dithering stink-pigs!"

Goldie's crew spat, one by one, on the ground. Mr. Beast, his nose also very red, spoke across the space. Not to Goldie but to Art.

"Cap'n Piratica, you've beaten her, that one there. She ain't pistol-proof no more. And so's she's bad luck now. Her dad'd turn in his watery grave. *You* take us on, Cap'n, we'll all be yours." (And the crew of *Enemy* cried "Aye!" at the top of their lungs.) "Faithful to the end."

Art lifted her head and laughed a terrible laugh.

And that was when the sea and the sky fell together.

The tinny boom of it turned every head and eye.

Near the cliff's edge now, at once they saw it coming.

It was a second sea, which jetted up from the first in a wide, curling wall of wave. Neither blue nor brown, this wave was like dark molasses, and on its top plunged the white horses of the foam. It roared as it came.

Behind them on the cliff, the parrot hordes squawked. Plunqwette, now on Ebad's shoulder, gave a lone wild cry.

"How high is that wave?"

"It looks a mile high—"

"It's the height of this cliff—it's the flood coming in again."

United in alarm, the men of both crews stood staring out. Art stood there, too, facing the rising sea. Only Goldie sat farther back in the grass, holding a handkerchief to her face, her back to everything.

Now the great wave was folding over. As it spread along the sea's surface, everything there in turn gushed upward. The flood tide raced toward them.

On the shore's edge below, already the boats had been lifted on water and were now being snapped in bits. Farther out, neither of the ships was to be seen.

Above, lightning and thundery bangs tumbled through the sky, which was dark now as evening.

"Move back," said Art, "and lie down flat. All of you."

"Aye," said Ebad, "it'll hit the cliff's face at the very least. Wash things over—"

The rock of the cliff was humming, buzzing. Still hauling the treasure chest that had brought them to this, they thudded back toward the nearest trees, where hundreds of parrots were already grouped, noiseless finally, in bundles of feathers.

The water struck the rock with a clang. Spray burst in white fireworks against the sky. Then it came down on them in salt sleet, stinging. In three drenching rushes this happened, but the second and the third rushes had a little less violence.

There were other rushes after—they heard them hit the cliff, but soon no longer saw or felt the explosion of the spray. The tidal waves were ending.

"This Isle is cursed." It was Goldie, whining. Ignored.

Salty water ran in trickles through the grass.

Art saw Felix, his hands still tied, huddled among the trees beside her. Though the ground was wet, the sea had withdrawn from it.

Wet parrots shook water off their feathers. The cliff top had stayed above the waterline, as always in the past, presumably. But below the cliff, when they went to look, the water ran sheer, about fifty feet below. Dark like the sky, it covered everything there, the beach, the orchard, the forest—the entry-exit of Tennmile's Up. Not even the tallest trees showed above the sea.

"Blacky lies down there."

"And our boats."

"The ship, too. *Unwelcome*'s gone to the bottom."

Some way off, the only other thing now to show above the tide, rose the wooded hill. More parrots were flying round there. The hill had become, like the cliff, only one more of the small islands of the Eastern Ambers.

"Marooned," said Eerie. "Shipless and lost upon this rock. Here we must starve and pine."

"Nay—look, mates—" cried Mr. Beast. "There's yer ship! Why—by the Cat's Tantrums—*our* ship, too—*is* it?"

Ebad took out the spyglass. He gazed away across the high dark sea in silence. In silence, he handed the glass to Art.

Not two ships, but four. Clear enough they were, through the glass, though many miles off, and well clear of the oceanic upheaval, only now turning themselves toward the Isle. The glass showed their flags, too.

"*Is* it the ol' *Unwelcome Stranger*, Cap'n? Is it rescue?"

"Alas no, Mr. Cuthbert. It's one ship flying a flag of an elephant with a coffeepot, and three more who fly the colors of the English Republican Navy."

The groan was nearly universal, and came from all throats but four (Art, Ebad, Felix, Goldie). Mr. Beast spoke the last speech. "Then we're tooken. We're doomed. It's the hangman's rope for every man jack of us."

∽⊃THREE℃∾

Walking the Planks ⎯

Felix found the captain of Naval Destroyer FRS *Utterly Match-less* very civil. Each night Felix dined with him and his officers, they in their navy blue, brass buttons, and gold medals, Felix in the gentleman's clothing they had given him, and which they kept, as they said, for guests.

So Felix was a favored guest again. And everything was going entirely to plan. That was, the plan he had made as a boy in the workhouse, after his white-haired father died. For the crews of two pirate vessels were being taken to Free English justice, and one of these was the crew of the *Enemy*, the copy of Goliath's ship. And it was three of Goliath's fleet that had, all those years ago, destroyed Felix's father's own ship, *Voyager*, and so his wealth, happiness, and life.

Felix had never confided that piece of the story, Goliath's involvement, to Art. She hadn't known that Goliath was the one pirate Felix hated best. Or that Goliath's daughter, Goldie, was the one Felix was prepared to see taken, in dead Goliath's place. When Felix had said to Art that he would have gone off with Goldie, because she was what he had been waiting for, not knowing it, all his life—*revenge* was what he meant. Not that he *loved* Goldie. That he wanted to help put her in irons.

He wondered if Art had now reasoned this out. He wondered, too, if actually he wished even Goldie to be hanged on Execution Dock. There was no need to ask himself if he wanted that for Art and her actor crew. He didn't.

It was all very well to dream of vengeance, and pledge yourself to it, and partly have it always on your mind—an impossible dream—if ever you got to sea, which had been, back then, so unlikely. Confronted with the fact, Felix knew he had changed. He had never disliked Art's pirates, try as he might. He had only felt himself a traitor—as bad as Black Knack and Hurkon Beare, Felix thought to himself now—for Felix had, in his way, betrayed his friends from *Unwelcome*. And also, by liking them, betrayed his father's memory.

At first, however, Felix had almost been included in the prison group.

That had been because of the fat Coffee Sponsor, and Captain Bolt, jumping off their ridiculous ship, with its flag of an elephant holding a coffeepot in its trunk, and being rowed over with the naval boats.

"Here's *another* felon! 'Tis the notorious highwayman Gentleman Jack Cuckoo-Clock—"

But the naval officers had laughed. "Don't be absurd. Everyone who knows anything knows Gentleman Jack is a *woman*—a blond called Dolly Muslin."

"Another *woman*?" had shouted outraged Captain Bolt. "Is none of England's crime in decent male hands?"

"Talking of hands, this young fellow's hands are tied, too," the Navy men said, hurrying to Felix's assistance.

(Felix remembered how at that point, Art, her own hands cuffed by strong rope, had stepped forward. "He's none of ours. Our innocent victim. I took him for ransom, gentlemen. Have him back with my blessing. He's been a pain in the ear all voyage.")

Art, stylish—generous—to the last. But the last was yet to come.

Felix puzzled over what he could do to save them from the gallows. And saw he could do nothing. Nothing at all. Which surely was what he should *want*?

All the ships kept close company as they sailed back toward

the Cape of Good Hope. Felix could usually see two or three of them just off across the water. And there were *six* ships, for there had been another big surprise for them once they were taken aboard. Neither the *Unwelcome Stranger* nor the black-sailed *Enemy* had gone down. Swept outward by the island's disturbed tidal sea, the Navy had found them both adrift, with anchor chains snapped, and claimed them for the Republic. Manned now by lawful sailors, they, too, were going to England. (Captain Bolt had argued some of this—*Unwelcome,* as FRS *Elephant,* had been his. "You'll be sorted in the courts," the Naval officers had replied.) The new Coffee Ship was also to be seen, though generally it kept farther back than the others, not able to make quite such speed.

Sometimes the vessels drew in very near. Then Felix noted the prisoners taking exercise on the decks. Obviously the Navy wanted to keep all the pirates healthy and fit for trial in England.

Each crew had been placed on a different Navy vessel. Goldie had made friends with *her* captain, Felix had already seen. She seemed not to be tied in any way, and walked up and down, *arm in arm* with the fellow, laughing deliciously at his apparently witty talk. That so-pretty laughter echoed over the water. Her crew, at exercise, were less jolly or attractive, and all in shackles.

The actor-pirates were also tied, Felix saw, but with cord not iron. They walked the planking of the deck of their Naval gunship, looking miserable. But now and then they gave the sailors dramatic performances—bits of Shakespur and applause came over the waves.

He ceaselessly saw Muck and Plunqwette, too. Muck had become a Naval ship's pet. Plunqwette sat on the rigging like another colored flag.

The Navy had taken *Unwelcome*'s egg-laying chickens on, too.

He glimpsed Art only rarely.

She still seemed to be roped at the wrists, but otherwise free, and she stalked along the planks, head up, smiling and nodding at her crew, the Naval officers, like royalty—exchanging banter. Her jokes made them laugh.

Felix's heart ached.

It ached so much he couldn't sleep, or eat the fine dinners at the captain's table, so the officers got all concerned about him, and brought him delicacies from the stores.

His heart ached as it had for his father. Although—not quite in the same way.

Really, she wasn't badly treated. The captain of FRS Naval Destroyer *We Do the Impossible* had spoken to Art at once.

"Well, madam. As you're a woman, I shan't imprison you below with your men. You can have the spare cabin below the forecastle. You'll be under lock and key, but when inside, not tied up."

Art had thanked him graciously. As Molly (in the play) would have done. Then she said, "But also, sir, I ask you treat my own eight men gently."

"They're *pirates*, madam! You're a *pirate* crew! All England rings with news of your robberies on the High Seas."

"A pirate crew who has harmed no one. Who never took a life, nor sank a single ship."

The captain blinked at her. He wasn't young, and his weathered face was not unattractive. He didn't, for example, for a *second*, remind Art of her hateful father. "Hmm," he said.

"Sir, I will also remind you that I and all my crew are actors." (She did not exclude Glad Cuthbert.) "We made our name years back in a popular drama. My mother, sir, was Molly Faith—" About to elaborate, Art found she had no need.

"By the Dolphin's Silk Stockings—! Your mother—was *Molly Faith?*"

"Yes, Captain. *Piratica*."

"Ah, *Piratica*," breathed the captain, glowing. "I saw that play a great many times. I have a poster of it at my house in England—signed by Molly Faith's own hand—a lovely creature, your mother, and a fine actress."

"My thanks. My ma, sir, indeed, was very fine. But if you've seen her play that role, then you've also beheld all of us—myself and all my men—save two, perhaps."

The captain stood up. He shook Art's hand.

"I see I have. And, too, I see Molly Faith in you, Captain Blastside. Now then. I shall have no choice but to keep all your weapons, and to tie your hands when you're on the deck—and your crew likewise. But we'll leave the ropes loose enough it won't cause you too much trouble. As for below, there's a good space with bunks your gentlemen may have. We'll all dine on deck, the lot of us together. If me officers don't care for it, they can go fly a peacock. Maybe"—he looked at Art with eyes full of blue memories—"you and your lads might put on a bit of a play for us? It's a long way home."

Art smiled. "I'm sure we'll be glad to, Captain. Though for us, perhaps, the longer it takes us to get home the better."

After she had spoken these last words—theatrical, as Molly would have—Art, now herself Piratica, turned them over in her mind.

No, she and her crew wouldn't want to hurry to England. In England they would be tried—they would be *hanged*.

Art looked at this thought, then kicked it out of her brain. *No*. She had decided, none of them would die. She had already lost two men—Black Knack, a rotten and fouled being, but she couldn't wish him dead. (The idea of his body lying on the floor of the flooded Isle irked her, made her sore.) Hurkon, of course, was the other one lost. Hurkon, also a traitor—doubly so—for a few days out she had learned, without much astonishment, a little more about him.

They had dined on deck. Art's men were up on the forecastle, practicing speeches to amuse the destroyer's crew. (Every one of the actors seemed resignedly unhappy, but they cheered up at mealtimes or when rehearsing. Even Ebad joked and swaggered, which she hadn't often seen him do. She had had no chance to speak to them alone, for others were always there—a guard or an audience.)

Art sat on with the captain, not unwilling to talk with him about her mother.

When the talk veered to Art's own deeds of piracy at sea, she told him everything. There was nothing she wished to hide. The captain nodded. He said, "But why'd you do it? Why not a stage?"

And Art quoted neatly, because anyway she couldn't explain, "All the *world's* a stage, sir, and all the men and women merely players."

Far off to port, a white swimming shape—like a swan. *Unwelcome Stranger,* in other hands, sailing, too, for England, and no longer under a pink-and-black flag.

The captain bowed to Art. He gave her time to look.

At last she said, "Who told you how to find us, or to find the Treasured Isle?"

As she had expected, the captain said, "That villain Hurkon Beare, who kings it on Mad-Agash. The *Governor,* as he's pleased to call himself. He had pinpointed the area of the Isle pretty well, you know. But too much a slug—or a coward—to go after it again for himself. He let others do his work—you. Goldie Girl. But then the Law gets wind of it all and pays him a visit. So he gives all over to us. I'll say, the sea helped, too. That tidal surge was like a beacon, and it led us in."

"Hurkon plays all sides then. Pirate *and* Law's informant."

"Yes. 'Tis why the governments of England and Amer Rica leave him be. He knows almost everything, and so he's useful to them. They pay him handsomely. For myself, I'd take a fleet and clean out his nest. But there."

Then came the other news. "Did you know Beare sailed with Golden Goliath himself, the worst pirate and murderer seen on the Seven Seas?"

It was Art's turn to blink.

"*With* him? As Goliath's prisoner, do you mean?"

"Nay. Those two were always partly friends. Finding the treasure map—one of the proper ones with the proper clues—that wasn't their first bond, though it made them closer."

"Do you mean, sir, even when Hurkon was one of Molly's troupe—"

"It would seem he knew Goliath even before that."

Art said no more. Her blood had chilled, thickened. Something terrible lurked at the fringe of her thoughts—she couldn't quite come at it.

The captain added, "And 'twas all for nothing, eh? At the end of the day, there wasn't even the treasure to be found. All gone—just that empty chest you showed us. At first I thought you must have hidden it—but how and where? No other inch of that cliff was dug up. Nor was there anything on your persons. Someone had got ahead of you, eh? Some other with a true map and the wit to solve the code."

"Precisely, Captain. It was a bitter blow."

The treasure . . .

Oh, the treasure—

Art winced, remembering how the crews of both pirate ships, *Enemy* and *Unwelcome*, had sworn, shouted, and yelled.

This was when they still stood there on the headland, gazing out at the three Navy ships riding slowly and surely toward them. And the chest between them, packed with its hundred or so maps, the keys to the greatest fortune, maybe, on earth. (By then, what the treasure *was*, was known to all.)

Only Goldie and Felix had taken no part in the noise. She

was keeping her head down right then. He was keeping his head turned away.

"We've time," Cuthbert had finally cried, "it'll be an hour afore they reach us—then they'll have to row over, the water's still not deep enough for those great tugs to come in too close. We can rebury that ol' chest."

Art said, "No, Mr. Cuthbert. If they know to come here, they know what this place is. Their first act, after putting us in irons, will be to check the cliff for the signs of digging."

"Then—we give up all *that*—to the *Law*?"

Thirty-one horrified faces turned to Art. Even Ebad—if not horrified, still angry. Her actors—now definitely pirates— Goldie's crew who had come over to Art. She had thought, It's how small boys in trouble look at their mother. How they'd have looked at Molly.

"This is what we'll do," said Art. "The map paper is waxed. We fold each map up into a little paper boat and drop it down on the sea."

Pandemonium.

She waited it out.

"Listen. If we hide the maps here, they'll find them. If we hide them on ourselves—they'll find them. But the sea—look. Lots of things are floating about on it, came up with the tide—sticks, weeds, leaves, jellyfish— By the time the ships arrive, those little paper boats will be away, just more flotsam on the water. And like us anyway, the Navy *won't* be looking for paper."

"But Captain Piratica—" Tattoo of the *Enemy* spoke respectfully, "if you float the maps off—we'll never get them back. *Others* may find them—"

"Fool," grunted the Beast, "*we* won't be coming back. Let's do it. We'll swing—but *They* won't get their undeserving mitts on our dosh."

Every face fell—and *set*.

Ebad said, now in a hard, calm tone, "Let's do what our captain says."

So sitting together in a group on the cliff top, like good children with their school lesson, they made the treasure maps into a hundred odd paper boats.

Art's crew, who had formed such boats out of posters at Grinwich on Christmas Night, in memory of a festival of the Inde, showed the *Enemy*'s men how to do it. The *Enemy*'s men's boats, however, were mostly not very good.

Down onto the sea they all dropped their handiwork. One by one, in twos and tens and twenties.

And away they sailed, the poor little boats, circling sometimes, sometimes turning upside down, several went all the way down—laments filled the air.

Yet soon, as Art had said, they only looked like more debris on the water—like waxy wet flowers.

When the Navy ships sailed near, guns ready, and the pistol-aiming naval boats were rowed in (some even passing through a few of the last maps, unnoticing), not a single treasure was left on the cliff.

Remembering it, Art walked up and down the deck of FRS *We Do the Impossible*, taking her exercise. How white the clean planks beneath her feet, under that bright Afric sun.

If she stared to starboard, she would see Felix standing at the rail of FRS *Utterly Matchless*. He was gazing fixedly across at FRS *We Do the Impossible*. At her? Maybe. Maybe gloating. The Law wouldn't even need his drawings of them now, though it might like his evidence against them.

She didn't look across at him.

She felt she must never look at him again. Because if she did—then she might break. And that wasn't going to happen.

On the deck of the third gunship destroyer, FRS *Total Devastation*, Little Goldie Girl sat under an awning with the ship's captain.

She had been allowed to cut her hair, and had done so carefully. Now it was in a short, but most becoming style, and recent washing had made it glossy and very curly. It framed her face like a black halo. They had found her female clothing—at her own request. On her mostly flawless face, the tiny cross Art Blastside had nicked there was healing well. It would leave only the tiniest scar—though *not* in Goldie's mind.

"Oh, Captain," cooed Goldie, "I never cease to thank God for your rescue of me."

The captain wasn't *quite* convinced. But he was very taken with Goldie. He couldn't really believe she was a villainess—it must be more like what she had said—her evil father—and then his evil crew—had forced her to acts of piracy. "How could such a weak, fragile little woman as Goldie," she had said, "resist? Oh, those awful acts—I would swoon with fright and distress." (Naturally she had left this evil crew to rot in the hold in chains. When they appeared on deck, Goldie vanished with the captain.)

She never mentioned Felix—or Art—directly. But she *had* told FRS *Total Devastation*'s captain about the fate of the treasure maps. Somehow, he in turn hadn't told anyone else.

Goldie had added, "I do believe, though, all's not lost, there. You see, the lower beach was littered—simply *smothered*—in gems and coins. Which of course we—I mean, my father's horrid crew—picked up—and you, gallant Captain, afterward took from us—them—as well you should have done! But you see, it made me think. The jewels must get swept out in the floods—so then they must also be swept *back* when the water goes in again. So why not the same with all those maps?"

"Art, you and I must speak. Alone."
"Yes, Ebad. But no chance here."
"It must be done. If I'm to hang in England—"
"None of us, Mr. Vooms, will hang."

"If I'm *likely* to hang, girl—you and I—I haven't told you all I might. It must be said."

"But look, Ebad, already three Navy officers and six sailors approach. They want to watch us rehearse. Or simply make sure we don't pass any secrets."

"Damnation."

"And we're separated always, except up on deck."

The Navy men were there beside them. Ebad thundered in his best voice, "And the royal sail, so called not for *royalty*—but from the meaning *Raised Over All!* The great royal sail shall hear my oath. Heed then—" His black eyes gleamed like swords, and the watchers stood transfixedly delighted at the performance. "Heed me, *Piratica*. Tonight, beneath the moonless heaven, thou and I. For I must reveal to thee the truth of thy beginnings."

Art's eyes narrowed. For a moment she couldn't think. And then, "Upon my soul, sir, thou shalt have thy wish."

And all the Navy gentlemen enthusiastically clapped.

In the Same Boat

Art stood waiting for Ebadiah Vooms at the rail of *We Do the Impossible* in the moonless dark.

It had been simple. She had asked for another airing in the cool of the night. The captain granted her two hours. Her request to be alone and reflect upon her fate, he also granted. A romantic, this captain. Luckily.

Plunqwette had flown down to join Art at the rail, which was something she seldom did when the Navy men were there. Muck was with the officers in the saloon. They were playing cards, and the dog, sitting on his parrot bone, was helping them by barking at a high score. ("Faithless hound," Eerie had declared. "You can't blame the old dog," Whuskery had said. "We're no use to him now.")

Art wondered how Ebad could escape the belowdecks prison. She sensed he would manage it. He did.

Suddenly he was by her, cat-footed as she—or Molly.

He told her quickly his method of exit. "They don't rope us down there. Muck brought me the door key."

"Muck!"

"Nosed it in under the door. An old trick we taught him. Out-of-work actors sometimes need such plans. Best dog in England, Muck. The cleanest, certainly."

"So Muck plays two sides as well." Lost in admiration, Art heard Muck yap again in the saloon.

Ebad unknotted the cord at her wrists and handed it to her.

Neither of them mentioned any chance they could all now escape—untied, prison door open—they couldn't. Two lookouts were aloft, eyes on the ocean. Any going that way would probably soon be shot in the water. While, shooting aside, not all Art's crew would make it—poor swimmers, or nonswimmers, and the coast far off. She had considered earlier whether or not they could take this ship. Believed they couldn't. They were unarmed and had no access to arms. The naval crew amounted to over sixty men, she thought—besides which, this ship taken, if they had even been able to do it, the other two would doubtless close in at once. The odds were too great. She tried hard not to think how frustrating this temporary freedom was, nor if she should persuade Ebad at least to take his chance in the water. She sensed he wouldn't leave her—and that he would know she in turn wouldn't leave her men.

"The watch'll come round," said Ebad now. "We'll climb up into one of the boats. Less likely they'll be looking in there. If they want you, you can call back—and I'll keep my head down."

In the boat, in the darkness, then. Plunqwette, as if to preserve their secret, had flown back to the main mast. By starlight alone, Art saw Ebad's face, the face of a former slave, the descendant of kings.

"I'll tell thee, Arty. Best be swift. Do you still think you remember being a child on the sea—the real sea, not machinery on stage?"

"Yes. Despite all you said to me. Despite the gunpowder knocking me senseless and forgetful for six years. I remember the sea. All of it."

"You're wise to, Art. By the topgallants, it's a fact."

She breathed out slowly. That was all.

Ebad said, "Molly was an actress. That was always true. That man, your father, Fitz-Willoughby Weatherhouse, he saw her and wooed her and somehow she gave in. Married him. She lived with him about a year, during which time you were born. Molly said this of you, you had no look of Weatherhouse. Only of herself. You were all hers. So, after the year was done, she took you and left *him*."

"I've always been very glad about that."

"What happened next, though, Art? She didn't go back to the stage. She was afraid Fitz'd follow her, cause trouble. She was in Lundon, and she was looking for a way to the coast. She wanted to take ship out of England. In Lundon, that was when I met her." Ebad sighed. "I can only tell this one way if I'm to tell truth. She and I, one look between us—her words, not mine, though it was true for me as well. One look and we were each other's. That ordinary. Sometimes love is."

"You and Molly?"

"Aye. Yes. Do you mind?"

"I'm glad. What next?"

"We took ship downriver and to the coast. We got to Battering-Ram's Gate and found a ship across to France. From there we found passage to the Amer Ricas. We were bound for a place at the foot of the southern continent, a place with a Spanish name that means *Brave Paradise*. But it was a rough town, had been in the wars. They said you could make your fortune there. Whether she or I believed that I don't know. But it was a fair name—and we hadn't been long together. And it was some-where far off to go."

"Valparaiso is the place you mean?"

"Yes."

Art thought of the movement of seas, in storm and lull. She thought of jolly boats towing a great ship through the static Doldrums, and the fire-opal stars of the South Down Cross—she spoke of what she thought to Ebad.

"You *saw* it all, Art. You were only a baby—one, two—three years of age toward the end—but you saw it, with her, and with me. That was when she started teaching you languages. And when she taught you to swim, like I'd taught *her,* off the Bay of Spain. And she told you about all that was happening on the ship. Even when there was a tempest— My God, Molly, your mother—she strode that deck without any fear. She held you up to see the lightning and the wind that turned us nearly over, and the phosphor fires on the rigging and the waves the height of churches—"

"I remember, Ebad. I remember."

"She said to you—"

"She said to me, 'What a spectacle! Look—how beautiful it is! Don't ever be afraid of the sea. She's the best friend our kind have got. And even if we ever went down, don't fear that, either. Those that the sea keeps sleep among mermaids and pearls and sunken kingdoms.' I know she said it in the play, too. It was a speech. But she said it on that ship to me first, in the middle of the storm."

Ebad grinned. "She loved that ship. She'd climb the rigging, with you tied on her back. My heart was in my mouth. But you were laughing and crowing. And she—she had no fear. No fear for you or for her or for me. Not on the sea. And the sea never hurt her. It was the land, the *stage* did that."

"Then why did you go back to England? What happened?"

Ebad said, as one other had said, "Don't you guess? Pirates."

Art said quietly, "Your ship was attacked by pirates."

"By the Golden Goliath himself. Yes, Art. If Felix told you his story, our own is similar—in its way. The very three ships that attacked his dadda's vessel sacked her—and then, not finding what they really wanted aboard her, they turned southwest and met *our* ship. It turns out they were mostly looking for that, an English or Amer Rican ship in those waters, with a treasure map aboard. Ours—had one. Only a few months stand between the date of *Voyager*'s sinking and the attack on our vessel. But the outcome was different. Our freighter had twenty guns, and she turned 'em all on Goliath. The pirate scum didn't like that much—you've seen the same with his daughter, Goldie. A good fight sends 'em running—and they ran. We got away. But the freighter took casualties, and she'd been holed by Goliath's own cannon. We limped into some hapless port, a long way off from Brave Heaven Valparaiso. One more thing. Our ship's captain had died in the battle, along with seven of his crew. He was a good man, and he'd had a soft spot for Molly—and for me. A black man, never a slave, from Port Liberty. Also a gun blast had knocked you and her right over—not a scratch on either of you—except for a mark in your hair. That was where you got your powder-burn streak—fighting off Goliath. And that did rattle Molly for the first time."

Art said, "And so you both lost heart."

"It shook us through. In those days we were young, Molly and I. You think you'll never be stopped. But Goliath showed us plain, we could be, just like our captain. And—how easy it was to die. And then—stuck in that nowhere port, nothing going out in any direction for fear of Goliath, Molly began to miss England. We had another friend with us by then, too, Hurkon Beare. He'd come aboard our dead captain's ship at the Blue Indies. I saw at once he fancied Molly, but she only liked me in that way. He tried to interest her, then seemed to accept she wouldn't turn. I always wondered. Sometimes, in later years, I'd see his eyes follow her—or me. I didn't trust him so well in England. Besides. There was that map."

"The treasure map."

"Art, the captain of our Amer Rican ship, he did have a map. It was the map I gave you in Grinwich, burned at the edge—the map that's caused all this. The captain said he bought it from an old trader on the Ivory Coast. He said he bought it as a kindness, thinking it worthless, and the old man's parrot, too."

"Plunqwette?"

"The same bird. The trader seemingly swore blind the map was a true one. The Isle it showed lay somewhere beyond Africay, he said, where the oceans meet. And the bird sometimes spoke a strange set of clues. Molly liked the parrot. She used to say the clues back to Plunqwette, and other things, and soon Plunqwette started to repeat everything, clues as well, in Molly's voice, not the trader's. And so, we still hear Molly's voice, coming out sometimes in the squawk of that parrot. But the captain, he'd told us one night, the map and the parrot were his inheritance he'd leave us, if anything happened to him. He said he'd meant one day to go east, try if it might be genuine. Perhaps he sensed his fate. He died four weeks later from Goliath's guns."

"So you took the map—and Plunqwette."

"Hurkon—it was Hurkon who *insisted* we take the map—Molly already had Plunqwette. And then, stranded in the port after, Hurkon was saying, 'Let's us go over east, let's see if we can find this Treasured Isle—' "

"Wait," Art said. "I've been told—Hurkon was a friend way back with Goliath."

"I've heard that by now, too. I think this. I think Hurkon came aboard that Amer Rican ship to suss out if the captain had a map, and if the map was real—and if Hurkon was Goliath's all that while, maybe he got word to Goliath. For sure, Goliath came after us. But then couldn't take us. And Molly and I, now *we* had the map. So Hurkon wanted to stay in our company. I'll tell you, he stuck to us in those days like a wasp to wet velvet. And back in England, he was the one who said we should, all three of us, keep quiet about ever having traveled on a ship. Keep quiet even to our own troupe of actors."

"Wanting the map, for Goliath—or for Hurkon himself."

"And wanting Molly, too. And wanting me dead."

"Ebad." Art hesitated. "No, go on," she said.

"He was an actor from Canadia then, Mr. Beare," said Ebad. "And Molly was training me to be an actor. You have the voice, she said, all you need's the training. I'll give you that. She did. We'd all sit and say what we wished on Goliath—aye, Hurkon'd say it, too—Molly and I certainly were still raw at the captain's dying. Molly would say, if *she* commanded a ship, she'd chase Goliath seas over. And out of all that, the idea came for the play. In the end, we found a vessel'd take us and got back to English shores. We were well over a year traveling—that ship we'd had to take, she called in everywhere, even the Cape and Free Cape Town. Molly would say, at least when we get back, no one will still be looking for me. And when we did get back, no one was. Your jewel of a father had never bothered. So she looked up the actors she'd known, and formed her own company—her notion caught on—the play caught on. The rest you know."

Art said steadily, "Hurkon left you after the accident with the gunpowder. After Molly died."

"Straight after. He was off his head with it. But so were we all. That was when Weatherhouse finally appeared. It shames me I let him take you—though the precious Law was on his side. I'd meant to be a father to you, Art. I should have been, not him."

"With that I agree, Mr. Vooms. And I should have been proud to have you as my da. But there's this other thing."

"I know, Art. I know. It's begun to pick at me, too."

They sat in silence awhile. Neither spoke this thought (though it was the same in both of them), which was: Had Hurkon set out to destroy the act, maybe to kill Ebad, definitely to cause such confusion that Hurkon himself could steal the Treasure Map? Had Hurkon spiked the gunpowder in the stage cannon named Duchess? No accident—but murder?

If he had, the plan went wrong. Molly died, not Ebad. And the map—already hidden by suspicious Ebad—Hurkon never found.

"I recall," said Art. "Hurkon and my mother—always them—on the ship, when Goliath's *Enemy* came at her. And I recall the crew from the play. That's where my memories are mixed up. But Ebad, now, sometimes, I dream you're there with Molly. Just you and her, and me. And so I dream, even if I don't quite remember otherwise how you two were together."

"On the way to Valparaiso."

Overhead, Plunqwette, whispering, "Pieces of *Freight*."

Muck, still toting his bone, scampered below and barked loudly. He was up from the saloon—warning them?

Ebad eased to his feet and prepared to slip down to the deck.

"We need to talk again," said Art.

"We may never be able to, in this world. But I'll see you in the next, Art Blastside, Young Piratica. Just as I'll see your mother."

Ebad was long gone by the time the ship's officers walked out on deck. Art called them a pleasant good evening, from below the mizzen, where she now stood, her hands neatly retied.

But her head was full of her past. Full of Ebad's loss—and both her own. He had lost his love. So had she. Twice.

Mother, then . . . Besides, her second love had never even been won over. Across the water, on the next ship, Felix Phoenix would be sleeping, happy in the thought Art's days were numbered. And *were* they? How near was England, and the rope's end?

Trial and Error

"Death."

In the prisoner's dock, the young woman stood, head high, her fox-streaked hair streaming down her back. She wore male clothing. They had let her keep it on, to show the judge, the jury, and the crowd, that she was beyond saving—nor *worth* saving.

They had also told the woman, who was known mostly by the name *Piratica,* that, since she had once been trained as an actress, she must answer questions now only in less than ten words, and make no speeches of any kind.

When she came in, the crowd applauded. Which caused the judge, in powdered wig and fur-trimmed robe, to shout (jealously?) at the officers of the court, "Still that noise! Hush 'em or bash 'em."

Presently the crowd was quiet.

The trial didn't take long.

Many people spoke of Piratica's awful deeds, among them a Coffee Sponsor, and a Captain Bolt, and of how she was a fiend among women. How, too, if a man were a pirate, he was a devilish felon—but if a woman did such a thing—she was the devil itself.

A captain from a naval ship, FRS *We Do the Impossible,* attempted to say that Piratica had behaved tremendously well during the long voyage home. He had found her intelligent, honorable, indeed charming, as were her crew. (But everyone knew Piratica's crew had already been sentenced to swing, by this same judge.) The captain was quickly dismissed, the "impossible" not done.

For highway robbery and for piracy, only one penalty was available by Law. The judge put a black cloth over his head to announce it.

Once the word had been said, Piratica turned on the judge and his cloth her icy gray flame of a gaze.

Though he had sentenced her to hang, he then decided, it seemed, on one last cutting remark.

"You go to your death then, girl. You have earned it. You are a disgrace both to your country and to your female sex."

Art answered in nine words, clear and faultless on the cue:

"And you, sir, are a disgrace to this world."

Despite the clubs of the court officers, the crowd stamped and cheered her as she was led away.

Keys rattled, and the cell door croaked. The jailer's snouty face appeared around it.

"Oh, Mistress Piratica, may I, ever so humbly, enter?"

"If you must."

In he came—as far as he ever did, his head and shoulders and one hand and leg round the door, afraid to advance more, in case the pirate-woman—or her parrot—lunged at him.

Art stared at him coldly. "What is it?"

Plunqwette, perched on a rickety chair, made a chicken noise.

"I wondered, ever so humble like, what the Mistress would like for her dinner?"

"I'll get what you usually give me, I suppose. Rancid bread and half-cooked rat."

"Ho!" said the jailer. "Such wit."

Art turned away. (So did Plunqwette, closing eyes and wings, sleeping.) Art looked instead out through the narrow, thickly barred window of her solitary cell.

It was winter in England again—coming back, it had looked to her as if English winter had never actually *stopped*, just started before she left, and then gone on all the time she was away. Snow had fallen, by now a sooty half-thawed mess. Outside the window, the River Thamis flowed sluggishly between cloud and mud. It seemed bored here, the river, bored with the city of Lundon and its outskirts, too bored even to hurry off. Along the shingle beach below Oldengate Prison, which right then cast its black shadow on the slushy stones, was famous Execution Dock. And the special place there saved for Art's kind, the place called the Lockscald Tree.

Art had a view only of one high beam. Which was enough. She had been watching them build the scaffold.

Did she believe it at last? She thought she probably did. And yet, it seemed miles away, as far away as it had seemed on the Navy ship.

They hadn't let her keep any coins or money—even though the romantic captain of the *WDtI* (the man who had spoken of her virtues at the trial) had given her gold to bribe jailers and other prison staff—which was the only way to get decent food or any comfort. However, the Lundon Constabulary had sternly relieved Art of all that.

So, she hadn't any bribes. Which had been a pity, for she did have a single small plan—

The jailer in the doorway, not coming in or going out, was shuffling around. He said suddenly, "The papers are full of you. I'll bring you some to read, if ya like—full of you and yer crew. *They're* all reading them, I can tell you. Dauntless actors, they call you, Heroes of the Seas—Robina Hood and Her Merry Men—the *Lundon Tymes* even has your name in the Acrostic. And it goes on and on about 'Piratica's dignity and spirit—fearless and gallant,' well, the journalist was in the court. He praises yer crew an' all. Says they're *noble* pirates, the first of their kind."

"Why are you telling me all this?"

"Oh—ah. Well, you *see*, like"—he sounded nearly sheepish now in his snouty way—"it's, er, our *book*."

Outside, a big ship hove into Art's sights, going down the river. A strong vessel, half-rigged masts like pillars. They were pulling her down for speed, three ship's boats, with sailors at the oars, like the Doldrums—The ropes shone silver in an unexpected ray of wintry sun, and the trim on deck shone gold. Even in the white-gray, she sparkled and made the water sparkle, waking it up.

Art couldn't read the ship's name. She was too far off. Like everything that had happened.

The gallows down there was much nearer.

"Y'see. This book—"

"What book?" she impatiently asked the jailer.

"It's just we wondered if you'd sign it—you can write, too, can't yer? Maybe leave a little message about how you've found it, staying here—"

Disbelieving, Art forgot the ship and turned to glare. *"What?"*

"You're a celebrity, Mistress," snouted the jailer. "It's yer famousness. Like, when you hang like, er—three days' time I think it is—well, you'll draw the biggest crowds—hundreds— they're booking up their places right now—buying *tickets* for it—even thousands, maybe. To see you off. And some of them pays for things of yourn you've had—like your hair with that orange blotch in it—"

Art didn't shudder. But he saw one of her hands make a capable fist.

The jailer backed off—only his nose now still poking round

the door. "They'll pay to look at the book, you see—the rich ones as come. Some of 'em'd like to look in at yer, too—just a quick glimpse."

Art drew in a breath. "You should have been nicer to me, if you want something."

"I've bin as nice as I can—I've give you the best of everything—"

"*That* was the *best*?"

"Well"—reluctant, but putting face, one foot, and one hand back round the door—"er, what'ya want then?"

Art said, "It's cold in here. I want a cell with a proper fire in it, for me and for my crew. I want a decent meal, for me and for them. We'll all have some proper blankets and sheets, too. Another thing, unchain my men for their dinner, or they won't enjoy it. And I want to see them then, one last time. A chance to say good-bye."

"Cor, you want a lot. That'll *cost* ya!"

"No. I'll sign your disgusting book. *That's* the cost."

"Bloody cat-spit pirate-witch," yattered the jailer, forgetting his fear of Art in righteous indignation. "You don't deserve a *crust*. Oughta be in chains yerself, I told 'em so—chained to a wall, not stood there giving me orders—fires—foods—*blankets*—where'm I to get all that?"

"Up to you."

The door banged, the keys turned. Even through all that stone Art heard him, bundling along the passage, shouting to himself about wicked unreasonableness, until all the other prisoners were yelling back, and the prison rang like a bell.

The grim judge, who had by now sentenced Art and her crew, and also the crew of the *Enemy,* to death, looked up as the latest vile pirate was brought into his dock. Surprised, he looked harder.

A young and quite gorgeous girl, with short curling dark hair, and eyes the color of fresh-cut lettuce.

She wore a plain white dress, which showed off her pretty figure and lovely skin. (Someone must have brought her things in prison. . . .)

She glanced timidly at the judge, and two crystal tears limpidly fell from those green eyes.

"Who is she?" The judge consulted documents. "*Little Goldie Girl*? The daughter of that monster the Golden Goliath—?"

As Goldie's trial went on, the judge began to interrupt Goldie's accusers. Instead, he called on Goldie to speak.

When he frowned at her she visibly trembled, yet for a moment, their eyes met. And in them, the clever judge, who prided himself on always judging ably, saw what she was—a fragile and tender maiden, an *angel* indeed. And—he saw, too, she trusted him, for she could tell how wise he was, and that he could see through everything to the truth.

She spoke. "Sirs. Sir *Judge*. My story is a tragic one. I have been a prisoner of my own cruel father, Goliath, who forced me to sail with his ship. And nextly of his heartless men. I have been made to wear male clothing, which isn't suitable for a girl, and made to stand by as horrible piratic deeds were performed—I dared do nothing to prevent them. I have been in terror, gentlemen" (her eyes were turned now on the jury), "for all my young girlhood. But, if I must, I will now answer with my life—not for my own crimes, for I have done nothing—I am a victim, too—for what can a poor weak girl do against the sharp intelligence and strength of men? Yet almost I welcome death. I've suffered enough."

The judge, waving down the voices of all others in his court, leaned forward. "What, if you were spared, would be your dearest wish?"

"Oh, sir"—Goldie lifted to him her face, on which the tiny crossed scar, a symbol of her ill treatment, was now only like the tiny X mark of a kiss—"I would long to become that which

I was never permitted to be. A proper woman. A *real* woman. Oh, if only someone might teach me how."

The judge cleared his throat and said no more.

About ten minutes later, Little Goldie Girl, pirate captain of the *Enemy*, was pardoned. In fact, proved quite innocent.

Art heard the news of that, when the jailer came back.

She said, "What about Goldie's crew?"

"The gallows, like your lot."

"It sounds as if the ropes will be busy," Art said as if she were Molly in the play.

Then the cell door widened, with two prison toughs guarding it—and in were brought several dishes, steaming, a bottle of wine, a pot of coffee—plus an iron fire basket with lit coals.

Plunqwette flew sedately across the room and landed on a plate of potatoes.

"Filthy bird," grumbled the jailer through his black teeth.

"I asked for a cell with a fireplace, jailer."

"Can't be done. This is the special cell, reserved for your kind. You're to stay in it." He sidled nearer, fawning again. "Moved yer crew, though. Nice big cell—they've got a great big fireplace, one of our best. Real cheery."

"Do I believe you?" Art felt her heart punch against her side.

"You can take a look after your din-din. Yeah. You can visit your crew, full twenty minutes. How's that?"

"'Twill do."

"Ungrateful Bat-Bucket."

Strange. It reminded her of how she had found them first, that morning at The Coffee Tavern in Lundon's West End. There they were. Her pirates.

They were sitting on benches drawn up to the hearth, on which burning logs and pinecones crackled. It was a fire and a half. The jailer hadn't lied. One black iron bar crossed the fireplace.

For a second, Art looked round for Muck. But Muck, of course, wasn't there. (He had bounded straight off the naval ship when she docked and run away, yellow tail high, careless, on his own business—and with that parrot bone still in his mouth. "Don't get all upset," Dirk had said to Walt. "Muck always did that, didn't he. Always going off—then coming back—" "This time if he comes back, he won't find us," said Walter.) And Muck anyway hadn't come back. That dog knew, as Eerie had once said, which side his paws were buttered.

Plunqwette rode on Art's shoulder, head and beak stuck forward. The moment the parrot was sure the group at the fire were her crewmates, she let out a piercing cry and went flapping toward them.

They leaped up, tankards and coffee cups flying.

"Plunqwette!"

"Art—it's Art!"

"Have they put thee in with us, to share our last hours, all as one?"

"Sorry, no. Just a visit," she said.

Their enthusiasm was like the smallest twig in the fire—flaming quick and bright—burned out almost at once.

What else? There was nothing to get excited about. In three—two and a half—days' time, they would all be down at the Lockscald Tree.

But they made the best of it. They sat together at the fire and told a jest or two, and uttered a speech or seven. They told Art she looked a wonder, you'd never know she'd been shut in a cell. She told them the same.

Then they lapsed into their cups.

"Mr. Vooms," she said, "step aside a minute, if you will."

Ebad, who as so often had been the most silent among them,

seemed also to have been waiting. He got up and walked with her to the one narrow window.

"How did you buy all this for us?" he asked.

"The jailer wants my signature for his celebrity book. Listen, our time's almost up—he only gave me twenty minutes. Ebad, I see you're not in irons."

"They let us off the chains for dinner, said we'd stay loose till the rounds at six tonight."

"It had better be before six then. Maybe, too, when I'm gone, make out you're all drunk." Ebad looked at her searchingly. Art said, "Have you guessed it? The *fire*."

"It's possible. If we make our moves just right. The chimney seems quite generous in size. We can act drunk, as you say, sing loud to cover when we smash the iron bar out, which will make the entry wider. But are they such fools here, they don't see we might?'

"That's it, Ebad. Fools never seem to think of chimneys. It was the same as the Angels Academy. *That* chimney was wide enough for me to get out by—this one's a giant next to it. There'll be stepping rungs, too, for the chimney sweeps."

"Some of it may be hot going if other hearths connect to this pipe. Where does it come out?"

"On a roof, where else? There'll be guards below on the ground, but they won't expect this kind of bother. Mind how you go, stay quiet and keep hold. Did they give you sheets? Then take them for ropes to get down over the wall. We can all climb up and down, can't we; we're used to ship's masts in a gale. It's the best chance you've got."

"What about you?"

"I'll think of something, Ebad. I've got three days still. It'll leave my mind free if I don't have to worry about the rest of you."

Ebad took her hand. Art finally thought, *Yes, it's good-bye.*

Then Plunqwette came back, dipping down to Art and

Ebad's outstretched, linked hands. The bird balanced there, standing between them, one claw each on either side of their wrists. "I'll leave her with you, Ebad. I was wondering how I'd squeeze her out through my cell window. This is better." Art stroked the top of the parrot's soft, smooth head, the feathers of jade and ruby—colors of Molly Faith's two gowns for dancing. "Take care of yourself, Plunqwette, old girl. Take care of yourself, Dad."

Ebad smiled. "You're Molly's," he said. "You remember that."

"Oh, come on. I only forgot for *six* years."

Art embraced her crew. Eerie wept. That set off Dirk and Walter, Whuskery, Peter . . . Honest's face looked like one enormous round tear. "Ere, watch it, mates," said Glad Cuthbert sadly, "you'll put out the ol' fire."

"Mr. Vooms will explain to you that putting out the fire will be, very soon, a wonderful idea. Good night, gents. See you in better times. See you—in some brave Paradise."

When Snouty undid the door, without a word Art instantly emerged. The jailer grunted. He locked the door. "You'll sign the book now, right?"

"Right."

"Then a couple of landsirs and ladies just want a peek at you. One minute each—five of 'em—that's money, that is. I'm going to chain you up an' all. They expect it, y'see. Mustn't disappoint yer public. You'll understand, being a hactress."

Let them escape. That's all I ask. I can't. They must.

Alone now. Had she *ever* been alone—all those times before when she thought she had been—but oh, not like this.

Felix, she thought. No, not Felix. Ebad. Molly.

But she thought of the Shakespur sonnet Felix had sung on the Coffee Ship. The song that had *meant* Molly, to Art. *Shall I compare thee to a summer's day? Thou art more lovely . . .*

thy eternal summer shall not fade . . . Nor shall Death brag thou
wander'st in his shade . . . so long as men can breathe, or eyes can
see . . .

Two days more, two nights. Curious. They were all she
had left, but would they seem the longest of her life? Or—the
shortest?

Do I believe it now, *death—*

No, she thought. I don't believe it. But it seems it will happen anyway.

The *Tymes* bannered the headline: "Notorious Night Flight of
Actor-Pirate Crew and Parrot, Who Cunningly Evade the Jaws
of Justice."

All Lundon seemed loud with cries of "Up a *chimney*!" All
Lundon—all "low" Lundon—laughed and toasted the daring
and brilliant pirates who had escaped the Republic's prison of
Oldengate, got clean—or not so clean, being covered in soot—
away over the roofs, the walls. None of them yet recaptured.
Heroes. Lovable rogues.

"But they still have Piratica in jail."

"And she was the cleverest of them all."

It was red, the sky. Winter dawn. But of which day? The first—
the second—the *third—*

Ah.

The third.

"Rise and shine," pealed the jailer, supported now by several
armed guards. "It's your big morning."

But Art was ready. Coat and hair well brushed. Her boots
rubbed to a gleam. Unfaltering. She looked at the jailer, and
said, "Did you read what I wrote in your book?"

"Yer know *I* can't read," said Snouty, with great scorn for all
who could.

"Get someone to read it *to* you, then." (A few days later, he would. And the air would ring once more to his snout-felt roars of fury at Art's description of him, just as he always did at any reminder of his mistake over the fireplace and chimney.)

Meanwhile, however . . .

"A blowy day for it," said one of the guards as he undid Art's chain that the jailer had left on, after her crew got away. "There's a big crowd out there. Biggest I've seen. No doubt you've been hearing the noise. By the Stars!" he added gleefully. "'Tis what I like to see. A bit of public interest. Supersweet."

Bells dinged in the city. The wind was getting up along the river. But no more ships were going past, sailing free and bright toward the sea.

Last Scene—Lockscald Tree

Just as Mrs. Orchid, powdered blue of wig and in blue spectacles, came into the parlor room of her inn, a cheer rang out on the floor below. It wasn't, however, for her.

The Last In, First Out stood well down on the mud of the Thamis riverbank. The inn was on a platform and raised, too, on stilts, clear of the high-water mark. It was a rickety building of two stories, and appeared itself almost like a peculiar scaffold. The real scaffold, however, was the reason for the inn's being there. Last In, First Out overlooked the choicest place on Execution Dock—the Lockscald Tree.

Visitors came from far and wide at the best hanging times. And for the hanging of this female pirate called Piratica, all Lundon—and half of England—seemed to have arrived.

Ahead of Mrs. Orchid, as she stood with her ginger cat, named Burst, under one arm, and the tray of fine wines and coffees on the other, was the inn's upper parlor, with its one large, clear, crystal window. This window gave an unrivaled view of Lockscald gallows. And as always on hanging occasions, several rich persons had paid well to gather at it in private and watch. They would certainly see better than those others everywhere out there on the mud around Execution Dock. This bank of the Thamis was invisible under the crush of humanity—and even over the river there was a crowd. Three hundred thousand, the multitude, someone had said.

And all this for a girl who was a pirate—

Today, no women were at Mrs. Orchid's gallows-watching window. Instead, five men grouped there. Impressive men, though, who had paid in gold.

"Ah, the refreshments," said Landsir Snargale of the Admiralty, one of the most powerful blokes in England.

"Call this coffee? 'Tis never any of mine!" rudely called the Coffee Sponsor, Mr. Coffee, dressed in a brocade coat the color of coffee when black. But Mrs. Orchid only shook her head indifferently.

Captain Bolt downed his drink without comment, and went back to glowering at the gallows.

The other two were young fellows, one the nephew of the Coffee Sponsor.

"That dem wind's got up out there," said Harry Coffee to his friend, and once dueling partner, Perry. "That'll blow the ropes about a bit, eh? By the Goat's Trotters, I tell ye what. I went along and took one of the one-minute looks at this pirate queen. Dem my stars, Perry. Terrifying girl, innit."

"Too right, so I heard. Wish I'd thought to take a look at her, too."

"Paid through the Pig's Nose for it, though. That jailer chap. I'd dig a pit and drop the grasping tockalot right in it, innit."

Landsir Snargale turned with a frown back to the window. He disliked this noise and lightness, when a young woman was about to lose her life. Of course, she was a pirate and deserved it. (But he had been told the *other* female pirate had been let off. Snargale hadn't liked that. He understood this other piratess was the daughter of the Golden Goliath, and Snargale, like many more, had a long-standing grudge against Goliath.) Besides all that, this Piratica's crew had all escaped—due, Snargale had been told, to *her* tricking the idiots in the jail.

It really was too bad.

He had sent a letter to her father as well. George Fitz-Willoughby Weatherhouse. But the man hadn't turned up, nor had he even had the politeness to reply.

"Couldn't even be bothered to come to his own daughter's hanging," Snargale remarked, more to himself than Captain Bolt, who stood black browed and vengeful beside him.

The Captain's only response? "'Pon my soul, by the Sardine's Trumpet, I promised this young wretch I'd see her hanged, and I *shall*." Thinking back then to Plunqwette's parting shot at his hat, Captain Bolt added, "I'd hang that bloody parrot, too."

Mrs. Orchid had heard enough. She went to get more drinks. Below, her less powerful (or rich) customers were raising another loud cheer. But the cheer was for Piratica, Mrs. O could hear that now, and also that they were singing songs about Piratica's bravery and cunning.

Had she *really* taken so many ships? Mrs. O had thought perhaps not. . . . Five hundred was the number in one of the songs—

Burst *burst* (reason for his name) from Mrs. Orchid's grip and cantered away down the wooden stairs to the main room of the inn. He had no time for the rich and powerful, and needed to make none, lucky cat!

> "*O sing of the valor o' a pirate so bold,*
> *Who robbed the seas over, and took all the gold*
> *Of captains and traders, from Carrib to Inde,*
> *And slipped by the nets of the Law like the wind.*

> *O sing of Piratica, Queen of the Sea,*
> *Took now in irons and bound for the Tree.*
>
> *O sing of her courage, her mocks and her jests,*
> *From the South to the North and the East to the West,*
>
> *For never was like her another so fine,*
> *When she slipped from the jaws of the Law like cool wine.*
>
> *O weep for Piratica, Queen though she be,*
> *She's took now in irons, an'll swing from the Tree."*

Ebad Vooms heard the song, which had caught on now, all along the waterfront. It was like songs written for the play—for Molly, long ago.

But above the bank and the song, that evil stage set, the gallows, with its upright and crossbar, and the ready rope.

The wind was blowing up a tempest. Even the murky water of the Thamis was whipped and bubbling. Rain was starting to fall, but the crowd took little notice.

Ebad stood there, near the very front. He had wrestled a ticket for this place off a man late last night. Ebad didn't look much like himself. He had flour-whitened his hair and eyebrows, painted on two or three most convincing scars, padded out his body with straw. He seemed stout, bent, and old. Well, he was good at disguises, even if he had to steal flour, straw, and face paint to do it. He had been an actor.

No one else of the crew knew he was here. They would have tried to stop him. For, once they had done that chimney climb, and got away into the fields beyond St. Martins, they had talked about an attempt to rescue Art. And they came to the conclusion it wasn't to be done. Art had thought of a way for them to save their skins. What use would that be, if they lost them immediately after, trying to protect her, when *she* hadn't a chance. They knew the score. For such a famed prisoner as Art, her guards would be numberless, all armed, and the Constabulary of Lundon also standing by. (Which Ebad now saw to be true. Plenty of those constables were already present.)

Going through the chimney had been fairly simple. They were by then thin enough, and still fit enough, to worm their way up and along. In the couple of spots where the route was too narrow, Ebad and Whuskery had used the iron bar, wrenched out of the hearth, to knock away bricks. Getting off the roof and down the wall by means of the knotted bed sheets and blankets was nearly easy. No one saw them. The prison guards had been drinking off across the yard.

In the fields they found a barn to shelter them. There they talked through the night, cold—and not caring, for they were free.

But they cared about Art. And couldn't help her. They all agreed to that by the time daylight came. Then they split up, disguising themselves already as best they could. In the low areas of Lundon, which as out-of-work actors they had come to know, the fleabite taverns and hole-in-the-wall shops of the poor, runaways could often find assistance, or at least successfully hide.

They had vowed to meet at Grinwich in a month.

None of them would remain in Lundon. They didn't want to witness the hanging of their captain, Molly's daughter, Art.

"She nearly made us some of the richest men on earth."

"She nearly got us killed, bless her."

"Well, she'll pay for that in two days time, so shut your mouth."

"Aye. 'Tis shut."

Now Ebad, in disguise, alone in the crowd, and so near the scaffold he could almost reach out and touch it, nursed the

pistol he had got on credit in the back alleys. His plan was perhaps hopeless—to fire, to wound—or kill, he didn't mind that
now, to create confusion during which he might be able to spirit
Art away. It wasn't much of a plan. But what else could he do?

Behind Ebad, probably about sixty feet off in the thick of the
crowd, a wild-haired peddler in ragged garments and a brown
beard was selling sweets and hot baked apples to the people.
"Oh, go on, dear, it'll do you good, nasty chilly day like this."

Dirk had embraced Whuskery in the door of the Tottershill
hayloft where they had gone to hide. "I'll be back a bit late
tonight, Whusk—don't worry, I'll take care I don't get caught.
Just need to see someone before we make on."

"Well," Whuskery had said, "I've got a couple of errands to
attend to myself."

Dirk had been relieved. He had thought Whuskery might
argue about Dirk going out alone.

Now Dirk sold his apples (taken from a drunk peddler over
the river), aware of the also stolen gun and knife under the flapping old coat he had exchanged for his own with a tramp near
Sheerditch Lane. Dirk didn't have much of a plan. But he
thought he might succeed. His life had never been that easy till
he fell in with Whusk—and that stroke of special luck had
always made him think Someone might be looking out for
him—though Who, he couldn't say. So he didn't expect to die,
when he dived in, waving his pistol, to drag Art off the scaffold.
He was glad Whuskery wasn't involved, though. He would have
been afraid for Whuskery's safety, and it might have spoiled
Dirk's aim.

The fat, elderly, blowsy washerwoman down by the river's
edge, her powdered face marred by the blue shadow of a thick
mustache she had obviously shaved off carefully—but too early
last night—was forcing her own way through the crowd. She
was very strong—but her arms would be like that from the

washing she did. She whined, though, "Go on, let a poor girl get a bit nearer the Tree—how can I see anything from down here?" "Oh, go on then, Ma. Poor old soul. Let her through."

Whuskery, whiskers off, his heart in his mouth, also had a thieved pistol concealed in his skirt. While the rest of his gear he had nicked off a washing line near Rabbit Warren Street. Also he had a plan he knew must fail. But he had to try—maybe Art, in the confusion, might still get away, even if Whuskery didn't. At least Dirk hadn't got involved. Dirk was safe now, so that was all right.

The Honest Liar was right over by the stilts of the Last In, First Out. The name of the scaffold-overlooking pub had puzzled him. He hadn't seen its dark joke—for whoever was hanged at Lockscald was always the *last* of the crowd to arrive, and the *first* to be thrown out, as it were, when the rope did its work.

Honest was also disguised. He looked exotic. His skin was deep brown, and his head wrapped in a white turban. His robe was embroidered—it had been a curtain before he begged use of it, from old theater friends in the city. "I'm still an actor," he had explained innocently. The dreamy friends lived in another mental world and lived on scraps. Although they could possibly have named every play ever put on in Lundon, they knew nothing about pirates or hangings.

Honest had a pistol Ebad had already given him. But not the faintest notion of how to really fire it. He hadn't even fired guns on stage. Didn't like them. Unlike swimming, or learning lines, they had never been natural for him. He thought a plan might come, some chance. He knew, even if it didn't, he would try to save Art's life. None of the others, who were more sensible, had dared.

Salt Walter meanwhile, tangled in the crowd, had dyed his red hair black with bad dye—it had gone a rusty green. The crowd liked Walt's green hair. They kept on about it, when all he wanted was not to be noticed. And to think himself into being brave enough to rush, when the moment came, Art's guards. He was thankful Peter hadn't suspected Walter's plan and hadn't tried to come himself.

Salt Peter *had* come, though, but only managed to get stranded on the opposite bank of the river. Shaven-headed (having seen Walter's plight with the dye), Peter had also bandaged over one eye and covered himself in three stinking sacks. This had been meant to make people give him plenty of space so, when the time came, he could draw his sword and leap at the hangman. Unfortunately, though, his smell had meant instead he was hustled all across the river at Scald Bridge. And now, trying to get to the gallows side, no one would take him on a boat—only partly because of the rough wind— He was thankful, nevertheless, Walt had kept out of all this.

Eerie O'Shea was *in* the inn, dressed in a priest's robe and holding a huge Bible—a fake that concealed his gun. He was having a last several drinks, adding to the Piratica songs his grand tenor voice, and crying. But many were moved by Art's fate.

None of the others realized Eerie meant to try to rescue Art, he had made sure of that. He knew what he would do. He would hold his nerve till she was on the rope—then shoot *through* the rope—as it broke, he would catch her and run with her, the crowd scattering in startlement at his wild warrior yells. He had tied up a stolen horse just round at the inn's back. Not much of a horse, but it might do. Eerie had never felt so tragic, or such a hero. Nor so entirely on his own.

Glad Cuthbert had actually just looked into the inn—and hadn't recognized Eerie. Cuthbert was, himself, unknowable. Though no actor, he had outdone them in disguise.

Creeping up on a constable at the edge of Ox-Ford Street Market, Cuthbert had stunned him, tied him up, and put him in a handy hovel. Cuthbert then took his official uniform. It quite suited Cuthbert, the brass buttons and so on. Less appealing was the thin mustache he had grown, or the bread-formed warts he had stuck all over his nose and cheeks.

Cuthbert was thinking of his wife and of his hurdy-gurdy. He might never see either of them again. And *his* plan? Bluff. When they brought Art along, he, having worked forward through the crowd to the scaffold, would start some nonsense about one of her guards. Cuthbert would shout the man was a wanted thief—cause a rumpus. It might work. Probably wouldn't. But someone had to do something. He had been disappointed at the others. They were like Art's family and had known her since she was a kid.

Muck, the Cleanest Dog in England, was now perhaps the dirtiest. He had *rolled* in muck and slush and garbage, till he was sticky and tufted gray-black all over. Then, having buried his giant parrot bone safely in the garden of a nice house off May-Fair, Muck had run toward Oldengate Prison and Execution Dock. *Perhaps* he had a plan. Perhaps he *thought* he had a plan. Perhaps he didn't. Perhaps it wasn't likely that even a yellow dog covered in wet, stinky dirt could have a plan of any sort. But there he was.

And Plunqwette?

Anyone looking at the highest chimney of the Last In, First Out might see Plunqwette. And doubtless not recognize her, either. That red-and-green thing, like a feather ball ruffled by the river wind.

Plunqwette had no plan at all. She was old as a century, and more. She knew, for parrots *know*, that all this was in the hand of Higher Powers. But also, she was there.

And then through the wind and rain came the sound of the great iron door of Oldengate scraping open. It was like a screech from the mouth of Hell.

Snargale peered down through the rain-flecked inn window.

"Is *that* the girl?"

"Without a doubt. Look at the horror. Dressed still in man's clothes. Confound her. Small wonder I took her for a boy—"

"Two Goats to a Box of Ducks, that's her for sure," said Harry.

"Brill," said Perry, craning forward.

Captain Bolt folded his arms, speechless with satisfaction.

Snargale said quietly, "She is to suffer a sad end. But her face is calm and thoughtful. She shows no fear. A brave woman."

"An actor," said Mr. Coffee in loathing. "She's an *actor*. She's acting, sir."

"Then, sir, she acts extremely well. Bravo, lass," said Snargale under his breath. "A pity it's come to this."

Art glanced upward, walking between her many guards, only her hands cuffed now with steel. She looked ahead at the upright and the bar and the rope.

Ten miles up. Yes, the gallows seemed that high. Ten miles. Ten—J was the tenth letter of the alphabet. J for Judgment, Judge, Justice, Jury—

Act your part. Yes, act. It's all that's left. You're on a stage. Look at the audience.

The audience—they were clapping and cheering. So glad to see her hang? No—they were calling her name. That name from the play, Molly's name—now Art's name—

"Piratica!" "Here's to you, Piratica, Queen of the Seas!" "Good luck, Piratica!" "Good luck! Godspeed!" "Piratica, we love you!"

The guards were uneasy. Clubs and flintlocks, people pushed back—but still—the cries and cheers—and now—not flowers, for it was winter here—but sprays of evergreen—flying over, the fierce wind helping—so the guards shied like horses.

"O sing of the valor o' a pirate so bold—"

The song.

Bemused, Art stares round her, but she doesn't dare let go of her trained actor's control. So, instead, she bows to the crowd, more a nod, there's not much room for any flourish.

And the crowd—her audience—goes crazy with delight. Trying to join in, the wind kicks and bellows. Rain rattles.

But now here are the steps.

It's a stage. All the world's a stage. Nor shall Death brag . . . Valparaiso, Brave Paradise . . . Ma—

Upward. Each one of her steps rings on the wood. She is on the scaffold.

Ten miles up over her head, the rope, now near enough it gently brushes her cheek. And the hangman is—tying back her hair—she has refused the blindfold. The loop of the noose drops over her head.

Silence comes down like a bowl, covering everything. No crowd noise. No *weather*—for the wind, too, and the rain, suddenly end. It is like a lull at sea—

Then something—

Someone-

Guns raised, muskets, but—

He is on the scaffold with her. Just there. Like a trick in the theater, a magical *effect*—how ever did he do that?

He turns and looks at the hangman, and the guards, looks down at the police all getting ready to blast him apart. He isn't armed—shows them that he isn't. His eyes are so blue, his face so—*different*—something, and maybe not this—or maybe *only* that—makes them all hesitate.

"Give me," he says in a musical voice that travels to every inch of the riverbank, along it, upward, down—the voice of a trained singer, "time to speak."

Then he glances again at the hangman, the guards. With the

most charming smile, Felix Phoenix says to them, "Just a few minutes. It won't matter. You can spare me that?"

And "Let him speak!" a voice bawls in the crowd. Then a hundred, three hundred, a thousand voices—*"Let him speak!"*

Nervous, the hangman. Stepping away. Though the noose he put around the throat of the pirate Piratica still lies there, quietly. The guards are alarmed. *They* argue. The crowd's shouting goes on and on. The guards' weapons are lowered.

"My thanks," says Felix as the crowd again falls still. He turns his back on them again, those armed men on the scaffold. And on the young woman with her neck encircled by a loose rope. His eyes go over the crowd. (Perhaps vaguely, at the edge of vision, he does notice a disturbance up at the top window of the inn—yet takes no notice of it.)

Felix speaks to the crowd.

"Do you want her dead?"

Utter silence again. Awe at this curious question. *Want* her dead? No—but what choice? The Law of England has decided—

"But," Felix says quite humbly, "you have a song about her. Piratica, Queen of the Seas. A song of admiration and affection."

He is dressed in clean but poor clothes. His hair is moon white. Never has Felix looked more beautiful. And his heart is in his eyes.

"She's your heroine, this woman here. Captain Art Blastside—Piratica. One of the great women of England."

From beneath the stage, a constable speaks loudly and harshly. "Nay. She's a pirate. Scum." (Oddly, another constable beside him kicks him in the ankle—an accident, perhaps. . . .)

"A pirate," says Felix to the crowd, "who gets her loot by tricks and cleverness, but who harms no man, who takes nothing that is truly sentimentally precious to those that have it, who sinks no ships."

Across the crowd the upper window of the inn flies open

with a bang, and the glass cracks. Captain Bolt stuffs out his raging head—

"She stole my ship!"

"And there you stand, sir, howling. Not a wound upon you. What other pirate would leave you so? Or am I mistaken? Did Piratica *kill* you?"

The crowd *laughs.*

Captain Bolt makes a lunge and nearly topples from the inn. Someone—it seems to be Landsir Snargale of the Admiralty—pulls him back.

Felix concentrates again on the crowd.

"My uncle," says Felix, "had a ship taken by pirates. Mercilessly they killed him, and all aboard, men, women, children. That in turn killed my father and my mother. My brothers, too. I swore revenge on all the pirate kind. Then I met Piratica."

Felix looks round now, looks full at Art.

Her eyes looking back are like silvered mirrors. Can she even *see* him with them? She says nothing.

"This woman you'd let hang for piracy is to me my only friend in this world," says Felix frankly. "I meant to bring her down. Instead I fell in love with her. Why was that? Because she is like no other. She is a heroine, and an ornament, both to her sex and her country. I would have spoken at her trial—and was shut out. There's English justice. *I was shut out.*"

The crowd growls.

Behind him, and below, Felix hears and sees the renewed movement of readied guns.

He roars at the crowd, *"Do you want to kill her, then?* Be sure of it. She is yours, a woman of just seventeen now, a being of honor, and the wife of my heart. I tell you, people of England, you rose up before and threw away your oppressors. Rise up again now and save English justice with your chosen heroine. Or—" With a gesture only an actor could have managed, Felix has the rope up like a cobweb over Art's neck and head. Down and over his *own* head and neck. In the noose he once more turns to Art. He looks at her. *Looks* at her. "Or, fellow Republicans, let me die at her side."

Art—the silvering on her eyes goes. She stares at Felix. "You're mad."

"Sane. What do I care? I *was* dead. You gave me back my *life*."

She puts out her hands and takes him softly by the hair. She pulls off the noose quite roughly. It drops away. No one intervenes. She takes him in her arms.

When they kiss each other, there on the scaffold under that storm sky stilled by Plunqwette's Higher Powers, everything— the crowd, life, *death*—is forgotten.

And in that moment, the world trims her sails and changes course.

Eight *persons* leap for the scaffold—an old man with white hair, who looks too elderly to jump like that—a peddler throwing off his tray—a washerwoman with a blossoming mustache— a constable, who uses *another* constable as a launchpad—a priest with a bottle in his hand—a fellow with green hair—an Eastern grandee in a turban—and not quite last, nor by any means least, the filthiest dog anyone present has ever seen.

But this weird assortment is only the first spray of a tidal wave.

For now, sixteen more men fling themselves onto the scaffold. Sixteen men, followed by thirty women, followed by—sixty, ninety, two hundred *people*—and the tidal wave comes in, knocking up the guns, knocking over any opposition—resisting constables tumbled—the hangman flat on his back, guards gone flying like a pack of cards—bullets whirling harmless through air—away and away—

While over the river a shaven-headed beggar prances and sings with joy, which isn't really forgivable, considering how he smells. . . .

The crowd, the whole city—up in arms.

"The Republic!" the multitude screams. "The Law of the People!"

"Save our heroine!"

"Piratica—Queen of the Sea!"

"Justice!"

Captain Bolt in the opened window of the Last In, First Out now has his pistol aimed. He is about to shoot Felix Phoenix through the head, when Landsir Snargale floors Bolt with a well-placed uppercut to the jaw.

"Bedevil you, sir. You'll not shoot that man. By the topgallants, when I was at sea—his uncle Solomon was my friend. His father, Adam Makepeace, too—thank God I recognize the lad at last—he's the boy I tried to find when I got home, after that four-year voyage, to save him from the workhouse—and discovered no trace—my oldest friend's eldest son. He shall be rich. And Piratica shall be pardoned. And her crew, by the Flag's Ferret. *Pardoned,* by God. As for you, Bolt—shoot my friend's son would you? I'll see you exported to Australia. I'll see you flown up to the planet Mars."

But Bolt doesn't hear, being out cold.

Nor Harry and Perry who, overexcited—"It's that rotter Cuckoo Jack—wouldn't fight a duel with us, Perry!" "Rubbish—I shot him, OK? Six Foxes on you, Harry—do you say I lie?"—are arguing and slapping each other's faces with gloves— there'll be another duel tomorrow—

Outside, Execution Dock is a riot. A riot without shots, a riot that laughs and sings. But Art and Felix don't seem to hear either.

Plunqwette, now seated atop the gallows, saw the goose first. It was flying south, along the Thamis, and below, taking no notice of all the chaos of the banks by Lockscald, a boat was lumbering on thrashing oars.

"Stop that goose—fellow told me it'd be seen to—all plucked and *ready*-roasted—but there it was—you go and catch it, he says—and I'm still trying—flew straight off, it did. I've been chasing that blatted goose since yesterday—"

The rain and storm were over. It was more than a lull.

The goose flew straight, still, and Plunqwette watched it go.

Far down the Thamis, as the afternoon tide came in, the big bird stooped a moment to the water, but not to the by then long-lost boat of its pursuer. Something else was there. A little sodden waxy paper, shaped only *something* like a boat. To anyone else it might, if unfolded, still resemble a map—a treasure map—which had traveled a very, very, very *long* way—but to the cunningly escaped flying dinner, it meant instead some other thing. The white goose closed its beak around the map from the Treasured Isle and bore it away into the free and open sky.

Turn the page and
plunge into

Piratica II

HOUSE AND PARDON

Every time she saw her house across the sweep of its grounds, day or night, Art was both amused and perturbed. Thankfully it wasn't at all like the house of her father, Richman's Park. Even so, it was grand, large and pillared, hung with carved stone wreathes, and surrounded by an army of statues. She'd tried to get to know it.

'Hail and hi, Diana,' Art called lightly to the marble hunting goddess up on a plinth. Diana, of course, took no notice of the young woman cantering by on the black horse.

The trees poured down, oaks, cedars, pines, to the long-sloping lawn, silver gray in moonlight and stained yellow where the house windows were beaming. On the far side of the mansion the ground was rough and few trees grew. The headland framed a view of the black circling sea.

Felix was on the terrace here. You could hardly miss him. Several stands of candles had been arranged, and by their light he was standing painting, his head bent toward the canvas.

Art rode in and Felix, not looking, raised his hand in greeting. 'Just let me finish this detail...'

She sat on her horse watching him, Felix Phoenix, her beautiful husband, who, by his wit and courage, had saved her from the gallows.

Was he happy now?

She wasn't quite sure. But then, how could she judge? They were so different, and he so intent on his work, these wonderful paintings of views and people. He had even painted Art up on her black horse. (This picture now hung in the Republican Gallery in Lundon.) But Art had called her horse Bowspirit. That said it all. If Felix had mislaid the sea—which anyway he had never been that keen on—she had not. No, the sea was in her hair and skin and bones and blood.